Praise for *Seraphim* by Michele Hauf

"A rich medieval tapestry woven of fantastic tales of revenge,
women warriors, faeries and demon fire. Michele Hauf
captures your attention with vivid, powerful, sexy characters.
What I wouldn't do for a man like Dominique San Juste!"
—Award-winning author Lyda Morehouse

"From her first word to her last, Hauf weaves a magic spell.
You'll root for Seraphim and sigh over Dominique as they
risk heaven and hell in this heart-stopping adventure."
—Emma Holly, author of *Hunting Midnight*

"This book kicks butt—in a lush and lyrical way."
—Susan Sizemore, author of the "Laws of the Blood" series

Gossamyr

MICHELE HAUF

LUNA™
www.LUNA-Books.com

LUNA™

First edition May 2005

GOSSAMYR

ISBN 0-373-80220-X

www.LUNA-Books.com

Printed in U.S.A.

For all who Believe

Enchantment is Faery's *raison d'être*.
Many moons ago—during a blue moon's reign—a rift was
cleaved between Faery and the Otherside.
No one—man, beast, or fée—can say how or why,
Only, the act decimated a great source of Enchantment.
The curtain between Faery and the Otherside has become transparent;
fée travel back and forth with ease;
mortals, once banned from Faery after one visit, find return less difficult.
It is a challenge to keep that which should not be in Faery *out.* And vice versa.
Time wends forward, widdershins, and thus.
Such conditions shall remain until a champion
can restore the Enchantment complete.

PROLOGUE

Faery—betwixt and between

The revenant swooped down from out of nowhere. Wide gaping maws, fanged and stretched to maul, loosed a shrill cry, shaking Gossamyr de Wintershinn from her petrified stance. She stumbled backward and landed atop the blue marble floor of the circular castle tower. Eyes fixed to the danger, Gossamyr groped blindly at her side, slapping the stone, in seek of her fighting staff.

The very flesh had been stripped from her attacker's bones. Swathes of tattered muscle clung to the skeleton. Red glowed within the skull's eyes, molten and dripping, as if blood. The pellicle wings, void of lustrous color, were but a ghostly mesh of flight flapping madly between the shoulder bones. It looked like a winged one—a fée—but it could not possibly be. Never before had she seen the like.

Be this one of the relentless creatures that had been tormenting Faery for a summer of moons?

Tattered wings siphoned the air in foul hisses. The wraithlike thing lunged. A skeletal arm slashed out. Claws cut the air—and flesh.

Gossamyr stroked a finger across her cheek; slippery blood flowed from the cut.

Whence came this creature? 'Twas full sun. She had been tending her own pleasures, looking over the muster of peacocks trampling the wild rose garden below that hugged the inner curtain wall. Why did it attack her?

Shuffling backward, her hand slapped upon something—her fighting staff.

With a hue and cry to strip the senses, the creature again struck. Gossamyr dived to the right. Gripping the applewood staff and, facing down, she kicked back and up. Her bare toes connected with bone. The creature shrieked as it spun into the crystal-white sky.

Pushing up and landing a ready stance, Gossamyr swung the longstaff to mark her periphery—the applewood sang a battle cry—then prepared for a return attack. Keenly, she marked her surroundings for additional threat.

Skeletal arms slashed the air. Bone fingers curled into claws as the creature rushed her. She swung hard, using the force of the staff and counterweighting her body into the defense. The end of her weapon cracked skull. Bits of the creature's head scattered like a harvest gourd cleaved by elf-shot.

Landing the swing, she steadied her bearing. No time to think, only react. Deft twists of her fingers spun the weapon in a hissing figure of eight as she turned to challenge the opponent. Now headless, the creature hung before her, arms spread—yet the wings flapped. Still alive. If bones could harbor life.

"Remarkable." Gossamyr stepped back. How to defeat the thing? "Can I kill it?"

"Either that or be killed!" came the unbidden answer.

The stiff barbs of a feathered cape stroked her cheek. The *shing* of an obsidian blade drawn from a hip sheath sliced the air. One slash of the fire-forged sabre sectioned the creature at the waist, dropping the leg bones to the tower floor in a clatter.

"Shinn—"

"Stand back!" Shinn swung and hacked through the rib cage of the creature. "These things don't know how to die!"

Frayed wings—severed from the skeletal body—furiously beat the air above Shinn, her father. The dauntless fée lifted his blade up under the left wing, cleaving it asunder, and brought the blade down through the right wing. He spun toward Gossamyr and shouted, "There!"

Pulled from her awestruck stare, Gossamyr jumped as a foot trimmed with muscle shreds stamped her toes. Together, the legs of the creature attacked. Sweeping her staff low, she dashed it across the anklebones, sending them crashing against the marble embrasures. Reduced to dust on impact, the shattered bone glinted as it floated to the tower floor.

"What in all of Faery is it?" Gossamyr called as she swung and caught a disembodied arm with the tip. Fingers clenched the end of her staff. Shake as she might, the evil fist clung. "Shinn?"

Residue from the crushed creature glimmered in a mist about Shinn as his sabre obliterated the wings. "A revenant!" the implacable fée called.

Ill clad for battle, Shinn's everyday vestments of flowing arachnagoss tunic and elaborately stitched hosen would not protect him from injury. But he did not waver, instead standing proud and defying the thing with a swing of his sabre. He dived to avoid the other arm as it sailed toward him, fingers fisted.

"Let me to it!" Gossamyr cried. An audacious smile crooked her mouth. She had trained for this sort of challenge. Opportunity had finally fallen to her. "I've been craving some fight."

She rushed the attacking arm and connected wood to bone in a hollow crack. "Yes!"

The return swing of her staff proved the attack had not jarred the creepy passenger. Gossamyr slammed the carved applewood upon the tower floor. Finger bones gave loose, but as quickly, scrambled across her toes and gripped her ankle, shaking her off balance.

She landed the marble floor with a jaw-loosening *dumpf.* A skeletal hand scurried up her leg and over her hip moving farther.

Wheezing breaths gasped from her mouth. Dropping her staff, Gossamyr clutched the hand that squeezed about her throat. Probing fingertips threatened to pierce her flesh. She struggled to wrestle the thing off, but it possessed strength immeasurable. It was futile to fight, to kick at the air and pray she connected with some part of an attacker that just wasn't there.

A murky blackness muddied her thoughts. Shinn—where was he? Needles of numbness loosened her grip on the hand. Her shoulders dropped. She could see nothing, smell not the scent of fresh morning dew and lush rose oil, nor sense the smooth polish of the marble beneath her fingers. An angry peacock mewl echoed Gossamyr's longing to cry out.

As death crept closer one final sound summoned her audacious smile. The shrill of finely honed obsidian cutting through bone.

ONE

High above the lush cypress and laburnum treetops that encircled the curtain wall Gossamyr followed her father through the carved marble loggia. The castle she had lived in all her life nested at the peak of the Spiral forest as if a bloom upon a verdant bouquet. Pendulous yellow flowers hung heavily on the laburnum that grew only at the top of the forest, contrasting marvelously with the castle. The blue marble was deeply veined with streaks of midnight and palest sky; it mimicked both day and night and shimmered with a fée dust of the ages.

The village of Glamoursiège fit like a twist about the marble screw of the Spiral. Blue marble segued to granite and finally to sand at its lowest where it met the grounds in a mire of marsh and reticulated tree roots. For the entirety was laced with the roots of cypress, ash and hornbeam. The Edge—very few places where the trees did not grow—was ever to be avoided, at least by the unwinged ones.

"I can do this, Shinn! You cannot deny I am the only one able."

Shinn moved swiftly toward the south tower, speaking his impatience with his strides. "Many are capable," he called back to Gossamyr.

"Capable, yes," Gossamyr had to agree.

Faery worked counter to the Otherside, and a war of almost one hundred mortal years had been keeping the mortals to blood and wrath, while Faery enjoyed fellowship and peace. Tribe Glamoursiège had been formed of trooping warriors before the great Peace, a Peace that had existed since long before Gossamyr's birth.

How long? Time indeterminable, Shinn often answered when Gossamyr would question, for Time was of no concern to the fée.

Though Faery claimed Peace there were still the occasional rises amongst the various tribes. Shinn's troops were indeed capable and, with the recent arrival of the revenants, increasingly vigilant.

Gossamyr picked up her pace, as well her confidence. "If not for this very challenge, what then has all my training been for? Naught? I am as skilled as any in your troop, male or female."

"Child of mine, you know well you have been groomed to sit the Glamoursiège throne," Shinn said over his shoulder. "It is not an idle, benevolent woman who can rule in my absence, but one who possesses all the martial skills I have taught you, and the mind for diplomacy, honor and valor."

"I will not neglect my duties to Glamoursiège, but...I want this, Shinn. It is such an opportunity!" She hurried up beside him. Where did he go in such a hurry?

"Convince me it wise to send my daughter on such a singular and dangerous quest."

Ah, there, he had not given an unequivocal no. This gave Gossamyr hope.

"Your fée warriors will not survive the Red Lady's seductive allure. As you've told me, she seduces Disenchanted fée into her clutches. They have not the fortitude to resist!"

Any fée who left Faery for the Otherside risked Disenchantment. Necessary trips to the mortal realm were swift, coached in the knowledge that glamour dissipates quickly and Time could not be trusted. A risky venture for a fée warrior.

A risk chosen by some.

There were those rogue fée, who, seduced by the lure of the mortal, and that intricate city called Paris, chose to remain on the Otherside. To stay meant sure Disenchantment; a condition that saw the fée completely drained of glamour, and often they lost their wings to a shriveling malady attributed to the baneful touch from a mortal. Enchantment gone, they became nothing more than a shell that survived as any mortal. Return to Faery was difficult but not impossible. But never again could the Disenchanted regain Enchantment whole.

Of course, one did not have to be fée to fall under the seductive spell of the Otherside. Gossamyr had lost her mother to the mortal passion ten midsummers earlier. The lure of the unknown was ever beguiling, but Veridienne de Wintershinn had always known the Otherside, for she had been mortal complete.

Shinn stopped abruptly, causing his daughter to collide against his back. Savoring the faintest scent of hyacinth that marked her father, Gossamyr stepped back.

The south tower overlooked a riot of white roses and speckled foxglove in the gardens below. Overhead, the carved marble open-work cast a lattice of shadows across Shinn's tightened jaw. His blazon, an iridescent tribal marking, curled down his chin and neck and across his upper chest, and shimmered in the blocked patches of sunlight. Glamoursiège blazons showed on neck and upper extremities; placement varied from tribe to tribe.

For all his stern posture and commanding demeanor—even the recent announcement that his marshal at arms should marry Gossamyr—Shinn would ever occupy a soft place in Gossamyr's heart. All planes and hard slopes his face, only in his eyes could she ever find compassion. And such a find was a rarity to be hoarded. Shinn's manner switched from cool to disinterested, and then suddenly to genuine concern with such ease. One moment he was gentle and attentive, the next, the battle commander wore a fierce mien. Gossamyr had not known him to be any other way. Attribute to his trying history, she could only assume. They had both loved and lost. Love being one of those mutable words the fée toyed with in exchange for lust, hunger or envy.

"I listened last night to the council's discussion," she said. Shinn required she sit as a silent member at council, for her future demanded she take an active role in Glamoursiège matters. "The revenants' presence in Faery increases. But I was surprised to learn about the rift." She bent to meet Shinn's straying gaze. "It has never before been discussed by council. Why did you not tell me of it sooner?"

"It is just something that is…known. The rift has existed since before your birth."

"That long? And all this time you haven't once thought to—"

"It has never been in my mind, Gossamyr. Until recently. There are none who can name the reason for the rift cleaved between Faery and the Otherside; only we know it exists. Such a tear in the fabric that separates our worlds allows the revenants to return with ease. I am sure I mentioned it when I explained the revenants to you."

"You did not." Hand to her hip, she paced in short turns, pointing the floor with the tip of her staff. Shinn had explained the revenants two midsummers earlier when she had witnessed a natural fée death. Normally the fée essence leaves the body and experiences the final *twinclian*. But there are those fée—those of darker natures—who do not *twinclian* to the Celestial. Instead, their essence merely pops, and the revenant follows, its destination—the Infernal. It is a rarity.

The sudden appearance of revenants in Faery—not newly emerged from a natural fée death—had given clue someone on the Otherside was stealing the essences. And so was discovered the Red Lady.

As frustrated as Gossamyr was to just now learn something she should have known about, she took it all in. Knowledge was required for a successful mission. "Still, I do not understand why, or how, those skeleton creatures return to Faery. Are they not dead?"

"Did that creature *look* dead?"

Actually, yes. However, not if death implied stillness. "So it was alive, yet...I don't understand."

"That thing I killed—"

"*We* killed."

"Yes. We." A nod verified her participation in the event. But too brief, Shinn's reassuring smile. "The Red Lady stole its essence, leaving the revenant in limbo. Somehow she can feed off the essence of another—the essence holds the former body's glamour—delaying her Disenchantment interminably. The revenant is a shade of the fée that cannot find final rest without the essence, so it returns to Faery in seek of a new essence."

"But why Faery? Can it not locate a fée on the Otherside?"

"It is compelled back to Faery. The rift literally sucks them back home. I don't believe it could remain in the Otherside if it wished."

"This essence..." Gossamyr leaned against a blue machicolation, tapping the cool marble with a thumb. "When I witnessed the fée death something blue rose from the body. Is it something the Red Lady can draw out and...possess?"

"Yes and no. Inside the body it is our very being. Outside the body, well, it either *twinclians* or it pops." The elegant fée lord tilted his head to look upon his daughter. A sigh hung in the air between them, a resolute pause. "The essence is akin to...a mortal soul."

"Ah."

There was so little Gossamyr understood about mortals. About that part of herself.

Her mother had been mortal, but Veridienne's sickness—the mortal passion—had kept her focus from her family and eventually lured her home to the Otherside, leaving Gossamyr alone to comfort her heartbroken fée father. And to ever wonder. Why had not her mother taken her daughter with her? Surely she might have wished to raise her own child? Had it been so easy to leave her family behind for the mortal world? She had once begged to stay in Faery—but that desire hadn't lasted long.

Of course, in terms of emotional distance, Veridienne had much over Shinn. Likely, she had not seen beyond her own self-satisfying desires.

Following her mother's abrupt departure, Gossamyr had vowed not to become mired in her own selfish wants. And what better way to prove it than to track the Red Lady and protect Faery from further torment?

So this sought-after essence was like a mortal soul. What did it mean to have a soul? And mortal, at that. Gossamyr had known no other way but of the fée. Fathered by Shinn, would she possess both a soul *and* an essence?

"There are things I would have liked to give you," Shinn said, looking off into the sky, avoiding her gaze. "Truths."

"I don't understand."

"There is no time for confessions. The revenant is single-minded," Shinn said, "focused on obtaining that which was stolen from it. So much so, it will kill to obtain the final *twinclian*." He focused briefly on her cut cheek, but gave her injury no verbal regard. The fée were not so emotionally delicate as mere mortals. "They are becoming more frequent, the encounters. Streklwood was attacked last eve."

"The cook?"

Shinn nodded.

A lump the size of an uncooked goose egg formed in Gossamyr's throat at memory of this morning's still-shelled offering. She'd thought to complain, to send her maid, Mince, marching down to the kitchen…

"The revenant must be reduced to a fine glimmer," Shinn continued. "For to leave a single bone intact will not defeat the creature's quest for wholeness. They are difficult to kill."

"I noticed. But it felt good, the challenge."

Avoiding his daughter's enthusiastic declaration Shinn strode the curve of the tower, hands akimbo, his raven-feather cape flitting gently above the length of his folded wings.

This demesne of Faery was not so much ruled by Shinn as protected and guided—a position Gossamyr knew she would one day fill. Descended from a long line of trooping fée, Shinn had once commanded the Glamoursiège musters. He'd become lord over Glamoursiège following his father's death. And he'd trained his only daughter to follow in his footsteps, should he cease to stand upon the Glamoursiège throne.

Much as she did not like to consider that fate, Gossamyr realized it would happen some day. And she was prepared to take Shinn's place, physically. Mentally, she wondered if her lack of battle experience would make her a weaker ruler. She could sit council and talk politics with the best. But would they respect one without time spent in the musters?

Pressing her palms to a cool marble crenel cut into the tower, Gossamyr leaned forward. A swirl of white cottonwood kites billowed out from the dense forest spiraling the castle. Laughter smaller than a bird's tweedle glittered in the air like sunshine upon purling waters—a few skyclad piskies clung to the tails of the seed-kites, stealing a ride.

Despite the fées' frustrating lack of regard for Time, she did know it governed the Otherside. Veridienne had been the one to explain to her how the mortal realm used Time to measure everything. During that conversation, she'd told Gossamyr she was eight years in measurement, and that a year could be marked once every mortal midsummer. Which meant Gossamyr was twenty-one mortal years now. It filled her with pride to know that one mortal measurement, but she did not mention it to Shinn. The fée did not measure a lifetime with tangible numbers of years. Once on the Otherside, the fée struggled against Time, Veridienne had said. Time stole Enchantment.

To race against Time would afford a challenge.

Faery needed a champion to defeat this vicious succubus.

A thump to her chest thudded against the arachnagoss-stuffed pourpoint Gossamyr wore when practicing—which was more often than not. "You know I am fit for this mission," she said with conviction.

She had absorbed Shinn's lessons on the martial arts until he had declared her more skilled than he. Since childhood her father had honed her skills to counter the true glamour birth had denied. (She had a bit; her blazon shimmered as bright as any other.) But she knew he would balk. Always Shinn had forbidden her from visiting the Otherside. (*Forbid* was a favorite word of Shinn's.) Forbidden to journey beyond the marsh roots, forbidden to take the sinister curve to market, forbidden to court a Rougethorn, forbidden to even suggest a visit to the Otherside.

Mortals who left Faery could return, but their swift loss of Enchantment—and the fact they could never again regain such Enchantment—made their return visit to Faery dangerous and unthinkably fleeting.

Time, Gossamyr thought, the true evil.

But Gossamyr was only half mortal. Might she risk a trip to the Otherside and then return without fear of never regaining her Enchantment? Shinn *twinclianed* there often.

"And if you look beyond my skills," she said, "there is the obvious—my mortal blood. The Red Lady is not interested in mortals, or females, for that matter."

"But—"

"I am not a man. I can easily—"

"Gossamyr."

"—gain her lair and take her out!"

Gossamyr twisted her neck to find the glint in Shinn's vivid violet eyes. The trace of a grin bracketed his pale mouth. Always his emotion manifested in small measure.

Reaching for the applewood staff—her *vade mecum*—she turned from Shinn, spun the weapon in her fingers, then swung it out before her, spanning a full circle before she snapped it back to rest against her shoulder. She may not be able to shape-change or *twinclian* at sign of danger, but Shinn had made sure his half-blood daughter could stand and fight. Much as he forbade her to participate in the Glamoursiège tournaments, she had managed a few on the sly.

Gossamyr had developed a penchant for adventure. Danger even. Unfortunately danger had eluded her. Until now.

The thought of this mission verily sizzled inside her. She wanted this! For many reasons. But fore, she wanted to protect her homeland from the threat of the revenants.

"It is the mortal passion, be that so?" Shinn's quiet words made Gossamyr wince. "It blinds you to the real danger."

"But I crave danger!"

He caught the end of her staff as she swung it in declaration. The tension strumming from end to end of the staff—Gossamyr's grip to Shinn's—felt palpable. Unwilling to concede, she lifted her chin defiantly.

"You have not experienced real danger." Her father's stern tone curtailed her swagger a bit. "Bogies and hobs—"

"And that core worm a few days earlier! The thing spat dirt balls the size of a spriggan's head."

Shinn turned a wry smirk upon her. "Gossamyr, core worms do not spit."

"It was spitting at me."

"Think about it, daughter. How is it a worm exudes dirt from its body?"

"Well, it—" Throws up casts. Oh. She hadn't thought of that. So the thing had been— Ah. "Don't you trust I've the ability? You have trained me for this opportunity."

Her father released the end of her staff with a gentle shove. "You are skilled, this I know."

"Then I am ready. I will return to you—"

"Will you?" So much unspoken in those two words. And the sigh that followed.

"Yes. Of…of course I will return."

Did he worry that her mortal blood would prevent her safe return? Gossamyr had ever coached herself to resist the mortal passion. If it had seduced her mother, she, as well, risked such temptation, for Veridienne's blood coursed through her veins instead of Shinn's ichor.

Or was it that he could not abide her to leave him? The pain of losing Veridienne had changed Shinn, closed his heart. Emotion was difficult to mine from the stalwart fée. Gossamyr would not bring further heartache to her father.

And yet, Shinn had bruised her heart with his own cruel indifference. The memory of a Rougethorn's kiss would for ever live in Gossamyr's being, and for evermore close her heart to the mutable love faeries feared.

But it was all for naught. Love was not to be hers. Shinn had already announced her engagement to a most frustrating man, his marshal at arms, Desideriel Raine. Frustrating to Gossamyr's heart, but certainly deserving where skill and knowledge of the Glamoursiège musters were concerned. When Shinn had first suggested such over a meal the diffident fée had suppressed a sneer as he'd looked across the table to Gossamyr. She had read the young warrior's look—*she is not true fée.* The humiliation had prompted her to excuse herself before the final flower course.

She was perfectly capable of ruling Glamoursiège on her own, but tradition required marriage—marriage being reserved for royalty and the upper-caste lords and ladies. And, Gossamyr suspected, Desideriel would represent true fée blood when all in Glamoursiège merely tolerated Gossamyr's half blood.

"Truth," Shinn said.

Drawn from her troubling thoughts, Gossamyr approached Shinn.

Truth? Studying the sun-laced tower floor, the blue veins purling through the marble like cold blood, Gossamyr vacillated on admitting the truth. A truth that sat in her heart like the pulses of mortal Time that fascinated her so. How to do it gently?

"Truth," she murmured. An exhale released reluctance. "I do long to visit the Otherside. You know that." She met Shinn's gaze, half-concealed by a fall of his long raven hair. He sought the truth of her, and yet he would hide behind his own hard emotions. "I want to understand that part of my heritage most alien to me. I want to…experience."

She followed Shinn's pace to the tower's edge. The evening primrose that grew in the roots attracted night moths, which then attracted frogs. He nodded. "And find."

Frustration, muted and held back far too long, oozed throughout her. He would not close out her desires. Not this time. Even more, Gossamyr would have her father know her heart. She whispered, "Love never dies, Shinn."

"You think to know love?"

"I…yes." And not the fickle love faeries know. "I know the fée cannot truly—"

Too fragile, the memory of Veridienne, to speak of it. And so Gossamyr would not. But what of *her* lover? The one her father had banished from her very arms? Then, he had claimed she could not begin to know love. Did they both fool the other with their secret longings for fulfillment?

To continue would gain her no ground.

"Here is my home, Shinn."

"Yes, because you believe."

Yes, yes. Always he repeated the mantra to her: Believe and you Belong. She believed. She belonged! Nothing could change that.

"Faery is your home," he said. "Should you venture away…you must then return."

To marry Desideriel was the unspoken part.

"Indeed. And my home is no longer safe unless someone stops the Red Lady. I want to help Faery. How will I ever stand in your place if there is naught a place to stand?"

The summer breeze lifted Shinn's jet hair over his shoulders and twisted fine strands around the horns at his temples. Gossamyr read the pain in his tightened jaw. His own memories haunted. It had been much simpler for her to place aside the memories of an always-distant mother.

"Grant me this opportunity, Shinn. I will return to you."

"You vow to me?"

A father's fear: violet eyes unwilling to focus upon hers; hyacinth, heady and oozing with an expectant pulse.

"You won't lose me, Shinn. I vow it upon my fée essence."

Gossamyr noted the twitch at the corner of her father's mouth. Suppression always tightened his features. "This mission is deadly. Time cannot be tricked or defeated."

A stab of her staff rang against the marble. "I am skilled."

"A—" Shinn looked to the summer-pale sky "—champion is needed."

A champion. "Oh." Her bravado mellowed, Gossamyr bowed her head.

Indeed, a champion.

When had she ever proven herself in battle? Fighting dirt-casting core worms and drunken bogies? Night-creeping spriggans rarely offered more than a few moments' struggle before scampering away from challenge. Werefrogs were vicious but stupid. Tournaments offered her but display of singular combat skills. There had not been opportunity for real challenge here in Glamoursiège. And she'd never been off the Spiral, not even a near fall from the Edge.

The touch of Shinn's finger lifted Gossamyr's gaze up to his. His eyes glittered. With tears? She had not thought to ever see the like. Certainly it was a mirage created by the sun and the glimmer of his blazon.

"Of course you do know champions are not simply ready and able?"

She lifted a brow.

"They are made. Truly, you are the only one for this mission, Gossamyr." He bowed his head and clasped his fingers, the moue of his mouth frowning. But in a remarkable recovery he lifted a confident eye to Gossamyr. The former commander relayed battle details. "The Red Lady is malicious and is unlikely to rest until her penchant for feeding off fée essence restores her ability to return to Faery. She scents them out, newly arrived in the city, just as Disenchantment has begun to set in, for then the essence still retains its glamour."

Gossamyr touched the faint blazon curling up her neck in a manner of twisting design. Would Disenchantment steal her blazon?

"But most important…" Another heavy sigh released what Gossamyr guessed to be regret and fear and the intense compulsion to protect his only child. "You are ready."

A champion? Gossamyr straightened her shoulders and lifted her chin. *Have at me.*

Eagerness uncontained, she blurted, "How will I know the Red Lady? Is she…red?"

Shinn's smirk teased at a genuine smile. "You will know her when you see her. Banished long ago, she bears the mark."

The mark. Yes. Horrid memories flooded Gossamyr's mind. She had witnessed a banishment. The curl of red pinpricks boring into flesh. *A cri de terroir.* The suddenness of expulsion. And her bruised heart.

"You have seen the mark," Shinn had the audacity to remark.

A nod confirmed Gossamyr's understanding. Bile stirred in her throat. "Speak no more on it; I will know it when I see it."

Swallowing back memory, Gossamyr sorted the facts. A succubus fée. Red. Banished. An unmistakable mark. Paris. Her father never elaborated beyond the necessary information.

"How long ago was she banished?"

"Before your birth."

"Ah." And yet, only now the succubus had begun to havoc the Otherside? Hmm…

"Mortal time is different than in Faery," Shinn commented. "You will find it faster, startling. But most important, you know much about the Otherside; that will serve well."

"I have gleaned what I can while studying Mother's Bestiary of Humans—" Gossamyr stopped. Shinn did not appear startled by her confession. She had ever used stealth to steal into the locked study to snoop, much to the horror of her maid, Mince.

Veridienne had been detailing the mortals, magnifying them on amphi-vellum in the most remarkable detail, diagramming their manner and social ways from memory—re-creating her natural history. Gossamyr pored over the articles any chance she could find. The drawings were marvelously rendered in gild and such pigments created from madder, azurite and verdigris. Text gave splendid descriptions of clothing, food and custom.

I know you are half-mortal, Gossamyr. Your brown eyes intrigue. You are exotic…

Shucking off the cloying memory of a Rougethorn's enraptured voice, Gossamyr looked to her father. He studied her, his jaw tight. Ever visible, the hurt in Shinn's eyes.

"I wanted to touch a part of her," Gossamyr offered in a quiet voice. "It was difficult trying to get close to her. She was ever busy."

"Veridienne loved you, Gossamyr. The mortal passion led her astray. Nothing more. You two are devastatingly alike, so…passionate about life. Rebellion runs like ichor through your veins."

Ichor? Not in this half-blood's veins, she thought wistfully.

Gossamyr felt her father's sadness ran far deeper than he would ever show. Had Veridienne's departure been rebellion? To journey to the Otherside had always been her dream, but a dream tainted by the reality of her mother's absence.

"I have been nothing but clear regarding your never Passaging to the Otherside."

A shiver prinkled up Gossamyr's spine. Would he yet deny her this mission? Forbid her from yet another enticing fragment of life? Champions were made, not hired! And such an experience for the future lady of Glamoursiège! There was yet opportunity…

She scuffed her palms across her leather braies and scanned the gloss shimmering in her father's violet eyes.

"It is dangerous. We both know that." Shinn's breaths settled in the air between them, heavy with something akin to dread. "But the time has come to release you from a father's protective obsession."

Apprehension tightened Gossamyr's limbs so she stood boldly erect.

"Yes, you see, even I have my obsession. I cannot protect you once you leave Faery."

She needn't protection. With staff in hand and a keen eye for danger, Gossamyr invited the experience.

"Just remember," he said. "Always Believe—"

"And I will Belong. I know, Shinn. Worry not, I will never lose mind of my home. Will there be revenants on the Otherside?"

"No, they flee to Faery as quickly as the essence is stolen."

"Which is why you must remain here."

"Indeed. A fée can only travel to the Otherside on so many occasions before Time masters his body. I have journeyed there many a time. Would that I could accompany you."

"You mustn't risk it."

"I will muster my troops and prepare for a sure battle. I sense their numbers will only increase as the Red Lady remains unstopped. I have been witness only to those who return to Glamoursiège. I expect other Faery tribes have been attacked, as well."

"These revenants, what happens when one does manage to obtain an essence?"

"That would leave an innocent fée dead, and the revenant would have its final *twinclian*."

"Would not the innocent become revenant?"

Shinn nodded. "You understand this vicious cycle could cripple Faery."

Further reason to avoid delay. Time must be faced. "I can do this."

His smile didn't quite reach his eyes. "I know."

Why did a prinkle suddenly cleave to Gossamyr's spine? This is what she most desired.

"I should not send you alone."

"There are none in Faery who can accompany me." For there were none with mortal blood to protect them from the Red Lady's seeking lure. "You'll need your troops here to fight the revenants."

"Perhaps a pisky guide—"

"What of Mince?"

"She is far too aged, and honestly, much too plump to keep your pace. The Disenchantment would take her swiftly."

Indeed. Gossamyr would not risk the matron, even as she dreaded leaving her maternal influence. The only kind arms she had known following Veridienne's departure, for Shinn did not express his concern with sympathetic touches but with stronger actions, such as teaching her to fight.

"I will fare well on my own."

"Mayhap a fetch?" Shinn nodded, pleased with his notion. "Indeed, I will send one along to repeat back to me your successes."

She liked that he already thought of her success.

"Now, Disenchantment occurs quickly," he warned. "Once you

set foot on the Otherside you've perhaps less than a day before you lose all glamour."

"I have no glamour!"

"You've a cloak of glamour." He splayed his fingers before her face, raising a sensation of warmth in her flesh, drawing the shimmer of the fée to the surface. There in the blazon tracing her collarbones and upper chest did she feel the magic, the innate *being* of her kind. The prinkles dancing on Gossamyr's spine subsided.

"It has seeped into you over the years," Shinn assured.

So she twinkled. That did not mean she could perform *twinclian*. Hers was a false glamour. No flight, no *twinclian*, no glamour. Lousy fée she had turned out to be. Half-blooded was nothing more than mortal.

Gossamyr tightened her grip about the staff and strummed her fingers across the clutter of stringed *arrets* dangling from her braided-leather hip belt. "What of my skills, my speed?"

Shinn set a hand on her shoulder. Violet eyes looked into hers, as if to leap into her being. "The skills you have honed over the years are yours to own, Gossamyr. Nothing can strip your physical prowess or your battle technique."

She nodded and slid a hand upon the Glamoursiège coat of arms that she also wore on her hip belt, her family's sigil, it was carved from the same applewood as her staff. "What of my essence, er...my soul? Do I have both? Can the Red Lady take either from me?"

"Your mortal blood—as well, the fact you are female—will serve a boon. The succubus will not have the slightest interest in you."

Her father's voice, deep and strung with a melodious harmony, vibrated within her. Ever and anon he had protected her—even when that protection had hurt her heart. When all other fée would look upon her with a strange reluctance that would keep them an armshot away, yet still amiable, Shinn stood at her side, his pride in her apparent in the determination that pressed back the naysayers.

"Desideriel will be glad of my absence," she remarked.

"He is a fine match, Gossamyr. We have discussed this overmuch."

"I do not like him. Do you not sense his distaste for me?"

"You see things only you wish to see."

With a sigh she offered a silent agreement. So, too, did Shinn see only what he wished to see.

So little to look forward to with her marriage to a man who saw only her faults, and yet, she did anticipate taking the Glamoursiège reign.

"I have groomed him." Reluctance cautioned Shinn's voice. "He understands what is expected."

"As well do I." A marriage for Glamoursiège, her heart be cursed to suffer for it. But she did respect her father's choice.

She would speak to Desideriel Raine. Perhaps look again into his eyes and determine if it truly was only her that thought to see his reluctance.

Shinn reached for her staff and drew it between the two of them. One toise in length, the steel-hard applewood had been carved by the Glamoursiège sage and fire-forged by dragon's breath. Intricate ribbons weaved into a crosswork of roses and flame about the rich wood.

"I will not bid you farewell," he offered as he pressed the staff into her hand. "Because you are unable to *twinclian*, you will have to Passage. There is no way to place you immediately in Paris, so a journey awaits. Take this purse of coin, purchase a swift horse and make haste."

Slipping a leather pouch from his hip, he then tied it to her belt. His fingers lingered on the coat of arms before relenting and stepping back.

Gossamyr spread her fingers around the ample pouch, feeling rich with its weight. Never had she required coin, for her father's steward and Mince had seen to her needs and desires. How she would miss Mince!

Shinn touched her forehead with his thumb and closed his eyes, imprinting the whorls of his life upon her flesh, connecting with her hidden eye, the all-seeing and all-knowing. No lack of glamour could dispel intuition.

"Come back to me," Shinn whispered.

A sudden hollowness in her chest forced her to swallow back a strange sense of loss. It wasn't as if she would never again see him. And Mince, the fretful matron, would only worry should she seek her for a farewell. Such discovery waited her on the Otherside!

"I will," she promised. "Set me off, and I shall succeed."

"I send you forth with my blessing, child of mine. Make right what you shall, and may you discover the solace to the ache that has been your nemesis."

With a nod, Gossamyr silently vowed that ache—the mortal passion—would not defeat her.

The soft press of Shinn's lips replaced his thumb. Gossamyr lifted her head and in the violet gaze looming over her she found all the strength she would ever need. "I am off, then?"

Shinn stepped back and nodded.

"Very well, but I've no *twinclian*. How shall I enter—"

TWO

France—1436

"—the Otherside?"

The droning alarm of a cicada announced her arrival. Wobbling off balance, Gossamyr swiftly recovered. She bent her knees and, hands spread, scanned her surroundings.

Every pore on her body sensed the world had changed. The air smelled verdant. Tightly sown moss, plush in density, cushed beneath her bare toes as they curled into the thickness. The musty vapor of earth rose about her. 'Twas a muted aroma of decaying wood and fetid bracken, similar to Faery but…different.

Gone, the Glamoursiège castle of blue marble.

Gone, the crystal Faery sky devoid of cloud or shadow.

The Spiral forest, why…it was gone. She stood on horizontal ground, not a mass of forest and marble and reticulated roots all twined and flowing at the slightest of angles.

A squeeze of her fingers reassured her staff was to hand. The carved ribbons pressed into her palm tingled with glamour. She had not natural glamour, but over the years Faery had seeped into her being, imbuing her with a latent glamour that could be briefly utilized.

Gossamyr touched her hip belt, clasping a narrow *arret* string. Scanning the ground she sighted within the brushy grass bright red toadstools dotted with white warts, closing her into a complete circle. *Amanita muscaria;* long ago her mother had taught her the strange name for the mushroom; Latin, she'd named the identifying language.

Names possess power. A litany fed to her every day since she could remember. *Use that power wisely.*

The toadstool circle had risen up below the castle tower overnight. Gossamyr had marveled that the peacocks had walked a wide berth about it. She had been standing in the tower immediately above the circle—indeed, a Passage.

A copse of pendulous cypress rose to her left, shadowing the thick grasses with a silky gray lacing. Pine and earth and grass flavored the air in a pale mist. Gossamyr drew in a breath. Gone, the sweet aroma of hyacinth. Shinn did not stand beside her, his hands clasped before him. The glimmer in her father's violet eyes was but a twinkle in the air, a breath of fée dust shimmering to naught.

She reached out, grasping at the absence of all she knew, all she had come to depend upon—Faery. Opening her palm upward, she spread her fingers. Gone.

But still there.

Faery was neither here nor there but betwixt and between. Though she could not see him Gossamyr knew Shinn could see her. *I will send a fetch.* She looked about, but sighted not a hovering spy.

According to what she had read in Veridienne's bestiary, mortals did have ways of peering in to Faery.

Indeed?

A mischievous tickle enticed Gossamyr to test that theory. Tilting her head forward, she peered back through the corner of her

eye. Swiftly, she jerked her head the opposite direction and nar-
rowly stretched her gaze.

Hmm. Not a glimmer or vibration in the sky. No flutter of iridescent wings, not a single flicker as fellow fée *twinclianed* elsewhere.

A trickle of panic tittered in Gossamyr's belly. She rubbed her
palms up and down her bare arms—the quilted pourpoint stopped
at hip and shoulder—and turned about, eyeing the ruffled canopy
of treetops. Grapelike clusters of bright yellow laburnum flowers
speckled the greenery. 'Twas clearly the edge of the same forest
that limned her father's castle. There! She recognized the hol-
lowed-out yew stump—a youngling's favorite hiding spot. But this
forest edge was no Edge. There was no risk of falling to a crush of
bones amidst the marsh roots should she step off the Edge, for the
land beyond this forest stretched on. The Bottom. Everywhere.

Gossamyr gulped. The Bottom was a dangerous place. But
where there were no marsh roots there would be no kelpies. No
kelpies meant no werefrogs. Blessings.

But what situation was she in now?

She had asked for this mission. And wonder upon wonders
Shinn had relented. What was once forbidden now lay before her.
The Otherside was hers to explore.

But not to forget: the fate of Faery relied on her success.

A decisive nod stirred courage to her surface.

"Champions are made. I will return to Faery the victor."

Until then— "Achoo!"

Spreading her arms to adjust her balance, Gossamyr settled a few
steps from where she had landed. "Achoo!"

What tickled her senses?

Sniffling, she thought briefly her watery eyes were tears. Tears
were a sign of weakness, of unfettered emotions. One could not
Be amidst a fury of conflicting emotion. She had once cried enough
tears for a lifetime, so it surprised now there should be any left.

Mayhap they were tears caused by the mortal atmosphere?

"It is merely the dust." For indeed motes of dust floated, and close loomed a skein of buzzing gnats.

Turning, Gossamyr scanned the dark emerald lacework of the forest canopy and the blackened trunks of oak trees she recognized, but had known in a more spectacular image. No exposed roots twisting and trailing down the length of the Spiral forest. 'Twas her favorite activity to swing and climb amongst the network of roots, chasing night moths. And where be the canorous frog song that so twinkled from amidst the shadowed roots?

Shrugging her hands up her arms, she scanned the forest. A rabbity moan brewed in her throat. Gossamyr pressed a hand to her chest. *Calm yourself.*

How to return when her mission was complete? She wasn't sure how she had entered the Otherside. Born without *twinclian*—the ability to twinkle in and out from a place—she could only imagine the task had been accomplished via Shinn's glamour.

Perhaps she should have gotten the return method clear with her father before setting off on adventure. Always, Shinn had tried to crush her penchant for rushing blindly into situations. A warrior must assess and plan. But Gossamyr liked the danger, and the thrill of dashing into the fray—as much as the peaceable kingdom of Glamoursiège had allowed. There were the occasional vagrants from the Netherdred that crept into the Spiral; excellent opportunity for Gossamyr to put her training to use. Always, though, Shinn had been there to aid.

Mayhap she had leaped a bit too far this time? Who would catch her should she stumble?

The buzz of a large insect spun Gossamyr about to spy a harnessed dragon fly. Pale blue wings spanned the width of her forearm. Zip, zip here; zip, zip there. The bejeweled harness glinted in the sunlight. It hovered before her—*see me, I am near*—then jettied up into the forest canopy.

"So he did send a fetch." A bit of Faery close by to reassure.

A breath of confidence filled Gossamyr's lungs. "Shinn would have never sent me did he not trust I would be successful. I will find the Red Lady and put an end to her vicious reign. If more of those revenants return to Faery, my father will have a full-scale battle on his hands. I must make haste."

Which way lay Paris? Perched high atop the Spiral in her father's castle *down* was the only direction she had ever learned. To navigate horizontally instead of vertically would prove…interesting.

Gossamyr searched her memory and envisioned a finely detailed page from Veridienne's bestiary, a map of the mortal city with the various tribes of Faery inscribed over all. Glamoursiège sat downsouth of Paris.

Lifting her foot, she remembered the Passage. A precarious position for one just arrived. Stabbing her staff outside the circle, she swung her legs up and out and landed the ground.

She stared wistfully at the empty ring of toadstools. 'Twas how the Dancers arrived in Faery. A Passage should, by rights, work both ways.

Should she? Just a test?

Gripping her staff, Gossamyr lifted her foot and pointed a toe toward the circle, then…she stepped inside. One foot firmly planted on the ground. Shallow breaths quietly exhaled. The chirring finale of the cicada's song rattled to silence.

Nothing.

"Hmm…"

Removing her foot from the circle, she then tried the other foot, and waited, breath held.

Again, naught but the pulse beat of her heart inside her ears.

Looking about she did not spy the fetch. It saw all, she knew. Dare she jump inside with both feet? What if it did work? She would return to Faery. To Mince's sheltering arms. And Shinn's disapproving eyes.

Her father had granted her this opportunity. She must to it!

"I can do this," Gossamyr said. A shrug of her shoulders and a loosening shake of her limbs summoned bravery. "I *will* do this. I know how to protect myself. I know how to track and defend. Oh yes——" a smile crooked her mouth "——I want some adventure."

A few strides put her to a narrow wheel path gouged along the horizontal purlieu of the forest. The packed red dirt felt warm beneath her bare feet. She must have landed the edge of Glamoursiège territory, for the Spiral forest spun down to the border between tribes.

The Netherdreds inhabited the perilous flatlands that surrounded large mortal cities, for their kind thrived in the unstable atmosphere that separated Faery from the Otherside. (Faery simply did not exist in the large cities. Densely populated mortal lands tended to tamper with the Enchantment. As well, the mortals' use of magic drained any Enchantment that seeped too close.) Gossamyr would have to traverse the Netherdred, albeit, she now stood on the Otherside, so there was no fear to encounter any from the nefarious tribe.

However, if she had come to the Otherside, what then, prevented a Netherdred from doing the same?

Flicking a keen eye about, Gossamyr assessed her surroundings. Alone. And keep it that way.

The fetch buzzed overhead, its wings glinting copper against the settling sunlight.

"Not alone," she reminded. And was pleased for it.

A skip to her left and she scampered onward. A smile was unstoppable. Her high spirits lended a lightness to her steps. Gossamyr splayed her arms out to her sides. A shimmy of her hips nearly lifted her bare feet from the ground. She felt...less heavy.

"So light," she marveled.

Always in Faery she had fought her natural awkwardness. Cumbersome in the air there, and often tripping over roots or rocks. Yet here? The air barely skimmed her being. Performing a spin, Gossamyr let out a squeal and set again to her pace.

A tilt of head took in the vast horizon. Fascinating to view the sunset from its parallel and not above.

Fragile wings skimmed the scabbed cut on her cheek, and the skitter of legs tapped at her nose and forehead. Faster than a wing-beat, Gossamyr lashed out, capturing a damselfly by the wings. She dangled the annoying insect before her face and tilted a defiant smirk at the pivoting jade eyes.

"Thought you possessed swiftness, eh? The air here is better suited to me— Achoo!"

Nearly toppled from her feet by that powerful sneeze, Gossamyr stumbled and stabbed her staff into the red dirt.

The damselfly escaped in a spiraling ascent through the crystal sky, a sleek distraction for the fetch.

A silly grin followed Gossamyr's explosion. While the air seemed to fit her like a charm, it did not want her to get too comfortable.

Of a sudden, a strange, mournful tune touched her ear. The small *clink* of saddle furnishings punctuated the song with synco-pated notes.

Gossamyr spun to eye a horse and rider ambling down the path. Her right hand stiffening and fingering the waxed cord of an *arret,* she homed in on the approaching target and crouched to strike.

Paris—downnorth

Aaee aaaa...mmm...oooo....

The melodious call beckoned him along the rough limestone garden wall, arms stretched to flatten his body and meld with the twilight shadows. Wings scraped against stone, but for the task he did not mind the pain.

Again came the sonorous call, a seductive beckoning. He closed his eyes and rode the shiver that vibrated his very bones and bub-bled his blood. A strange and overwhelming desire always transpired at the call. For a moment it blocked those just-beneath-the-surface longings to flee, to mutiny.

Down the alley the door to an inn opened to emit or eject. The beat of drums, pounding to a rhythm of the Indian isles, escaped and fixed a tempo inside his breast. It synchronized with his heartbeats and played dull tympani to the succubus's call.

His fingers curling around the corner of a darkened cobbler's shop, he peeked to spy the nondescript black lacquered carriage across the empty market square. Red curtains of heavy plush covered the glassless windows; a thin, painted red line danced an arabesque across the gut of the carriage. The equipage, plumed in even more red, stood motionless, sleeping upon their feet. The coachman slept as well; a forced rest, that.

Aaee...aaaaa...mmm...

He dived into the shudder that swelled in his muscles and centered in his groin. Moans leaked from his tight lips, aching for her touch, to be controlled by his mistress. Though the call spoke of private pleasures and selfless devotion, he knew this one was not for him. He only received the call in the privacy of his lady's manor.

So he watched as from out of the shadows crept a lone man, tall and armed at his left hip with a sword. They always approached with cautious steps and plumed hats pulled low. Elegantly dressed in doublet and thigh-high boots, a chain of ornamental gold hung heavily about his shoulders—rich, then.

Fée, the watcher deduced, for their kind betrayed themselves with their carriage. Ever haughty and slim, unable to sulk under the oppression Paris pressed down upon all. Regal rogues. Yet Disenchantment had melted away this one's wings.

Not mine, the watcher thought. *Puppy still has wings.*

The fée ran a glove, palmed in mail, along the carriage body, inexplicably tracing the fine red line—when a lithe hand swept out from the window. Flinching as if singed, the fée's hand recoiled, but as quickly dashed back to clasp the female's fingers. He bent to inhale the aroma of lemon soaking the fine kidskin glove.

The watcher rubbed together his bare fingers. Dry cracks from squeezing lemons to extract the oil from the slippery rinds tormented his flesh. *Good Puppy.*

One final call. This melody lingered, wrapping its music about the fée's volition and securing hold.

As the carriage door creaked open, the watcher hated her. Slipping a hand into the leather sheath at his hip he drew up a long thin needle of silver, capped with a smooth, perfect ball of winter-forged iron.

Pin man.

No. *I am your puppy, yes?*

Moonlight danced on the pin's tip. Fixing to the thin shimmer of silver he mesmerized himself, falling into the moment and the singular admiration of the narrow shine. Anything to avoid thinking of her…and what absence denied him.

Moments later the carriage door again creaked open. One long leg thrust out, followed by a torso and the other leg dragging closely behind. The fée stumbled, catching himself upon the ground with his gloves. Mail *clished* across the cobbles. The tip of a steel-capped sabre sheath drew a metallic line in the wake of the clatter. Curious, the Parisian fée choose metal weapons over the finer stone instruments. Did the Disenchanted no longer fear the bite of iron or the burn of steel?

The watcher pressed his back to the wall and closed his eyes, clutching the pin near his thigh. Silver, yes, but a strange magic protected him from its devastating burn.

The fée managed to right himself, wobbled as if soused, then sauntered toward the shadows. Boots, spurred and jingling, trudged closer. A racket of riches announced the fée's approach. The watcher felt the wind of movement as a gloved hand smacked the wall near his ear—steadying, grasping a moment to catch a breath that from this moment on could only be a dying cry.

The fée passed without notice. Almost.

The pin held firmly in his palm, the long needle sticking out between his first and second finger, tugged at fine silk hose and pierced. The small cry from the fée preceded his jerk to swing and eye his attacker. He stared at the pin man for but a second—memorize those strange-colored eyes and smooth silvery skin dotted with red—then staggered onward.

Drawing the pin along his torso, one deft twist tilted the point to his nose. The pin man drew in the scent of the fée's blood, savoring it as if a bung-cork plucked from the cask of aged Bordeaux—not so much sweet as sour, and laced with an earthen origin. Scent of Faery. Had he ever lived there? *Yes!* But…when?

He dashed across the way, and lifting the carriage door open without making a single creak, entered the dark box. Crawling upon the carriage floor and coiling his legs up under him, he stretched an arm along the soft, sensuous damask skirts, feeling beneath all the frill and lace her thigh, the sharp curve of her hip and waist. Burying his face into her lap he sighed and snuggled into salvation.

The tips of sharpened fingernails grazed his scalp as his mistress raked a hand through his long hair. "Such a good puppy you are."

He snuggled his face deeper into the warm thickness of bone-colored damask and lemon and the cloying aroma of woman. Always she allowed him this small moment. A reward for a task begun.

But not completed.

THREE

The horse seemed more a mule for it did not span half so high as the eighteen-hand destriers Shinn's troops had once ridden into battle. Gossamyr loved to ride the stallions across a flower-dappled meadow, her arms stretched wide to catch the wind—it was as close as she ever came to flying. But never too close to the Edge.

The careless tune suddenly ceased and a dark-hooded head looked up at the block in the road.

"Well met?" called Gossamyr, waving to appear unthreatening. She had no intention of attacking until she determined a menace. "Be you friend or foe?"

The male snorted. "You shall have to divine that for yourself."

Taken aback, Gossamyr straightened and unhooked an *arret*. It wasn't so much the rude reply but the tone of it. Harsh and deep, and not at all friendly.

The man heeled the mule toward Gossamyr until they stood but two leaps from her. Truly a mutant, the beast. For what purpose did so small a horse serve when its master's feet toed the grass tops?

The rider remained astride, unconcerned the proper greeting

should see him bowing before her. Green-and-black horizontal-striped hosen, tight as spriggan-skin, emphasized his long legs; a shock of pattern weeping from the blur of black wool cloak and hood. His pale face was severely scored by a thin beard and mustache the color of burnt chestnuts. Following the length of his blade nose, Gossamyr focused on his blue eyes filled with more white than color. Eerie. She had not before looked into eyes of such color.

"I…offer you no bane," she tried. How to address a mortal? "Er…kind mortal."

"Oh?" He leaned forward, balancing his palms on the saddle pommel. "And do all ladies fair welcome a weary traveler with such a big stick? And wielded in a manner as to appear threatening?"

Gossamyr stabbed the staff into the moss at foot and shrugged. "You offered no answer to my query, so I cannot be sure if I face friend or foe."

"I am neither," he said and stroked a hand over his bearded chin.

Those eerie eyes assessed her from head to bare toes, a gaze that boldly brushed her being. The sensory assault unnerved her for she was still startled by the tone of the man's voice. So rough. Not at all melodious. The urge to step forward and scent him was strong, but she remained. Caution, her instincts whispered.

"What is that dangling from your hand?"

She gave the *arret* a twirl; the sharpened obsidian tip cut the air with a hiss. A simple weapon she fashioned herself. Not fire-forged, but deadly in its swift and accurate flight.

"Looks like that device would hurt," the man bellowed in notes that knocked at the insides of Gossamyr's skull. "At the least, leave a mark, should a man find it lodged in any portion of his anatomy."

Amused by his jesting tone, Gossamyr agreed with a smirk. She had never placed an *arret* to any part of a man's anatomy—mortal or fée—but there was always a first time. She lowered the weapon but kept it in hand.

She hadn't expected to encounter a mortal so quickly. She had just been getting her bearings! Nor was she prepared in any way to converse with him. Did all mortals emit such raw and echoing sounds when they spoke? Gossamyr was accustomed to the musical lilt of fée speak; she had never guessed that mortals would not sound the same.

Well! Her first mortal. (If she did not tally Veridienne—whom she did not—for she, too, had worn a blazon of glamour). The fascination with standing so close to one did stir her blood. She had only ever dreamed to meet another mortal besides her mother. There wasn't much physical difference between mortal and fée in body height or appendages, save the fée's defining swish of wings, horns, scales and the occasional spiked spine. And the telling blazon.

Gossamyr gripped her throat. Was it noticeable? Is that why curious blue eyes fixed to her?

"You are alone, fair lady of the strange costume?" Not so grating as the initial tones.

"I am," she replied. Strange costume? Her arachnagoss pourpoint? It was certainly very average. Mayhap he did not notice the sheen of glamour on her flesh. Better even, mayhap her blazon was concealed?

Two steps took her right up to the mule's side. She gazed up into the mortal's hooded visage. Musk and earth and a curious scent of sweetness intrigued.

"Remarkable," the rumble-toned man said. "And most bewildering."

"Why so?"

"My lady, do you not fear attack?"

A short burst of laughter preceded Gossamyr's cocky grin. A spin of the longstaff cut the air in a swift gulp and she stabbed the tip to ground near her foot. "As you have remarked, I carry a big stick."

"Indeed. As well you could take a man's eye out with that spinny thing."

"It is an *arret*," she explained, then tucked it away on her braided amphi-leather belt. "Achoo!"

"Bless yo—my lady? Did—did you just...twinkle?"

"What?" *Twinclian?* She hadn't moved. Well, the sneeze had shaken her fiercely—

"You just glimmered!"

Impossible—ah! So her blazon was visible!

A step back was necessary. A tug of her pourpoint did not lift the soft fabric any higher than her collarbone. The blazon started under her chin and flowed to the bottom of her collarbone, wrapping around her neck to under her ears.

The fée did not reveal themselves to mortals. Nothing but ill could come from discovery. Another step placed her in the shade of a fat-leaved mulberry.

Yet another startling thought unsettled: this mortal *could* see her. Mortals were not capable of seeing the fée. Not unless they possessed the sight. Hmm... Unless—no, she knew the fée visited the Otherside completely unseen.

Mayhap a half blood was visible to mortals?

So long as he did see her, she had better distract attention from her blazon, the only telling sign of Faery.

She summed up the man's attire, long dark cloak, striped hose and an open white shirt with blue peacocks embroidered around the neck. About his fingers danced colors of ruby, sapphire and gold. Various silver symbols hung from a leather cord about his neck. Alchemical symbols, she surmised. A sure sign of the sight. And that she must beware, for surely he dabbled with magic. "You are...a wizard?"

"Far from it."

"A mage?"

"Are they not two of the same?"

"What are you?" *That you can see me!*

"Why, I am a man." Still sitting upon his mule he bowed to her and introduced himself. "Jean César Ulrich Villon III." Casting a wink at her, he said, "But you may call me Ulrich."

Ulrich. Who saw her. And whose voice blasted inside her skull and rippled through her body like tiny sparkles of sunlight heating her flesh. Everything about him called to her attention.

Was it the same for him? Did she sound so different? How soon before her blazon faded? Surely the Disenchantment would wipe it away?

And until it did, and she could walk undetected by mortal eyes?

"I shall call you gone." Gossamyr nodded over her shoulder and made show of spinning the staff in a twirl of defiance.

"The lady is not a conversationalist. And I must heed she is well armed." The man heeled his mule and ambled past her. "Very well. This forest remains the same. The trees are the same. All…is well." His hood did not conceal the curious eyes drinking her in from crown to toe. Bare toes, Gossamyr realized as she turned her toes inward. "Fair fall you, my lady. Good…day." He paused, blatantly staring at her, then, snapping his attention away, nodded. He muttered to himself, his parting words low but audible, "Could she be?"

Gossamyr watched until the man disappeared beyond a rise on the red clay path and the whistles of his renewed dirge became but a figment. Only then did she release her held breath. And only then did she realize she had been holding her breath.

"What sort of skittish maid am I? He presented no threat. He was but a man. A mortal man. I should have…asked him things. Questioned him!" She kicked a tuft of grass.

For all her frustration she had not been trained on mortal relations. Shinn had ever made it clear a trip to the Otherside would never occur. Martial skills served well against the spriggans, hobs and werefrogs of Faery. One did not have to converse with the rabble, merely lay them out.

So what hindrance had befallen her tongue? 'Twas not as if she had never before stood so close to a male. So close as to once kiss, she thought wistfully.

You are exotic... A Rougethorn's wondrous declaration to love.

Yes, I can love. It is the mortal half of me who loves, I know it!

My lady, did you glimmer?

Ah! 'Twas the man's notice of her blazon that had thrown her off! That is why she had sent him away so hurriedly. She had not expected to be seen. And if so, she required time to plot how she would move about in this new and alien world.

Yet, for as strange as she suspected her surroundings, the man had made an odd remark about the sameness of the forest. Verily, in a stretched-out, horizontal manner. And yet, far removed from all she had ever called home.

Fact remained, the mortal had seen her. Mayhap they all could? Her half blood had never before been tested by unEnchanted eyes. And if all could see her then all would remark the blazon.

A disguise must be summoned to cloak her fée shimmer. Shinn had told her of those mortals who would keep fée as pets. A caged spectacle to be presented at fêtes and in market squares, forced to wallow in the Disenchantment until they literally shriveled to bone.

She had not true glamour, though by merely living in Faery she had absorbed a bit of the skill. With a decisive nod, Gossamyr closed her eyes and began to concentrate, to summon her latent power of glamour. If she simply thought *plain* that would mask the blazon.

"Ho!"

Drawn prematurely from her attempt, Gossamyr twisted at the waist. There he was *again*. The man with the eerie blue eyes and clinking silver charms about his neck. Had he traveled a circle? This forest, dense and large, would surely require any casual traveler much time to circumnavigate—even should his journey spiral. Was mortal time so spectacular then?

Time is the enemy.

"What sort of witchery be this?" the man said as he heeled his mount beside Gossamyr.

Her fingers toyed with the carvings on the staff, and one hand flattened to her throat. "You jest with me."

"I beg that I do not, my lady. I traveled straight; there was not a turn in the road. And yet—"

"No time passed?"

"Exactly." Pressing a hand over his brows to shade his view from the setting sun, he peered at her. A flicker of ruby flashed in his ring. "I do not believe your sparkle is merely the sun—"

"Impossible you did not turn and cut back through the forest."

He shrugged, and the hood of his cloak fell to his shoulders to reveal a scatter of tangled hair and a trickle of crimson running from temple to ear. Might have been scratched by a branch, so small the cut. Yet there, to the side of his right eye, a bruise the color of crushed blackberries tormented the flesh. What had the man been to? Fighting? Defense?

"Be gone with you, stranger," Gossamyr said. She had enough to sort through without him tangling her thoughts, making her wonder when wonder was best abandoned to focused attention.

The buzz of the fetch zoomed past her face, too quick for a mortal to regard as any other than an insect. Shinn kept watch.

"Ride straight and do not look back."

With a surrendering splay of his hands, the man huffed out a grand sigh. "As the lady wishes. I've my own sorrows to keep me this day." He again heeled the mule. With a bristle of its dirty hide the beast carried its master onward.

Over the rise in the road, Gossamyr watched and listened keenly for his return, for a signal he veered from the path and into the underbrush that paralleled the pounded dirt. A bluefinch soared overhead, chirring a greeting that made her smile. Exactly as the birds in Faery. The bird verified the traveler neared the edge of the forest—

"'Tis a spell!"

Behind her, Jean César Ulrich Villon III reined the beast to a halt and jumped to the ground. Fists planted akimbo, he looked over the mule, then up the verdant wall of the surrounding forest. Gossamyr thought she heard him mutter, "The same."

"Be you a witch?" he called.

"Most certainly not." That would imply she dabbled with forbidden magic! She stomped over to him and jabbed her staff under his chin. "Tell me true, you traveled straight?"

He nodded, raising his spread hands to his shoulders to keep them in view. Small cuts gashed his palms and wrists. Had the man battled his way out from a prickle bush? Where then had he found such a nasty bruise?

Gossamyr scanned the forest, seeking a tear in the curtain to Faery where perhaps a sprite might be seen spying on his mischievous deed. Wide hornbeam leaves remained still as stone. Tree trunks gripped the earth, silent stately sentinels. Pale ivy twisted about the grasses and journeyed toward the toadstool circle. Not a dryad in the lot.

Gossamyr could not be sure if it was because she no longer stood in Faery, or simply, the Disenchantment befell more quickly than expected. She saw nothing out of sorts. *Save that everything was horizontal.*

"Pisky led," she decided, then snapped the staff away from the man's chin.

"What?" Ulrich followed her as she turned and stalked down the rough path away from him. "I've not seen a pixy."

"Pisky," she corrected sharply.

"Piskies, pixies, what have you!"

"They are very different. Piskies fly, pixies…they trundle. As well, pixies do not glimmer."

"Only thing I've seen that glimmers of the enchanted is you, my lady. On your neck there— Oh, Hades!" He clamped a palm to his forehead. The action resulted in a yelp, for obviously his bruised face pained him. "Not again! Pray, tell you are not a damned faery."

Gossamyr winced at the unfamiliar word. Not a favorable oath, she guessed from his tone.

"You are not? You cannot be. Dragon piss!" He pressed beringed fingers between them in an entreaty. "Have they sent someone to bring me back? Where are they? Do they lurk? No! I will not go. I refuse!" He curled his fingers and wrung the balled fist at Gossamyr. "Your kind have done enough to foul my life."

"I am n-not a faery," Gossamyr managed. She pressed a hand to her throat where the blazon was visible. *They keep them chained in cages.* "No, not faery," she reiterated more confidently.

"You lie, trickster! Your sort never speak the truth, only in circles." The man drew tiny frantic rings in the air before him. "Circles, circles, circles. Oh, but those damned circles! It is not the same! Changed, damn them all. It has all changed!"

"Believe me or not," Gossamyr said over his ranting. "I am m-mortal, like you." A quick twist of her fingers clasped the highest agraffe on her pourpoint, closing the vest to an uncomfortable tightness.

"Mortal?" He jerked a sneer at her. "My lady, we *mortals* do not have occasion to call ourselves mortals. We are men, women, coopers, bakers, fishermen—but never do we say *mortal*. Tavern keepers, tanners, magi and—"

"Enough! I am…a woman then." Yes, he must see that! She managed an awkward curtsy—a quick bend of one knee—and forced a smile. "Are you well pleased?"

"Pleased? To stand in the presence of a faery?"

"I am not!"

"What of your clothing?"

"What of it?"

He peered closely at her. Gossamyr controlled the urge to reach for the discoloration on his cheek. Did it feel hot? Tender? What *did* a mortal feel like? His face was such a display of movement and lines and sighs and outburst. So emotional!

Oblivious to Gossamyr's curiosity, Ulrich eyed the sleeveless pourpoint, slid over the applewood sigil propped on her hip, then stretched his gaze back up her neck. Stuffed with arachnagoss and sown in a fine quilting, the garment protected from sharp or slashing weapons.

He finally said, "Are those leaves sewn together?"

Clutching the rugged fabric fitted snugly to her body, Gossamyr lifted her chin. "Mayhap," she offered stubbornly, thinking a lie would be just that—so obvious. Lies served nothing but to prolong the inevitable bane. But the truth of her was a necessary misappropriation, lest she find herself in a cage rotting in a market square.

"Leaves! Marvelous!" A brilliant smile revealed white teeth and he clapped his hands together—but the smile straightened sharply, as did his mood. "Well, I am not going with you."

"I did not ask your accompaniment, mort—er, Ulrich."

"So be off then." He shooed her with a flip of his fingers. "Back to Faery where you belong."

"Do you not hear well?"

"Perfectly."

"Mayhap you are daft? I said I am n-not a faery. It is ridiculous of you to assume as much." Gossamyr crossed her arms over her chest and assumed a defiant stance.

"What then places you here in my path, charming my mule to return at your bidding? If that is not faery glamour, I don't know what is. Have not your kind toyed with me enough?"

"What torments have you suffered at the hands of Faery?"

"You don't know?" A skip to his right, his feet nimble and sure, twirled him around once and ended with a mock bow. The man changed moods so quickly he was either barmy or a lackwit.

He blew forcefully from his mouth, which fluttered his lips into a slobbery sound. "Is not a dance of the decades damage enough? Oh!" He thrust up his arms, then as quickly, snapped into a wary crouch and scanned the dense forest. "Am I in Faery now? If you mean me no harm then get me gone from here. I command it of you, wicked faery!"

Gossamyr rolled her eyes at his dramatics—then narrowed her gaze on him. The remarkable thing about the man was not the bruises and blood but that contour of hair above and below his mouth. Fée men did not sport facial hair. It wasn't necessary, for, unlike dwarves, they did not require body hair to protect from the elements. And those eyes. Blue, a color Gossamyr had never before looked into. Her mother's brown eyes were the only anomaly from the fée violet. And her own. So much color twinned on the man's face, and yet, that color drowned in a sea of white.

"We stand in the mortal realm, Jean César, er—"

"Ulrich Villon. The third—hell, what am I doing? I have just given my name complete to a faery!"

If he only knew how little glamour she could wield with that information.

A poke of her staff into the ground spoke her impatience. "Not a single faery taunts you this day." Or so he must believe. But he seemed to know about her kind. And the forest, it seemed not to want him to leave her side.

Hmm... An enchanted bane or boon? She must...test. If he could leave her, then it was mere coincidence. If he again returned to her side, then they were meant—for reasons beyond her grasp—to travel together. It is all she could figure with so little experience of this realm.

"Get back on your mule and ride off. I will follow you over that ridge in the path to ensure your success."

"She is not a mule," the man offered as he mounted. His shoes, strapped and circled in thin leather ties, grazed the grass tops.

"Fancy is a rare breed, yet while lacking in height makes up for it in endurance."

Fancy? A miserable waste of horseflesh. But Gossamyr did not speak her annoyance. Surely the only reason for the man's return to her twice over was that someone or thing in Faery saw to make mischief with her. But to speak to Faery—the trees, as the man would view it—would not put her to advantage. And where was the fetch when she needed to communicate?

Gesturing the mortal and his mule follow, Gossamyr walked up the path. At the rise, she saw the forest stretched ahead for endless lengths. Not a visible root or marsh kelpie in sight. Impossible he had traveled the distance and returned to her side in so little time.

Could Shinn be behind this? What reason had her father to place this man in her path? He had wanted her to accept a guide...

"You are a faery," Ulrich muttered, the mule ambling to make pace with Gossamyr's light-footed strides. "I know it. I am not going with you, foul one."

"Suits me fine and well. I have no need of such misery to accompany me on my travels, you barmy bit of breath. Go. Once more," she said as the man passed her by. And then he was gone.

Assuming a defiant stance, shoulders back and one knee slightly bent, Gossamyr counted her breaths, waiting, wondering. A strum of her fingers across the dangling *arrets* produced a multitude of obsidian clicks. Deadly aim, Shinn had once remarked of her skill. She'd taken the prize in tournament three years consecutive.

With a sigh, she shook away the sudden rise of apprehension created by her encounter with the mortal. Time threatened. Her father and his troops must battle more revenants even as she stood here.

She felt a familiar presence first at the base of her skull, the prinkles of warning, of sure knowing.

Gossamyr reluctantly turned to face where she had started her adventures in the Otherside. There lumbered her pisky-led mule and rider. It was too ridiculous to wonder. And so she loosed a chuckle and splayed her arms out in surrender.

"It appears I am destined to remain at your side," Ulrich called. "Oh, to tap into the source of such magic!" Then he narrowed his blue gaze on her and muttered, "Mayhap I will, luck be with me."

"I possess no magic." And that was truth. Magic was a mortal device, forbidden in Faery. (Though there were those who dabbled.) For every use of magic, be it good or for evil, tapped Enchantment. Mortals literally stole Enchantment (most unknowing) to conjure their spells and charms and bewitchments. Should a fée be accused of dabbling, banishment was immediate.

"I do not know why you lie, faery, but I will allow you are a lone woman who must protect herself. Of course, lies be the way of the faery."

"Faeries do not appeal to you?"

"Faery circles, my lady. And we are far from— Yei-ih!" He flicked his gaze back and forth between Gossamyr and the ground. "What is that? It's…that's it. A toadstool circle?" Ulrich heeled the mule, but it remained stubbornly stationed beside the Passage from which Gossamyr had disembarked. "Move, beast! Get thee gone!"

Gossamyr reached out. A tweetering whistle enticed the mule to wander toward her as she walked widdershins down the path. "They are merely toadstools. No harm will come to thee."

"Speaks one who has not danced!"

A Dancer? Gossamyr peered at the mortal, seeing him newly. Much as she loved her parents and her home, she had ever been curious about the mortal realm. A curiosity that had flowered since the day she'd witnessed a Dancer. So very much like herself. Wingless and clumsy, with a lumbering body that had made his dance steps wobble—almost as if the air was too heavy for him to acclimate.

Had this man really Danced? Or did he merely babble nonsensities? To make a determination proved yet difficult. Too new this mortal realm, and this man but her first mortal. Nothing to compare him to. He could be luna-touched for all she knew.

But he had returned to her side, thrice over.

"You have been placed in my path for a reason. I must accept and move on, for urgency is fore. Come!" The mule followed as she walked onward. "Do you ride to the nearest village?" she asked, her pace slowing to mirror the mule's laborious trudge.

"Mayhap I do."

"I've great need to know how far away it lies. What is the time from here to the next village? How many suns will rise before I arrive?"

The horizon held his attention. Young, he appeared, though the gashed flesh on his hands lended to hard labor, or struggle. Definitely struggle, to gauge from the condition of his face. He could well be her peer.

"Aparjon," he offered, without looking her way. "That be the next village. And following…who knows." His heavy sigh intrigued Gossamyr. "I go where I am led. Tell me true, you have not been sent to retrieve me to Faery?"

"You continue to assume I am from Faery when I tell you I am not." She winced at the lie. And she fooled herself to believe the blazon was not visible even with the highest agraffe secured. "I am on a mission."

"Ah. A woman on a mission. And she wields a big stick, so watch out world!"

Ulrich scruffed a hand through his tangles of dark hair and offered a genuine grin. A missing tooth to the side of his front teeth spoke of certain battle. "You are not like most women."

"Why say you such?"

"You are confidant and commanding."

She bristled proudly at his expert observations.

"And…well, you do twinkle."

"And you bleed."

He touched the cut on his forehead and studied the minute flakes of blood on his fingers before dismissing it with a shrug. "A mere scuffle, which found the opponent most unfortunate."

"You sure it was not a tangle with a prickle bush?"

"Would that it had been so. I hate bloody banshees." He narrowed a suspicious gaze at her. "You're not a banshee, are you?"

"No. Merely mort—like you. What of that bruise?"

Trembling fingers smoothed over the modena on the man's face. He grimaced and shook his head. "If I told you a woman gave it to me, would you believe such foolery?"

Gossamyr shrugged. "A woman like myself?"

"I see your point."

"Your insistence you see faeries and banshees leads me to wonder if you've the sight?"

"That dance changed everything. I'm still a bit dansey-headed from the whole event. I want Faery from my eyes!"

So he did see. Yet obviously it was not a gift he enjoyed.

Striding lightly, Gossamyr clicked her tongue to encourage the mule to pick up pace. It did not, and so she slowed.

"Now, explain to me why, if you are not a faery, your dress is so strange. Leaves for clothing? And those braies, they appear to be leather, but never have I seen so remarkable a color. Only the fair folk could fashion such a garment and make it strong and so flexible."

Gossamyr smirked. The remarkable color was utterly average. Fashioned from frog skin, the amphi-leather was strong but flexible and comfortable.

"It would not be wise to be seen by any in a village or otherwise dressed in such a manner," he stated. "Women conceal their forms with dresses and silly pointed hats. And sleeves. And shoes. Braies and hose are for men. As are weapons."

She had not considered as much. Why had not Shinn? Of course, male and female were equals in Faery. Though Veridienne's bestiary had detailed the misbalance between the sexes in the Otherside. For all Shinn's visits to the Otherside, he should have known.

Gossamyr glanced over her attire. The fitted pourpoint stopped at her thighs. The weapon belt hung snugly across her hips. The Glamoursiège arms were carved in fire-forged applewood—faery wings upon a sword and shield; a holly vine wrapped about the sword signified the peaceable times. Amphi-leather braies wrapped her legs, and secured about her ankles a thin strip of leather kept the loose braies from catching on brambles or sticks.

The bestiary had illustrated mortal women wearing dresses sewn from ells of elaborate fabric trimmed with furs and jewels. Gossamyr wore gowns when it suited her—for balls and celebrations. Rarely though did such cumbersome garb suit her.

Had Veridienne insinuated herself to the Otherside with ease? But of course, her mother had known the ways of this world, for she had been born here. Gossamyr sensed now it would require much more than mere study of pictures and text for a rogue half-blood fée to find equal success.

Keep the blazon concealed.

"As well—" Ulrich leaned forward "—you travel alone, and are far too lovely to put off a man's advances."

"Let no man test my mettle unless he wishes to pull back a nub. Or, lose another tooth."

Ulrich whistled through the space in his teeth. "I believe you, my lady. I believe you."

She stepped through the grass and leaned in close to him. "Stop smiling."

"Can't."

"Try."

He spread his arms wide to exclaim, "'Tis the bane of my existence, this smile." He paced a grand circle about her, as if announcing to the masses an exciting performance. "For all the tragedy I have endured it did little to remove this false glee. For it is false. I feel only sadness in my heart."

"Be that the reason for your mournful tune when first you approached?"

He stilled in his circle of footsteps. "You heard?"

"Your world is filled with echoes—er, *this* world." She grimaced and punctuated her frustration by stabbing her staff into the ground with each word. "*My* world. The continent."

"France?"

"Indeed."

She caught his bemused grin. Far more appealing than his frown or shouted oaths. The sudden thought that this mortal appealed to her only vexed. *You've no luxury to dally!*

"As for my smile, women drop like flies in a swoon when they see my pearly chompers."

"Are you sure it is not your smell?" Peering through the corner of her eye at him, Gossamyr teased, "Flies dropping in manure?"

He puffed out a protesting huff.

"Well, *I* am still standing," she offered, unable to hide a playful grin.

"You, my lady—" he stabbed the air before her with a finger "—are not a woman."

"I am so!"

"You are a faery."

"The correct term is fée."

"Fée, faery, banshee, witch! For all my troubles are caused by the like." He kicked the dirt path and dust rose up about his parti-colored ankles.

Swoon? More like clap him with the tip of her staff. A banshee? Truly? Gossamyr knew of no root swamps—the banshees' usual haunt—but the rift had increased the likelihood of mortals in Faery, as well it let out more from Faery to torment the Otherside.

This moment she likely stood near Netherdred territory.

"Have you a name, faery? Or would that be encroaching upon

your person to inquire such? I do know should a faery give his name complete he would hand over his power."

As well, a fée garnered much control over the mortal with his complete name. Jean César Ulrich Villon III. Quite the mouthful. Were she full-blooded, Gossamyr could work an *erie* upon his tongue to silence him.

"I am not afraid of your taunts."

"Prove it with the gift of your name."

A challenge? Such daring stirred her blood. She was beginning to like this man, despite his barmy nature.

"It is…" Gossamyr paused.

Never give your name to a mortal. They use magic, and can command your compliance by repeating it thrice. You will be beholden to their cruel wishes.

Caged and taunted, kept as a pet…

"My lady?"

A *schusch* of wind danced the leaves overhead into a rising cheer. Nearby, Fancy snuffled over a patch of clover.

'Twas only her name complete which would give away her power. The mortal had no means to discover that. "You may call me Gossamyr."

"Gossamyr." He whistled through the space in his teeth. "What sort of name be that? Gaelic? Irish? Not a bloody Scot, are you?"

"You talk too much."

"And you are far too impudent for a woman." He danced with his speech, as if it a natural extension of his thoughts. Into a circle about her, but too far for her to touch or even scent. "What be your destination? And whom have you left behind? Surely there is a father or husband who mourns your absence. And so alone."

"I am not alone—*achoo!*—I am with you."

He eyed her staff, held at shoulder level like a pike ready for launch. "Mayhap not. But there is something about me you should know."

"What be that?"

A splay of his beringed fingers before him caught the fading sunlight in a rainbow of glints. Moving his hands like snakes slinking through the air, he bemused with his extravagant motions. "I have always had a weakness for sparkly things." Another wink seemed to please him immensely.

Sparkly things? Gossamyr felt a strange warmth rise in her face. She lowered her staff and looked away so he could not see her discomfort. The blazon must be shed. Soon.

"I merely require direction to the next village," she said. "Is it very large? I must purchase a swift horse and, as you suggest, some clothing."

"Yes, I favor a fine dress of damask for you. And long red ribbons for the plaits in your hair."

Gossamyr snorted and flipped the silver-tipped end of one of her thick plaits back over her shoulder. "Ribbons? Do you romance me, then? I'll have you know I do not succumb to a man's charm so easily—"

"Bloody hell!"

Gossamyr froze, the tone of Ulrich's voice alerting her to the vibrations now obvious in the ground. Vibrations increasing in strength and moving toward them. She'd been so busy chaffering she hadn't been paying attention.

"Don't look now, Gossamyr, but you are soon to discover consorting with Jean César Ulrich Villon III is not for the faint of heart."

Gossamyr did look. And what she saw loosed her demon-take-me smile.

The silhouette of a wide, squat figure barreled toward them. Dust plumed about it in a furious cloud. It wasn't a man. It wasn't even mortal.

Danger had arrived.

FOUR

Gossamyr swung her staff, bending into a defensive stance. She hooked the applewood parallel beneath her outstretched right arm. Peripheral vision sighted Ulrich, stalking up beside her, his fists bared and swinging for fight. "If you've not a bigger or pointier weapon, then stand back!"

"I've the will to survive, my lady, so you stand back."

"I know what I'm doing!"

"As do I!"

"Do stay out of my way!"

She spun to catch the bogie in the gut with the steel-hard staff. Impact shook her feet from the ground. Tottering two steps to the left, she found her balance.

Ulrich yelped. She spied him shaking a fist that obviously had more impact on himself than the bogie's hindquarters.

The beast let out a yowl and gripped her staff. The span of that grip covered a third of the longstaff. Gossamyr leaned backward to counter the attack. Landing her derriere shocked stinging prinkles up and down her spine. Shaking the vibrations from her skull she leaped to her feet, drawing the staff before her in a half arc of warning.

Bogies were dumb as wood, but when enraged were difficult to contend. Usually they were more breath than roar—and oh, did their foul breath wield a malodorous bite. Their square bulky bodies were solid as stone, save, their bald, flat heads; the skull proved thinner than parchment. Only problem was climbing the mountain of bogie to reach the prize.

A vicious wind of foul breath and gnashing incisors rose up behind Gossamyr. She spun, prepared to defend. The bogie shrieked and tumbled midair, soaring over her head, and landed the ground behind her.

Gossamyr pierced Ulrich with a dagger of a look.

The man countered with his own cocky wink and a tilt of the crossbow he wielded. "I'm keeping my distance!"

Rolling and shrieking, the squat brown bogie stirred up the dirt from the ground in a billowing cloud. The crossbow quarrel—wedged in the bogie's gut—splintered and was crushed to pulp. Now the beast lay prone, its skull level with Gossamyr's shoulder.

"Leave him for me!" Gossamyr yelled. Levering her leg back to force momentum through her body, she swung hard, meeting wood to skull. The definite dull crunch of shattering skullbone thundered in her ears.

A deft twist of her staff placed it like a spear in Gossamyr's palm. Stabbing it into the bogie's eye, the applewood met with little resistance. The body shuddered, jittering the staff in her sure grip. The ground shook. The mule brayed. Yowls to stir up a slumbering swamp beast from a bed of muck assaulted the air. With a final shudder of stout hairy limbs, the bogie gave up the ghost. The stench of such finality coiled into the air, wilting the freshness with a heavy veil.

Brown matter oozed from the skull. Gossamyr tugged out her staff and tamped it on the ground to clean it off. The ooze clung.

"Nasty bit of business that," Ulrich commented.

Heavy breaths panted over her lips, but a smile stole Gossamyr's disgust. She had done it. Her first challenge—alone, without Shinn looking over her shoulder—and she had been successful. The thought to retreat hadn't even occurred. Danger had approached and she had stood at the ready.

"Yes!" Gossamyr said in an elated whisper.

Crossbow tilted against his shoulder, Ulrich stomped over and studied the oozing carnage. "Now *that* shall leave a mark."

Spinning on the insolent, Gossamyr landed her staff with a *click* aside the crossbow. "I am going to leave a mark on you should you persist in interfering."

"My lady." He pressed out a placating hand. "There was a challenge to be met!"

"Expertly mastered by me!"

"You? Ha!"

"You laugh? I—"

"It was *my* quarrel brought down the thing."

"I killed the beast!"

"Yes, and with great savor, I note. The thing is dead as a doornail." Ulrich strode to the mule and, flipping open a tattered saddlebag, poked about inside. Drawing out a small horn, he uncapped what Gossamyr guessed to be cleaning oil for the weapon.

The fetch fluttered down from the sky. She offered it a smart bow. Danger annihilated. Shinn would be pleased. Circling the beast to take in the carnage, the fetch then alighted into the crystal sky to *twinclian* in a shimmer of dust.

Unaware of the exchange, Ulrich tucked the oil horn inside the saddlebag and strapped the crossbow across Fancy's back. So he had assisted. Next time she would not allow him such opportunity.

"I cannot promise to stand idly by should such need again arise." Ulrich strode by Gossamyr, finger to lips in thought. "It is my manner, fair lady, to help when a damsel requires saving."

Damsel? Gossamyr slid a look to the left then the right. Where be this damsel? She was the only— Ah. So he thought…?

She spread her shoulders back, lifting her chest. Fisting her fingers before her, she hissed, "Do I look like I need saving?"

Dancing blue eyes took in her obstinate pose in a quick *cap-à-pie* flight. "Actually…no."

"Just so. In the future keep your mortal weapons to yourself."

"Indeed? *Mortal* weapons. Ahum." He assumed a haughty pose, thumbs hooked at the waist of his striped hose, one foot stretched forward and his body cocked at an angle. "So says the damsel with the sparkly throat."

"I—" Gossamyr slapped a palm to her throat.

"I suppose I must thank you," he added.

"For saving thee?"

He chuckled. "No, for reminding me of which I forget. There is a damsel in need of rescue. And she will not argue my help. I must be off."

"Saving damsels? What sort of pitiful, unoriginal quest—" She stabbed a proud thumb into her pourpoint. "I've a mission to save the—"

"The what?" Mirth tickled Ulrich's lips into a slippery smile and now his tone danced teasingly. "The world? Is not such a quest reserved for armored knights and champions wearing their lady's favor on their sleeves?"

"I am not here to save *your* world. It is my world I…must save." Bogies and blight! Very sly, Gossamyr. Really blending well. Why did she not simply reveal her fée origins and hold out her wrists for the chains?

"Ah! I see. There is a separation between our worlds. But since you claim *not* to be a faery, I can only then assume you speak of the minuscule world that populates the inside of your skull."

Ulrich approached and made show of tilting his head this way and that as he looked into her eyes. A vicious preening. The look was so familiar, like that of a fellow fée who deemed Gossamyr lesser because of her half blood, and yet, the rank of her father elevated her above all. Fluttering beringed fingers near her head, he insulted with silent menace. "My master once treated a victim of psychomachia."

"Psycho-what?"

"It is one who lives within their own mind. Entire worlds are invented. An extraordinary life is led walking through the imaginary world, while the victim's very feet tread the earth of reality."

Gossamyr stepped right up to the man to meet his mocking stare. The embroidered trim of his cape brushed her knees. Must and earth surrounded his air. No longer did anything about him appeal, not even his fine white teeth. "You. Are rude."

"And you are most snappish. And much too close. Have you no sense of propriety? Back off, warrior woman."

She hooked her hands at her hips and fixed him with the mongoose eye.

"Not at all the same," Ulrich muttered as he stepped away and drew a glance down her form. A sorry shake of his head shook his loose curls. "In twenty years women have truly lost all their graces. Pity."

"What do you mumble about now?"

"Nothing that concerns you, Faery Not."

That moniker, most cruel, set Gossamyr to a stomp.

"Very well." Ulrich slapped his arms across his chest and faced her again with that preening expression. "I promise to stand back and allow you all the glory next time we are set upon by supernatural beasties."

"It was a bogie."

"If you say so."

"I do."

Next time? Hmm… Very possible, considering they walked the edge of the Netherdred, and would soon have to cross through it to reach the mortal city of Paris.

A scan of the horizon sighted a line of lindens and a wispy ghost of smoke, likely a fire roasting a family's evening meal. The distant yowl from a night creature gave her wonder to the rampant wolves her mother had documented in the bestiary. Not so vicious as a Netherdog, frequently found wandering the sandy borders of the marsh roots, but certainly ferocious. She'd had no time to gather expectations of her journey, but already it proved more perilous than she might have imagined.

Adventure? Yes, please. She could stand down any threat that challenged.

I hope, a small voice deep inside whispered.

"I wonder what it was doing here?" she said with a glance to the block of bogie lying in a growing puddle of brown ooze. "Is it common for bogies to charge from out of nowhere? Such creatures generally keep to cinder caves and the night. For all the rage it possessed, one would think we'd done it a grievance."

"Do you wish me to answer according to *my* world?" Ulrich tugged at the saddlebag, secured to Fancy's flank. "As opposed to your skull world?"

With a glance to the battleground, peppered with brown bogie blood, Ulrich let out a heavy exhalation. He squeezed an eye shut at the blast of setting sun that beamed him in the face. "Never, in my extremely pitiful life, have I seen one of those things. Said life being much too short of late. Or be it too long?" A tilt of his head revealed the modena on his cheek. "But I trust you have encountered such? You knew exactly how to take the thing out."

"Training."

"Oh? Did I miss something in my schooling? Attack and conquer abecedarian?"

She delivered him a sneer to match—nay, defy—his mockery. "Just answer me this: are we close to a village? I tire, and have worked up a hunger."

"One would never guess from the brilliant sparkle you put out."

His constant reminder she glimmered troubled. A touch to her throat discovered the highest agraffe was open. The carved bone clasp had broken, most likely during the fight.

"A village? Indeed, Aparjon lies just ahead. But tell me, why do you not simply fly there? Ah!" He made show of bending and peering around to study her shoulders. Gossamyr twisted her back away from his view. "No wings!"

"We have already discussed this."

"Indeed. Not a faery." Now his jesting tone returned and that brilliant smile flashed like a beam of sunlight. "But plenty faeries do not have wings."

"How know you such?"

"Every child learns the facts before they are out of infant skirts." He made a merry skip and danced around Gossamyr. "Faeries come in all manner of shape, size and wing. Some walk amongst the mortals undiscovered, some flitter up to a man's ear to stand inside it. But one thing they all have in common is a glimmer—" he drew his palm between them in a curtain of fluttering fingers "—that sheen of the unnatural."

The blazon.

"Though, I must say, you do appear a trifle…faded."

"What mean you by that?"

Ulrich pointed to the hem of Gossamyr's pourpoint. "Your clothing. The leaves look as though they are fading. More so than when we first met."

Gossamyr touched a curve of supple hornbeam at her waist. Indeed, the leaf had lost some of its glossy resilience. The arachnagoss threading was strong, but no more so than the outer layers it stitched together. She smoothed a hand over her braies. They felt secure; amphi-leather was virtually indestructible, even a fire-forged blade must draw a precise line to cut through.

A bend of her arm tugged a crack in the leaves at her shoulder.

"I must make haste," she said and picked up her pace along the dirt path.

"And so I shall hurry alongside you, Faery Not."

They walked onward, Ulrich leading Fancy as he ventured first. His strides were light, jumping to kick a stone in the path, as free as the air made Gossamyr feel. When he finally spoke, though, he sounded suspicious. "You are quite skilled in defense and attack."

She smirked. "And you are adept at getting in the way."

"Why, thank you, fair lady. It is a skill. Pity 'twas my last quarrel. Though, rest assured, I can hold steel to the enemy should the need arise. That is…if I had steel." He patted his hips and scanned the ground. "I seem to have misplaced my dagger a few leagues back."

"Would that be when you won the prize dripping down your forehead?"

"Do you think it will leave a mark?" He touched the wound.

Ever changing, the man's moods. From suspicion, to anger, to a teasing charm. Despite the danger his learning of her origins could pose, Gossamyr found it difficult to dislike the man. For he tread the earth as if he had wings. To have him accompany her even a short distance could prove a boon. She would study him, prepare for future contact with mortals. They weren't so different from the fée. Even his deep voice she had grown accustomed to.

"So, Gossamyr who isn't from Faery, I did notice you were particularly surprised at your success over the beast."

Gossamyr tripped ahead, enjoying the warm air skim her bared flesh. *Right,* was the only feeling she could summon. She spun in a dancer's twirl and rejoined Ulrich's side. "It is the first time I have engaged in hand-to-hand combat."

"Ah. Well then, good show, Faery Not."

"Don't name me that—achoo!" Halted in her tracks, Gossamyr grasped her head.

"Touché!" Turning to walk backward Ulrich smiled at her. The gap in his teeth distorted his mirth. "So you like to dance?"

Skipping, Gossamyr shrugged and offered an unexpected "I think so!"

"You take marvel at your own wonder."

"It is just, the air…I feel light."

"Pray tell what the air is like whence you hail?"

"Not like here," she called out and jumped to the grass to skip through the cool blades.

Flight had ever alluded her, no matter how often she had attempted it. Which had been often in the rose garden behind the castle buttery. Mince had once witnessed her fruitless attempts and had laughingly joined in. The matron's small wings, attached to a generously rounded body, had served little more than to lift her shoulders. She could not leave the ground, either. It had bonded them in laughter, and a smirking confession from Gossamyr, which revealed her jealousy of the winged ones.

"You are the daughter of Lord de Wintershinn," Mince had stated simply. "You needn't envy; you are envied."

Mayhap. But Gossamyr had not missed a single averted gaze or cruel stare in her lifetime. Envy hurt. And the only way to overcome was to prove herself. She needn't the Wintershinn name to stand proud; to defeat the Red Lady would prove her worth and perhaps put to rest the suspicious whispers.

She spun now, and leaped into the path immediately before Ulrich. He had no wings, and yet, he took to the air in his strides. And that made him all the more appealing.

"The dirt from the fight," Ulrich commented as he angled forward to study her. "It covers your face."

Gossamyr wiggled her nose. Another sneeze tormented.

"It is bone," he said of her dirty covering. "It hides your glimmer."

"Bone?"

"That means good."

"Then why not say good?"

"For the same reason you say mortal. We have our own slangs, do we not?" A click of his tongue beckoned Fancy onward.

Gossamyr paralleled him but a leap to his left. He suspected; she knew that he did.

"I wager you are safe from wonder so long as you do not favor bathing. Though your clothing—"

"Will be changed anon. I need only locate a seamstress. May-hap something bright, like yours." She glanced over Ulrich's attire. The cloak swung merrily with his strides, intermittently revealing the tight striped hose he wore.

"I'm afraid a change of costume won't be so easy in Aparjon," he said. "'Tis a very small village, as most villages are. It is not fortified, which will prove bone. Our entry will not be questioned. If I recall from my travels there is a stable behind the one lone tavern that rents out to riders. Plead to Luck to find a horse for purchase, especially a swift one. As well, it may be difficult to get a room for the night." He turned and scanned back down the road.

"Dead as a doornail," Gossamyr reassured. And who decided when a doornail was dead? "What lends you to believe I wish to stay the night in the next village?"

"You said you were tired?"

"Yes, but a rest and some hearty fare will serve. I am off to Paris."

"Indeed?"

Ulrich handed Gossamyr Fancy's reins and skipped ahead, turning to walk widdershins in front of her. His cloak billowed as he gestured and filled the air with the rumbling tones Gossamyr found she favored more and more.

"I cannot resist questioning when there is so much of interest about you, fair lady. Whence do you hail? And, skill aside, what finds a lone woman trekking to Paris with so little fear of danger?"

"I am in search of a…woman. She goes by the moniker of the Red Lady."

She picked up her pace in hopes of the man stumbling, but he tread backward with ease. His arms pumping, his robe splayed open with each stride, to reveal long legs and ankle-high suede boots with pointed toes.

"And where in Paris does she reside?"

"I know naught."

"Paris is a big city. Mayhap I can help you locate her?"

"How might you discover a woman you've never met?"

"I found you."

"But you weren't—"

"I've a location spell that may be of use."

A spell? Caution fired. "You said you are not a wizard."

"That I am not."

The last thing Gossamyr needed was to align herself with a practicer of magic. She had come to stop the damaging effects done to Enchantment, not contribute.

"But I did pay attention when His Most Magical—er, my former patron—needed to locate a lost dream or dragon."

"You practice magic?"

"Not enough to make it real."

But did his attempts tap Enchantment? And with the rift, the damage caused was increased immeasurably. Mayhap choosing to share the road with this man had been a mistake. Where was the fetch? If Ulrich proved a threat, would Shinn intervene?

Quickening her footsteps, she commented, "I fear the woman I seek be more dangerous than a fire-breathing dragon."

"You say so?"

"I've said enough. We must keep to ourselves. We've only to accompany one another to the next village."

"You're not keen on friendship, eh?"

Gossamyr shrugged. Not with a man who practiced magic.

Mince was the only friend she had ever known. Not even a good friend if one considered Shinn paid her as nursemaid. Gossamyr had been schooled and trained exclusively by her father, and kept from most situations that would see her surrounded by vindictive fée. The few times she went to market or escaped to participate in a tournament were such wonders. There were food stands offering honeyed petals and toadstools carved like miniature castles. Lavender creams and smoky beetles enticed. Children were rare, but few ran about laughing and playing challenging games. Women dressed gaily and men ogled them with soused grins. Brownies socialized with hobs and the curiously tall dryad would draw a lingering stare. Who could be bothered to look for a friend?

Besides, Gossamyr was ever studied from afar—like a curious bug—but rarely approached with a smile.

You are half-blooded, and that is fine. You are the daughter of Lord de Wintershinn. They know you will ascend to the throne one day, and they respect you, for you are of Shinn's bloodline. Still, the fée will never completely accept you. It is best you avoid the central markets in Glamoursiège. Half bloods, while rare, are cruelly teased.

Unless a fée was attracted to her *because* of her mixed blood.

You are exotic, Gossamyr.

He is a Rougethorn. They dabble in magic....

"I say——" Ulrich turned and rejoined her at her side "——that a man can never have too many friends."

"I am not a man."

"You fight like one."

"Bespell your tongue to silence," she hissed and then under her breath murmured, "Or I shall do it for you."

"I've rudimentary knowledge of magic. Would that I could bespell myself!" he called out grandly. "'Twould be akin to smiling myself into a swoon!"

But Gossamyr wasn't listening. Evening traced the atmosphere with an orange line on the horizon. Surrounding gray illumination loomed. An eyelash moon slit the sky. Soon the countryside would be black. A unique experience, for the light bugs that populated the Spiral forest produced such illumination Gossamyr had never found herself to fright because of darkness. She sensed mortals viewed the world in a darker shade. Were there light bugs in this realm? The compulsion to cling to this final moment of sparse light, to see all—and remember—overwhelmed. For soon she would see that darker shade, as well.

That is why you must be of haste! No time to rest this night. Leave the mortal to his foul magic and be off.

A line of fire-ravaged treetops frosted the western horizon with a macabre lace. To the right, a creaking windmill chomped on the silence, wood bearing against wood, commanded by the wind. Crickets chirred and long grasses *schussed*. Evening sounded much the same, and that was, as Ulrich might say, bone.

"Achoo!"

"Sneeze on Tuesday—"

"—clobber a stranger," Gossamyr finished the childhood rhyme.

"So touchy, my lady. I'd fare to wager we are strangers no longer."

"What happens when one sneezes on the morrow?"

"Sneeze for a letter. And Thursday sneeze for something better. Mayhap by Thursday you'll have shed your sparkle?"

"Or even better, I'll have shed one mule and its jabbering passenger."

Jabbery? Indeed! Why the nerve of the...the...well, Ulrich wasn't exactly sure *what* Gossamyr was.

Feisty, fine and female. Mayhap a faery?

The woman who strode in skipping steps ahead of him by ten paces was like no woman he had ever before known. Or seen. Or dreamed of. Well, mayhap he had dreamed a tempting siren once or twice—hell, dozens of times. But never had she been so skilled in the martial arts. Killing bogies? She had moved without thought, swinging that beautiful carved stick of hers and taking out the bogie with but one stroke. Masterful.

His rusted crossbow had been less than splendid when matched against the woman's mettle. Made him feel a bit lacking.

On the other hand, with a traveling mate of such skill, he could pay heed to that which required attention. Ulrich patted Fancy's withers and slid his hand back to smooth over the saddlebag. A certain hum, much like the throat of a purring cat, vibrated against his palm. Safe. But for how long? Would his quest be ended most violently before he had opportunity to save the damsel?

Or was it already too late? So little remained the same. It had all changed. Everything. Twenty years had been stolen!

He should have been there to save her, his sweet Rhiana. Instead, he had been…dancing. That hellacious toadstool ring!

Ah, but he would have Rhiana back. And he would die trying.

But he mustn't think overmuch of his quest. For one brief thought—just back the road a ways—had called up the bogie. Myriad strange and malevolent evils could sense him, even—he suspected—hear his thoughts.

What should happen if he were to dip into the saddlebag and draw the thing out into view? He'd barely avoided death last eve when the wailing white ladies had followed him through the mist-fogged swamp. Not being corporeal they could not touch him, but such hadn't prevented them from flinging sticks and stones and the like at him. And finding target with each attack. Recall prickled the hairs all over his body to alert. And the realization this quest was insane.

How to locate what he sought? Was this feeling—a calling that led him toward Paris—sure?

What a task, what a task.

An ally from Faery would make all the difference.

Ulrich eyed the sure, muscular form striding ahead of Fancy. She was as a man in strength and prowess but with the curves and beauty of a siren. Those double plaits of summer-wheat hair tipped in delicate bone clasps beat at her back with each lilting stride. And the clothing! Braies and pourpoint? Leaves? No mortal man or woman could fashion such. And that glimmer, it almost seemed to form a pattern under her jaw and down her neck. Did it spread across her chest?

She was a faery; he sensed it. For he could lately *see* the damned things. A gift of the dance. How to give it back?

A man should like to have a confident fighter at his side if he had set to an insane quest that would surely bring about many more a challenge.

As well, a faery would attract the one thing he most needed to find.

FIVE

The iridescent fetch was not to be seen against the dull flatness of night. Must have twinclianed to Faery. The quiet warmth of protection Gossamyr felt whenever she sighted the dragon fly tremored for reignition. Sure, she could stand off a bogie, but...

But...she wondered now if Mince was asking for her absence. What must her maid think? Did she fear for Gossamyr, all alone in a strange land? Mayhap Shinn had not mentioned her departure. And if he had, only the facts—details were unnecessary. Surely, Mince worried.

Something so insignificant as a sigh now felt a heavy burden as Gossamyr marched along the rutted path alongside her mortal traveling companion. She kept turning to look back, thinking to spy the marble castle from the corner of her eye. She didn't like feeling this way. Uncomfortable. At a loss. For all purposes she should charge ahead, thinking only of the task. All of Faery relied upon her defeat of the Red Lady.

"All," she murmured. "That is...quite many."

So many, she wondered now if Shinn had made a wise choice.

It was not a choice! You begged.

Yes.

I hope you discover the solace to the ache that has been your nemesis.

He knew. It had been time to set her free. If only to fulfill the personal quest she sought before settling upon the Glamoursiège throne. To experience the Otherside, and to claim victory.

Ahead, torches flickered and wobbled along the path. Night had settled, completely blacking the sky save for spots of starlight.

Gossamyr skipped ahead. About a shout down the road an equipage with two armored destriers in the lead pondered slowly forth. Both carried torches. Following, a carriage and a large covered wagon behind, trailed by yet more mounted riders. Every corner of the carriage was hung with yet another torch.

"What is that?" She turned to Ulrich. "Royalty?"

"Unlikely." A bounce on his toes scanned the coming caravan. "No banners or coats of arms that I can see. It is likely a traveling merchant who has just passed through Aparjon. We should move from the road."

Gossamyr stabbed her staff into the red clay. "Why?"

A chuffing breath preceded Ulrich's sharp retort, "Do you wish to be trampled?"

Gossamyr held her tongue. She held no position here in the Otherside. While normally her equipage would command the road, she was supposed to be lying low. Waylaying suspicion. Besides, a mule and a dancing fool could hardly be considered an equipage. A touch to her neck; she spread her fingers down over her collarbones. Darkness hid her blazon.

Leaping from the path, she landed Fancy's side and gave the mule's neck a smooth of her palm. "Will they be dangerous?"

"Not unless provoked." Ulrich eyed her suspiciously. "You, er…won't provoke them?"

Did he think her so unhinged? "Not unless they give reason for such."

"Of course. I should expect nothing less from a bogie-killer. Just…do not speak," he muttered in low tones as the equipage neared. Iron-bound wheels creaked under the load and armor clanked with the pace of the horses.

The mounted men leading the band were attired in black armor with black leather straps and polished silver buckles that glinted with torchlight. Black leather braies and boots blended with the velvet-black hide of the horses.

"Perhaps not a merchant," Ulrich whispered over Gossamyr's shoulder. "Not with an armored escort. Stand back and allow them passage. It is safest."

Solemn in expression, the men's eyes turned to Gossamyr and Ulrich as they slowed to pass by. The lead rider wore a bascinet helmet sporting a brilliant red plume. Gossamyr looked boldly into the dark eyes of the man. A chill touched her breast. Malevolence followed her gaze, but offered not a word. Only when he had to turn away or force himself to twist in the saddle did their contact break. Not friendly, but neither did she feel threatened. They would offer no challenge so long as they were not pressed.

An entire band of mortals!

Eager to take it all in, she propped her chin on the hand she fisted about her staff and watched as the carriage approached. Filigreed iron lanterns dangling at the four corners of the boxy vehicle glittered across the highly polished wood body. Simple narrow red flags hung limp in the lacking breeze; the fabric ends were frayed and dirtied from the road. The carriage rumbled slowly, the uneven path likely joggling the passengers inside to a jaw-jarring clatter.

Light from inside the carriage box set the heavy window hangings to an eerie glow. As a hand pulled back a curtain, Gossamyr's heartbeats quickened. A female peered out—her eyes were rimmed in thick kohl and bejeweled at the corners with glittering red stones.

"The Red—" Gossamyr choked on her declaration as she rushed the carriage.

"No!" Ulrich shouted.

A call from one of the leaders brought the equipage to a halt. Hoofbeats pounded up from the rear, drawing a half-dozen mounted men to defense.

Gossamyr gasped in the dust of the sudden upheaval as she slapped a hand to the carriage window and clung. The woman inside, not at all frightened by Gossamyr's hasty approach, stared curiously down at her. Long red hair slipped around her neck and dangled upon exposed upper curves of her pale breasts.

"It is she!" Gossamyr cried. "The succubus!" She stretched to touch, to grope, but her reach was shortened. Someone grabbed her about the waist and jerked her away, legs flailing and staff swiping the air.

"Settle." Ulrich held her. Gossamyr struggled, but the sudden dismount of the rear guards, and the barricade they formed before the carriage—crossbows to the ready—halted her in Ulrich's arms. "What do you think to do?" Ulrich hissed in her ear. "We are outnumbered with long pointy, sharp weapons. The woman is but a bit of damask and lace."

The woman in the carriage now leaned out the window. Gossamyr saw there was not a mark of the banished on her face. A very obvious mark that no one should miss. And her hair was but a rusty shade of red, not brilliant as a ruby or the blood of a slaughtered hare.

"I thought she was the Red Lady," Gossamyr said under her breath. A foolish act on her part to approach so boldly. "She is not."

The mounted rider who had held her stare appeared at their side. The sixteen-hand destrier unnerved Fancy with a snort of warning, and the mule backed away.

The tip of a sword drew up under Gossamyr's chin. "Mean you my lady harm?"

"I plead mercy," Ulrich said with a stunning swipe of his hand to deflect the blade from Gossamyr's neck. He approached the barricade and addressed the woman in the carriage over the warning crossbows. "Forgive me, my lady, for the rudeness of my, er—" he turned to Gossamyr and shot a glance up and down her body "—my sister."

Gossamyr gaped, stepped up to defend—but was stopped by the leader's sword. Leery of mortal steel, she kept still. Two dark eyes peered out from the narrow slit on the helmet, holding her more fiercely than a blade to her shoulder.

"You see, my lady," Ulrich continued. He managed, after a bow, to gain access between two of the men barricading the carriage, insinuating himself right next to the lady's window.

The woman propped a hand on the window ledge and, fascinated by Ulrich's gesticulating confession, gave him her full attention.

"She is daft," Ulrich explained with a wide stretch of his arms to encompass the enormity of his statement. "Luna-touched. She meant you no harm. Just a little difficult to keep…calm when the light of the moon threatens her very soul."

"I see," the lady replied in throaty tones that slipped into Gossamyr's ear so smoothly, she settled, and stepped back from the threatening sword. But not too far. A half circle of weapons were to her back. Kohl-lined eyes peered carefully at her. "She is dressed oddly."

Now Gossamyr gripped her pourpoint, trying to clasp the broken agraffe. It was too dark to make out details, so long as she stood out of the lantern's glow.

"My family indulges her whims," Ulrich explained. "Fancies herself a forest warrior, at times. Others, we must chase her cross the meadow to place a stitch of clothes to her naked back."

Blight that!

"How troubling," the lady said. Her eyes sought Gossamyr's secrets. So dark, and moving up and down, and along every portion of her being. "Yet you allow her a weapon? Might she not injure herself?"

"Oh, she does! The occasional hit to her head knocks her out for but a time. Blessed relief, I tell you, from tending her idiotic antics."

"I am standing right here!" Enough. Gossamyr would not allow them to make jest of her with such falsities. She knew what Ulrich attempted; but his suggestion she was a lackwit only drew more attention to her than masking it. She nodded toward what looked now to be a cage all covered over with a tapestry tied at each of the four corners. "What is in the attached carriage?"

"Allow her to approach me. Guards," the woman commanded lazily. "Step back. I see no harm so long as her brother stands beside her. I want to look upon madness."

Bloody elves. So now she was mad?

Yet, the woman announced her desire with such passion it shot a prinkle up Gossamyr's neck. And not a favorable prinkle.

Eyeing the covered cage, Gossamyr stepped cautiously past the men who smelt of horseflesh and sweat, and who clinked with every cumbersome step. Stealth avoided them, but, it mattered little; they could take her down with fight. She was no match to four men on their feet and wielding weapons. But if need be, she would give them a challenge. Oh, indeed.

Ulrich slid close as Gossamyr approached the carriage. His cheek brushed hers as he whispered, "Caution, Gossamyr. We want to walk away. I do not favor a sword to my gullet."

He did not leave her side, remaining just behind her shoulder. A presence that somehow stilled Gossamyr's apprehensions, almost as if grounding that part of her that wished to fly. With a glance to the well-armored men who stood but a leap to either side of her, Gossamyr then stepped up to the carriage. She did not get so close this time. Her enthusiasm must be restrained. This woman was not the Red Lady.

A movement from inside the cage alerted Gossamyr. Her sudden jerk to look to the side was met with a *shing* of steel as two swords were released from their sheaths and placed to threaten.

"Relax," the woman said to her men. "She is but a troubled girl."

Wincing at the bright light that beamed across her face, Gossamyr ducked her head to better view the woman. A small ruby had been pressed to the corner of each eye, distracting with each glint of lamplight. Her lips were glossed with an unnatural substance that also shimmered in the light. When she opened her mouth in a wondering observation, it revealed a row of small, thin teeth, almost as a fox's foreteeth. Sharp and made for exact cutting.

"Your costume is most creative," the lady commented. The sound of her voice reminded Gossamyr of the ungraspable past. A piece of mortal, whole and deep, very similar to Veridienne's voice.

Forgetting her interest in the cage, Gossamyr merely stood there, betaken by the woman's unnatural allure.

"It grows cold for her." Ulrich made a move behind her. Gossamyr turned to ask of his concern only to see the swing of his dark cape billow toward and around her shoulders. He fastened the embroidered peacock agraffe at her neck and pulled the hood up over her plaited hair. "I shouldn't wish my sister to take a chill."

He'd covered her blazon.

He had not—he was…touching her. *Mortal touched.* A fearsome condition whispered by those who would never dare to visit the Otherside. The touch of a mortal makes you shiver, and the shiver never leaves, eventually it eats away a faery's wings.

But Ulrich's hands were not cold, rather warm. Instead of a shiver, Gossamyr smiled as a relaxing loosen of her shoulders chased back her fears.

"Where do you journey?" the lady asked.

"The next village," Gossamyr replied.

"It is dangerous."

"I crave danger."

"Do you?" A chuckle again revealed those vicious little teeth. "But there are Armagnacs."

"You saw them?" Ulrich asked.

Sensing his sudden tension by a squeeze of his hand to her shoulder, Gossamyr peered cautiously out of the corner of her eye toward the direction they traveled.

"Indeed," the leader said from his mount. "We exited the city as a score of mounted Armagnacs, wearied and hungry, crept in."

"Mayhap we shall pass around the village," Ulrich said.

"It would be wise."

"Do you journey for a convent?" the lady asked.

"Oh, indeed," Ulrich spoke in Gossamyr's stead. "The best place for my sister, you understand. She is marveled too easily. 'Tis why she became so excited to see you, my lady. If I may be so bold, your beauty rivals quite any woman my sister has yet to lay eyes upon. Mine, as well."

Oh, but he was laying it on thick. It took all her strength not to swing about and knock him silent with a club of her staff.

"You like marvels, do you?" the woman asked Gossamyr. "Mayhap you wish to see what I've in my cage?"

Gossamyr followed the slender finger that pointed out from the carriage and behind. Lace threaded through with glinting strands of silver fell over her narrow wrist. Gorgeous, the mortal vestments.

"Yes, please," Gossamyr cooed. And then she found herself shaking her head. Snapping out from a strange fog. Almost as if a faery *erie*. Blight, what was this? 'Twas as if she was mesmerized by the woman. The mortal passion?

No! Concentrate. She was merely tired and hungry.

"What is behind the tapestries?"

"Look at me," the lady beckoned.

Spots of brilliant gold dotted her deep brown eyes. Gossamyr found herself leaning forward, to better scent. An indefinable odor, not like any flower or even the must of mortal earth, surrounded her. Almost cold, like the depths of a dark cave oozing with dribbles of ice water.

"Your eyes are brown," the woman commented. As if it were

uncommon. "Have you ever…" She leaned forward, clasping the rim of the carriage door with long fingers painted with rust-colored designs that swirled across her entire hand.

Gossamyr swayed closer.

"…looked into violet eyes?"

Struck by an unseen force, Gossamyr pressed a hand over the agraffe at her neck.

"Do you believe in faeries?"

"Wh-what?" A step back found her tumbling into Ulrich's arms.

"We should leave you to your travels," Ulrich said as he righted Gossamyr. "My sister tires. We need seek shelter."

Ignoring Ulrich entirely, the woman announced in spectacular breaths, "I've a faery in my cage. Do you wish to see it?"

"A f-faery?" Finding herself quite unable to stand upright, Gossamyr clung to her staff. *They keep them caged to display in market squares.* This woman had captured a fée?

Teetering her gaze between the covered cart and the woman's sharp smirking mouth, Gossamyr fought a sudden rise of fear. "I— I don't think I believe in faeries. No, of course not." She stiffened, locking her knees to remain upright. "This is the mortal realm. So many…mortals. Faeries are nonsense and so much blather. We are off, brother?"

"First you must look!" The woman's head withdrew from the window and moments later Gossamyr heard her call from the rear of the carriage, "Draw back the curtains!"

Utterly gasping for breath, Gossamyr fought to settle her racing pulse. Intuitive caution could not dispel the hard compulsion to seek the truth.

Using Ulrich to steady her on the left side, Gossamyr, much against her better judgment, but compelled by her curiosity, walked toward the cage. The armored men cautiously parted to allow her access. Mortal steel clinked; horses snorted. She ran a palm over the heavy tapestry; the weave was tight and heavy. The fabric pushed in through two thick poles—two of many dozens that caged whatever it was inside.

Fear dried her throat. Horror stilled her heart. Not a faery. It cannot be!

"Are you ready?" the lady whispered so loudly Gossamyr heard it as a scream.

"My sister—" Ulrich started.

"I am!" Gossamyr declared.

With little fanfare the tapestry curtain was drawn back and flipped over the corner of the cage. The contents were not initially visible, for a sheer curtain that glimmered like faery dust hung from top to the floor of the cage. The rear lanterns, while boldly kissing the woman's cruel grimace, barely lit the fore of the cage.

Steel glinted and one of the men poked his sword through the curtain and bars. A cry of pain pierced Gossamyr's breast. A female voice. Something within the cage shuffled into the torch glow. A frail, thin figure…indeed, a woman, clad in tattered brown cloth. And there!

Gossamyr let out a cry.

"Quite remarkable, yes?"

Gossamyr swung a look to the heartless woman peering out from the rear window. She kept a faery chained inside this foul cage!

Gripping the wood poles, Gossamyr scanned the poor creature. Bones were visible through her pale flesh. Arms clasped about her legs, the creature shivered. *Not a creature, but your own kind!* She would not meet Gossamyr's eyes. Just as well. Sure Ulrich's cloak concealed her blazon, Gossamyr could not know if another fée would recognize her. The cage floor was littered with crushed hay and the glimmer of faery dust. One wing swept a lazy trail across the poles Gossamyr held. The wing was limp, colorless, and a tear rent through the upper section. Unable to divine a scent, beyond the rotting straw, Gossamyr swallowed. Lifeless, or almost so.

"I usually charge admission to look upon my pretty faery," the lady announced. "But I won't ask one so troubled to sacrifice."

"Troubled?" Gossamyr swung around. Ulrich's arm barred her from approaching the rear of the carriage. "The only troubled one I can see is you, my lady! How dare you? She is not yours to own or display or to destroy!"

"Gossamyr," Ulrich cautioned.

"Your name is Gossamyr?" The lady's fox teeth parted and her tongue ran along them. "Unusual. Not a French name. Will you turn about for me?"

"I will not move another footstep until you release this poor creature!"

The clomps of heavy hooves rounded behind Gossamyr and Ulrich. The caravan leader marched his horse warningly close. Sword drawn and eyes keen to her, with a flick of his weapon he bid her turn.

"We thank you for revealing your prize, my lady." Ulrich tugged Gossamyr's shoulder. "Best we leave you to your path."

"You cannot own this faery," Gossamyr hissed, "nor treat it as a beast!"

"I cannot see," the woman directed the man on the horse. "Her cape must be lifted."

Caught up in Ulrich's arms, Gossamyr struggled against his firm grip. She swung out her staff, clipping the shoulder armor of one of the men. Forced backward by a line of drawn swords, she held her staff to the ready.

"Let us pass, my lady," Ulrich called. "It is the moonlight; she is so troubled."

"Indeed."

Gossamyr clenched her teeth. Ulrich tugged her backward, away from the carriage. She followed, but held a hard eye to any who would challenge her. Indeed, she knew it foolish to have reacted so, but in that moment her heart had led her.

The armored men, forming a shield before the carriage and cart stood with weapons aimed for Gossamyr's retreat. Ulrich turned and, dragging her along by the clutched ends of the cloak, began to jog across the grasses.

"Release me!" She kicked at him and managed to free herself.

He landed her body, a foot to her shoulder and bent over her face. "Cease!" he hissed. "You wish to lose your head?"

Twenty paces away the caravan began to move.

"She has no right," Gossamyr growled. Unmoving, she found she had no desire to leap up and run attack upon the carriage. For much as she wanted to believe she could win any challenge, the threat of so many mortal weapons becalmed her bravado. "The fée are not animals. Did you see her? She was close to death. Her wings…oh…"

"Stand up." With Ulrich's offer, Gossamyr clasped his hand and stood. "I know naught what you are about, my lady. But I can wager a guess."

She lifted a defiant chin. In the darkness it was difficult to determine whether he jested or spoke a challenge.

"We shall be off, without further mention——"

She jerked from his touch.

Beneath the wool cloak, she felt the hem of her pourpoint fall away from her waist. "Oh!" She clutched the fabric, hearing the dried leaves crumble.

"You are falling apart at the seams," he said. "Tough bit of luck."

Blight! Her father had not been jesting when he'd said the Disenchantment takes quickly.

Apprehensions brewing, Gossamyr eyed the caravan that wobbled off down the road. Oh, but she had looked upon Disenchantment. Pale and shivering and in chains. Let it not be so cruel to her!

A testing bend of knee determined her leathers still held. The tough material should hold. But who knew what the Disenchantment could do? Had Shinn known she would literally lose the clothing from her body?

Gossamyr jerked as Ulrich moved aside the cloak to look her over. The sweeping movement of the wool ripped the back of her pourpoint. Quickly, she pressed a hand to her chest.

A low whistle punctuated his astonishment. Ulrich tugged the cloak tightly over her groping arms and secured the perimeter with a scanning eye, though the night could not allow him distance. "You need proper attire, fair lady. Most urgently."

"There may be a seamstress in the next village."

"You heard the knight; Armagnacs have entered Aparjon. We will do well to pass around the city."

"But—"

"You are too quick to fight, my lady. I will not risk my neck standing aside you as we enter an embattled city."

He removed the saddlebag from his shoulder and carefully placed it across the mule's flanks. "We must make haste. I would let you ride behind me."

"Behind you?" She had never shared a mount with anyone. Why, there was barely room on the beast for Ulrich's long limbs and overstuffed saddlebag and the crossbow. "Impossible."

"You are a bit of a spoiled one, eh?"

"What?"

He turned, one arm propped at his waist, the other hand tapping impatiently upon Fancy's back. "I said, you are spoiled."

"You think I've gone bad? Do I...do I smell?" She attempted to scent her immediate air but only smelled the coolness of the night and a faint tang, which she attributed to Fancy.

"Spoiled, as in rotten. Everyone jumps to your whim. The princess demands her pleasures. Whatever you should ask is given."

"What be wrong with that?" She stabbed her staff into the ground.

They both looked to the ground to spy the clump of dry hornbeam fluttering out from beneath the cloak. Flakes of the enchanted, disarrayed and damaged.

"What is it I have heard about Faery finery and coin?" Ulrich pressed a wondering finger to his chin. Glee sparkled in his eyes, Gossamyr sensed, for it was dark save for the carriage lanterns bobbing down the road. Private as it should have been, he enjoyed her humiliation immensely. "It disperses to dust once introduced to the mortal realm." He toed the flakes of her decimated pourpoint. They disintegrated to a glitter of dust.

Gossamyr nodded. "Very well. Be there another village close?"

"Pray there is. Now mount behind me. I promise I shall not attempt to befriend you along the way."

"Splendid."

"Though I wager it shall be difficult to ignore a naked rider clinging to my waist."

"I am not naked."

"Steal not my hope, my lady."

The sky thinned and receded. A flutter of his wings proved ponderous. Never before had he felt as though the world might…slip away. That his footsteps would not take hold on a path simply not there. 'Twas as if he were falling through the roots.

Images from the fetch proved Gossamyr had successfully arrived in the Otherside. She had even found a companion for the road. Shinn was not overconcerned a mortal traveled at her side; the man would prove a boon. As well, Gossamyr had easily managed the attacking bogie. He would have expected nothing less. The vision of the caged fée had disturbed him perhaps more deeply than it had affected his daughter. She was strong. Capable. *Not a single reason for any mortal to cage her.*

And yet with every breath, Shinn felt the shiver that had become his bane more deeply. Mortal touched. The result? His mortal passion. A sweet punishment. And so much he had reaped from that risk. Greatest of all, his child.

Gossamyr was gone from him. Gone. *Child of mine.*

Should he have told her more? Revealed—

He just...he wanted her to return to him. But Gossamyr's truth would prevent that. *She must never learn her truth.* For if she continued to Believe she would Belong.

Clutching the curved crystal doorpull that opened into Gossamyr's bedchamber, Shinn stood for a breath, blinking, struggling to find hold. The spice roses Mince cut daily for her room seeped into him, cloying and powerful. Gossamyr's scent.

He had set his only daughter off on a dangerous mission. It had been the right choice.

There had been no real choice. Shinn had known for some time Gossamyr would be called to the Otherside. The mortal passion was ever persistent. He could not interfere. Would Gossamyr sacrifice to remain on the Otherside? Would she wish to do so?

"It is the bargain we made, Veridienne. For your home, you must sacrifice."

"I sacrificed my home for you, Shinn! To love you."

"I acknowledge that, but to have it back, you must—"

"Very well. I will do it. I will...leave her."

"Oh!" At Shinn's sigh Mince popped her head up from the floor by the bed. "Lord Wintershinn." She tugged at her tight blue gown, pulling it snugly over two gentle rolls on her stomach. Her small wings fluttered madly as she backed away. Eyes not meeting his, the rumpled fée backed right into the armoire and bent a wing.

"Is there something amiss, Mince?" Shinn strode by the bed. His fingertips grazed the cold, precise marble and danced through the hanging bed curtains. Nothing out of ordinary. He walked to the window where the long arachnagoss sheers fluttered on the breeze. He turned abruptly, catching Mince in the act of shutting the armoire—on a finger. "Are you looking for something?"

"Looking? Me?" The syllables shook more rapidly than her tell-tale wings. "Why ask you that, my lord? Oh, no, just...tidying up a bit. What of you? You're not looking for Gossamyr?"

"Nay."

"Marvelous. Oh! Er, fine. Just fine."

Now he understood. Mince sought Gossamyr.

"I'm out to the yard."

"What for?"

"Oh? To check...for something. Erm, the peacocks must be shooed from the roses."

"She is gone, Mince."

"She?" The matron paused by the door, turning to him with delicate fingers curled into one another. "Who, Lord Wintershinn?"

"Gossamyr has gone to the Otherside."

"No, I—I just saw her. I'm sure she's here somewhere, swinging from the roots—I'll start there, my lord. She never disappears for overlong."

"I sent her."

Mince gaped, seeming to momentarily choke on her own breath. "W-why? How?" she breathed. "Did you...tell her everything?"

"She seeks the Red Lady. I sent her through a Passage. You know her truth will keep her from returning to me."

"Oh! But she needs to know! You've sent her to face the very woman— Oh, dear."

SIX

Forgoing the village of Aparjon for what Ulrich claimed to be another not three leagues to the east, the duo plodded through unmarked grasses and followed a low rabbit-ravaged hedgerow for some distance until a narrower, lesser traveled road attracted them. There were no trees as far as she could see. The world was very silent. Eerily so.

Ulrich called ahead to Gossamyr. "We should seek shelter for the night, 'tis nearing matins."

"You don't think we'll make the village?"

"Likely not."

Sensing the man's exhaustion, Gossamyr conceded. "Very well."

Tugging Ulrich's cloak about her shoulders seemed to hold the crumbling pourpoint together. She hoped. She had dismounted earlier and now walked, finding the exercise more fitting than joggling along on the miserable old mule. She sensed the beast tread alongside the Infernal, and did not wish to put more of a burden on it than necessary.

The fetch preceded her at a clever distance. She had ever thought fetches only recorded noteworthy events. Mayhap Shinn missed her as much as she was beginning to miss him? To have the fetch follow her at all times?

Miss her father? It had been but part of a day.

The only thing she missed right now was the illumination of Faery. This mortal night clung to Gossamyr on all sides. Crickets chirped and unseen rodents scampered along the grassy borders of the rutted path. She could not see Ulrich for the gloom, but judged him less than twenty paces behind her.

His suggestion to stop was not entirely unwarranted. She did feel the strain of her journey tug at the muscles in her calves and shoulders. Yet the struggle to stride freely while keeping the cloak wrapped—blight!

Gossamyr dropped the ends of the cloak and let the sweeping fabric dangle. If her garments were to fall off, then so shall it be. For she wanted to skip, to revel in this atmosphere that welcomed like a warm embrace.

"Oh, Hades, be gone."

Gossamyr smirked at Ulrich's hissed remark. The man had babbled most of the way. He had a strange compulsion to compare things, or rather label them as either "the same" or "not the same." She could not figure what he was about. But she had to confess, having a companion eased a bit of her growing discomfort. Alone in a new land. Physically capable, but…her thoughts had begun to return to a place of safety.

She missed Mince. The matron was ever there, a companion, a confidante. A willing foil when Shinn would question Gossamyr's day, and she had snuck off to tournament. And always there to bring her whatever she may request, to know before Gossamyr spoke her need.

Spoiled? Never before had she heard that term to describe one who is given all she needs. *Such as a lady who travels with a caged faery in tow?*

Hmm…not like that. Nor did she smell.

An eerie feeling of disquiet shimmied about Gossamyr's body. It wasn't as though she were frightened by the darkness. Nor could she summon worry for any beastie that might leap out from the shadows at her. In truth, a tiny niggling at encountering further outcasts from the Netherdred did bother. Unfamiliar, this world. And yet, intriguing. Horizontal and stretching for leagues that fell off the horizon as if the Edge. Mayhap it was an edge? Veridienne had detailed the stretch of France in her bestiary. It was edged by a vast ocean—tribe Mer-de-Soleil territory; merfolk and selkies and kelpies abounded there. But she had no measurement for distance in this land. Unless it was down. So she must rely on Ulrich's navigation.

Many Faery tribes inhabited the realm the mortals called France: the Rougethorns, the Wisogoths, the Quinmarks, just a few. Yes, a huge nation, and she but an itty speck skipping toward sure danger. If she wasn't careful she might lose her grip and fall—as she had once amidst the tangle of roots that reticulated about Glamoursiège. Avenall—her Rougethorn; ever charming and chivalrous—had caught her then.

Who would catch her now?

"No." Ulrich's voice had receded. "Not now. A crossroads? Wicked luck. Now *this* is the same."

With every step Gossamyr felt the world close about her as if the cloak wrapped tightly against her flesh. Enchantment sluiced from her pores; she could feel it as a tangible prick. An ache hummed in her heart, a central tremor that called from the shadows of mortality. *Home,* it whispered. *Embrace it.*

No, no, no! Home was Faery. Not here.

Gossamyr fought back the invisible enemy, but the ache did settle to a fine pulse, ever there. 'Twas the mortal passion, vying to wend into her veins.

"Be damned with you all!"

Gossamyr stopped and swung about. Neither Fancy nor Ulrich were in sight. But she could hear him...talking to someone?

"I beseech thee to allow me passage. No? Very well, *that* way. Yes, follow my direction. You there, follow the finger. Up, up and away with you. Bloody saints, I shall be here all through the night!"

"Ulrich?" Gossamyr stepped cautiously through the sooty darkness. The whisper of a breeze through the long reeds that lined the path danced them to a crisp shimmy. Her bare feet made not a sound on the dirt road. The cloak whipped out behind her.

She spied Fancy, unloosed and grazing over a patch of clover. Another outburst from Ulrich stirred Gossamyr to a trot, her staff held horizontal and shoulder level, ready to spear.

"Another? Be patient; wait your turn. This way. Not so pushy!"

"Ulrich?" Now Gossamyr could make out the gray outlines of Ulrich's head, bowed and swaying as if in deep thought. She veered from her approach as he swung out a hand and pointed starward.

"You. Yes, you next!"

"Whom are you speaking to?" There was not another person in the vicinity. To be sure, Gossamyr turned a complete circle—staff cutting the night—scanning the circumference. Scentless, the air. Strange, she did neither smell the dirt or grass. She noted they stood at a crossroad, Ulrich exact center.

When she turned back to him his body jerked, as if tugged from behind, and he leaped about to face the empty darkness.

Could it be a creature from the Netherdred? One who stood yet on the Faery side of the rift, invisible yet capable of affecting the Otherside? She should be able to see anything that stood in Faery if it connected with this world. Why could she not—

"If you cannot afford me the virtue of patience," Ulrich announced to no one, "I shall see you to Hades where you belong. Be gone!"

"Ulrich!" She leaped forward and gripped the man by the shoulders. If he had succumbed to a glamour, perhaps her contact could unloose him. Because he was rigid and jumpy and jerking in her grasp, her fingers could not maintain hold. The vexing cloak impeded her and she toppled, but caught herself with the staff. "You speak to the night. What is to you, man? Be you luna-touched?"

"Get me free from here," he growled. A flick of his head to the left and he addressed another unseen entity. "Heaven? You who takes your own life asks very much!"

"Is it the Netherdred?" she pleaded.

"I know not of nether dreads—only the dreads that stand before me. Ah! I must concentrate!"

The man had stepped into a realm that frightened even Gossamyr. She could feel not a presence. No smell or sound could be pulled from the confusion of the moment. She tugged Ulrich's arm, but resistance tensed in her grasp. And yet, the man did not pull himself from her. 'Twas is if he were bestiffened.

Banshees? she wondered. No, they were visible figments of white wailing women. Ghosts? She had not experience with the sort; ghosts aligned themselves with wizards, witches and forbidden magic.

"I have not the leisure for you all," Ulrich shouted and twisted from Gossamyr's hold. "I will die of old age to send you each in his turn. Faery Not, pull harder!"

"I am trying," Gossamyr said. She clutched him about the waist and planted her toes in the loose dirt. It was as if he were being held to the center of the roads, fixed with nails pounded through the soles of his soft-bottomed shoes. Yet she felt not a single presence. "What is it? A spectral creature I cannot see?"

"Hundreds," Ulrich cried. "Take my hands."

Twisting under his outstretched arm, Gossamyr seized the man's hands. Though the darkness shadowed features, the agony on his face showed strongly. As their palms joined, Gossamyr felt cold tremor through her forearms and up her shoulders.

Horrors! A chill greater than winter's bite trickled through her bones. "I can feel them," she uttered.

Pushing with all her might, she succeeded in moving Ulrich from the center of the crossed roads while he shouted and protested with the unseen forces. Together they shuffled backward. Her toes stepped onto grass. Fancy snorted and clopped from their way. Finally, Ulrich tripped and went down. Gossamyr fell forward onto his chest, collapsing with a huff. The distinctive rip of dried leaves sounded.

Breath wheezed from Ulrich's lungs. Reaching back, Gossamyr felt over her pourpoint. A rent down the center, up to her midsection, she determined.

Now even the crickets silenced. Dark surrounded; the eyelash moon ignored this little crossroad. Lying atop Ulrich, Gossamyr grew aware of his breaths, short and hot. The chill had slithered off as if it had not bitten her so sharply. The man had been assaulted in a manner she could not comprehend. But that she had rescued him from an unseen assailant seemed apparent.

She gave a jerk of her head to swish back the heavy corner of the cloak from her face. "Are you fine and well?"

A burst of laughter shook him beneath her.

Gossamyr bent her legs and knelt over him, trying to assess his condition. Eyes closed, and his breathing still fast, was all she could remark. No cold—yet she had felt his flesh to be as ice when gripping his hands. She scented not blood, but when she thought to touch his face—check for wounds—she recalled the bruise. A touch would not be welcome to his tender flesh.

Pushing up, Gossamyr stood and struggled with the cumbersome cloak. The heavy fabric twisted between her legs. "Blight!"

Ulrich remained on his back. Short bursts of laughter continued, so she judged him safe. But sound?

Plodding up from behind, Fancy nudged her warm nose into Gossamyr's palm. With contact, fear flowed out from her. A glance to the crossroads sighted only stillness. Whatever had threatened was now gone. She took a breath and expelled it in a lip-fluttering blast.

"The saddlebag," Ulrich asked in a gasping voice as his laughter settled. "Is it safe?"

"Exactly where it should be." Gossamyr bent and this time stroked aside a clump of hair from Ulrich's temple. No fear in touching this mortal. Secretly, she felt daring to do so. "What happened to you?"

"A damned crossroads," he said in a tone that blamed her for not guessing the obvious. Moving up to prop on his elbows, he blew out a bluster of breath. "I wasn't paying attention, and walked right into the center of the infernal place. Hell would be most pleased to open a tavern right there." He gestured forcefully toward the spot he had stood. "Plenty of doomed souls for the taking."

"What has a crossroads to do with whatever it was that tormented you?"

"You don't know?"

She shook her head. "When we joined hands I felt something...so icy, I could have frozen."

"Ah. Yes. The chill of death. Do not faeries have their lost souls? Suicides and murders? They gather at crossroads."

"Who?"

"The souls! Lost and misdirected souls wandering a purgatorial nightmare. They convene at crossroads because that is where we *mortals* bury the forsaken."

"Ghosts?"

"Not exactly. Souls, Gossamyr. Souls. Disembodied and searching."

She turned to look over the place where Ulrich had battled. Souls? *The revenants cannot commence the final* twinclian *without an essence.* "Like...revenants?"

"I know not what a revenant is."

"They are—" Skeletal flying beasts with wings. She clasped both elbows. Better to keep that information to herself. "Why could I not see them? Did *you* see them?"

"Not in a physical way. But believe me, I felt their icy, possessive bones everywhere. Had you not dragged me away I would have been trapped until dawn guiding those damned souls to Hades. So horribly the same!"

"Guiding them? I do not understand. Be this magic?"

"Far from it. Let's walk, shall we?"

Ulrich stood. Bell-wavering forward a few steps, he turned and groped Fancy's flanks to steady. Had she not known him sober Gossamyr would have guessed him soused. "Distance, my lady, we need to get Jean César Ulrich Villon III far from this horrific place. I can yet feel them leering at me, waiting for me to stumble back onto their domain."

She squinted, yet sighted nothing but gray shadows upon darkness. A chirr of crickets resumed their night symphony, and a snort from Fancy drew her attention around.

"Come, my fashionably challenged misfit." Ulrich slapped a palm to Fancy's flank and the mule stepped into motion. "Let's be away."

They resumed the path, Fancy trotting hastily to keep pace with Ulrich's swaying strides. Gossamyr skipped alongside on the border of grass. Every third step she stabbed her staff into the ground and swung forward. "So, you are truly well?"

"Soon enough." He noted her swinging steps and smiled. "Just a little begroggled is all. My head will clear as I move farther from Hell's stain. What of you? I heard leaves tearing."

"Still all together," she said. "So…you were guiding those souls?"

"Not by choice."

"But…you…do all mortals have such an ability?"

"Ah! You are not up on we mortals, my lady. Your disguise wears thin. Methinks I can see the glimmer on your hands."

The night did not grant such perfect vision, so Gossamyr did not even check. He lied in an attempt to get her to reveal herself. He guessed he knew her. He *did* know her. And she sensed no danger from him. But she must remain wary.

Or must she? A scan of the sky did not sight the fetch. What horrendous danger must she encounter to bring Shinn to her side? Or was the lord of Glamoursiège too busy with the revenants to leave?

She whispered blessings for her father's safety.

As for help, she did not need it. Champions were bold. *Be bold, be bold, be not too bold.* A statement Gossamyr had once read in the bestiary, written in gold text below the image of a charging knight.

"This talent of seeing and guiding souls is not a common one," Ulrich said, drawing to a halt. A stretch of his arm to the sky and he announced with less than his usual flare, "I am…Shepherd to Lost Souls."

Their closeness allowed Gossamyr to see the grin slip onto Ulrich's face. Did he mock her? "Shepherd to Lost Souls?"

"Another of my royal appointments. One I've tried desperately to shuck, but it is the only one that ever really sticks with me. I was born one. Will die one. Likely, I shall perish at a crossroads, inundated by the miserable hordes that seek Hades." Ulrich reached to grip Gossamyr's shoulder. A firm grasp that demanded her attention. Here in the darkness she could not see his expression. "Truth?"

"Please."

"I am a guide for lost souls. Families either hire me before an imminent death to ensure their loved one goes the direction they believe it should—Heaven or Hades—or I am called upon after a death to guide a lost soul."

"How are they lost?"

"Ah, you see, they either aren't sure they led a good life and deserve Heaven, or well, would you go to Hades if you knew you should?"

"Heaven and Hades are not familiar to me. Be they in France?"

He gasped. Clutching one of the silver talismans about the chain at his neck he displayed a cross in the ill night. A holy symbol associated with the mortal church. Veridienne had once fashioned one from holly sticks for Gossamyr, but she had broken it when shoving it in a sap hole to collect a sweet treat. Ulrich's Heaven and Hell may be very similar to the fée's sacred resting places.

"Infernal and Celestial?" she tried.

"Yes, yes. The same."

Be that so? She wondered if the fée *twinclianed* to the same place as did mortals. It seemed unlikely.

"How do you guide them? Do you just point?"

"If only it were so easy. I trance. Then, I communicate with the soul—"

"Can you see it?"

"No." He smoothed both hands over his scalp, pushing back his tousle of curls. An extravagant gesture into the air startled Gossamyr back a few steps. "But I can feel it!" Ulrich announced with such declaration she thought him preaching doctrine. "And the sensation gives me a picture of the person, most in their death state. Murders are a nasty picture. As well, suicides." A forceful exhale lowered his shoulders and he toed a crop of clover that Fancy had taken to chewing. "Must we go on about this? I want to clear the crossroads from my mind."

"So you do not enjoy this ability?"

Ulrich turned up a palm and twisted on the rings circling his fingers. "It is my way; I have accepted it."

"And yet you've performed many other jobs?"

"One of many unsuccessful attempts to replace this particularly vexing profession. At all means I try to avoid what happened back there. It drains me. Makes me grumpy. Much like a tired faery princess."

"A what?"

"Well, I've guessed, haven't I?"

Gossamyr shifted, her toes hanging over the thick cleft of grass edging the path. Why was it so difficult to be forthright when she wanted to? An affection for mistruth had never been hers.

Because the dangers of the Otherside had been preached to her since she could understand. *They capture and keep faeries.* A truth illustrated not two jigs earlier. Should she have tried to free the caged fée? For what hope but death, for the Disenchanted, upon return to Faery, could never hope to regain Enchantment.

Yet you left her to live a tortured existence. Could she have given the fée death to end her suffering?

Gossamyr shivered. No, likely not.

"So many lost souls," she noted, "each wanting your complete attention."

"Exactly. Once again we change the subject. Well! Neither are graveyards a pretty spot to wander."

"You bury your dead."

"A wise observation for a mortal."

"No questions, Ulrich, not…now. Please?"

"Yes, we are, both of us, exhausted."

Gossamyr nodded. "Onward then."

"I require rest, my lady. I wager you could slip to Nod if only you'd admit such."

"What of that castle ahead?"

Ulrich stared off toward the horizon. A jagged line rose above a lush forest of trees. The single tower of a large castle—what once might have been a formidable stronghold—drew a black blot in the gray sky.

"Looks to be abandoned." He squinted. "On second thought, it looks to have been torn from its ramparts. Let us cross the meadow to that copse of trees and make camp."

"But if the castle is abandoned it may provide shelter." Gossamyr strode ahead while Ulrich trundled through the tall grasses. "A wall or two is all we need. Mayhap a bed?"

"My lady of the annoying questions," he called as his steps took to jumping dashes to navigate the meadow. "The few things that see a castle abandoned are plague, famine or siege. Either of the three leaves a heap of dead in its wake. And where there are dead, there are souls. Dozens of them, surely. Just…waiting."

"I see." Gossamyr turned and skipped after him. She would not subject him to further horror. She overtook Ulrich and rushed up to the trees. "Then we camp here, and I'll scout the remains in the morning."

"I've a blanket in my saddlebag."

A nest of thick moss at the base of an ax-tormented oak tempted for but a moment. Gossamyr settled down and tucked her feet under her legs. "The evening is warm. I am not accustomed to night coverings." Actually she often slept nude. And wouldn't bare skin feel much better right now than this itchy cloak? "I will keep the cloak if you would grant it."

"Please do. I shouldn't wish your virtue compromised."

"My—" She snapped her jaw shut. Virtue. Yes, the mortals were not so accepting of bared flesh.

"Sweet dreams." Fabric snapped. Ulrich laid out the blanket on the opposite side of the trunk. "I wonder, do you dream of mortals?"

With her staff clutched near to ready, Gossamyr closed her eyes. "Cease, Ulrich."

But her thoughts remained busy.

This information about Ulrich and his skill with souls intrigued. Gossamyr sought a woman who stole essences, which were similar to the mortal soul. Could the soul shepherd see a fée essence? And if he could, would it serve her a boon or merely a belated warning to an already stolen life?

Either way, he may prove valuable to her quest.

Now, to dreams of…Paris and mortals.

The decimated ruins of what had once been a great castle lured Gossamyr from the red dirt pathway. She had woken this morning to find the midportion of her pourpoint crumbled, where she'd bent her gut to curl into a comfortable position. The bottom half had fallen away as she stood. Ulrich's whistle had prompted her to tie the corners of his cloak about her waist in a wrapped manner that didn't so much conceal her bared belly as keep the cloak to hand should the remainder of her clothing sift away to dust.

Disenchantment attacked her Faery vestments. Yet, the braies remained complete. Her staff, the *arrets* and the Glamoursiège sigil were also whole. A curiosity. How soon before all fell from her body in a glimmer of dust?

The fetch darted ahead of her, veering back and skimming overhead, then turning to bank tightly toward her. Fancy wandered the border of the castle wall, picking amongst the fallen stones and charred ramparts for a choice blossom of her favorite, clover.

"Hasn't been abandoned overlong!" Ulrich called. He remained a good distance from the ruins. What he determined a "safe zone" from the lost dead.

Again the nuisance fetch darted at her. Wings flicked the crown of her head. Gossamyr batted at the insistent insect. "Be gone!" It was as if the dragon fly did not want her to go up to the castle.

Which only made Gossamyr all the more determined to do so. Dodging the fetch's incoming flight, she bent and ducked under the insect and ran up and over a pile of fallen limestone blocks.

Her feet melding to the moss-frosted stone, she stood at the entrance to what might have once been the bailey. Rusted iron spikes stuck in a charred length of wood. The clawed bottom of a portcullis? Gossamyr stilled and closed her eyes. The caw of a raven soared overhead. She could scent but the grass and a patch of nearby clover. Nothing unseen brushed her flesh. (Not even the fetch. Wise creature.) Which merely proved she could not sense what Ulrich had been born to see. Intriguing, his skill, though it be a vexing burden to bear.

No more vexing than the burden of half blood.

Desideriel has agreed to the marriage. Be that the reason for Shinn's need to pair her so quickly? Did he not want a half blood ruling

Glamoursiège? It was a startling thought. One Gossamyr had not before considered. It made sense. But that Shinn had not expressed such concern to her hurt.

The gentle hum of wind softened as she entered the destruction. Ignoring her conscience's dreadsome notions, Gossamyr poked through the rubble with her staff. Ulrich's guess might be correct; this castle had not been abandoned for more than a few years of mortal seasons.

A tattered tapestry, lifted with the end of her staff, displayed vibrant indigo and amber threading in the crease where the sun had not found purchase. A pod of bronze beetles were shook to the ground. She watched their haphazard scurry to find a shadow; pretty how the sun reflected on their hard iridescent shells like animated jewels.

A deep breath drew in the lightness of the world. Stretching out her arms, Gossamyr teetered playfully as she jumped from one stone to the next. Flight was hers in this lightness of being. No need for wings, merely a breath lifted her high from the usual.

She kicked aside a dented steel bascinet and squatted beside what looked to be human remains—a skull, the jaw cleaved in two to separate the teeth with a perfect line. Only a heavy slicing weapon could have done such. Much as she craved danger, Gossamyr said blessings she had not been raised when Glamoursiège had been a warring tribe. Shinn had intimated to his violent history in his attention to her training. Strife was far and rare in Faery, for the mortals thrived on opposition.

But tendrils of strife had now seeped into her home. What may become a full-scale battle of revenants versus her people must be stopped.

"What do you suppose happened?" she called as she marked what might have been the length of the keep. Wood beams spanning a thickness to match her torso bracketed the fieldstone hearth, the remaining rib-work that had supported what must have once been a formidable fortress.

"War." Ulrich's voice echoed easily across their distance. "Indifference. Greed. It is a common thing."

"Yes, the mortal war," she murmured, knowing from Veridienne's bestiary that near to a century had ensnared the Otherside in war. How many years formed a century? Had Shinn lived so long?

"Shall we be off? There is nothing of value to be had from the remains of another man's suffering."

"Anon," she called, disinterested in leaving just yet.

Gossamyr approached a burnt wood piling that might have once supported a ceiling beam. Thick as a man's body and charred at an angle on both ends, it stood upright, rooted in the rubble of stone and defeated pride. Faint smoke and coal tinged the air. A damaged shield had been fixed to the beam, literally pinned there with a rusted sword.

The fetch landed on the blade of the weapon, tucking its translucent wings against its streamlined body and eyeing her with wide golden orbs.

"You are not Shinn's conscience," she warned. "I will not be dissuaded. Merely record and be gone with you."

A flicker of wings glinted in the sunlight.

She touched the leather hilt of the sword; it bounced against her palm, setting the fetch to an abbreviated flight—up, then back to settle upon the blade. A fine, heavy sword—had it served a warrior? A tug proved it was fixed into the wood. Fine and well, she had no desire to touch mortal steel.

Gossamyr stepped up and traced her fingertips along the jagged edge of the shield, not touching, but close. The dexter corner had been torn away but did not destroy the faded white lettering mastering the shield. She had learned the mortal language from Veridienne in her youth; it was very similar to her own. Painted across the top were two words written in mortal script. Valor. Truth. An "r" preceded *valor;* mayhap the end of the first word.

"Valor," she whispered, feeling the need—verily, a compulsion—to trace above the letters.

To the side where the shield had been torn, the stone hearth had been marred with charcoal. Someone had written a word to replace the one that had apparently been ripped off the shield. Vengeance.

Gossamyr pressed her spread palm over the word but did not touch it. She verily felt the anger emanating from that vile word. Glancing up to the crumbled walls that were now crenellated from damage, she sighed. Great suffering had befallen this castle and its inhabitants. Vengeance, indeed.

A glance to the fetch. Did it wink at her?

Drawing in a breath, Gossamyr suddenly struggled with insistent thoughts of worry. Her heart felt heavy. She mourned for... something. Something lost.

A tilt of her head studied the shield, but her eyes unfocused and she merely listened to her heartbeats. So vigorous.

Vengeance, valor, truth.

All were not lost.

Stretching out a finger, she tapped the middle word—no sting from the steel. She would claim valor as her own battle standard.

As for the truth, she had it. 'Twas buried in her name complete—Gossamyr Verity de Wintershinn.

Ah, but she dallied and Ulrich waited. One day, her journey thus far. Paris was close. She felt the loss of strength, of Enchantment, as one might feel a layer of clothing peeled from their back. Time would not prove her boon. Even now Shinn must battle more of the relentless revenants.

She turned and strode out from the ruins. "I must be to it."

Ulrich hustled after her. "You are most urgent, my lady!"

"And you are not? I thought there was a damsel in need of rescue?"

"There is, but timing is not of import."

"What is?" she called as she reined in Fancy and tugged the mule back onto the path.

"Luck. I seek an elusive end."

"Care to elaborate?"

"No."

"Has it to do with lost souls?"

"I pray the damsel is not lost. But you may help my quest."

Quirking a brow and swinging a look over her shoulder, Gossamyr maintained pace. "How?"

"You are a faery," he called.

"I have only denied that claim."

"Not very effectively, Faery Not."

As she plodded forward, the mule slowing her pace, Gossamyr struggled between confession and keeping her secret. What was the harm? At the least, the truth would defeat that vicious name Faery Not. The man could not think it any more than a silly nickname, but oh, did it cut deep into Gossamyr's soul. A mortal soul? Or half-mortal soul half-fée essence? All her life she had been Faery Not, something lesser, not equal to any other.

"What think you to wed my daughter?"

Desideriel Raine sneered at Gossamyr. "Oh?"

That sneer could not be put from her memory.

'Twas time to accept and move on. Had not a good portion of her desire to come to the Otherside been to learn about that part of herself she did not know?

"Very well," she said, more to herself. Ulrich shuffled to catch her pace. A man she could trust, for he held more than enough trouble in his heart to make any more for her. "If you must know, I *have* come from Faery."

Ulrich punched the air with a triumphant fist. He skipped around in front of her, the talismans about his neck chinking. "I knew it! You are *not* the same!"

Grinning at his delight, Gossamyr left the road and trod through tall, cool blades to stop beside a massive stone. She squatted before the jagged granite lump and twisted a long ribbon of grass about her finger, then plucked it, pressing the wide blade upon her upper lip. Planting a foot upon the stone, she then offered, "But I am nearly so mortal as you."

"I don't understand." Ulrich dropped Fancy's reins, leaving the mule to graze. The man seated himself upon the rock, crossing his legs and pressing the heels of his palms behind him. "How can you come from Faery and not *be* a faery? You look like one."

"Have you ever seen a fée?"

"Hell yes! I danced, remember?"

Indeed. And something about his Dance seemed familiar to her. She had witnessed but the one...

"As well, I've the sight now, much as I'd rather trade it for a fortnight standing dead center at a crossroads." He entreated the skies with a grand gesture of arms. "How to get Faery from my eyes?"

"I do not know of a way."

"You sparkle—"

"Merely remnants of Faery." Gossamyr slid a finger over her wrist, noting the residual glamour was only visible when she tilted her arm and the sun glanced upon her skin.

"What of there on your neck. It looks a pattern."

And so she would confess all. "My blazon. It is the mark of the fée."

"So all faeries wear similar markings?"

"Yes, but not in the same places on their body. It is a tribal marking. Though some elders are marked overall with the blazon. Glamoursiège blazons the neck and upper chest. My father's chest, shoulders and back are entirely marked. One can determine which tribe the fée hails from merely by locating his blazon. But as you've said, it fades on me?"

He gestured she tilt her chin up and studied. Lost in thought, his lips parted and she noted the bulge of pink tongue pressing through the gape in his teeth. "Yes, it is difficult to see unless—oh! Do not stand in the sunlight, my lady."

"That bright?"

"The cloak will serve if you tug it closed." He reached to pull the cloak close about her neck. His finger brushed under her chin. The two met eyes and held.

Utter awareness crowded out all other sensory litter. Blue, so deep as the sea in which the merfolk swam, she wondered of the eyes so intent upon her. Gossamyr watched the heavy bob of Ulrich's throat as he swallowed. Different, in a manner that enticed. Yet again, mortal touched. And yet again, pleased for it.

"That is bone." She touched her chin, and at the same time Ulrich pulled away. Whatever they two had just shared in the silence of their eyes she wanted it kept silent. "The Disenchantment sets in slowly. Any fée glamour I have gained through shared blood with my father will be shed from me until I appear merely mortal."

"Don't knock mortality until you've tried it."

"I am trying it right now, Ulrich." She sighed and settled upon the rock next to him. "It is different. Yet the same."

"Much remains the same."

"Will you explain to me your need to label things the same and not?"

"If you will tell me how you did come to live in Faery? It makes little sense. Unless you stepped into a toadstool circle and danced the endless dance of joy? Oh, poor thing. Have you lost all your family and friends then? Are they old or dead?"

"I did no such thing. I was born in Faery! But you did visit, yes?"

"Danced twenty years, Faery Not."

"If you do not stop calling me such I promise to push you into the next circle of toadstools we pass."

"Touchy, touchy. Very well." He held up his hands. "So explain your life, lady Gossamyr. Faery or not?"

"Both. I am half-blooded. My mother was completely mortal, my father a fée. Though birth granted me more mortal attributes than fée. I've no genuine glamour."

"So your blazon is…?"

"Attribute it to years spent in Faery. Should a mortal spend a length of time there, they would eventually develop the same. As did my mother."

"Interesting. How did your mother come to live in Faery?"

"Shinn—my father—" Had he ever truly loved? Had lust been the origin of Veridienne's coming? How to judge the difference between lust and love? *It forges deep into your heart, fixes there and never relents.* Indeed. Love. Devastating. "Veridienne went to live as his wife in Faery."

"I have heard tales of mortals who fall in love with faeries. One cannot leave Faery without first bargaining for their very life."

"That…is not right." Gossamyr had not heard such. "My mother left Faery. The mortal passion led her home—here—to the Otherside. There were no bargains made."

"Ah, so that be your mission? You seek your mother?"

Gossamyr twisted her gaze to the man. Seek her mother? No. Well…no. She'd never considered such. Shinn had always told her Veridienne was dead; there was no sense in seeking a trail that would lead to nothing. "No."

"So why are you here? Is not Faery a far better place to be?"

"You say so? When you were so disturbed by the possibility you might be taken back by me?"

He shrugged. "I just thought, for you, one who has always lived there, it would be better. Such as this land, my home, is better for me."

Indeed. And yet Faery had never felt so right on her body as did this Otherside.

Tracing a finger along the carved ribbons on her staff, Gossamyr stared off toward the flock of crows that swooped overhead. Better in Faery? When her return would bring marriage? It disturbed her that Shinn was so eager to see her married. Did he suspect he was not long for this world? Gossamyr's heart double-stepped. "Shinn?" she murmured.

"What is that?"

"Hmm?"

"You were telling me why you are here. Then of a sudden you went all panicky."

"I am…well." But was Shinn? The fée did not suffer maladies. They died in battle or of long life, or…from the mortal passion.

"Gossamyr?"

"Hmm? I am…on a mission only I can achieve."

"Why is that?"

Dragging her thoughts from images of her father, limping, gasping for breath—no, not dying—Gossamyr focused on the conversation. "I possess mortal blood. The enemy seeks the Disenchanted. They are of true fée blood—ichor, actually—but have lost most all of their glamour including the ability to return to Faery. She will not see me coming for I will blend easily with those mortals who populate Paris."

"And this enemy—she?—why is she an enemy?"

"The Red Lady's actions threaten to destroy Faery."

"All of Faery?" Ulrich whistled. "A tremendous lot riding on your success."

"Yes." Gossamyr checked herself with a touch to her chest. That answer had been but a whisper. Not so sure of herself?

Vengeance. Valor. Truth. Gossamyr peered back down the path they had traveled. The sadness she had felt lingered as a tangible hollow in her belly. What had she lost in that castle?

"Why do faeries live in Paris?"

So many questions. Yet, Ulrich seemed genuinely interested. And she did take comfort in talking with him. "It is a passion for the unknown, the mortal, that attracts them."

"And this red lady is doing what with them?"

"She is a succubus who decimates the male population of Disenchanted fée with her evil killing kiss. I've been sent to stop her."

"Why not your father? Surely he commands troops?"

"He does. But they would fall to the same fate as the Disenchanted. The Red Lady can scent another fée and strike with forces as to overwhelm an entire troop. It is an enchanting song she uses to draw them to her, much like a siren's song. As I understand, the male fée is quite powerless to resist. Besides, there are revenants to battle in Faery."

"Revenants?"

"They are like your invisible souls seeking rest—yet they are very visible. The revenant is a result of a stolen essence; it seeks an essence in order to achieve the final *twinclian*. An essence is similar to the mortal soul."

Both clung to the other's seeking look. Much to comprehend, Gossamyr knew. She did not completely understand, herself. Should not Shinn be able to *twinclian* directly to the Red Lady? She could not be more powerful than the Faery lord. One moment away from Faery—no, it must not be possible, else Gossamyr knew the Glamoursiège lord would have already risked the trip.

It was Ulrich who nodded and let out a low whistle as he leaned forward on the rock. "You speak words I have never heard—*twinclian*, Disenchanted, revenants—but I understand there is a great need to stop this red woman. You think I can help?"

"Can you see faery essences?"

He shrugged. "If I cannot see a mortal soul I most certainly cannot see a faery soul. Nor, likely, these revenants."

"If one charged you with its skeletal arms clawing and its maws open for blood, you would see it."

"Sounds...like it would leave a mark."

"The revenants will mark Faery with their tirade." And a new war will begin, ending the long Peace.

Not going to happen. Not if she had a say; and she did. "But you understand now, Ulrich? I am not a full-blooded faery."

"I think I understand. You, being half mortal, will not be detected until it is too late. But what of the blazon and these faery powers you speak of? Will this red lady not judge you to be a faery, as well?"

"Like I said, these remnants of Faery will soon be gone. Besides, it is the males she prefers."

"Without the glamour will you be powerless against her?"

Gossamyr gripped the staff. "I have the skills taught me by my father." She saw Ulrich's squint and knew what he was thinking. "Oh, come now, Jean César Ulrich Villon—"

"The Third," he tossed at her.

"The Third. Have you no allegiance to me?"

"I have known you but a day and each moment of that day you concealed your truth from me."

"As have you!"

"Indeed." He leaped to the ground and stood before her, hands to his hips. "And in that time I have seen such remarkable skills as to believe you are certainly capable. But you say this red lady can take out an entire Faery troop? How then will but one single woman be successful against her?"

Drawing up her shoulders, Gossamyr released a huge breath. "I won't know unless I try."

"You've a hell of a mettle."

"I like danger."

"That you do. Stick around me, my lady of the hurting stick, and I promise you your fill."

"And why is that? Has it to do with your quest?"

"Er…"

"Achoo!"

Ulrich swung a gap-toothed grin at Gossamyr. "You're going to have to work on that. I wager not a few enemies will be pleased to hear you announce your arrival with such a powerful sneeze."

Rubbing her nose, Gossamyr stood and stalked past him. "I cannot prevent it. I feel as if I sneeze out a bit of my essence with each one. It must be this mortal soil. The very air is filled with...stuff. Faery is cleaner, brighter, more...vertical."

"Will you miss it?"

Ulrich's quiet query beat back and forth in her mind. "I will return."

The village of Juvisy was of good size—two taverns, a blacksmith and a cooper occupied the market square. Gossamyr tugged at the heavy cloak. The wool made her itch and taxed her long strides. Yet still, she remained buoyant. Difficult to sulk when surrounded by lightness.

At Ulrich's beckon they quietly entered the village through a stone portcullis that bore no heavy wood door. Neither were there city walls, so protection must come from armed guards, Gossamyr assumed. Keeping a keen eye to her surroundings, she strode behind Fancy. Children's laughter startled her so thoroughly, she spun to locate the sound.

That movement proved devastating. She jumped as the entirety of her pourpoint slid over her stomach and to the ground. The heavy weight of her hip belt caught upon the waist of her braies.

"Ulrich."

The soul shepherd turned to her. Blue eyes widened as they spied the heap of dried leaves at her feet.

"Dragon piss." Ulrich scanned the periphery. "This is not bone."

Clasping the cloak to her body as if a shroud, Gossamyr frantically searched about. The village rustled with carts and carriages and there a small herd of sheep scampered behind a rotund shepherd. Surely there must be a shop that sold premade clothing. The coin Shinn had given her yet hung at her waist, the Disenchantment had not eaten away the purse.

"Give me a moment." Spying a coach parked outside a white-washed hovel, she decided a little investigation could prove fruitful.

"A bit too late to stitch a patch here and there, my lady!" Ulrich called.

"I've a disguise to procure. I'll meet you in the market square, yes?"

"I wait with bells on. A hell of a lot more than you're wearing, I wager." And with a smile to charm devils, Ulrich clicked his tongue and signaled Fancy to follow him.

SEVEN

Outside and behind a smithy shop reeking of charred wood, Gossamyr tooled around behind a small carriage that sported a chest on the backboard—unlocked. Rummaging about the contents she found clothing stuffed around heavy, thick books. A scholar, likely. Though the clothing was minimal and spare—perfect.

Leaving a pile of Faery coin in her wake, she snuck behind a stack of hay to change and emerged feeling newly entered to the mortal realm. It was a good disguise, covering her from crown to ankle, most especially her neck. But it was hot and itchy. Couldn't be prevented.

Walking down the center road, Gossamyr's steps increased to a skip. Every building, cart and person remained horizontally placed. Nothing glittered or twinkled. Not a single pisky flew by. Yet, so much proved of interest. The sun played upon puddles of mud and in the glint of saddle furnishings. The metallic chirr of an iron horseshoe being shaped mixed with the bray of a goat being chased by a handful of children.

Her smiles were greeted with equal smiles. No one cast a disdainful sneer upon her. In fact, a few even crossed themselves and bowed to her. Hmm. Must be the necklace she had borrowed. Gossamyr patted the long chain of dried rosebuds that hung to her belly.

An urchin no taller than her knees bounced by and looked up to her. The goat chase momentarily forgotten, a smile cracked the boy's dirty face. Wide brown eyes glinted from the round, pink flesh.

Gossamyr had only ever seen the dark eye color on her mother's face and her own. "Like mine," she said to the child.

Child of mine, so precious, her father's favorite mantra.

When a fée woman was with child she usually stowed away for the six months of gestation. Such a delicate business, childbirth. Someday she hoped to have her own. Would there ever be another Avenall? A fée man who could love her for her exotic qualities and not turn in disgust from her brown eyes? Desideriel would not offer the kindness of interest. Alas, they two were destined to parent a child. Pray it was not born with brown eyes.

The child giggled and toddled off to cling to his mother's wool skirts. A half dozen women knelt around a central well, scrubbing clothing, their chatter frolicking with the smithy's clangs of metal. Gossamyr wondered if there was a misplaced pair of braies in the mix of laundry. She still wore her own, but couldn't guess how long the amphi-leather would hold.

The *shing* of steel alerted her to an armored man. He strode through the children's goat chase and past the well. Glimpsing his determined frown, Gossamyr followed his pace. She tugged at the sides of the headpiece she wore, knowing it covered her scalp and revealed but her face. He stepped into a tavern busy with shouts and general bustle.

To her right she spied a stone fountain trickling green water from the side of a building. Approaching with a thirst that did not care what color the water was, Gossamyr cupped a few gulps down her throat. Eyes peeled to her periphery, she noticed a huge shirt-

less man blocking view of another much smaller man wearing
bold green-and-black hose. Their conversation, though she could
not make out a word, did not sound friendly.

Splashing a palmful of water over her lips, she then called, "Be
there a problem, Ulrich?"

"Not at all, my lady. Just a difference of opinion."

She joined the men. The shirtless brute crowding Ulrich against
a wood stall wore a leather apron and wielded a heavy iron club.
If any required a bath, this stinking specimen took the prize.
Scratching an itch at the back of her right hip, Gossamyr propped
a hand to the wall beside Ulrich's head and looked the two over.

At sight of her, Ulrich banged the back of his head against the
wall of the tavern. He clutched his chest and babbled, "Bloody
saints, that's…that's…"

"A suitable disguise?" she wondered innocently, while keeping
a keen eye to the confused intruder.

He stretched his gaze up and down the costume. Her heavy plaits
were concealed, as were her legs, arms and any hint of feminine
shape. Seeing his dismay, she lifted the hem of her gown to reveal
beneath the leather-bound braies of such strange color.

Ulrich smiled. "My lady, you commit most delicious blasphemy."

"Who be you?" The man actually growled at her!

"Who be you?" she countered in equal gruffness.

"H-he thinks I resemble a man who tricked a bushel of eggs
from his lady wife," Ulrich offered, a wince multiplying to a nervous blink.

"You are the one," the brute spat. A meaty fist gripped Ulrich's
shirt and lifted him to tiptoes.

"I have not been to Juvisy before this day."

"Two days hence! I would not forget your ugly face."

Gossamyr smirked. The smelly man lied. While she knew little of Ulrich, the man was no thief.

A swing of her staff whacked the tormentor on the back of the neck. He went down smoothly and without a sound. The iron club settled in a plume of dust at their feet. She offered a smile to the gaping soul shepherd.

"You will stop that!" Ulrich hissed.

"Why? You were in danger. That weapon must weigh two stone."

"Da-danger? Only from the return swing of your staff!" He stepped over the fallen man and tugged her past the dribbling fountain. "You should not have done such. A woman has her place."

"Oh?"

"Yes. Women, they are—" Gossamyr caught herself against his chest, and he shoved her off "—well, they are to keep *behind* their males. They rely on their men to protect them."

"Really?"

"Indeed! They cook and keep the home and tend the children. They do not humiliate their partners by beating on the evil ironsmith."

"I see."

"Do you?"

She shrugged. "Not particularly."

"Obvious."

"Methinks such subservience sounds perfectly silly. In Faery all are equal. Women fight alongside men. Male fée tend their children and play with them as much as their mates. And since when did we become partners?"

"We are partners of the road." Ulrich slung his saddlebag over his shoulder and wandered to the shade beneath a massive oak stretching its gnarled limbs across the market square. The flickering white hide of the goat, tucked amongst a holly bush, revealed its hiding spot.

Gossamyr punctuated her frustration with a stab of her staff to ground. "I thought you were in a hurry?"

"Why think you so?"

"Be there not a damsel in need of rescue?"

"Sure," he said with a dismissive gesture. "But I also said time was no concern."

"Why not? Does your damsel sit in a high tower at her tapestry gathering wrinkles in your absence?"

"She is dead."

"Dead?"

Ulrich turned his shoulder to her.

"Oh, no." She rushed him and gave a shove to make him face her. "This is not some sort of evil psychopompery?"

Beringed fingers twisted before his face. "I don't believe there is such a word as psychopompery."

"Blight! It is what you are, isn't it, soul shepherd? What do you intend to do with this dead woman?"

"I plan to bring her back to life. Unhand me. Your closeness is naught seemly. Keep back. Do you know you've a problem with standing too close?"

Gossamyr swayed back at that remark. "What do you mean?" She wrinkled her nose and looked him up and down. Too close? How to have a conversation without the reassurance of a noncombative scent?

"Yes." He pressed two fingers to her shoulder and made show of carefully taking a step to measure distance between them. "See here. About an armshot. That is the proper distance."

"For conversing? Do you mean to tell me there are rules regarding—"

"Merely propriety, my lady. It is gauche to stand so close to another. Unless you've a desire for more intimate converse?"

"Intimate? Like—"

"Yes. Like."

She looked about. Across the way a man conversed with one of the washing women, the brown-eyed child yet clinging to her skirts. Indeed, a goodly distance, an arm's length, separated them. Not close enough to scent one another, as was custom in Faery.

"Why did you not say something to me earlier?"

"I did. But you are not adept at taking orders."

"Orders, no. But helpful suggestions, of course. So I must stand back?"

"Unless you wish us a greater intimacy."

Gossamyr took another step back. "Certainly not." Intimacy bruised one's heart.

"You've only half the costume," he remarked. "You do realize that is not a proper gown?"

"Oh? But it covers. A bit large, I tightened the seams at the shoulders here." She gave a tug to the sewn ties that circled the sleeve and connected it to the body of the gown. "There was a thick black robe, but 'twas cumbersome. This headpiece will conceal my hair and neck until the glimmer subsides. I found all this in the chest of that coach."

"You *stole* holy garments?" Ulrich crossed himself.

"I left coin. They are holy?"

"You have stolen a nun's headpiece, fair lady, and likely her undergarments. And the rosary!" Yet Ulrich's smile only grew as he entreated the heavens. "Blessed Mother, forgive this woman her sin."

"And who be you to invoke the holy?"

"I appreciate the finer points of the Catholic church. Trust me, there is but the one God. And be you layman, mage or faery, we all came from the same place. Well, mayhap."

"I have no wings," she insisted. "You'll gain no remuneration by displaying me in a market square."

"Think you must be a spectacle to bring me profit?"

"What do you mean by that?"

But the market square suddenly filled with a gush of life. One man spewed out from the tavern doors across the way to stumble forward and land the ground in a cloud of choking dust. Gossamyr's sneeze went unnoticed as a roar of men followed, cursing and shouting and kicking at the fallen man.

Shouts of plague and a bloody sickness carried over to Gossamyr. Stifling another sneeze, she nudged Ulrich with an elbow to clear her view. "What is about?"

Head bobbing to and fro, Ulrich discerned the melee. "Best to avoid confrontation," he cautioned. "We've our passage to Paris to concern— Oh! There she goes again, folks. Headfirst into trouble. Staff in hand and rosary beads swinging. What a perfectly delightful young thing. If I were not a married man— Hades, I'm not, am I? Or am I? Definitely *not* the same."

Unfazed with Ulrich's attempts at steering her from danger, Gossamyr pushed through the throng. Dodging deftly to avoid a boot to her bare toes, she slid toward the center of the ring of mortals. The man on the ground crooked his arms over his head to fend off blows, but in the moment he looked up—perhaps to sight an escape—his eyes met Gossamyr's.

She shoved aside a peasant stinking of dung. "Stand off!" she shouted. Roughly jostled, she made way to the man lying on the ground.

Mayhap it was because of her forceful shout, but more likely because the shout had come out in a female voice, that all the men ceased their violent antics and stepped back.

Women rely on men to protect them.

No time. And no desire. There were no protective fée lords to question her actions this day. Besides, this was the first clue to the Red Lady she had seen.

Gossamyr swept her eyes over the open cuts on the man's arms. From the kicks, no doubt, for the short, but deep lacerations looked to be self-defense wounds. He had vomited into the dirt from the torture. Slapping a palm to his forehead, she twisted his head to look into his manic eyes. Red with blood. But surrounding his eyes, where the dirt and dust and the browning from the sun had not touched, she noticed something even more remarkable.

Faery dust. Minute, likely unnoticeable to the untrained eye. A scan of his exposed flesh did not sight a blazon.

"What be this?" one of the attackers said, gasping from exertion. "Sister, there is nothing you can do for this man."

Sister? Ah, the wimple.

"Put him from his misery!"

"He is touched with the plague."

"'Tis the falling sickness!"

"He contaminates our village. Ride him out!"

The crowd held no mercy for this poor one. Gossamyr needed to get him from them if she might gain opportunity to question him.

She bent to study the victim's eyes. "Fée?" she murmured so only he could hear. "Glamoursiège?"

"Wi-Wisogoth."

One of the oldest and most revered Faery tribes. If he yet wore the blazon it painted across his back.

The fée sobbed and grasped at Gossamyr's arms, pleading for mercy. "I am but a victim," he murmured. "I do not want to die."

"Unclean!" shouted out from the crowd. "Plague!"

"This be not the plague," Gossamyr shouted, hoping to divert the madness that ebbed about the circle. She could hold her own against a Faery evil but this crowd of mortals honed an edge of uncertainty to her confidence.

The redness in the fallen fée's eyes formed a sheen of viscous blood. Gossamyr studied the flesh on his face. It was red, most likely from struggle—but no, the very pores were bright little pinholes of blood. Or was it blood? The fée bled ichor.

"Whence have you been?" she asked.

"I've come...from Paris." A thick glob of crimson gurgled up over his lips.

The surrounding men stepped back, cursing and crossing themselves. Whispers to—what Gossamyr guessed—various saints rapidly volleyed over and above her head.

"What is it, Sister?" Ulrich called.

"Grant me a moment."

"That's right," Ulrich addressed the crowd. "Step away. Allow the sister of the cloth to examine the victim. No trouble here. Be on to your private matters."

Gossamyr avoided touching the red substance, for there was no way to determine its virulence. "Paris? You are Disenchanted?"

"Yes," rasped out in a sputter.

"Winged?" He wore a cape. If the villagers saw—

"No longer."

Bone, she thought. But the absence of wings would only keep back suspicion of Faery. How to convince the angry mob to allow her to bring him away with her? Surely, if they suspected he was contagious they would escort her and him from the village.

Keeping a close huddle over the fallen fée, Gossamyr used her body as a shield.

"Did you meet any women? Touch them?"

"So many… Gorgeous and giggling and— There was one," the man gurgled. "Pretty. Pale and…wearing plush as white as snow. Her hair…like rubies… So curious the marking on the side of her face."

"What did she do to you?"

"She—" a macabre grin carved itself in the flesh on the man's face, and then his eyes flickered shut "—kissed me. Her kiss, it was marvelous. Like Faery. Her breath…drenched with…home."

Crimson gushed from the man's eyes.

"What be this substance? It cannot be blood."

"The red," he said on a sigh.

His face, lush with the bloodlike tears, reminded Gossamyr of her three-day crying jag that had changed her life, so subtly, and yet, for ever after. Tears salted with loss. Mortal tears were valuable to the fée—much sought after and traded for incredible sums.

Shinn had instructed Mince to clean away Gossamyr's tears—not mortal complete—following her fall to misery. What the nursemaid had done with them, Gossamyr had never questioned.

The man's head fell limp in Gossamyr's palm. Dead. From a kiss.

Gently, she set his head upon the ground and, using her staff, stood and made eye contact with the circle of morose watchers. 'Twas a remarkable moment to stare down so many mortals, and yet such fascination quickly grew bleak.

"'Tis the plague!" rose up from the crowd. "Do you see the blood?"

"Silence!" Gossamyr's shout eddied a nervous stillness to the marketplace. "It is not the plague. Nor is it—" No explanation for the red. "It is merely…"

How to explain without causing greater panic? And without revealing herself?

Threading her fingers through the beads hanging about her neck, Gossamyr pondered her dilemma. The sea of frightened faces circled her, seeming to move like a wave soon to crash upon the rocks. Aware they thought her a woman of their mortal religious ranks, she perused her options. How soon before the revenant parted from the body? The one death she had witnessed years ago had taken little time. Shinn had explained length of dying was unique to the individual fée. If only there were a way to stop the essence from leaving the body…or mayhap, guiding it to safety?

Gossamyr glanced to Ulrich. Could the soul shepherd help?

"Sister, help us!"

Studying the rosebud beads soaked in lampblack coiled about her finger, Gossamyr struck on an idea. Might she use their faith? A faith she knew naught. But all religions revolved around worship of a greater good, of a divine being, yes? The wooden cross dangling at the end of her necklace sat in her palm. A symbol they revered.

"This man…suffers a rare sickness," she said. Grasping the cross and holding it forth, she made show to wave it over the fallen fée. "There is no risk to others who might touch him."

"Be you a surgeon, Sister?"

"No, but I have seen this before. He must…be buried…beneath the…shadow of a cross." She caught Ulrich's disapproving grimace. "Yes. Er, before vespers."

"Why, Sister?"

The only reason she could summon on such short notice; that was why.

Twinclian occurred only with the untouched essence—a sacred extension of the body. The fée were averse to mortal consecration, so an Enchanted fée would never rest. But such might control this Disenchanted's *twinclian*. Might that keep the revenant at bay? Give Ulrich opportunity to attempt his soul shepherding?

"If you will allow it, my assistant—" she cast a stern reprimand toward Ulrich, who looked ready to protest "—and I will dispose of the body."

"No!"

"We know naught of you!"

"I am a Sister of your church. Er…my church."

"The Catholic church!" Ulrich shouted. And then he sternly said, "Gossamyr."

"Be you God-fearing?"

"You want him for yourself!" someone called. "We'll keep the body."

"You cannot!" She straightened, meeting the man who had spoken boldly. "You think to challenge me?" Certainly a proper challenge would require him to recognize her position by first kneeling into a bow.

But he merely tilted a queer gaze upon her. "Do I face down a woman of the cloth in a challenge?" He eyed her staff. "Or a blasphemer in want of her own suspicion?"

"Come along, Sister. Vespers to be said." Ulrich gripped the back of her wool gown and tugged. Gossamyr choked, and was literally lifted from her feet. "So sorry to have interrupted this gleeful, er, *dire* event. Go along. God grant you all peace and safety." He nudged Gossamyr. Hard. "We're off."

"You stand too close." A tug of the wimple unloosed it from the tight choke about her throat.

"Times like this we're both too close—to an imminent uproar that may likely involve pain. To us. Now move!"

Facing the crowd, she drew her finger across her chest then swept it down her stomach. It wasn't right, she knew, but on occasion she had witnessed Veridienne doing something of the sort.

"What was that for?" Ulrich hissed in her ear.

"I need that body."

Another tug swung her around behind a cart parked but ten long strides from the scene. Ulrich pressed a palm over her shoulder to the wooden body of the vehicle, effectively pinning her. "You need a change of religion."

"I don't understand you."

He nodded over his shoulder to the thick circle of naysayers. "They think you wish to sell the body."

"Why would I do that?"

"For coin! Why else would you want it?"

"Did you not see his eyes?"

"All that blood?"

"It is not blood." Itching the wimple, Gossamyr then palmed Ulrich's face and—closeness be blighted—explained, "The Red Lady. It is her kiss that releases the revenant from the Disenchanted fée men. The revenant must come *out* of the body. It cannot happen before the eyes of these innocents. Do you understand?"

Ulrich's swallow was audible. Gossamyr felt much the same. For a time he simply gazed upon her, his marvelous eyes not revealing his truths, but merely a solemnity that confused.

"What are you thinking? Can you work your soul shepherding on it?"

"Oh, no." He twisted his face from her hand. Two strides moved him closer to the crowd, a bend at the waist attempted to survey the scene between legs and shuffling children. He swung and hissed back at Gossamyr, "I don't, I've never— You're sure he's a faery? I don't see any wings— Watch it!" Ulrich dodged to avoid a hunched man wielding a dagger. He moved with the angry crowd around the body. "That man poked me!"

Gossamyr spied the man. She could not see his face, for a cloak covered all, including his hair, but she did see the weapon. It wasn't a dagger but a long pin of sorts. Fixing her staff under her arm, she joined Ulrich's side. "Shall I poke him back?"

"No!" Ulrich turned her away from the crowd and shoved her to a walk. "You've already brought enough suspicion upon our heads. Let's away from this place. It is creepy."

"We cannot leave." She dug her toes into the ground. "I must keep an eye on the body."

"They want to rip the body asunder and bury it deep for fear the plague will creep under their doors and kill them all."

"That is macabre. He will bring them no harm. Not unless the revenant escapes. Revenant, Ulrich. An indestructible skeleton with sharp teeth and a desire to rip out one's essence with its bony hands."

Ulrich eased a hand over his chest and winced.

"Yes," she answered his unspoken fear, "it *will* leave a mark."

"Fine, but let's keep to ourselves until the crowd settles. Show them we have no interest in stealing their plague-ridden body. We'll keep the dead faery in sight, I promise."

The body was unceremoniously tossed into a cart slimed with old greens and wheeled around behind the stables connected to the Pig's Snout tavern. Soaking it in oil was required, for the heavy substance would fill the shell of bone and coat its flesh, keeping the plague at bay until it could be burned. Old Basequin, who normally buried the unnamed dead, would have to be roused and a keg of valuable lampblack cracked open.

The man who had waited in the shadows of a dilapidated church for the last angry villager to leave now scampered across the grounds and fixed himself to the shadows that cooled the cart. A wisp of red hair slipped over his cheek and he tucked it back inside the hood of his cloak.

Very little time had passed since the fée had fallen, and yet, flies buzzed over the dead fée's face, settling on the red-filled eyes for a few beats before taking to flight and repeating the *danse macabre*. The flitter of a dragonfly's wings alerted, but the man paid the large insect no mind.

Glee in his eyes, the man raised a long shining pin over the fée's skull—and waited.

EIGHT

"You are not hungry?"

"I cannot abide strange meat." Gossamyr bit into a bruised yellow apple and proceeded to consume the mushy fruit in six more chomps. They'd slipped inside the tavern and sat near a window so dirty there was but an eyehole of sight to the crowd still looming around the body. Too anxious to sit and wait, Gossamyr had walked back outside. Now she stood next to the hay cart parked at the edge of the square, one eye on the ground where a lazy mongrel slept behind the shade of the cart's rear wheel.

"Strange?" Ulrich chomped on a thick chunk of deer. He balanced a bread trencher in his palm, not too thrilled to be eating on foot. "Let me guess, you eat toadstools and flowers?"

"You make it sound an unnatural diet."

"I suppose it is in the eyes of the chewer."

The cart the fée had been tossed into was now pushed around behind the stables but two buildings down from where they stood. Gossamyr remained alert, ready for the moment when the last of the angry villagers might leave the body alone.

"So you tell me this red lady steals the essences of disenchanted faeries?"

"Yes."

"How? And if the faery is disenchanted…why would this essence have any enchantment in it? It makes little sense."

Gossamyr stopped chewing. As elementary as the man's mind worked, he did raise a point. Surely someone had to *remove* the essence. For 'twas certain it was not with the revenant when it left the body, for then the revenant would have little reason to return to Faery in search of such. How then would the Red Lady get said essence? It was not Enchantment that lingered in the essence but the body's glamour. Mayhap the essence had been removed long before the fée expired?

"Do *you* not know?" she entreated Ulrich. "Surely the death of a fée is no different than your mortal deaths."

"I cannot see a soul. No one can. It is a feeling. I connect with the remnants of life as it leaves the body or after it has already vacated. But what I don't understand…is this revenant thing the same or is it separate from the essence?"

"Separate. Why must you label things same or not the same?"

"I…well, what would you do if twenty years of your life had disappeared in a snap?"

Gossamyr couldn't even guess. Though her concept of a mortal year was midsummer to midsummer—a very long time. She supposed she might react the same. *The same?* Most likely she would never again be the same should she lose a portion of her life due to her trip from Faery.

"Yes, the same," Ulrich whispered over her shoulder. The grease from cooked meat shining his lower lip appealed very little to her. "Though *you* are not the same."

"You have not before met me so you cannot determine my sameness." She stabbed her staff to ground and, with another bite of the apple, followed the billowing cloak of the hooded man she knew had poked Ulrich. What was he to?

"True. But as a representative of your common mortal woman you are *not* the same."

"What think you of me representing a fée woman?"

He poked at the gape in his teeth with his tongue; trying to dislodge food? "No wings."

"Not all faeries have wings, you said so yourself."

"You do sparkle."

"I thought this hideous headpiece covered—"

"There is a smear on your cheek. Let me get it."

She dodged his sticky reach and instead swiped her own dirty palm across her cheek.

"Fine and well," he offered. A chomp of the trencher filled his cheek with a bulge of hard bread. He silently offered the lump of finger-poked bread to her. Gossamyr shook her head. Ulrich tossed the morsel to the dog sleeping beneath the cart.

"I should slip around behind the building and keep an eye on the body."

"A death watch?"

"If I see anything come out from it I must kill it before it can flee to Faery."

"What if it is the essence you see leaving the body?"

"I know what it looks like. It is remarkable."

"Well, you'll not be able to feel the essence, that is my talent."

"Then you must come along." The more she thought on it, the more she realized she had no idea how the essence was removed. It could be long gone, or it may yet have been released.

"To the body. Quick!"

The color was beautiful, deep scarlet and speckled with luminous pockets of palest pink. It hovered above the dead fée's head, lingering, undulating, as if adjusting to the atmosphere outside the body. Or perhaps preening. The essence generally behaved as it had when enclosed within the body. Cocky, elegant and proud, as were most fée.

"Another prize for my mistress's collection. Come, pretty one."

The man stabbed the essence with his silver pin. A shriek of death accompanied the action. And following, the howl of the revenant as it began to clamber out from the fée's body.

Even as the skeletal fingers emerged from the core of flesh and muscle, the pin man scampered off. No need to remain and witness the hideous event. Or risk decapitation by an angry revenant.

"Do you see?"

Ulrich looked where Gossamyr pointed. What he saw stopped him cold. The blood slowed in his body and a shiver curled up his spine. Let the bold faery charge into danger, he had come to his limit battling supernatural beasties. Current supernatural beastie being half in, half out, of the dead faery's body. A skeleton, animated and jaws yowling, pushed out of the chest. Boned wings stretched wide in a *whoosh*. The tattered membranes between the wing bones shrilled a vile note through the air.

Gossamyr reached the cart, staff wielded for fight. The revenant had completely emerged and crouched upon the boneless shell of flesh and fabric, an incubus newly birthed from its host. It glanced to Gossamyr. Deep red glowed in the skull's eye sockets. Fangs glinted. Fingertips clattered, bone against bone, in a challenging gesture. Yowling to the heavens, the creature leaped into the air.

Gossamyr swung her staff, nicking the revenant's foot. Dust of bone and faery glimmer spumed from the connection point.

"She's going to be killed by a dead thing," Ulrich murmured. Clinging to Fancy, and to the saddlebag, he contemplated rushing to assist. A glance about ensured no witnesses. Another swing doubled the creature. Gossamyr stood tall. "On the other hand,

Faery Not is little afraid of anything. I would hate to interfere. Once already been chastised for that."

With each swing of Gossamyr's staff, the revenant's bones were broken and crushed. Faery dust veiled the air surrounding the battle. But the thing did not attack—more like it tried to defend so that it could…leave.

"For Faery," Ulrich gasped in realization. "Just let it go! Don't risk your life, my lady!"

"My life is to defend my own!" she shouted and took another swing. A bend of her waist, and she swung the end of her staff up behind her and knocked the thing's legs off just below the knee. "Did you see the man?" she shouted.

"What man?"

"The one who stood at the cart as we arrived? I saw him earlier."

Gossamyr's yelp put Ulrich to his feet. The revenant's fangs gashed open her wool sleeve. The half-bodied creature flapped its wings and soared too high for Gossamyr's swing to connect. And with another flap it was gone in a twinkle and a froth of glimmer.

"Take this vision from my eyes," Ulrich hissed. So much he did not wish to see! And all because of his dance.

"Blight me!" She swung furiously up through the air, fighting but the shade of the creature. "It is on to Faery."

"But only half of it," Ulrich reassured as he tugged her toward Fancy. "Come, we must be away from here. The entire village will be upon us after that ruckus." He shoved her up onto Fancy's back. "Let's be off!"

Mounting behind her, Ulrich heeled the mule, and was delighted the beast picked into a gallop.

Gossamyr tugged off the wimple and tossed it to the ground. "Wait!" She pulled the reins and turned Fancy toward the cart. "What of the essence? That man with the pin took it. I saw it leave the body before the revenant broke out."

"Why did not the bony creature go after the thief?"

"I don't know. Mayhap, the essence was injured by the pin."

Fancy plodded by the dead fée. It lay there, literally a bag of bones tossed onto the cart. Above and behind, Gossamyr sensed the flight of the fetch. With little fanfare the empty body suddenly fizzled to a fine dust. But a glimmer glinted at the bottom of the cart. Not the final *twinclian,* such was much more spectacular.

"Sorry, Father, I tried."

A swipe of her fingers through the dust in the cart drew a line. The hum of Faery jittered upon her fingertips. Bringing them to her lips, Gossamyr blew the dust away. It sifted through the air, slow and receding, until but one final particle twinkled to naught.

"If I were your father, I'd be here by your side, helping."

"Shinn must lead the Glamoursiège troops against this threat." It was for her to prove herself, to return the champion. "They risk falling to the Red Lady's allure. As I've said, I do not."

"This mission of yours seems a trifle ill stacked, and not in your favor."

"What mean you?"

"Your father *and* his troops fight these beasties, while you are one lone woman."

"But I have not been charged to battle an army of revenants. My task is much more singular."

"Would that you could simply attempt such a singular task. But I sense we've not seen the last of those skeleton things."

Indeed, the Red Lady's thirst for Enchantment would not wane, but increase.

"She attacks only the males?"

"Fear not, Ulrich. I can do this."

"Yes, but can I?"

An hour later, they arrived at a stable that offered change of horses for travelers going to and from the city for a fair price. Faery coin purchased the one remaining palfrey from the dark stall at the back of the stable.

"I must admit my surprise."

Gossamyr flinched as Ulrich touched a wet tip of his shirt to the cut on her arm. The revenant had not escaped to Faery without claiming some damage to its aggressor. He dabbed carefully, like a doting Mince. "What surprise?"

"You do not bleed ichor. Nor do you heal at a remarkable pace."

"Why should I? As I have said—"

"Yes, yes, half faery, half mortal. But not even a sparkle? I've no lint cloth to cover the wound, but it no longer bleeds. It is shallow and should heal aright."

"I've no worry for scars."

"Indeed, a remarkable woman." A snap of his bejeweled fingers called Fancy to his side. He tugged the saddlebag, checking that all was secure, then followed with a smoothing pat to the leather. "We should be off. You were able to procure a mount from the stables?"

"Yes."

A match to Ulrich's mule, what might have once been a fine riding horse, now looked to be ready for pasture. With little choice, Gossamyr had paid the stable owner for the palfrey, glamourizing the coin by suggesting he spend it quickly. Better luck that way, for Faery coin lasted only so long as it desired. A mortal who hoarded the precious coin might return one day to find nothing but a whisper of dust.

Leading the tired gelding toward where Ulrich waited on his mule, she saw him laugh and shook her head. "I saved him from becoming horse stew!"

"A most noble effort, my lady."

Mounting the horse bareback, she tucked the cumbersome wool gown up around her waist. Her leather-bound braies and bare feet received a lifted brow from Ulrich.

"Paris will offer the comfort of dress you seek." He handed up her staff.

The horse groaned as she heeled its flanks, but in its defense, it took off in a feisty gallop, leaving Ulrich and the mule in a cloud of dust.

Hours later the distance between windmills shortened and spirals of smoke from the grand city could just be seen coiling on the horizon. Eerie tendrils of the unknown shivered through Gossamyr's system. She felt traces of residual glamour coil away with every ponderous clod of the palfrey's hooves. 'Twas a heavy fall of something unnatural coated her flesh, invisible, but knowingly mortal. The air had become less light, but she could not determine if it was a foreboding to danger or a physical change.

A rub of the cut on her arm made her wince. *You don't bleed ichor.*

Once she had asked her mother to *twinclian* for her, and when Veridienne had lifted a refusing chin, Gossamyr learned that day how different they truly were from the common fée.

Do you not wonder?—she recalled Veridienne's mad query but days before her disappearance—*What we mortals are like?*

We mortals? Of course, her mother often forgot her daughter bore half-fée blood in her veins, so focused had she been on herself. Mortals must imagine loving a Faery lord as a grand vision. Yet, Gossamyr had never once dreamed to love a mortal man. Only, she did spend much time perusing the bestiary.

Had she savored the thought of meeting a mortal man? Mortal touched as she had become, she favored the sensation of Ulrich's flesh to hers. It did not spread a chill through her. Would a kiss be as favorable?

A shake of her head sorted her thoughts. What is this? Thinking to kiss the man? Truly, these delusions were not her own. Gossamyr would not allow the mortal passion to trounce this mission. Nor must she succumb to wistful dreams of stolen kisses.

Now she could not press her mount to more than a walk. Nudging her toes into the palfrey's side served little more than to make the beast whicker at her. A fat, pollen-loaded humble bee buzzing from one clover patch to the next marked a swifter pace than she did.

With thoughts to abandon the beast to a peaceful death in the meadow, she suddenly jerked up her head. Pricking her ears, Gossamyr homed in onto the minute thunder of hooves. Nowhere in sight, but the pace of their approach verily pounded in her veins.

"Ulrich" she whispered. Staff spinning, she tucked it under her arm, at the ready.

The man pulled rein beside her. "What?"

"Listen."

He shrugged. "A stream babbles nearby. We parallel the Seine by less than half a league—"

"No. Two of them. At a good pace. Heading this way."

"Travelers?" He shrugged again, but Gossamyr saw his move to slide a hand across his ever-coveted saddlebag. "Where? Behind or ahead?"

"Ahead. There!"

Two black chargers gained the horizon, their hooves beating the road to a fury in their wake. Could merely be an equipage with an urgent message. But Gossamyr suspected otherwise. They yet roamed Netherdred territory. And the oncomers charged lick-for-leather.

"Armagnacs!" Ulrich yelled.

The same they had avoided by traveling around Aparjon. "What beast be they?"

"Frenchmen! But fear them, my lady, for they only have mind to annihilate."

Leaping from the horse and giving it a slap to flee toward the meadow, Gossamyr slid her staff along her arm and assumed a defensive pose in the center of the road. Drawing up straight, she nodded. "Have at me!"

"Gossamyr, I don't think you should—"

"Follow the nag," she hissed at Ulrich.

"I don't think so!"

If he had intention to start that again. "There are but two of them. I can manage!"

"Come, my lady, toss the poor man a bone. At least let me *appear* I can defend myself."

"You cannot fight clutching that saddlebag as if a favorite child."

Gossamyr heard the oncoming shout, "He's got it!"

She lifted a brow. Who? The soul shepherd? Got what?

She hadn't time to consider what the Armagnacs wanted from Ulrich. Aligning the staff along her forearm, she flung her arm around, landing one of the riders across the chest and successfully unseating him.

Spinning to the left, she planted the point of her staff in the ground and swung up her legs toward the rider tormenting Ulrich with a wickedly curved falchion. She succeeded in kicking the horse's flank, bringing the angry beast around. Landing her feet, she swung up the staff and clocked the rider between the eyes. The horse, angered at her assault, tried to stomp her. Seeing the obsidian-glossed hooves rise over her head, Gossamyr dropped to a roll and spun under the horse's belly. A shimmer of glamour snuck beneath the horse, spiraling it on its hind legs to land away from Gossamyr.

Steel cut the tension. Equine snorts misted the air. Gossamyr stood, spat out a mouthful of road dust, and faced both men clad in black leathers and shining mail, their falchions swinging in tandem as they approached. Gold fleur-de-lis decorated their gray tabards. The symbol of Paris; Gossamyr recalled it from the bestiary. Indeed, Frenchmen. So why should they attack?

Thrusting up her staff before her, she blocked both weapons. The applewood had been forged of an ancient tree and of dragon fire. Hard as steel, it would not be thwarted. Nor would she.

"Achoo!" Wavering off balance, Gossamyr sensed the sweep of sharp steel and followed her equilibrium to the ground. She landed palms first. A curved blade cut into the dirt but a breath from her littlest finger. As quickly, it was cleaved from the earth in a spatter of fine dirt that again tickled her nose.

The shrill of another blade alerted Gossamyr. She rolled, twisting her staff to catch the bravo between the legs. His slicing attack abruptly veered from her and he collapsed in a groaning tumble.

"What do you want?" she said, jumping up and spinning to strike the other across the knees, and bringing him down with a yelp.

"We want what he gots!"

"The prize," the other grunted. "Ouff!" Gossamyr connected to his throat. Bloody spittle sprayed the air.

"What does he gots—er, have?" she asked.

The two exchanged vacant looks. "Don't know. But it has power!"

"Have at me!" Ulrich shouted. Bravado splashed the air with an abbreviated punch of his fist. Yet he had moved safely to his mule's side.

Ulrich? A prize?

Gossamyr felt steel slice her shoulder. She brushed a hand over the wool undergarment, touching blood. A shiver drew up a mist of faery dust. Not completely Disenchanted then. The flitter of the fetch's wings hovered high above.

Her eyes watered. A sneeze threatened. But through the blur of tears she assessed the situation. Both men felled and groaning, yet on their knees and recovering.

A *thwap* of her staff to the men's skulls—swing, connect, spin and connect—knocked them out.

The midnight chargers huffed out foamy breaths behind her. One falchion had landed the ground, point first. Glinting steel quivered.

Elation from the fight made her jittery and loose. A swing of her staff and a decisive stub of it into the ground placed a mark of triumph before the Armagnacs. Who be willing to stand with a fix to challenge her? Standing over her carnage, Gossamyr swiped a hand across her brow. A nod and a satisfied smile. "Most splendid."

Hand-to-hand combat delivered double the thrill of a well-met tournament. This danger was everything she had hoped it to be. "Blight, I'm good."

Over her shoulder she sensed the fetch's *twinclian*.

Do not worry, Shinn, she thought. *I fare well away from your side.*

She cocked a look over her shoulder. Ulrich bristled with pride. "I took out one before he could jump—"

"Very well. So you did."

Retrieving the falchions—careful to grip only the leather-wrapped hilt—Gossamyr handed them to Ulrich. He took them, awkwardly and unsure what to do with the vicious blades that were the size of his thigh.

"Now." She strode past Ulrich to Fancy and slapped a hand onto the saddlebag. "To what they were after."

"No!" Blades clattered as Ulrich dropped them. One of the falchion tips landed his shoe. He fell to his haunches, clutching his foot. "That is my private cache!"

Gossamyr ignored his protest. She did see no blood, so the blade must have missed toes. Instead, she upended the saddlebag upon the thick summer-sweet grass and out spilled a twist of black linen, which splayed open to reveal its long and glittering treasure.

"Bloody elves." She fell to her knees, not daring to touch the item. "What have you done?"

NINE

Gossamyr gripped Ulrich by the hair and forced him, scrambling on his knees, over to the spilled contents of the saddlebag.

"What evil have you done?"

"My lady, have mercy, I am not evil!"

"Why then, do you carry an alicorn in your saddlebag? What madness possesses you?"

"Release me, foul faery!" Pushing from her grasp, the man made to cover the contraband horn with the thin black cloth.

Shoving him aside, she plunged to the grass on her knees before the sacred article. The alicorn sparkled with Enchantment. Carved with interlinking symbols of purity, innocence and wisdom, the twisted bone verily hummed a canorous song that Gossamyr felt in her bones. She recognized the curved, intertwined symbols from her school studies. 'Twas an unpardonable crime to remove such from a unicorn—far more wicked than murder; more devastating than to dabble in magic. All of Faery wept when such occurred, for the severing of any source of Enchantment crippled Faery profoundly.

"It is mine." Ulrich smoothed the cloth over the sacred object and clutched it to his chest. "I purchased it from a hawker a week ago."

"A hawker?" Gossamyr huffed. Unbelievable!

"An old man with a cart hobbled roadside betwixt Sées and Tourouvre."

So much she wanted to say, to tirade, to condemn and accuse— and yet what could she say? Did the man know the significance of what he possessed?

"I do not believe you," she said firmly. "Some roadside hawker sold you this? Unknowning?"

"Indeed! Displayed amidst his wares of various distinction; wood sabots, candles, obsidian blades, wicker baskets; it sat amongst a basket of shells and stones. Pretties, he called them."

"He knew naught what he was selling. He could not!"

"Oh, he knew. The man did look to have survived a journey through Hades. He wanted to be rid of it something desperate. And I now know why."

"Why?"

"This pointy thing is evil!"

"It is a sacred object, how dare you—"

"Sacred? This bedeviled horn—" he shook the wrapped horn before her, causing Gossamyr to veer back "—attracts evil like flies to the plague, my lady. You mark my words. Everywhere I step, evil senses this thing and evil wants it." He gestured to the men sprawled on the ground behind them. "Do you not find it at all unusual that we've been so oft attacked?"

"I did. But we stand adjacent to the Netherdred; it is to be expected with the rift—"

"We stand on French soil, my lady. Paris looms to the north and the soil beneath our hands is not sprinkled with faery dust. France! Nothing but!"

"If you have Danced then you should not be so quick to discount those who travel here from Faery."

"Oh, I do not discount them, I merely wish they were not so determined and so well armed."

Gossamyr paid him no mind, for something she had said bothered her. The rift? It made trips to and from Faery much easier. The rift let out things that did not belong—such as bogies? And let in the revenants and dancing mortals with an ease that should not be.

We know naught what caused the rift, only a great source of Enchantment was decimated.

That source be a unicorn.

An unbidden moan preceded Gossamyr's sorry shake of head. She lifted her head and eyed the wrapped horn Ulrich clutched so covetously. Surely the Enchantment had bespelled him. But, could it truly be, the very cause for the rift, held in a mere mortal's hands?

"What are your plans for the alicorn?"

Tilting the horn this way then that before his eyes, Ulrich said, "Not your concern."

"Not my— Be this the reason for your quest?"

"It may be. Yes. Don't look at me like that. I plan to return it to the beast!"

"The unicorn? Why?"

"Not your concern."

"You've plans to use it? How? And don't you dare say— This *is* my concern!"

Gossamyr swung up her staff, preparing to catch him under the chin, but Ulrich slapped his palm across the end of the stick. His boldness raised her ire. How dare this pitiful mortal handle the alicorn!

"Very well." He held the alicorn like a sword. It peeked from the black cloth, threatening with its beauty. "It is legend the one who returns the alicorn to its rightful owner is in return granted one wish. I need that wish, and I will have it."

"To bring life to your dead damsel?"

"You are most perceptive."

"It is a cruel magic you seek to employ. I will not have it!"

"It is not your place to have it or not to have it. The alicorn is mine, paid for with real coin—coin that does not disperse to dust."

"It belongs to no man! Least of all no mortal man."

"I told you I intend to return it."

"For your own gain!"

Ulrich tipped the air with the horn. "Yes, my gain. But tell me how else this thing will ever find its way back to the unicorn. If I simply succumbed to evil and let it ride off with the prize it would never again see the unicorn. Someone has to bring it to the beast. That someone will be me."

"Oh? And where do you plan to find a unicorn? And a hornless one at that!"

"I am…following my heart."

Gossamyr snorted. The man actually bristled. He had no right to take offense!

"It is a real feeling I have had ever since taking claim to the alicorn. I am being led. And so I follow."

"To Paris?"

"Indeed. So, if you wish to keep an eye on the thing then remain by my side. But I promise a fight should you even consider taking it from me."

"I would not touch the alicorn if the only other option were facing a throng of revenants." Only the pure of heart could press flesh to the alicorn and not suffer burns or great calamity. Everyone knew that!

"Well then, your argument fades. Shall we be off?"

Such dread filled her gut, completely opposite, Gossamyr felt, of how she should feel to be in the presence of the sacred horn. The song of the alicorn was muted, wrapped within the black cloth. Wicked portents caressed her bones. Evil wants it?

"Keep it tucked away."

"Trust me, I will. But it will matter little; evil will find us."

"Evil…" Gossamyr was suddenly struck by a realization. But of course—it must be! "You say you follow your heart?"

"Yes, a calling; as if I am being led."

"Why Paris? The mortal city is as far from Faery as one can possibly travel. Certainly no place for a unicorn."

"As I said, I am merely following my instincts. I sense that is where my troubles will find relief. So Paris it is."

Instincts? *I am being led.* Could the Red Lady be luring Ulrich to Paris? It made sense. Because a unicorn in the great city of Disenchantment defied all logic.

Gossamyr paced, her eye keen upon the wrapped horn in Ulrich's grip. Suddenly the lightness of this mortal air had been stirred to a wicked simmer of intrigue and confusion. From the moment she had set foot on the Otherside Ulrich had been impossible to shrug off. Had her original instincts been true? Did he accompany her for a purpose?

Had some part of Faery known what he carried in the tattered saddlebag? And so the enchanted wood would not have allowed her to march off alone, but to accompany the one thing that could restore Enchantment complete to Faery.

"The alicorn is the key," she said.

Swiping a hand across his dirt-smeared face, Ulrich stared at Gossamyr. He handled the horn with such disregard. Impossible that he knew its true power. Mayhap that was a boon, for in the hands of the unknowing the alicorn could be little more than a nuisance—which stirs up evil.

Wherever I go, evil follows. And evil wants it.

It seduced all far and wide. So why had *she* not sensed it? So close for two days and not even a hint of the Enchantment within a stride? To think on it overmuch troubled. Time—her mortal enemy—would not allow more than reaction.

Gossamyr retrieved her staff, and with a glance to the prone men, then scanned for the mounts. Both chargers and her palfrey galloped toward the horizon. "Isn't that some luck?" She patted Fancy's saddlebags. Briefly she sought for something, a vibration, some call from the contents. Nothing. "We are in this together now. She knows."

"We are? Wh-who knows?"

"The Red Lady. I believe she entices thee toward Paris. An alicorn in the hands of that woman would prove chaos."

"You mean I'm being led to Paris by—by evil?"

"You said so yourself."

"But I thought…well, I assumed… By the same red woman who has been sucking the innards from your rogue faery men? Let's turn around. I'd prefer to keep my insides intact, if you don't mind."

"You told me you followed an instinct. That you can think only to travel to Paris."

"Indeed." Fingers to chin in thought, his eyes darted furiously across the ground. Fear brightened the blue to overwhelm the white. Gossamyr could verily scent his distraction, taste the fear brewing out from his every breath. "So we were meant to travel together?"

"It may have been Enchanted, the forest."

"That must be it!" Spinning into a grand gesture, arms punching the air and head tilted back, Ulrich ended with a stomp and a splay of arms before her. "A man mustn't question destiny. We were meant to come together."

"I knew nothing of the contraband alicorn you carry when we first met. Which begs to wonder now why you were so eager to remain with me."

"Truth?" Ulrich shrugged. "When I thought you were a faery I couldn't summon a better traveling companion. If there is a unicorn in seek of its horn surely an enchanted being will attract it more quickly than a mere mortal."

"I cannot believe you simply intended to ride about Paris until your path crosses with the unicorn."

"Dangling my half faery as bait."

She sneered at him. To be called bait made her feel low as a slithering insect. He said it in jest, surely. On the other hand, he held no fealty to her or Faery. He simply sought his own means, with no regard for her fate. Not an ally.

"Is there a simpler way to call the beast to my side? I forgot my virginal maiden at home." He swallowed. All angles on his face fell and tightened with a quickening grimace. "Rhiana, she died a cruel death."

A name? Yet another truth from the man's past. But such information softened Gossamyr's stern need to push away the mortal who held Enchantment hostage. "I am sorry for your loss."

He splayed a sweeping hand through the air in a lost gesture, ending it with a powerful punch. "Every road I take I meet a bad thing that wants to crush my skull and make off with the alicorn. And you've been little help thus far."

"Me? I've— I have fended off two attacks, you thankless bit of…!" No, she did not wish to name him ill. Heavy, his heart. It was a familiar sensation. Gossamyr recalled the time Shinn had mourned Veridienne's absence. Yet, her father remained morose and stern. Had Ulrich lost a wife?

"I could have protected myself." He brandished the arrowless crossbow. Gossamyr shoved it from her peripheral view.

She blew out a disgusted breath and pounded the ground with her staff. "I'd walk away from you right now if I did not think the wiser."

"And what holds you here? Be gone with you!"

"What keeps me at your side is the alicorn, and the knowledge it may well fall into the hands of a vicious succubus. And wish you to believe a mere fée would have attracted the unicorn to the alicorn, imagine then what the Red Lady might do. Go ahead. Imagine it. Right now. I'll wait." She slammed her arms across her chest.

The enormity of the situation must be dealt with. For if they carried a lure for evil, their journey to Paris could only grow more perilous.

"I have no idea, Faery Not," Ulrich snapped. "I have little knowledge of this red lady. Is she queen supreme of the Faery realm? Does she possess powers untold?"

"She hails from the Netherdred and was banished for crimes to which I am not privy. The essences she steals feed her glamour, keeping the Disenchantment at bay."

"There is that word again: Netherdred," Ulrich said. "Just what horrors should I conjure to match that?"

"The Netherdred are a tribe of fée who inhabit the borders of Faery. Said borders surrounding any major mortal city, such as Paris; Enchantment cannot exist in such densely populated mortal lands. They are the outcast, the rogues and thieves of Faery."

"I see." Approaching with finger to chin, he disregarded his plea for propriety and stepped right up to Gossamyr. Blue eyes darted about her face. A smile started, then fled, then burst into fullness. "And what be you?"

"Tribe Glamoursiège." Tugging up her tucked skirt, she tilted the crest attached at her hip to display the coat of arms.

"Ah." He perused the applewood sigil. His fingers moved over the raised carvings, once brushing her hip so briefly, the shimmer of mortal touched but singed. "Wings and a sword."

"Wrapped by holly. We are peaceable now."

Ulrich nodded and straightened. He touched her more frequently, and with an ease that should be reserved for mates.

"There are others: the Wisogoths, Merovech, Mer-de-Soleil."

"Small cities within Faery?"

"Of a sort."

With a twist of his feet he began to pace a circle, arms clasped across his chest and all focus on her. Ever moving, the man possessed an energy that appealed. It had been a time since Gossamyr had commanded a man's attention. And for as many tears she had cried, and had then sworn to never open her heart again, it was difficult not to react to the flutter of interest that tickled her belly.

"So the red lady rules the Netherdreds?" Ulrich asked.

"No. Since Banishment she is no longer a part of Faery, yet—according to Shinn—she ever attempts to return. The essences, as I've explained."

"Indeed. And essences are like our mortal souls. Wait right there—faeries don't have souls, everyone knows that."

"They do, too."

"Do not." A forceful fist pounded the air above his head. "Faeries are heartless and cruel and lack emotion and they are nothing but tricksters!"

"They do not lack emotion!"

A grin slid onto Ulrich's lips. "Well, I'll give you that."

"What?"

"You finally rose to the bait, Faery Not. So maybe you do have a little mortal in there somewhere. You anger easily enough."

And what was that about? She was not quick to anger. Just moments ago she had been near to mooning over the man's fierce blue gaze. Blight, but the introduction of the alicorn had twisted her from sorts. "The fée do have souls—rather, they are essences—and it is their essences the Red Lady steals."

"Before or after their death? Have you figured that?"

"It can only be after their death. We saw the red essence in the last village."

"Yes, and then that…thing."

"Following the Red Lady's kiss the fée become deathless revenants, unable to incite the final *twinclian* until they claim an essence."

"Do you think that man with the pins stole the essence?"

"You saw, as did I, the *thing* he speared onto his pin. It was the essence."

"Mayhap he brings the pinned essence to this red lady. What does she do with them?"

"I know naught, but I will learn, right before I take her out. Now—" she leaped astride Fancy "—mount behind me and let's be off. There is little time for chatter."

"As my lady commands of me, so shall I follow."

With little room for the two of them, Ulrich sat close, propping his palms upon her hips, but not holding firmly. Gossamyr reined Fancy onward. She felt a solid warmth against her shoulders and guessed Ulrich had laid down his forehead. A heavy sigh preceded his weary question, "Can she take a mortal man's soul?"

"I know little more than you do, Ulrich."

"Fair enough."

He lifted his head. Their contact, so brief, quieted the deep hum of worry.

"So no more lies," he murmured.

"All truths are out."

"They are? So say you?"

"Yes, all truth."

"Well then! Obviously we both need each other."

"I don't *need* you."

"Oh, yes you do. You just don't know it yet. You watch, you will need me, Faery—"

"Gossamyr, please," she entreated.

He could be right. She may need him. She may not. Right now the alicorn needed her. Since she was headed the Red Lady's direction anyway…

"So we continue on together?"

"I'd say I was delighted," Ulrich said, "but for some reason I can only feel foreboding. Onward then. Mayhem awaits."

TEN

Paris looked a pincushion for the fleched stone church spires piercing the gray afternoon. Dozens of windmills dotted the periphery outside the stone ramparts, the creak of sundried wood competing with the chirp of hidden crickets. Not a frog song to be heard; Gossamyr missed the evening concerts. What a perfect ending to a day to find oneself dangling upside down, knees hooked over a root, and whistling to the tune of a frog symphony.

A strange croaky rumble, unfamiliar to Gossamyr, wavered somewhere off by the stream. That be not a frog.

A fine mist fell upon her head, raindrops bejeweling the interlocked ropes of her plaited tresses. Fancy's mane, dressed in round droplets, rendered the beast Enchanted. A storm brewed in the heady miasma crowding her nostrils. Gossamyr could not judge when it would fall. She had not learned to portend the weather. But here in the Otherside the heavy future of rain tingled her to an anticipatory expectation. So familiar this air. Yet she had not skipped since yestereve. Far too occupied by threats. And happy to do so.

The click of a wood beetle brought her to alert.

Standing upon a hill, Gossamyr observed the distant crowd hovering about the gates to the city. Not a quiet bunch. Shouts of declaration and good-natured tussle spiked the sky. Eyes, some alert, most tired, darted here and there. Mules broke rein and kicked up the dirt. Children wailed from their aching bellies, and dogs barked at everything that moved.

"We must be cautious," Ulrich said. He waited at Fancy's side for Gossamyr to venture onward. "The Armagnacs stalk travelers to the city."

That curious word again. "You said they were Frenchmen? Be they enemy or ally?"

"I'd like to call them enemy but they appear to side with our dethroned king. Yet they kill their own to gain control over the Burgundians."

"And what is a Burgundian?"

"Northerners; vulgar, stupid beasts—Frenchmen, as well. And then there are the English—" he reached around behind his thigh and waggled a finger in display "—drunks with tails, they are. Hell, this war is a farce. Methinks it is every man for himself. A woman must be most cautious."

"I will be."

"Your pretty stick will serve little against a gang of blood-thirsty Frenchmen. Best to now consider every man our enemy. These are impossible times." He scanned the horizon. "But you mustn't judge by what you have seen. There is goodness. Somewhere, surely."

"Yes, in the eyes of a child," she answered rotely. For she remembered yet the dirty grin of the village child who had smiled upon her earlier.

"Come." Ulrich slapped Fancy's flank to stir the mule to a walk. "We will stop at the water mill at the base of the hill before moving to the gates. See there, a convoy of carts approaches. Likely they carry provisions such as flour and weapons—open game to marauders. Be on your guard."

"I will."

The decimated water mill had seen better days. Planks had been torn from the wall frame, rendering it a skeleton with a massive grindstone for a heart. The water wheel looked to be lodged in hardened mud. Faint scent of milled flour hung in the air, and the surrounding trampled grass was matted with gray powder. View of the Porte St. Jacques was sheltered by a line of stacked hay piled so high Gossamyr guessed a spry goat must have laid the last bits to the top.

"Refreshment?" Ulrich winked at Gossamyr and tramped around behind the mill.

A crystal stream but four strides in width beckoned both travelers and their mule. Marching ahead, Ulrich noted the fetch, which fluttered overhead. It dodged and swooped, teasing the last rays of sun with iridescent wings. "That dragonfly is huge!"

"It is my father's fetch."

He followed the fetch's flight, hand to his eyes to block the sun. "A means to keep an eye on you?"

"Indeed. You mustn't heed it. It comes and goes as needed."

"So long as it has no intention of attacking."

"Worry not. The fetch is merely an instrument."

Squatting near the massive wood wheel that once moved with the water to grind flour, Ulrich cupped water to drink and splashed his face and hair, though his eyes took in the surroundings, ever vigilant. Content, he swiped the moisture from his chin and smiled over at Gossamyr. The road dust and grime had been washed from his face. 'Twas the first time she had seen him looking so clean.

Keeping her own vigilant scan of their surroundings, Gossamyr pricked her ears, but could not hear any brigands who waited before the gate to Paris. Assuming such an attack would first stir a warning noise, Gossamyr relaxed.

Kneeling to stir her fingers in the cool water, she cupped a few palmfuls to drink. Sweet, finer than honey wine.

"So what—" A croak like she had heard previous would not go unnoticed. Gossamyr turned her head to seek the noise. "What, by an elf's twelve toes, is that horrible noise?"

"Frogs." Ulrich leaned back and spewed out a spray of water, misting their heads.

"Frogs?" Gossamyr searched the sky and the darkening shadows of a nearby apple tree for a fat amphibian. "Where?"

"Why do you look up there?"

"I cannot see a frog." She made a shape with her hands to demonstrate the girth of the creature. "They are usually big enough to spy."

With a laughing grin, Ulrich said, "I know naught what manner of frog accustoms your dreams, fair lady—ah, so frogs are unique in Faery?"

"Not really. They are usual. About this big." She caressed the air in a circle about the size of her head. "They usually fly during the night. But their song is more melodious than that bleating racket."

"Frogs do not fly. Trust me."

"They do."

"Do." Ulrich bat an admonishing finger at her. "Not."

"Where are you off to?"

Cape abandoned in a lump, Ulrich wandered to and fro along the stream, his head down and searching. Skinny legs blocked by brilliant green stripes bent and twisted. A comical sight, his dance at stream's edge. After a few moments he returned and squatted before Gossamyr.

"That—" he placed a small slimy creature in her cupped palms "—be a frog."

Gossamyr tilted the brown, warty creature this way and that. Slime-glossed eyes filmed over. Its viscous body heaved in breaths. And the smell, like dirt, was the furthest from the sweet scent Faery frogs emitted.

She held the creature out on her splayed palm. "Looks like a toad to me."

A heavy sigh preceded Ulrich's inspection of the amphibian. His eyes crossing as he peered closely, he smirked and gave a defeated nod. "So it is."

Smiling not too large, Gossamyr set the toad on the grass at water's edge.

"So Faery frogs be so big as a man's head?"

"And winged. They make excellent leathers."

"Don't tell me. Your braies?"

She slid a palm along the still-intact leather braies. "They are thin and soft but strong."

"And violet. I suppose they are not dyed, but the actual color of the beast?"

"Do you find that strange?"

"As a mortal, yes, I find that most unusual."

"Then I suppose wee frogs may seem even more strange. They are a deep violet with yellow toes."

"Wee frogs?"

"Yes. Nasty bit of wings. They've a tendency to fly up a fée's nose should they be unfortunate enough to stumble into a pod flying head level."

"Up one's— I don't even want to know. I can only be thankful the time I spent in Faery was brief. And yet...here in my own world..." He clammed up quickly. Too quickly.

Thinking of his lost years, Gossamyr guessed. Time had stolen an entire chunk of his life—because of her own. She should be thankful he had not attempted malice against her in retaliation. He had every right. Twenty years stolen was hardly fitting punishment for but an afternoon of dance.

Bowing her head and wincing at the horrible creaking frog song, Gossamyr studied the shore stones, smoothened and slick. Her thoughts skipped over to the mule's saddlebag. Just her luck she had taken as her partner on this journey the one man who roamed the earth with a contraband alicorn in hand. She could hardly cut him loose to wander about on his own, most likely, to fall victim to evil.

But she could not simply take the alicorn from him. He was the rightful owner. Should she touch the sacred object, well—she wasn't sure what would happen.

It was a wonder the man had gotten this far with it. Only the pure of heart could actually handle the alicorn without protection. Remarkable, merely wrapping it in cloth shielded it from harm. And to even approach the unicorn to return it? Should not the man be an innocent? Pure and strong of heart. A virginal maiden or a valorous knight—those were but the choices.

What of a champion?

Gossamyr lifted a brow. She had yet to do anything worthy. Fighting off beasties had merely proven distraction. But soon. Somewhere in Paris the Red Lady lurked.

Now, to keep Ulrich and his prize safe from the succubus.

"It would fetch a mighty fortune."

Gossamyr looked to Ulrich, who now stood over her, shadowing her troubled silence.

He nodded toward the mule and the tattered leather saddlebag. "You're thinking about it, I know."

"Is mind reading another of your skills?"

"Not at all."

"Obviously, because you are wrong. I should never barter a sacred object."

He squatted beside her. Suddenly aware of the man's size, Gossamyr took him in on the sly. Wider and more muscled than she, he smelled sweet from the stream and a fresh scrubbing. Earthy, as she had before noticed. And…hmm, what else made her close her eyes and sniff the air? Almost as if to breathe him in. To put him into her senses like a new flower she wanted to memorize and cat-alog under the heading "favorable."

'Twas not a sensual attraction—but certainly she wanted to know this man. Mortal, so grounded. A man like one of those Ar-magnacs who would kill their own? Far from it. Jean César Ulrich Villon III somehow gentled her uncertainties. How, she could not determine. He be not a man of fine words or chivalrous actions. He cursed her and complained endlessly. Mayhap it was simply be-cause he accepted her and treated her as an equal.

Mayhap they two were more alike in ways she had yet to learn.

Ulrich toyed with the thick grass tops. A cast of his gaze over the horizon snagged sun glints in his eyes. "What is it like to leave a place that must be truly magical and come to this...mortal hell?"

Gossamyr shook out of her reverie. "Faery is not magical."

"It is to a person who can only imagine it."

"Magic does not exist in Faery. Magic is evil."

"You say so?"

His curiosity fixed sparkling blue eyes to her. What they searched for on her face Gossamyr could not know. But he looked, and took great leisure in doing so.

"For every act of magic practiced on the Otherside," she said, "a bit of Enchantment is sluiced away through the rift. It is outlawed."

"Really? Yet, it is quite common in my world."

"Oh, of that we are aware. Magic be a mortal device, yet it cannot exist without Enchantment. Every act of magic, be it good or for evil, is felt by Faery. Makes me wonder if the fine lady in the caravan practiced. To wield such control over one of my kind?"

"But if the caged faery was disenchanted?"

"Yes, but one touch from a mortal has made her weaker."

"Merely by a mortal's touch?" Ulrich rubbed his palms together and peered over his paired hands at her. "I have touched you."

"Yes."

"Am I...making you weak?"

"No. In fact, I feel no chill when you touch me. That is what happens when a fée is mortal touched."

"I see. What do you feel?"

"Splendid," Gossamyr said. She clapped her mouth shut. The man cocked a brow at her. "I didn't mean to say that."

"Oh ho?"

"No, I...blight." She *had* meant to say such. This conversation tread an intimacy that made her uncertain. "This Otherside is..." She splayed out a hand. "Different from my expectations. Not so vibrant. And dirty and slow. The sky here is sluiced with dull and the grass and trees are but a shade of the vibrance of Faery."

"But it makes you dance."

"Yes. I feel light. There are children in abundance here."

"Not so in Faery?"

"Newlings are rare. Faeries generally mate for life; a pairing that sees but a single child."

"Sounds like we mortals—though we do tend to have hordes of children. So you marry and have children and settle long and happy lives?"

"Marriage is not common. It is reserved for royals and the upper caste. Commoners merely...I don't know...join and have children. I believe it is called honeymooning. But a faery's fickle heart affords much time to discover a life mate."

Desideriel was rumored to romance a new woman every new moon. A rogue who might never be tamed following their vows? She hoped he would turn true to her, but did not expect something so untouchable as love.

"Oftentimes, they never wed, and instead choose the singular life with assorted partners. A child is never born of such a situation."

"Sounds freeing. To sort through a variety of choices before finally settling?"

He shrugged at her wondering lift of brow. A soft, deep chuckle, innately male, was followed by his dazzling smile. "I am a man, Gossamyr. We men...fickle though our hearts may be, do enjoy our women. And if given the freedom to pick and choose?"

Such freedom was far from Gossamyr's reach. For Glamour-siège, as Shinn would remind.

"I should like to marry for love," she said. Trailing her fingers over the surface of the stream, she fell into the fantasy of a life she would choose for herself. "My mother loved a man who sought her out every morning merely to watch her wake. The blush of waking, Shinn had once told me, is the most beautiful color on a woman's face."

"It is true. So smooth and perfect, a woman's lips, like tiny little sweets upon a king's table." Ulrich's sigh evoked a longing in Gossamyr. How she would like a man to look upon her with such reverence. "Er, I suppose you will wed a faery man? Can you ever return?" Ulrich asked.

"Of course."

When Shinn saw to retrieving her, for she had not an idea in all the Spiral how else to return. Without *twinclian* she was a literal prisoner on the Otherside.

"And...you will return?"

"Anon. When my mission is complete."

"Of course, you must. So! Are all faery warriors women, then?"

Gossamyr smirked and stroked the base of her throat. "I explained before, male and female fée are equal. I took this mission because I was the only one qualified for it. My father was reluctant to send his daughter to the very land that stole away his wife——"

"Your mother was stolen from you? Be that something like the Dance?"

"Not at all, it was the mortal passion." She shifted on her feet, moving closer to Ulrich. The need to scent him remained fore.

"And do you have this mortal passion?"

"I pray not."

Those words came out more quickly than the truth registered

in her brain. Of course the passion festered within her. Else she would not at this moment stand ready to enter an embattled city. And she would not be sitting so close to a mortal man merely because he intrigued. Nor, she suspected, would the air entice with every light step she took.

The mortal world lay beneath her feet. No one stopped her from seeking. Perhaps—following their defeat—she would listen to the mortal opera and watch a comedy in the theater. Ride upon the great barges floating the river and listen to the choirs sing under a lusciously arched nave in a grand cathedral. The bestiary had illustrated the beautiful colored windows and alluded to the tempestuous religions that reigned in the center of many a war between the mortals.

And then there was the chance she may stumble across *him*.

But to stay? She did not wish to go rogue! And there was always Time of which to be wary.

Ulrich's open expression beseeched her to continue.

"I do not have the leisure to think on anything but defeating the Red Lady. She will not see me coming until it is too late."

"You are brave." He reached and touched her forehead, smoothing aside a strand of hair that had escaped the tight plaits. Gossamyr flinched at the touch, but Ulrich made a soothing sound deep in his throat. Ah, that throaty rumble, initially frightening to her, but now it fit in her breast—*right*—as she fit here in this air.

"I mean you no ill." He lingered as his fingers traveled down to her shoulder.

"It is said," she offered, "that a fée who is touched by a mortal receives a chill that cleaves to his bones ever after."

"That be mortal touched."

"Yes."

"Do you wish me to stop touching you?"

She clasped his wrist, but let it go immediately. "Your touch… gentles."

"Your hair is soft and shiny. So elegant these twists of summer sunshine," he marveled.

"Witch plaits. They keep away—"

"Witches?" He gave a soft chuckle. "So faeries are as superstitious as we mortals?"

She twisted her head, tugging at the tips of her plaits, and eyed Ulrich's hand, which, in the strangest way, claimed. She regarded the touch as personal for it lighted a flame in her breast and stirred—just a little—her reasoning. What did the man want from her? She would never again wager her heart. Not for the ache that still pulsed within. *You could find him. Mayhap he has thought of you?*

"Your closeness causes wonder, Ulrich."

"Ah. Indeed. Not minding my own caution." He snapped back his hand, but did not change the distance between them, which was fine for Faery but far too close for his mortal reasoning. "Mortal touched aside, have you never been touched by a faery man?"

She twisted her neck, tilting her chin away from him. "Why ask you that?"

"Just a little jumpy. You don't like my being so close." A tilt of his head hushed his breath across the bridge of her nose. "How is it when you deem it fine, it is, but when I decide to, it is not."

"It is...uncomfortable."

Now he caressed her chin. Commanding fingers forced her to look back at him, yet the gentlest smile filled his eyes. "Perhaps there are a few wonders for you to discover in this *Otherside,* eh?"

"Mayhap you guess at something I know well?" She pushed from his touch and began to march alongside the stream. But frustration kept her from treading too far, so she turned back. She wanted to look him in the eye. To challenge his teasing. Gossamyr de Wintershinn stepped from no challenge!

"Ah, so the woman *has* had a lover."

"You imply very much!"

Putting up both palms to placate, he then stood and brushed off his cloak. "Just making small talk."

A slash of her staff connected just below his chin. A jerk lifted his head so he had to look down at her. "It is small when you seek intimate means with someone you know so little."

"I merely seek to know you better. I did not intend to offend."

Gossamyr followed his parti-colored strides as he paced over and stepped inside the shell of the mill. Tall and lithe, a quiet fluidity marked his movements. If she must sum him up he was a fine mortal man. Not so cocksure as the fée male.

Marry your daughter, my lord? Er...

One fée man had not seen the usual in her. Exotic, he had labeled her. And his kisses, even now, stirred a longing in Gossamyr's belly. Arousal tended to show in the fée wings, turning the normally pellicle appendages a deep color. His papilonid hind wings, with elegant projections that curled and uncoiled, had shaded to a lovely violet, stirring his long black hair to elegant waves across his back...

The memory of her loss hurt, and so Gossamyr pushed back the urge to re-create their tender moments. Her father had been cruel, reacting before considering his daughter's heart.

"Faeries know little of love," Shinn had warned. "It is merely lust you feel."

Lust was not what her heart knew. It could not be! Nor could lust have driven a man to arrive at his wife's bedside every morning just to watch her wake. It was something more. And the only something she could summon was love.

If her father's words held truth, why had it been so easy for Shinn to marry Veridienne? Had he loved her? Should not his marriage have been arranged, as was hers? Rarely did a fée lord marry by choice. Love? Or was it merely lust wanting to be so much more?

Gossamyr could guess. Mortal women were compelling to the fée men. Exotic and easily seduced by the Enchanted. Though, no fée would make it known, they carried on illicit liaisons against the commands of their elders. Gossamyr had not heard the fée women mention such desires for the mortal male, though it was possible.

Half mortal in blood, flesh and soul—who was she to discount a mortal man?

"Do you hear that?"

Turning to the man's voice, Gossamyr stood and strode toward the water mill.

Ulrich propped himself in the doorway beneath a surviving wood awning, one leg dangling, his head tilted back and his eyes closed. Suddenly the rains increased. Now the wooden slats were beat upon by heavy drops. The fresh scent smelled good enough to eat.

"Sweet, redeeming rain," Ulrich said reverently. Then he twisted his attention to Gossamyr.

So fierce his gaze fixed to her, she stepped back. A slick of her palm erased the rain from her nose and cheeks. "What?"

"I've an idea." He gripped her wrist and tugged. "Come with me."

"But—"

Cool, fat raindrops skipped across her face and soaked into the dusty wool gown. Gossamyr raised her face to the rain and closed her eyes. She felt Ulrich move his hands over her eyelids, her cheeks and her jaw but did not protest what he was doing.

"Forgive my touch, my lady."

"Blight that. Is it working?"

"Yes. Look!"

She opened her eyes to see his palms glittered with faery dust.

"It is washing from your hair, as well."

Gossamyr lifted her thick plaits and made to brush away the offensive glimmer, but she paused. *Do I really want this?* The surrender of all Enchantment? Her last tie to Faery and the father she relied upon for return. *You yet have the fetch.*

"What is it? Gossamyr? Ah." Ulrich's voice moved close to her ear and he embraced her.

She remained stiff, fingering the carved bone clasp tipping a plait, not sure how to react, or what to say. Embraced without her consent, she initially felt violated, and yet, the feeling was immediately replaced with relief and reassurance. How long had it been since she'd been embraced by a man?

"I understand," he said against her ear, his wet lips cold. "Perhaps you should take cover?"

Close, this man. Close, this mortal realm. And she but a step away from completely joining it.

Gossamyr held out a hand, palm up, to catch the rain. Pulse, pulse, against her hand. Beat, beat—her heart favored this man's closeness.

Can you do it? Wash away all trace of Faery?

Can you become a champion?

"This must be done. It is…bone." Gossamyr lifted the hem of the sodden blue wool and pulled it up over her knees and hips, exposing her braies. Striding around the windmill and toward the stream she called back to Ulrich, "Don't look!" And she pulled the gown over her head and tossed it to the ground in a tangle.

"Oh, mercy." His groan made Gossamyr smile. "Why do this to me, woman? I have not looked upon a naked woman since my wife. There you go and— Hades!"

She trusted he walked around to the opposite side of the mill, for his voice trailed off. It mattered not. With or without a watcher, 'twas splendid to stand in the rain and sluice off the dust and dirt from the road.

Shivering, she slicked her hands down her rib cage and undid the hip belt and amphi-leather ties at her waist. Kneeling, she made quick work of the leather strips bound about her ankles. She slid her fingers over the braies and they dropped at her feet along with the Glamoursiège sigil, her purse, and a clutter of *arrets.*

Earth and grass, soggy and thick, squished between her toes. A warty gray toad hopped to and fro along the stream bank and Gossamyr followed, plunging to her knees into the cold water. She gave a squeal and sank down and dipped her head back, surrendering to the moment and the inevitable Disenchantment.

"To mortality," she whispered and closed her eyes.

The water barely deep enough to cover her to the waist, she floated. The bone clasps closing the ends of her plaits were shucked off with a tug. Quickly, she worked the braids open and splayed out her hair. Long pale tresses took on the weight of the water, then clung possessively about her naked flesh.

The notion of a lover's possessive embrace took shape and memory filled her thoughts…

Gossamyr wrung her hands in frustration as she looked up to Avenall. He hovered outside her bedchamber but could not enter. She had not, until now, been aware of the shield of glamour surrounding the castle.

"There is no way through this." Avenall punched out a fist. The shield glimmered and wavered like ripples on a pond then stilled. "You think it is only against me?"

"Not sure." Gossamyr stepped back, a finger to her lips, and thought. "Perhaps it is merely against my room. Yes! Go around to the south side, I'll meet you in my mother's study. No one ever goes in there."

Avenall flew up and out of Gossamyr's sight. Her cobwebby robes sailing out like the wings she would never own, she scrambled down the corridor and pushed open the door to Veridienne's room. She did not need light to navigate the room, so many times she snuck into her mother's private chambers to study the bestiary.

Trailing a finger across the dustless book as she passed, Gossamyr sailed to the far side of the room and pulled open the curtain. Silk shinged to the side. Pale twilight entered. The summer night was hot and a moth that had been clinging to the curtain, seeking refuge from a predatory root frog, stretched out its wings and fluttered inside.

Avenall descended from above and landed the rose-festooned deck of the gallery with ease.

"You are sure it is safe?" Avenall folded his wings against his back and thighs and crossed his arms over his chest in a dashing pose.

"It is. I swear it to you."

Aware now she wore but a robe and her hair unbound, Gossamyr took a tentative step toward the grinning man. Young man, no longer a boy, but not quite a warrior. His shoulders were as broad as any of Shinn's warriors, and his muscles hard. The air, tangible against her skin, brushed her nerve endings to an alertness that prinkled.

"You are beautiful this evening," he said. "I don't believe I have ever seen you, my sweet, with your hair unbound."

My sweet? Gossamyr's heart lunged up her throat.

A rush of anticipation pressed her up onto her toes. Twilight danced in Avenall's eyes, making them liquid, a rich violet wine Gossamyr wanted to drink until she wobbled. Close enough to kiss, to smell, to taste.

"Brown," he whispered. He held her face so she could not look from him. "I have not before noticed your eyes. They are...exotic."

She smiled at that description. "Avenall, why did you ask to court me?"

"Isn't that apparent?"

"Tell me."

"Because I favor you."

"But why? I am half-blooded. Is it I am so different?"

"A bit. I saw the mortal passion in your heart when you witnessed the Dance."

She bristled. That had been many years earlier. She'd snuck out to witness the Dance, something Shinn had forbidden, for her father forbid more than granted.

"You did?"

"You reached out and touched the Dancer's hair as he spun past you. I know you wanted to touch the mortal."

Surprised Avenall had stepped so perfectly into her thoughts, Gossamyr could but shrug and gaze into his delicious violet eyes.

"You don't care what others think of you," he said. "I watch when you stride through the Glamoursiège markets. You are strong and smart and beautiful. I admire you, Gossamyr. I always will, even after your father marries you to another man."

"Don't say things like that." For indeed, Shinn had only days ago forbidden Avenall from courting her. His only excuse: he would not have a Rougethorn in the family. "Let's be in the moment tonight, please?"

"Can you feel it?" He took her hand and placed it over his chest.

Indeed, his heartbeats were strong and, when Gossamyr concentrated, she thought surely they did beat in synch with hers. But even more, the hardness of his body beneath her fingers intrigued. She slid her hand up to the part in his sheered silk shirt and drew a finger along his flesh.

The wind of his wings, spread wide and full, schussed her face with a sweet breeze. Heliotrope; his distinctive scent. Gossamyr closed her eyes and surrendered to the sensations that stormed about her. Heartbeats increased. An urgency vibrated in her bones. She wanted him closer, next to her, inside her...

The weight of his hand sliding down her neck and parting her robe made her gasp.

"May I," he whispered into her mouth, "touch you?"

"Yes."

The air cooled her briefly as gentle, wide hands cupped her breasts. The touch making her buoyant, Gossamyr rose to her tiptoes. An unbidden mewl crossed her lips.

"They are so...large," he said with a smiling titter.

"They are?" Gossamyr laughed. "I had not thought them overlarge."

"Fée women have nothing compared to this," he said as he smoothed and tickled and then bent to lave at her breast with his tongue. "They would hinder your flight, I imagine."

"Pity, I've not that worry. So that is the only reason you fancy me?"

"Don't be foolish, Gossamyr."

"I'm teasing."

And that was all she could say, for the sensation of Avenall's mouth and teeth and tongue working at her breasts drew a shudder to her bones.

Gossamyr tilted back her head, lifting her breasts higher. It was then she *noticed the flutter of Avenall's wings behind him. The pellicle wings, normally translucent, had deepened to a rich violet. Most remarkable!*

"*Your wings,*" *she said on a gasp.* "*They are gorgeous. Why have they changed color?*"

"*That, my sweet——*" *He lifted his violet gaze to hers. A smile could not be erased.* "*Is arousal.*"

"*Oh. Oh! I've never before seen the like.*"

"*Good. I should hate to discover you are overly familiar with male arousal.*"

"Gossamyr?"

Ah! Might she not simply enjoy this moment before all crowded in and became a battlefield?

"Ohhh…Gossamyr?"

Ulrich's voice sounded strange. Unsure.

Wading to shore, she looked for her abandoned gown. What appeared a mushy rock was actually a tangled heap of wet wool.

"You might want to get dressed, Gossamyr!"

"You've a naked woman behind that windmill?"

She stiffened at the sound of a gruff male voice. Not Ulrich's. A chill clamped to her spine. Instinct shot to the surface. A bravo? More likely a vicious Armagnac. She had not been too alert. Fool!

Scrambling to untangle the wet gown, Gossamyr cursed her need to linger in the stream. Her hair, heavy and dripping down her back, clung like deflated eels.

"She's…my mother actually. In the name of King Charles VII, I beg you do not go back there!"

The *shing* of steel alerted Gossamyr like an *arret* to the gut. No staff to hand, for it sat in the windmill. Not even a dry piece of clothing! She managed to untangle the gown and worked to open the hem.

"This should prove interesting," another voice said. Not the gruff voice. Nor, again, Ulrich's. But male. How many were there?

"You take him, I'll get the mother."

"I don't think so!"

One of the men let out a yelp of pain. Gossamyr cringed, hoping upon hopes it was not Ulrich.

"Bastard!" The gruff one. Another slash of steel sliced the air. A metal clang—armor?—and a groan akin to having the air punched out of one's lungs.

"I'm coming!" Gossamyr yelled as she shrugged her arms into the sodden sleeves. The water soaked into the wool and hampered the ease of dress. "I think."

A glance to her braies found the amphi-leather merely a pile of dust. The last raiment of Faery had left her body; the Enchantment had gone. She spun, the gown settling about her knees, her bare legs not finding purchase in the slick grass. The braided hip belt lay there, reduced to fine dust in the shape of a leather strap. But the weapons and her sigil remained solid—stone and wood traveled easily from one world to the next. She gripped an *arret* in each hand and began to spin them.

In her peripheral view she saw a body land the ground. The man tumbled backward, his legs flipping over his head. Steel flashed and a dark leather-capped head shook off the fall and glanced her way.

"Got it under control," Ulrich reassured. He dashed forward, but his feet slipped on the rain-slick ground and he went down as his aggressor swung. Fortunately Ulrich's head was sailing toward the ground.

A huge barrel of a man rumbled around the water mill, sliding into Gossamyr's view. He growled like a bear and charged. Sword down and at his side, the bear heading toward her looked ready to pounce rather than slash. And he did.

The *arret* connected with his forehead, bringing him down in a soggy slap of flesh. Gossamyr marched up to him and yanked the obsidian tip from his skull. Not much blood. He was still—

A meaty hand lashed out, catching her ankle and knocking her off balance. The sodden wool twisted between her legs, making a quick jump to her feet impossible. Pinned by the shoulders, Gossamyr's head submerged in the stream. She felt massive hands grope her neck and then—

As the bubbling of water in her ears dissipated, the sound was replaced by a gurgle of death. A final gasp of life spewed across her face. Gossamyr looked into the dismayed eyes of her attacker and watched his dark eyeballs roll upward. She shoved at him but his lifeless body remained, dead weight forcing out her own precious breath.

"Be right back!" Ulrich called. Having taken out her attacker, he now raced toward the mill and with a powerful grunt, delivered a blow to an unseen assailant.

Her breath fast leaving due to the oxen that lay on top of her, Gossamyr noticed the stream of blood ripple from his skull where the sword had cleaved it apart. She pushed but could not lever the giant from her body. She groped for a hold, but slick grass lined the shore and her fingers slid and slipped. Her heavy head splashed into the water and she gulped in water and strands of her loosed hair.

Of a sudden she could breathe and it was possible to lift to her elbows. Leaning in to the space where the oxen had been slain was Ulrich's dazzling smile. "Did I not remark you would need me sooner or later? Looks like it was anon."

She couldn't prevent a smile. The man continued to surprise.

He offered a hand, and Gossamyr clamped hers into it.

"Armagnacs?" she asked, standing and shaking out the heavy wool gown.

"Mayhap. Any man with a sword and a growl is fair game, remember that."

"I won't forget."

Bending to grab the last few *arrets,* she thought what to do with the applewood crest. She could not abandon it. It was her banner on the field of battle. Clasping it to her chest she strode from the stream, fighting the wet wool with kicks and stomps.

Ulrich followed her to the mill. "So you don't fight naked, eh?"

She turned to deliver a scathing remark, common—but unexpected—relief tamed her tongue. "It is not in my repertoire, no."

"Pity, I would have given a lifetime's coin to see that."

"Ulrich, I wager a lifetime of your coin would not see a family of peasants through one prosperous winter."

"You may have a point there." He tapped one of two dead men on the skull with the tip of the sword he'd heisted during the fight. "You think they were after the alicorn?"

"What else?"

"Well, you *were* naked."

"Will I ever live that down?"

"Not if I can prevent it, my Naked Faery Not. Not if I can prevent it."

ELEVEN

They passed a tree bare of leaf and vigor; as well, the body hanging from a sturdy branch by a frayed stretch of olive hosen had been drained of life and reduced to bone.

Not Faery, Gossamyr thought horribly. *Not the same.* Though she had heard tales skulls were found in the marsh roots. She liked to twist and twine her way through the roots spun about the upsweep of the Spiral forest, and occasionally descended close enough to peruse the gloomy marsh waters—but had never seen a ripple of danger.

She followed Ulrich as he led her and Fancy past a makeshift table of boards where three men played what Ulrich explained was called *hoca* and swilled dark beer as they waited to pass through the gates to Paris. The men who had attacked at the water mill had not been part of a larger raid; these people would remain, to their boon, unaware of that trouble.

Her wool gown had dried half through. Upon Ulrich's insistence she put up her hair so as not to draw undue attention, twisting it in a chignon loosely at the back of her head. Ulrich had suggested the applewood sigil as a means to secure it. Without a hip belt to secure her *arrets,* the weapons were kept to hand in a coil. Feeling completely without origin in the odd-fitting gown, Gossamyr drew in a breath. This was it. The city lay just beyond those gates.

"Might as well get comfortable," Ulrich said as he tossed the reins over Fancy's back. The mule did never wander far, so long as a patch of clover enticed. "I think the gatekeepers take joy in making everyone wait. Pity, for the Armagnacs take advantage of our delay. It may have been a boon they attacked us instead of these people. There are children here."

"Why put people in such danger? The gatekeepers are admitting the provisions before the children!"

"One cart loaded with flour sacks be far more valuable than a mere child. 'Tis the damned English. Think they run the town, they do. 'Course, now I think of it...they do."

Ulrich removed his cape and, with a scruff of his hand through his hair, gave a mighty shake of his head, then sought a comfortable nest on the compacted grass. He lay back, tucking the saddlebag beneath his neck for a pillow, stretched his arms over his head and yawned. "Think I deserve some rest after our skirmish. You mind watching Fancy?"

"Not at all."

A cursory check of the surroundings counted six men, two women—one with babe to breast—two children no higher than Gossamyr's elbow, and a goat rounding the batch. The cartsmen who manned the convoy busied themselves with counting, while a reed of a man, bespectacled and wielding quill and paper, followed and marked down figures that were called to him.

Gossamyr did not sense danger. But when, since arriving in the Otherside, had she actually beat danger to the notice? How these people sat about—in wait of attack—with such calm stunned. Had they become accustomed to the violence it seemed a mere interruption to a game of stones?

She squatted near Ulrich's head and studied his ease. So quickly he dismissed the danger after nearly being killed himself. He tilted his head to see her behind him. The effect was strangely enthralling, those celestial eyes beaming up at her.

"You intend to sit right there?" he wondered.

She shrugged. "I thought to."

"Then—" he lifted his head and gestured with his hand "—would you mind? I could use a soft pillow."

She realized he wanted to lay his head on her lap. Gossamyr scanned the travelers sitting about, playing stones, drinking and dozing. None paid her or Ulrich any mind.

Ulrich still waited her decision. He ruffled his hand through his hair. "I've not the lice if that be what you dread."

"I did not think as much." Though, now he mentioned it... "Very well."

She seated herself against a sheep-size rock, her spine melding to the warm curved stone, and stretched out her legs. Ulrich laid his head on her thighs and closed his eyes. Wriggling into a comfortable position, the saddlebag splayed across his stomach, he let out a satisfied groan.

"Your head is heavy."

"Your legs are bony," he murmured. "Wake me when the provisions have passed inspection."

Stunningly, the man drifted to a low snore within a few blinks. Sure he faked it, Gossamyr leaned over his face and studied his eyelids, smooth and motionless. Real sleep?

As Ulrich's soft snores segued to a somnambulant rhythm, Gossamyr rested her head against the boulder and closed her eyes. The sun warmed her face and made her smile. This Otherside was made even more beguiling by the flaws or differences from perfection. Even the dangers appealed. For when, in Faery, had she been so thoroughly challenged?

Smiling again, she realized she increasingly found favor with the Otherside. Her side, for the time.

Better here. The thought, unbidden, flashed in her mind.

To stay would be to embrace Disenchantment. Unthinkable. Glamoursiège needed her.

Just beyond the fortressed walls lay Paris. Lure for the Disenchanted, and home of the Red Lady. Soon her adventure would prove itself and she would finally realize her worth.

Gossamyr skimmed her hand over Ulrich's scalp, mowing her fingers through the strands of tangled hair. Heavy and dirty, the texture intrigued. And there, she traced the curve of his ear, small and close to his head. Her fingertips moved down and across the hard line of his jaw until sharp bristles of beard set her senses to a fine alert. She toggled the pads of her fingers back and forth over the bristles, thinking their texture so much rougher than the hair on Ulrich's head. How be it not the same?

A strange murmur, like supreme satisfaction, drew Gossamyr's attention. She flashed her eyes open and looked into Ulrich's upside-down gaze. Awake? She jerked her fingers from his face.

"I thought I dreamed," he said with a sleepy smile. "Don't pull away. That felt good. First tender touch I've had in a long time. Or has it been mere weeks? Ah! Almost makes me..." He closed his eyes and turned his head to the side.

"Makes you what?"

"*N'importe.*" He rolled onto his side and tucked his hands up by his chest, moving his head farther toward her knees. "You have no idea what you just did, eh, Faery Not?"

"I...well..." Gossamyr could but stare at the fingers that had moments ago been tracing the man's face, feeling his features as if she were blind. What *had* she been doing? Following her lover's abrupt banishment she had stashed away any feelings of desire or need. And yet, they strived for release with every moment she spent with Ulrich.

"So lacking in emotion, these faeries," Ulrich murmured, his words drifting to a sigh, and then to a snore.

"I…" Gossamyr crossed her arms and tilted a snarl at the sleeping soul shepherd.

I do have emotions, she thought as gruffly as she could. *I just…* Well, she wasn't sure what to do with them, so they were quickly pushed back. Left to wither.

Why punish yourself for your father's cruelty? Is it not your right to seek another lover? Before you tie yourself to one man? This world is bursting with men. Look at them!

She looked at her fingertips. One hand bracketed the side of Ulrich's face; a finger strayed down to the dark beard. Contact. And…connection. Of a sort that intrigued. Mortal touched, and happy to do so.

Ulrich's eyes opened to look right at her. "No time to consider romance, Faery Not?"

"Romance? You are begroggled. I am just—"

"Lusting?"

Had she been lusting over a mortal? A man who could not care if she was half-blooded. But would he think her exotic? "That would please you?"

"Surely."

"What of the damsel?"

"You think I have a romantic connection to her?"

Gossamyr nodded.

"I no longer have connections to any, be they woman, child or lover."

The sadness in his voice clued Gossamyr he had lost a great piece of his heart. Had he loved and given so much?

A finger to the circle of violet and green that stained Ulrich's right cheek intrigued. He winced at Gossamyr's touch. "I'm sorry. Does it hurt verily?"

"It aches—" he placed a hand over his heart "—in more places than my face."

Gossamyr wasn't sure what that meant. She saw no other

bruises. "How did you come by such a bruise? It looks a few days old—"

"A week, to be exact."

"And?"

A heavy sigh puffed up his relaxed gut. "You really need to know?"

"If you wish to tell."

"I received this bruise from a stone. A good-size stone that easily fitted into a woman's palm."

"A woman did this to you?"

"Indeed. My wife."

It never took longer than a day for the Red Lady's taint to extinguish her victims. Atimes but an hour passed; other times the sun would rise and set before the tainted fée would stumble and finally collapse. The pin man preferred the event happened in privacy. The disgust or sudden shock of the public never aided his retrieval. The essence he claimed yesterday behind the stable in Juvisy had almost been witnessed.

Why did they not keel head to ground immediately? He would never understand the working of his mistress's deadly kiss. Nor must he care. Maybe? No. No reason to.

This day, the sun sat high and bright; one could not determine where the ball of light ended and where the crystal sky began. A tug to the leather brigandine he wore shifted the amigaut between his shoulders blades. One of the bone splints sewn into the doublet had poked through and irritated the base of his wings something horrific. He gave ichor daily for the success of his mission. Did the red bitch appreciate the sacrifice?

How she wounded with her indifference.

The streets bustled with midday marketers en route to purchase the rotting remains of fish from the skiffs moored on the Seine. Precious few boats tied up for no longer than it took to pillage their stores and burn the boat, but this day the English patrolled the

riverbank with a keen eye to marauders. Cobbles beaten smooth
by the centuries echoed with the clop of horse hooves, the call of
fishmongers, and the scrambling feet of those who literally starved
inside this great city of riches. For the gates were a risky leave to
purchase flour for bread from the millers who would rather shelter away from the attacks.

Assuming a straight-shouldered pose—tall and fine—the pin
man scanned the bleary day, tainted with a fine mist. The succubus's mark had meandered from her embrace early this day and
had been wandering the narrow streets in a thrall. Clothed in
simple black wool, the barest of lace crept out from the mark's
doublet sleeves. The fée must have fallen on hard times since the
Disenchantment.

The pin man shrugged at the irritation scratching his back. Hard
times, indeed.

Fine rain slickened his face. He lashed out his tongue to drink
in the minute liquid and tasted the sooty air and briny muck of
the Seine.

Now the victim began to slow. The pin man scampered to within
a leap of the Disenchanted. As the fée stumbled, a palm catching
against a wall for surety, lithe shoulders swayed in an attempt to
find that easy balance. He turned his head to scan whence he had
dallied; red-glossed eyes sought nothing, only squinted at a bleary
crimson sky.

The pin man cringed when the fée started down the massive
stone steps to the Seine. Would he attempt to drown his agony? It
would make retrieval difficult, if not impossible. Even in the miserable weather so many bustled about. The silver glinting river
hoarded dozens of slender boats and skiffs. The bridge, pressed
with houses and humanity, verily oozed an awareness of the river
so close. Someone would witness.

Tugging his hood securely upon his head, he stealthily descended
behind the victim. To reveal his strange hair coloring amongst the

crowd would elicit stares. It had not always been such a color—
he sensed as much—but he could not recall a time when it had simply been black, as remained the lower half of his tresses. There
had been a time—that time—when…

Brows furrowing and his entire face squinting, he sought the origin of…of…

Ah!

Lost the notion.

Here, along the river's edge a log bench beckoned, its rotted,
warped legs coated in clinging ivy. Stench of scale and sewage
crowded against the walls of the riverbank. A rusted iron ring
larger than a cow's head hung a leap away, waiting to moor up a
visiting skiff.

The fée folded onto the bench, a surrender to his body's loss of
will. Now he noticed the pin man's arrival and managed a grim
smile and gestured he join him on the bench, which the pin man
did eagerly. No words were spoken. A fine pounded-gold sheath
was missing the sword the pin man had remarked this morning
when the fée had first stumbled out from his mistress's embrace.
Most likely abandoned in a whirl of dizziness, for so suddenly the
Red came upon them, choking from within, or rather, drowning
its victim with thick viscous fluid. Blood? Or somesuch. Couldn't
be blood, for ichor ran through the fée's veins. But the pin man
never pondered the conditions of the death overmuch. He lived
for but one task. Always had, always—

—well, not always. Yes? Or…no? Tricksy, the remnants of
memory that cloyed.

The fée, smiling woozily at him, laid his head back against the
moist stone wall that fortressed the river. A seabird careening low
scanned for food. The creak of moorings secured wooden boat
hulls kissing against one another.

The fée blinked. A red tear slithered down his cheek. He whispered, each syllable a husky dying hush, "'Twas…a remarkable kiss."

The pin man nodded, slid his thumb along his rain-slickened braies. Memory teased him. He knew he'd had the similar experience of longing but could not place the time or face or even name.

Be gone stupid flickers of a different life! Be gone or be whole!

"A kiss, yes." He said what he knew the fée was thinking—what they all thought. "Much like...Faery?"

"I—" a sense memory appeared across his face "—miss it so..." Death relaxed the fée's neck muscles. His head lolled, dragging his body down toward the pin man. He caught the fée by the shoulders and pushed him back, taking a moment to straighten the wool doublet. Silk frogs clasped the black wool from chin to loin. Valuable. Of little concern.

Anticipation making his fingers shake, the pin man dug into his leather sheath and pulled out a fine shiny pin. Pure silver, the pointed shaft, a ward against glamour—not that he need fear such from the Disenchanted. As long as a man's forearm, the shaft, but no thicker than his littlest finger. The polished iron knob, a perfect ball, hummed in his grip. Not completely safe, the winter-forged iron, but endurable. It negated the power of the silver. Why though? He could not guess

He held the pin poised over the dead fée's skull, and the wait began.

And he replayed her seductive voice in his head. *Aaahh... aaaae...eee...mmmmmnooo.* How he desired his ruthless red mistress. And how he despised her. Her song meant: *Come to me. Come to me, kiss me, drink from my life. Taste Faery. And die.*

Only, the pin man was not dead. He remained in limbo ever after. For she toyed with his essence, keeping it high above all the others. 'Twas the difference between the Disenchanted and those yet Enchanted. Or so he figured. The Red Lady could steal but a spark of an Enchanted essence, a portion that did not kill them, but instead dangled the hapless fée between the Infernal and the

Celestial. A cruel mastery, for only death would grant relief. May-hap her control over the Enchanted was greatest then, for it toyed for an eternity rather than granting a quick escape to Death.

Twinclian. Final.

The odd words visited briefly. *Twinclian?* Whatever that meant, he could not know. But should.

Ah! Banish the pesky thoughts!

A brilliant spark of corporeal property arose from the fée's skull. So brief, the moment of release, but the pin man had honed his skill. Stabbing expertly, he speared the essence. Tiny cry of death, defeated in its softness.

Tilting the needle up, he watched the blue globulus mass of un-dulating glimmer slide down to the iron-ball head.

Success.

A gargling yowl loosened as the revenant escaped its shell. Al-ways blind to the speared essence, like a banshee the revenant soared up into the sky and flitted over Paris. Its destination, the pin man did not know. So long as the skeletal apparition did not tor-ment him it could descend to the Infernal for all he cared. All oc-curred within a blink; none on the riverboats or walking the bridge took note.

Careful now to hold the pin upright, the pin man backed from the deflated corpse and skipped up the stone steps to the street. The shell of a former life he'd left behind would disintegrate with but a powerful gust of wind, faery dust dispersing across the Seine in a twinkle.

Twinclian? Hmm…

A bell toll later, the pin man danced merrily down the white marble floors of his mistress's lair. Along the walls clung huge white marble gargoyles bearing candles as wide as a knight's thigh in their wax-encrusted dragon-claws, brilliantly illuminating his skipping journey.

"Malchius," the pin man sang as he passed the first stone-eyed creature. "Maximianus, Dionysius, John." He always named the silent watchers as he passed. A blown kiss to the fifth was caught with a void stare. "Constantine, you precious thing."

The pinned essence glittered madly, as if all of Faery had been crammed into one globulus mass.

Spinning and kicking up his feet, the pin man celebrated his triumph. Such a good puppy he was!

"Seraphion and Martimanas, *amours* all!"

The doors to the Collection were open, as they always seemed to be, spread in wait of his return. Forgetting the seven sleepers, the pin man entered the air filled with myrrh and citrus. The scent dived into his brain, seducing and numbing.

Twirling into the room, he eyed the Red Lady, sprawled upon a massive bed bedecked in crimson silk with gold-tipped fringe. Her luminous white flesh enticed for but a spin—soon enough would come his reward.

First, he turned and danced his way up the two marble steps arced before the curved wall. Thrusting, he pressed the pin tip into the marble, feeling its fine point enter the cold stone as if gliding into a thick, creamy cheese.

And it was done.

He stepped back, the high of the moment dissipating as he looked over his handiwork.

Finished. Once again surrounded by so many stolen bits of life.

"A blue one," his mistress cooed deliriously from her bed. "So pretty!"

Indeed. Dozens of pins quilled the marble wall, each spearing a glimmering fée essence. Essences of white and indigo and palest violet. Coral and lime and bloodiest red. Orange. Lavender. Lucid blue. Every color danced to a rhythm that could only match its former body—vigorous, languid, proud or cocky.

The collection delighted his mistress to giggling peals. "Come, Puppy!"

He heard her pat the bed behind him. The soft *cush* of Turkish silk beneath a fragile yet strong palm. *Pat, pat.* Lemon scent dispersing with each smear of flesh to satin. Every portion of his being pined to rush into her arms. Remove the scratchy brigandine and slither across the cool sheets. Reward so sweet.

But wait. Prolong the moment.

Admire.

The pin man stepped another pace backward and stretched his eyes up the wall. Not far above the collection—more than a stretch, but certainly less than a jump—one single essence pulsed. Pale and soft, yellow as the sky on a lazy Sabbath morning. It glimmered boldly, defiant above all the others.

Tears welled in his eyes. He clutched at his throat, then swallowed. Desire overwhelmed triumph with bittersweet sorrow.

"Mine," he whispered in the barest of voice.

TWELVE

Gossamyr gasped. "Your wife?"

Ulrich eased his palm to the bruise on his cheek. "She was a trifle upset with me."

"You are married? Why then do you travel the road alone? I—" Touched you, she thought. Most intimately. And he had done the same.

He had a wife? And he sought a damsel in her absence? Why, the man's heart be more fickle than a fée heart!

"Lydia, my wife, would not accompany me on this quest for all the gold in the world. Just as well."

Ulrich stood and stretched his arms high above his head. His hose bagged behind his knees; he gave a tug to them just over his buttocks. Behind them, Fancy snorted. No patches of clover to be found here on this plot of beaten earth. A glance at the surrounding people, mired in miserable wait, and Ulrich beckoned she follow him.

Gossamyr remained on the ground, unsure.

"My lady, do you want to hear my sorry tale? It is my final truth."

"I had thought all our truths out?"

He shrugged. "Oops."

"Oops?" She stood and walked beside him, her bare feet padding in pace to his. "Blight these mortals and their puzzling words."

They strode toward the end of the convoy, Fancy in tow. Gossamyr kept a keen eye on the horizon and the forest that edged the hill for marauders. Why did the city not post guards outside the gates?

"That dance stole two decades from me," Ulrich said. He kicked the cracked wood wheel on a cart piled higher than his head with chopped ash logs. "Lydia had twenty years to mourn me. Rhiana, a babe in infant skirts when I left, could never remember me. Yet it was but an afternoon to me. What if you returned to Faery and all had changed?"

"Faery time is so mutable. This is my first journey away...."

Would it all be so different upon her return? How to know she would not lose Time as Ulrich had? "So Rhiana, the damsel, is your daughter?"

"Yes, you thought otherwise? Silly faery!"

"I am no such thing. I merely—" Had suspected he'd a lover. But she'd never thought the lover to be a wife. Blight! "Tell your tale, soul shepherd."

"Very well." Leaping around to the back of the cart, Ulrich leaned against the gate that barred the wood from tumbling to the ground. "I passed but a few hours of dancing in Faery. But here in France, er—the Otherside, for those of us unfamiliar with the terminology—twenty years passed. I had returned two decades after stepping into that evil circle."

"That is quite remarkable."

"Yes, and I had aged not a moment. So many things change," Ulrich said, "and yet, much remains the same."

"That is why you are always muttering about things being the same or not?"

"I am in a constant state of befuddlement."

"Sure madness."

"Is it mad to wish it back? Twenty years." He groped the air between them and made to fling it away. "Stolen! I did no harm to the fée." Checking that those waiting to pass through the gates were not eavesdropping, Ulrich then lowered his voice. "I did not covertly enter that damned toadstool ring. I was but wandering along, whistling a tune, when I stumbled into it with little knowing." He gripped her by the upper arms and entreated, "Why did they do it to me?"

The shimmer in his eyes looked to be tears. Gossamyr prevented herself from reaching to touch his face, from further connecting when the connection could only feel so illicit. Yet so strongly it intrigued. She ignored propriety more and more.

"I have always been told the Dancers are returned," she offered, "without harm."

"I was not harmed physically. But here!" He tapped his skull and swung around in a circle of outrage. "My thoughts, my memories, my *very life* has been altered." He wrung his fist in a useless gesture before his face then punched the air. "It is as if a chunk has been cleaved out from me—right here." He thumped his chest. "A chunk of time, of love and life that should have been mine."

Gossamyr pressed a palm over her chest. Not missing, but…slowly falling away?

"Lydia remarried!" Ulrich again checked his volume, and then hissed, "Upon my return to St. Rénan a strange man stood in the doorway to my home. Just stood there! Protecting it from *my* entrance. Lydia's new husband had taken over my home!"

Swallowing, he caught his forehead with shaky fingers. The ruby ring flashed like the glossy eye of a succubus's victim. "And my Lydia…she had aged. Still lovely, you understand. But lines had creased into her forehead. And her eyes—those glass-blue eyes— they had dulled. She recognized me immediately, but…such horror in that pretty blue gaze that had before looked upon me with love. Most likely she thought me a spirit, one of the very souls I have all my life shepherded onward. Can you imagine?"

"No." Gossamyr crossed her arms over her chest, the nubby wool gown still moist under her stroking fingers 'Twould be as if her mother returned to her, but aged beyond comprehension.

Gossamyr had been aware of a few of Shinn's brief visits to the Otherside. He never changed physically. Yet, the fée lord always reminded, to visit the mortal realm too often taxed all fée. Time would have its due.

Propping her shoulder against the corner of the cart, Gossamyr observed the soul shepherd pace before her. Remembering. Reliving.

"To Lydia I had been absent two decades, and yet I looked the same. But the worst of all?" Ulrich looked to her for permission to continue. "Rhiana was gone. Lydia screamed at me, 'She has been sacrificed to the dragon this day!' This day!"

Dragons were as unfamiliar to Gossamyr as mortals were. She did know the creatures usually ate mortals offered as a sacrifice. They were creatures of such old and enduring Enchantment they did not rely upon Faery for survival.

"I was that close to saving my daughter. And I will have her back! I will."

"What cruel fate your Dance has granted," Gossamyr whispered as the man paced off toward the woods. "It is not right." And now, far from Faery, she could not summon argument in favor of the fée. Tricksy, be her kind. But to the detriment of one who had only shown her kindness? "I will help you to make it right, Ulrich."

The gates were pulled wide to admit what had now become dozens. The final cart of provisions had been counted and covered and rolled on into Paris. Gossamyr had let Ulrich wander off, sensing his need to grieve. But soon the gates would again close.

She tromped through the fallen twigs and tall grasses edging the forest, making no effort at stealth. If the soul shepherd still be in a sad mood her noise would alert him, give him opportunity to adjust his demeanor.

Where had he got to? Mayhap he was off with the alicorn to serve himself. Or had he been set on by brigands? The alicorn was a beacon.

"When I find him, I am going to track the nearest toadstool Passage and shove him in."

Ulrich swung around a wide oak trunk. He flicked an acorn at her, missing by an armshot. "Shove me in? That, my lady, is positively evil. You should be nicer to me. I am grieving."

Yet his smile compelled her to wonder might his thoughts be more flirtatious.

"You shouldn't...disappear."

"I was answering nature's call."

"For so very long?"

"My thoughts were dark." He tossed another acorn at her. Gossamyr caught it and clutched it to fist. "I needed to be by myself."

"Sorry."

"No worry. I won't let this out of my sight." Ulrich patted the saddlebag. "I can feel it draw in power. The unicorn must be in Paris."

"You understand you cannot bring back the dead. Well, you can, but in exchange, Faery will lose something. It is like when magic drains the Enchantment."

"I care naught. Rhiana should be alive as we speak. She is an innocent, Gossamyr, a little child simply needing me, for her mother had not really loved her."

That statement peaked Gossamyr's attention.

"Nor had she opportunity to get to know me or her real father."

"Her *real* father?"

Shuffling a handful of acorns in his palm, Ulrich turned and slid a shoulder against the tree trunk. A sigh and he tossed the acorns to the ground. "I am not Rhiana's blood father. The child was... queer-gotten. Unsure parentage. Doesn't matter; I loved her as my own."

"You have embarked on a harrowing quest, rife with evil that wishes you dead, for a child not of your blood?"

"Yes!"

Flinching at his emphatic outburst, Gossamyr twisted the tip of her staff in the ground. The acorn dug into her palm. "Impressive."

"Think you?"

"I don't know I could risk my life for something not my own. My father, Faery—they mean so much to me. That is because they are a part of me, my very blood."

"It may surprise you the things a man will do for someone he loves."

"Will you tell me who your daughter's father is?"

Ulrich stared off toward the gate where the tired travelers filed through. "When I lived in St. Rénan, there was rumor a madman stalked the forest that edged the sea. He wandered the night naked, moaning and shouting insanities. All were cautious when passing through the wood, and never would any broach the forest after nightfall. Lydia was late from market one eve—but a se'nnight after we had wed. She arrived home well after moonrise, frantic and shaking. The madman had violated her."

Gossamyr sucked in a breath.

"Rhiana could be mine, but she is—was—pale of hair. Dragon piss, it was stark red sprouting unnaturally wild like a witch's broom from her scalp." Ulrich tilted his head to look at Gossamyr. "Lydia never did take to the child. So distant she kept, almost as if she feared to touch the poor thing. I could not fault her; she had suffered for that child. Mayhap that was why I was drawn immediately to her. I fell madly for her wide green eyes. Such a gem, she was, and so innocent of her coming to this wicked world. Do you believe a man can love a child not his own?"

"Such a man would have to be selfless, honed of impeccable integrity. If you say that you can, then I suppose I believe you."

"Such trust I've gained in so little time from you, Faery Not." Hooking an arm about the tree trunk, he swung forward, dipping his head to peer up into her face. "Not so quick to brush me off now. Must be the Disenchantment. It has made you more susceptible to we mortals."

Gossamyr touched her throat. She had abandoned the wimple somewhere along the way. "Do I yet sparkle?"

He stroked two fingers across her brow and pushed back a loose strand of hair over her shoulder. "Not so much. Actually…" He tilted up her chin. "I don't see the pattern at all. That bath in the stream must have washed it away. Nice."

His breath swept her cheek and Gossamyr blinked open her eyes to look upon his face. He smiled. "You are difficult to resist, you know that?"

"Resist how?"

"From kissing."

"But, your wife…"

"Never again to be mine. Condemn me naught, I still love her. Or maybe it was but the child I truly loved. Indeed, it was difficult atimes to withstand Lydia's blatant refusal to love Rhiana. Ah! *Mon Dieu,* it has been but a week! And yet, already I look to my fancies. You can steal the marriage from the man, but you cannot take away his desire."

Desire, Gossamyr knew. Desire, she had felt under Ulrich's scrutiny. But to know now that he was married and had a child…

"What will you do if you *can* bring back your daughter? It has been very long; she will not remember you."

He twisted, resting his back against the flaking birch trunk near where she stood. "I had not thought of that. Rhiana will have forgotten the father a two-year-old once knew. As Lydia forgot when she took another husband. But I have not had the years to forget. No one deserves to die so cruel a death. Dragon fire." He shuddered.

Gossamyr slid her hand into his. They stood there, looking into one another's eyes—close, but for the mortal propriety.

Yes, you do forget, she thought. You forget a promise to never love again, the feel of your lover's embrace and the power of his kiss. You forget. And you desire.

THIRTEEN

The twosome stood twenty paces from the large wooden doors. Great cuts hewn into the weathered pine gave Gossamyr to wonder who had tried to hack their way inside. The road, rutted and muddied from the procession, sucked at Fancy's hooves. An ominous calm fell over her. Mere wood and mud to welcome her to so great a city? This mortal kingdom be not so frightening!

"As much as I know I am being led to Paris—and must proceed—I don't particularly care to pass through these gates."

"Why your reluctance?" she asked Ulrich.

"Do you know how many people die in this city? Every day?"

Gossamyr shrugged. She pressed the staff to her cheek. Smoke littered the air with a heavy odor.

"How many die in Faery a day?" Ulrich asked.

"Not many. One or two every season."

"Well, it is many here in Paris. Plaguelike proportions."

"Ah."

"So you understand?"

"No." So there were dead people—oh. "Sorry, Ulrich. Do the souls assault you from all angles?"

He tugged his cloak up over his face and gave a yank to bring Fancy around.

"Will that help?" she wondered.

"Pray that it will, but likely not. Now, mount Fancy."

Gossamyr bristled as Ulrich shoved her up onto the mule's back. "What are you—unhand me!"

"Time to follow my plan, Faery Not. We will find safe passage through the gates if we appear a couple. You must humble yourself and give me that staff."

She gripped the staff as Ulrich struggled with it. "This is mine, soul shepherd."

"Please, fair lady, step down from your proud pedestal for but the time it takes us to pass through the gates."

Two guards stood at either side of the gate, fully armed, pikes longer than her staff in hand. They did not question but she could feel their eyes behind the metal bourquinettes taking in all. "Very well." She released the staff. "But you guard that—"

"Yes, yes, with my life. As if I've not already a life-threatening task with this bedeviled horn riding my back. You've the wimple?"

"I think I left it by the stream."

"And your hair is all ascatter."

"The sigil is too heavy to hold."

"Not bone. Here, take my cloak."

"But your protection?"

"Cloak, or no, if there is a lost soul about, it will find me. Tuck back your hair into the hood. You should have twisted it into plaits."

"I don't know how." Catching Ulrich's bestartled gape, she merely shrugged. "Lady's maid."

And though Ulrich muttered something like "spoiled fairy princess," she ignored him.

"One must be ever alert for thieves, brigands or worse—your fellow countrymen," he instructed. "You are far too pretty not to draw attention." He clicked a sound to Fancy and they were off.

Pretty? The compliment lit a sizzle in Gossamyr's breast. He thought her pretty? Proved almost as favorable as exotic.

They were allowed entrance through the gates at the Porte St. Jacques with little more than a question of their intentions. Come to visit relatives was Ulrich's cool reply. His sister was to cook for his ailing uncle. (Much better than the excuse of luna-touched, Gossamyr thought.) And not a moment too soon, for the sun had fallen behind the horizon and the pale scythe moon was beginning to glow in the gray sky. Heavy chains were laced across the iron-studded pine gate, keeping out all until morn.

Leading Fancy away from the gate and toward a tavern that bustled with shouts and feminine calls, Ulrich made to hand the staff over to Gossamyr, but she passed him by.

"There be a postern gate to pass through before the Sorbonne," he said.

"How many gates?"

"Just the next one. It may already be closed for the night. I wager there are no rooms between here and there," he called ahead, sensing she did not care. He had decided Gossamyr would curl up and sleep at the base of a tree should it be necessary. She was a woman of the earth, forged of the land. He wondered how she would fare in the big city of Paris. She did carry no sword or dagger. Though this big stick served her well, and those spinny things did lodge quite neatly into a man's skull.

So he had revealed himself complete to the half faery. She had not condemned, nor had she commiserated. Yet they had stood there holding hands. A simple act swollen with promise.

Did she fancy him as he had begun to fancy her?

Had he no fealty to Lydia? The bruise on his cheek yet ached. He could not fault his wife's fears. Had he loved Lydia? Or was it as he'd explained to Gossamyr—the first time he'd witnessed Lydia's indifference to Rhiana his love had only grown for the child. So much he'd given to love a woman who no longer appealed to him. Lydia's refusal to see the joy and innocence of her own child had troubled him. He did not know her suffering, but indeed, it had cooled his ardor for her.

And now he had found another who stirred his desires. He was old enough to be Gossamyr's sire. Or should be. He still felt a man of six and twenty. The Dance had not aged his body or his mind. Should not his desires remain young?

Or did he simply replace his innate need for the feminine with whatever was to hand? He had never denied himself the simple pleasures, nor his love for sparkly things. Pity, the rogue faery did no longer twinkle.

"Be you hungry?" she called as she tripped ahead along the cobblestones. "I could consume an entire rabbit, and the ears to boot. Do hobble the horse, Ulrich."

"Do hobble the horse, Ulrich," he mimicked at her retreating back. Attractive, yet bossy. She sauntered off in search of said rabbit. "What am I, a servant?"

Ulrich quickly hobbled Fancy to a hitching post and rushed after the half faery into the smoky ill-lit darkness of a rousing tavern. The place was round in shape and filled to the curves with all sorts of men, wench and even a child or two. He choked at the haze of humanity and soot clouding the air. But it did smell delicious—lamb, no mistaking.

Rubbing his palms together in hopes of some fine belly-timber, he picked out a flash of pale hair. Faery hair.

A lone woman in rumpled undergarment parted the crowd to lift a tankard of ale would startle more than a few, yet Gossamyr mastered the room within minutes. Shouts settled to grunts and soon the entire tavern stood around the rumpled and uncoiffed visitor.

Feeling the air verily harden about him, Ulrich sensed this was not a good silence. He also knew Gossamyr had as little clue she was the item of interest as she had known what she was doing earlier when she'd stroked her fingers through his hair. Pity she had the instincts of a faery, swift and deadly, but mute to human intention.

Looking about, Ulrich noted he was relatively ignored. All eyes were on Gossamyr, pale strands of her hair hanging messily over her shoulders. So pretty. So…naive.

King Henry's coat of arms, bearing the Tudor rose, was displayed on more than a few tabards. Englishmen.

"Not bone."

Now, to grab the girl and run, or figure a way out? Ulrich scanned the room, his eyes falling on the beams overhead.

Warm ale served in a dirty cup. Oh, but this was splendid. Refreshing after their evening lingering outside the gates to Paris, her nerves heightened for fear of the unknown mortal forces that savored a dangerous match more deadly than a herd of bogies. Behind her, meat sizzled on a spit, and her mouth watered to test such fare for it smelled delicious. Not rabbit, but her hollow belly would not protest.

Drawing away the pewter tankard from her lips, Gossamyr looked up to the circle of dark and weary eyes. The room had silenced and all looked upon her. What? Was she dribbling?

"Sister." A man a full head taller than she stepped forth from the line of gawkers, his meaty hands at his hips where she assessed a dagger on one side, and at the other, a leather-wrapped mace. "We don't often see a woman of your calling in our humble inn. And drinking so heartily."

Gossamyr peered into the tankard of piss-warm dregs. Did not nuns consume ale? Surely mead was hard to come by in this mortal realm.

A thick scar gashed her inquirer's cheek. A gouge of flesh had long been removed from the curve of his right ear. Both wounds looked recent, for remnants of dried blood crusted his flesh. Straight black hair cut in a bowl shape exposed pale skin where the sun had not touched. The arms on his tabard were dirty and streaked with brown blood. A rose decorated the sinister half of his coat of arms.

Do not travel the sinister curve! Always Mince had preached against Gossamyr traveling the sinister to the Spiral marketplace. And the one time she had taken it? Carriage door flying open, and her body springing free, she'd almost fallen to her death.

Feeling a prinkle of discomfort ride her spine—an imminent fall?—Gossamyr straightened her shoulders. Thick trails of her hair clumped upon her shoulders; the cloak hood had slipped from her head. Not bone. Ulrich had fastened her staff to Fancy's flank. Outside. So eager had she been to quench her thirst, she'd merely strolled right in, blind to defense. Disenchantment had softened her prowess.

Not bone at all.

Now the glint of all manner of weapon, from sword to dagger to the ugly mace and even a deadly curved scimitar, appeared from sheath and in hand. Shinn would remand her for her half wits. Were these the bloodthirsty Armagnacs or the English?

"Bit of hard times come to you, Sister?" Her tormentor lifted her loose hair with the tip of his grease-shined dagger.

"Er...God grant you a good eve," she said, and bowing shortly, backed up. Only to discover the half curve of men's faces was, in reality, a circle that surrounded her. Torchlight flickered in admonishing licks. She scanned the crowd, finding no gentility in the dark, greedy eyes, only a hard curiosity. Mayhap even lust. A foul look that had not a morsel of love in the glinting pupils. "Er, may your God look upon you with faith?"

The tickle of a sword tip lifting her gown at her ankle alerted.

But not to action. She could yet leave this establishment as peacefully as she had entered. Her peripheral view took in the whispers of two wenches who sat upon a nearby rough-hewn wood table, their heads pressed together in shared whispers and their bosoms exposed in jiggling display.

"The lady wears no shoes," a man behind her commented.

"Indeed, hard times." The man with the mace tilted his head in question. "Doesn't seem right, a nun all alone, without protection."

Gripping the wood cross dangling about her neck, Gossamyr thought to seek out Ulrich, but did not. Unnecessary to endanger him. If he were lost in the crowd then more the better. Someone had to guard the alicorn.

"I can protect myself, *monsieur.* Now, if you please, I will be leaving."

She turned, ultra-aware the man with the mace stepped closer behind her. Before her loomed yet another wall of man. A scar cleaved his cheek into a crater and his right eye was but a white marble.

Danger. How she did enjoy the prinkle it rippled up her spine. But she would not smile, no, that would only provoke.

"Step aside," she said firmly.

"The woman demands Sir John Casson, lieutenant of His Highness's royal army, step aside?"

Giggles from the women sprinkled over the silence like mischievously spread faery dust.

What Gossamyr wouldn't give to conjure a trace of glamour. Blight! Half a dozen mortal men should not prove any more difficult than a few large trolls.

Slapping an ax in the meat of his palm, the man cracked a brown grin. "Two coins," he said, and looked beyond her to the mace man.

"Three," she heard from behind.

"I will give you ease, my lady!"

"Four, and you can hold her down," called out from the crowd. They were...bidding for her debauchery?

And the melee began. Shouts for five and six were matched by the man with the mace by ten sous. One promised a corn-fed fowl along with his coin.

What manner of vile creature were these people? Did they not revere their holy sisters? Was she not worth at least twenty gold pieces?

A glint of silver captured her notice. One of the women had handed a dagger to another liveried man and nodded. *Do the deed.*

A hand grasped her around the waist. Gossamyr lunged forward and spun out of the clench, grabbing the handle of an ax as the heel of the blade hit the man's palm. Using the wooden handle to steady herself, she kicked up and behind and caught the mace man in the jaw with her heel. Using surprise to her defense, she easily plucked away the ax and spun it in her fingers, landing the heavy heel of the steel blade in her palm. The metal did not burn. Bone. A twist of her wrist slapped the handle between the eyes of the scarred man.

Then, as if the floodgates had cleaved wide, all men poured in upon her. She feared no man in combat. It was the many, many blades and assorted weapons that would hamper her. Had Shinn known she would encounter such opposition? The fetch had been strangely absent since passing through the gates to Paris.

As quickly as it began, the heavens suddenly rumbled. Dust sifted down from the roof upon the heads of the men. Women screamed. Gossamyr ducked to avoid the swing of a kris dagger. While down, she beat a fist into the saggy-hosed crease of a knee, bringing down another man.

A soot-blackened beam creaked and fell into the center of the crowd—*thunk*—dispersing her attackers. Thatching and heavy field stones from the chimney began to shower the tavern. Not caring what was happening, Gossamyr used the distraction to escape.

Slipping through the melee, she reached the door. Ulrich gripped her hand and pulled her outside.

"What was that?"

"A rotting beam and a length of rope."

"Well timed, Ulrich." She leaped to embrace him, closing her eyes and squeezing him dearly.

"Someone has to look out for you, Sister." He pushed her from him. Wonder brightened his eyes. "How often is it the English are served a treat like a nun? You would have been ripped to shreds by those licentious beasts—and their women would have cheered them on."

"You did not try to heed my entrance."

"I was busy doing your bidding, hobbling the horse."

A sneeze erupted and Gossamyr blindly followed her rescuer to the mule. He shoved her onto the saddle and mounted behind her. "Where are we—*achoo*—headed?"

"Someplace new mortals won't stand out so conspicuously."

"I cannot."

"You must." Ulrich pointed to a line of laundry strung between two buildings. "What of that one? It is brown, simple yet stylish."

"I require braies and a shirt or doublet."

"Nay, my lady. There is not time for the spoiled princess to be choosy. A gown it must be. I see no light in the house. Let's to it."

She reached to pull Ulrich back, but he scampered to the laundry line just ahead.

Searching the darkness, Gossamyr leaped from Fancy's side and joined him. Tall buildings leaned in on one another, blocking the sky and, pray, their antics.

Ulrich pulled a chemise and gown from the laundry line and offered it to her. "Take it. It is less conspicuous than the underthings and rosary." He shoved the gown into her arms and turned to pick over the other items on the line. "So, a spoiled faery princess convinces her father to let her go off and save the world."

"Faery."

"Sorry, *Faery.* What *was* daddy thinking?"

"My appreciation for your rescue declines. Rapidly." She studied the gown. More itchy, heavy wool. But the white chemise he tossed on top of the gown was a soft thin fabric.

"That goes on beneath," he explained.

"I know that." She almost made a snide face, but prevented it. The man did not deserve such treatment after saving her hide. And that hug. He'd made no comment. Best to leave that slip in propriety unmentioned. "I could wear it alone—"

"Oh, no, it is an undergarment, Gossamyr."

"To wear both would prove cumbersome. Just the ugly piece then?"

"Very well. Go there, in the shadows behind that horse cart, and change."

Momentary indecision held Gossamyr beneath the laundry line, holding the clothing to her chest. She could just tug on the clothes right here. Before the eyes of this man. Who she suspected desired her as much as she desired him.

"I know what you're thinking."

She tilted her head. "I wager you do not."

"You think I don't know that women turn and gaze when I pass them by?" He smiled, revealing brilliance. "It's the teeth, yes? Difficult for any sane female to overlook. You cannot decide whether to tease me with a display or to follow orders."

"Tease you? You think very highly of yourself. Are all mortal men so..."

"Cocksure?"

"I don't think that is the word." Now he'd completely gone and decided for her. No way would she display anything for this lusty mortal. Not when he expected it. She turned and sauntered into the shadows. Sure of anonymity in the darkness, Gossamyr quickly pulled off the habit and tugged the brown fabric over her head.

Itchy and short. Gossamyr lifted a foot; her ankle was bared well above the knobby bone. Should serve, until she spied a line with braies. Tugging at the snug fit about her arms, she skipped out from the shadows. A tug to the shoulders worked at the tight seams. Too small by far, this gown.

"Lovely," Ulrich declared with a nod.

"Think you?"

"Why, yes."

A stroke of the back of his finger across her cheek stirred a sudden shiver to her spine. Mortal touched! Gossamyr jerked away.

"Sorry. I forget you are touchy."

"And I cannot forget you have a wife."

"Just so. Let's be off, then."

"Ulrich, this is stealing."

"Not if you sprinkle some faery coin in our wake."

She dug for the purse she'd placed in the saddlebag. Crystal coins tinkling on cobbles, Gossamyr tugged Fancy along, into a walk. They would keep to the narrow streets, Ulrich had instructed. Easier to avoid a patrolling guardsman, or a ruckus.

"My wife wanted to come to Paris," Ulrich offered in the quiet of their walk. "I promised her the trip when Rhiana was old enough to manage the travel."

"How young was your daughter when you…disappeared?"

"Two years. That was a little over a week ago. And twenty years ago. She was this high to my knees and used to wobble when she walked."

"Did the other man—the real father—ever visit?"

"He was never found." Gossamyr looked to him for explanation but he merely shrugged. "Lydia is a strong woman. She does what she must to survive."

"Like marry again when her husband goes missing?"

"Indeed. I must concede it was good for them both to have a man in the home. A female needs a man—well, unless she be a faery warrior. I cannot get the enormity of what has occurred into my skull. It yet aches."

"You have had but a week to grieve. Your wife has had twenty years." Gossamyr used the measurement with growing knowledge. She was little older than twenty years. So odd that Ulrich had lost the length of her lifetime, and yet, they were peers.

They walked onward through the dark streets, Fancy's hooves a singular echo in the night. But close, the whisper of liquid called to Gossamyr's senses. "What is that sound?"

"Hmm... The Seine! Filthy and muddied, the river is the life-line of Paris."

Yes, but where there was water... "Might we step down to the river? I'm in need of a splash. I hadn't chance to quench my thirst in that tavern."

"Sounds perfect." Ulrich skipped ahead and pointed out a stone staircase at river's edge. "Though I wouldn't swim in this brew," he called as he descended the wide limestone steps. "It's an awful mix. 'Course, I could endure a splash myself."

Gossamyr paused on the top step as she watched Ulrich skip down the wide stone stairs and bend over the brown waters to dip in his hands. Twenty years. Stolen. Unthinkable that any fée could be so cruel to one who had merely stumbled by accident into Faery—even Shinn.

"We are a mischievous lot," she muttered.

Tying Fancy to a post near the stairway, Gossamyr then descended the steps, taking each wide level in a skip.

The saddlebag abandoned behind his feet, Ulrich poured hand-fuls of water over his face. Kneeling forward, he had to check his balance. He didn't want to take a dip in waters rumored to receive the king's privy, the Greve's victims, and any other waste the city dumped in it. It did not smell bad. But neither did the taste rimming his tightly closed lips entice.

But bone, it felt refreshing to wash away the day. Too much had happened, and his confession to Gossamyr had only dredged up misery. He regretted his life for the family he had lost. If only there were some way to take back control, to return it to how it should be.

Only a fool entertains foolish thoughts. He must accept—

"Yeow—"

The snarling beast that leaped for Ulrich's head had not in mind for mental suffering. Jaws wide and long fangs bared, it spat drool and slimy water as it neared Ulrich's face.

FOURTEEN

Gossamyr spied the kelpie as its oval nostrils emerged on the calm surface of the river. It approached with stealth; kelpies were not known to attack. It was the werefrog clinging to the kelpie's head that set Gossamyr sprinting down the wide steps to Ulrich.

She reached the soul shepherd as his upper body submerged. Lunging, she managed to grab an ankle. Struggling fiercely, Ulrich fought the werefrog underwater while Gossamyr strained to keep hold of his ankle. If he was pulled completely underwater, the kelpie would swim over him and weight him down, drowning a fine feast for the werefrog.

There was nothing on shore to anchor her foot to. Gossamyr leaned back and managed to pull Ulrich with her. An arm slashed out of the water, spraying the sky and her with water and frog slime. An abbreviated yelp was instantly drowned.

The werefrog sprang up from the surface. Jaws dripping blood, it twisted its fat slug body and dived. In the next moment two arms slapped the surface.

Gossamyr gripped Ulrich's hands. He grasped hold—good, he

was still conscious. She tugged and struggled with his weight and the slippery limestone that was more intent on serving as a slide than good purchase.

"Help!" Ulrich clung to the limestone, fighting against the unseen werefrog, which most likely clamped on a leg with fangs as long as a man's finger.

"I've got you!" Gossamyr called. "Do not thrash about!"

"It's chewing off my leg!"

Her grasp slipped from his left wrist. Ulrich slid back, submerging to his chest.

The werefrog sprang into the air.

Using her free hand, Gossamyr grabbed her staff and swung. Bits of violet frog splat the walls of the riverbank and her face and the water surface.

The kelpie's nostrils sank. Ripples undulated away from the river's edge.

Ulrich, gasping and moaning, clung to the limestone.

Gossamyr levered him up and out to lay like a drowned rat upon the stone. She went immediately to his leg. Below the knee, exposed bits of flesh and blood revealed a neat bite, but small, considering the width of the werefrog's jaw.

"I think you'll live," she commented, but went to ripping off the shredded part of his sodden hose to tie about the wound.

"What…" He coughed and choked and spat out drool of vicious brown water. "Hades!"

"A werefrog," Gossamyr answered. "Just rest." She swiped a hand over her forehead, dislodging a chunk of frog. "It is dead."

"Werefr—" And he fainted.

Fine and well— Gossamyr swung, smashing her staff upon the chattering fangs that inched toward the saddlebag. The action sent the leather bag flying against the wall. It opened and out spilled the alicorn.

"No!" Gossamyr lunged for the horn and tipped it back inside the bag with her fingers.

A scan of her surroundings sighted frog bits, but none moving. Tucking the saddlebag to her stomach, she looked over the river's surface. Be the werefrog as irascible as a revenant?

Deep in the lush wilds of the Valois woods, in the exact center of the dense forest, sat a circular wattle-and-daub cottage with a low door to protect the inhabitants from charging marauders. A meadow thick with dandelion kites, the buzz of pollen-laden humble bees and gold coltsfoot blooms flourished twenty strides from the cottage.

In the center of the meadow stood a brilliant white stallion, its moonlit mane carefully twisted into witch braids and its tail protected from ill deeds with the same.

The beast lifted its head, pricking its ears. The very fabric of the universe had suddenly…sighed. And following that sigh fluttered a keening cry only the beast recognized. It snorted in recognition and twisted its head toward the sound. South. Toward the village with so many dwellings and many more people.

No Enchantment there. Save the one fragment of the beast for which it had been longing.

Soft white dandelion kites stirred into a fury as the stallion stepped into a cantor, and then a gallop. It sped toward the cottage where the fée man who had cared for him over the years stood with his arms about his mortal wife, both taking in the warmth from an evening bonfire.

Dominique San Juste startled out of the embrace at the pounding arrival of his equine companion. "What is it, Tor? Did a humble bee sting you on the flank?"

Tor bowed before the man, beckoning he mount his back.

"Looks like he wants to take you for a ride," the female said.

"Very well." Dominique slid onto Tor's back, his long black cape slipping across the stallion's hindquarters. "I—yeow!"

Tor took off. The faery's parting words to his wife were but bumpy gasps.

"I will return to you anon! Easy, Tor. What be the hurry?"

And then the sensation of recognition was abruptly cut off. But the unicorn did not cease. He knew the direction he must journey to become whole.

Ulrich claimed an uncle, Armand LaLoux, who lived behind les Augustins in a dark little corner of the right bank that sported a baker's shop and a plume dyer. Monsieur LaLoux would offer bed and some fine cooking, for he worked in the baker's shop stoking the fires, and was always bringing home new creations.

Gossamyr wondered how fine the cooking could be after Ulrich explained that the constant warring between the Burgundians, the Armagnacs and the English kept food scarce and the prices high. To Parisians bread was precious, for the milled flour was imported from outside the city. Often the flour was ransacked before a brave seller could even broach the massive gates. Leeks and field roots made up the diet.

Appreciation for having grown up during a peaceful time in Faery grew as they navigated the inner walls of the city. Alms beggars rushed in throngs, grabbing at her tight wool sleeve and tugging her staff. Gossamyr shoved gently at an elder man with a face so black with dirt she first guessed him one of the Moors Veridienne had sketched in the bestiary.

"Keep your head up and walk swiftly," Ulrich muttered. He slid a hand into Gossamyr's free hand and directed her steps. He limped, but had not complained since they'd left the shore of the Seine. Likely putting the incident with the werefrog far from thought.

Overhead, the flutter of the fetch's wings occasionally captured a glint of moonlight. So it had returned. Not soon enough to catch Ulrich's attack; good thing. Shinn would question her inability to protect her travelmate from danger.

"I should give them coin." Gossamyr dodged to avoid stepping on a child, a dirty adult-size shirt hanging from its thin shoulders. "Ulrich, you cannot turn from their need."

"Can you perform a miracle of loaves and fishes with your mutable coin, Faery Not?"

"I don't understand."

"It means, no, you cannot. You have but a few disks of faery coin in your purse. Of course you cannot increase it. Can you?"

She shook her head.

So she pressed ahead, clinging to Ulrich's hand and using Fancy to part the crowd. They were trailed for a few steps, then the crew veered off, likely in search of more giving marks.

"How does your leg fare, Ulrich?"

"Those fangs were like needles, a straight pierce and then out. They did not tear the flesh so much, so I feel little pain."

"Either that or your leg will fall off before we find shelter."

"Be you the bearer of such fine tidings, my lady?"

"Sorry. Methinks it is this gown. It binds and digs into me. I will split the seams anon."

"I shall keep watch for a string of laundry. If you can wait until the morning, the shops will be open. All the braies your coin can purchase."

"Very well."

Gossamyr followed the trail of a fat rat as she strode alongside Ulrich and the mule. The rodent looked overly plump, not sleek and speedy as the meadow rats. Truly, this city of evil corrupted even the vermin.

High above, the shadowed shape of the fetch reassured. She wished the fetch worked both ways, that she could get images from Shinn. But, alas, she could not connect to the fetch, much as Shinn had attempted to teach her the mind-share required. She mentally sent blessings to her father. Be he lacking in enemy revenants to battle.

Beside her the soul shepherd sucked in a breath. She sensed Ulrich's leg did hurt, no matter his concessions to lacking pain. Interesting to find both a kelpie and werefrog here in the city of no Enchantment. Had they been called up by a magical spell?

Where in this tangle of humanity did the succubus hide? Shinn had not known, beyond that she lived deep in Paris. Gossamyr could guess the Red Lady would place herself at the perimeter of the city, far from the draining influence of the mortal population. But the perimeter seemed to be the most violent, attracting brigands and cruel Armagnacs.

Might there be a central gathering location where the Disenchanted congregated? Fée were attracted to splendor and elegance. They would not be found in filth and destitution such as Gossamyr had seen upon passing through the gates. A palace, surely they would insinuate themselves into the court.

Startled back to the now by a touch to her shoulder, Gossamyr looked in the direction Ulrich pointed. Here the streets were quiet, save one single man fit out in finery and staggering as if soused.

Skipping across the wide gutter gurgling down the center of the street, Gossamyr approached the man who clung to the corner of a building. He moaned and spat blood. A dueling injury?

It wasn't until Gossamyr got right up to the miserable wretch that she saw his stare. Now she assessed the fine gold stitches darting up and down his slashed doublet of crimson plush. Gold chains swung at his hips, decorating a graceful stretch of limb.

He groped through the air in an attempt to clutch at her. She dodged, yet moved right back into his face to study his eyes. The red did not drip down his cheeks but instead clung to the eyeball as a convex shield. Close then, she thought. Death stood near. Though, why the unfortunate things did not immediately die was unclear to her. Why did the succubus not directly take the essences? Or had this one merely escaped? The one in the village had gotten far away.

Looking about, Gossamyr scanned down a narrow alley that was nothing more than a whisker of space between towering buildings. Something rustled within.

"Watch him," she hissed at Ulrich, and dashed into the shadows. When the rustling became a scramble she picked up speed and thrust out her staff, catching the man who ran away under the chin and effectively pinning him against the rough stone wall. A black leather hood shadowed half his face and covered his head, save a wisp of unnaturally red hair.

"Who are you?"

Even with the dim light that poured through the end of the alley where Ulrich knelt over the dying man, Gossamyr recognized her captive's face. It could not be!

The entire world slipped from beneath Gossamyr's feet.

FIFTEEN

To find this one man in such a place? Memory flooded with glimpses of happier times: a sensuous discovery, followed by a heart-wrenching betrayal. Swaying, she fought against a sudden rise of dizziness.

The man she held pinned with her staff kicked out, a bare foot jabbing her in the gut. In his right fist clacked a conglomeration of—Gossamyr slid a look over the gleaming instruments—pins.

But the man. *Him.* He— Did he not recognize her?

"Gossamyr," Ulrich called. "Methinks he is soon gone!"

"No!" Her quarry struggled.

She did not relent, keeping her staff tucked under his chin.

"It is time!" he moaned. "Release me!"

"Did you injure that man with those pins? Tell me!" She pressed closer, staring deep into his pale eyes. Violet. And yet, each blink glossed them over with a receding sheen of red. Curving around his left eye were fine pinpricks of red, forming an arabesque design.

Was it truly? It could not be! Yet, her heart knew. *Banished.*

"Ave—" She choked on the name. Three days of tears. Never

again had she wept. She had not thought to ever see him again. "Do you not recognize me?"

A globule of spit hit Gossamyr's neck. She twisted her staff, wrenching a yelp from the man. Pins scattered and dropped to the ground in a sinister clatter.

It could not be coincidence, this—this fée who smelled of summer flowers and blood and who wielded sharp pins had been lurking so close to the dying fée. Was he connected to the Red Lady? The succubus's signature gleamed in the man's crimson violet eyes. Mayhap he had received her killing kiss? What manner of weapon be those long pins of steel? This man had been...

So close.

A stolen tryst.

More than a tryst. True love?

Faeries cannot love.

Why then did her heart ache so?

With a bend of her elbow, Gossamyr lowered the staff and jammed it into the man's gut. He doubled and sank to the ground. Long groping fingers curled about the carvings wrapping the end of the staff.

"Look at me!" she commanded.

The pin man jerked his face up at Gossamyr's command. Eyes narrowed, he stared at her, looking so deep and yet, skimming but her surface. Did he see her? Know her? How could he not?

"Remove your threat, wench!"

"It is me—" she crouched before him "—Gossamyr."

"He is gone!" Ulrich shouted.

Gone? Dead. A long suffering death, so unlike the immediate *twinclian* that signified a normal fée death. And the reward for such suffering? The revenant would soon claw from the body.

Blight, but she hadn't time for reunions. But oh, how her heart pulsed to watch this tatter of a man look upon her. Such confusion on his face. He did not recognize her! He could not have forgotten.

Reaching to shove back his hood, she stopped when he snarled. Brilliant crimson hair sifted across his shoulder. Red as blood. It had never been that color. Black, black as crow wings 'twas what it should be. Could she be wrong about his identity?

"Quickly!"

Gossamyr turned to Ulrich. The soul shepherd, one hand clamped to his wounded leg, gestured madly that she join him. Vacillating between his urgent pleas and her troubled heart, Gossamyr surrendered to the mission. She pushed up and stalked back to the street. With one last look to the pin man—how had he come to such a state?—she bent over the body. Red streamed from the dead fée's eyes and bubbled up in his pores.

"His essence," she said. "Ulrich, can you…see it?"

"Unless the fée are different—and they well could be—the essence should not be visible."

"But…can you feel it?"

"Get away from him! I must witness!" preceded an attack to Gossamyr's back. The wily pin man jumped her shoulders and gripped her loose hair like reins on a horse.

"Cease!" she shouted, but to no avail. Hands at her temples yanked. Strands of hair let loose in pinching pulls. She swung her shoulder to the right, but the man wrapped his leg about her waist. Impossible to put a bruising blow to him.

To Ulrich's favor he did deliver a punch to the man's jaw, only to dodge a steel pin slashed through the air. Her angry passenger sprawled across the cobbles, Gossamyr spun an *arret,* but stopped, arms falling to her sides at sight of Ulrich's frozen state.

The bespelled soul shepherd whispered, "What in all of Hades?"

Gossamyr turned to the dead man and witnessed a most remarkable sight. Emerald light quivered and jelled and began to rise above his head.

"I guess you *can* see their souls," Ulrich said, awestruck.

"Make it go back in the body," Gossamyr hissed.

"No!" the man with the pins cried.

She snapped out her staff, catching him across the gut. The blow sent him reeling into a spin against a wall. Red hair spilled about his face. His hand, pin held gleaming, stretched to follow the floating green light. "Lost!" he cried.

'Twas the fée's essence. It shimmered with glamour, gorgeous in its undulating movement, slowing rising from the body until it hovered eye level with her and Ulrich.

"I can feel tendrils of the former life," Ulrich said, his left hand thrust before him. He moved his fingers delicately, as if stroking the essence, but not touching. "Very much like our souls. But this one, it knows where it is to journey."

Of course it did. 'Twas the final *twinclian*.

A searing red pain erupted in Gossamyr's cheek. Slapping a hand to her face, she spied the retreat of the steel pin and the fleeing heels of her attacker.

Blood streamed in the lines of her palm. He had cut her!

"How could he?"

That he did not remark her, or even remember?

The tremendous ache that had been planted in her heart not so long ago pulsed, reminding of the bruise that would never heal. *He is a Rougethorn. Never will I allow that sort to court my daughter.*

"It's so beautiful." His vision fixed to the green light, Ulrich backed up and walked right into Gossamyr.

She shoved him away and staggered. The fact she had taken a cut so easily astonished her. That it had been by a man she'd long thought lost to her, a man she had loved—

"You're hurt? Let me take a look."

"No, I must follow him." She vacillated between the shimmering essence and the retreating pin man.

The light suddenly dispersed, stretching and thinning until it was but a shimmer of fée dust sifting to the cobbles. No revenant. This death, though prolonged, was true.

"The final *twinclian*," Gossamyr whispered. "I think that one is safe," she decided. "The pin man did not get the essence so the revenant was not released. I hope."

Pin man? Her Avenall? It *had* been him. Red pinpricks circled his left eye. Banished. Just like the Red Lady. Could the red hair be a side effect of banishment or a taint from the Red Lady's *erie?*

She skipped down the street and looked around the corner. Moonlight trickled across a line of laundry and the curious stare of a mongrel mutt sitting on a doorstep. "Where did he go?"

Ulrich strode up behind her, and she walked right into him. "Watch out!"

"Let me look." He gripped her wrist so tightly Gossamyr paused and granted him her attention. He touched her cheek, imbuing her stiff jaw with a settling softness. "It looks deep."

"No deeper than the bite marks on your leg. I must go."

"No." He squeezed her wrist. "He's gone. And you are injured. We must wash and stitch it. There may have been poison on the tips of those pins. We will to my uncle's home, it is not far from here."

"The pin man," she whispered. "'Twas him. He serves the Red Lady, spearing the essence on his pins. He…I…Ulrich, I know that man."

"You have such friends?"

"Once a friend. He has changed."

"A fellow faery?"

"Yes. He was—" A lover, or very close. The only man she had ever desired. The one man her father had banished in a fit of rage.

"First, rest."

"Ulrich, there is no time to pause, we must pursue…"

Blackness snuffed out her words.

Ulrich caught Gossamyr's limp form in his arms. Her weight was fée, much like her history. More faery than mortal, he thought now as he turned about in the center of the street, scanning for the escaped pin man. But so mortal in that she was not invincible. If she had plans to rescue Faery from an evil succubus Gossamyr required rest.

"He's gone," Ulrich said to himself, satisfied he'd searched, then tugged Fancy along behind him. His leg did pain him, but he would not reveal such. This refugee from Faery needed him to be strong. As he needed much the same from her.

Ahead, a crowd of clothing hung low over the street. Leading Fancy through the rippling fabric he acquired a man's pair of braies. Faery Not would be pleased.

Pins jangling and his left leg dragging behind him, the pin man entered the lair of his red mistress. Cowering already, he feared her wrath. He had returned without the essence. Fury would design her rage deliciously.

Stopping beneath Malchius, he wheezed out huffing breaths. Something oozed down his back. No matter how he wriggled his shoulders the becursed boned plate continued to inflame. But pain cried louder from elsewhere. He'd taken that blighted staff right across the thigh. Mayhap the leg was broken. His mistress could heal him—but for his bare pin, she would not.

That cruel warrior bitch! She had looked at him so strangely. Peered deep into his eyes, as if gazing into his very essence. She had commanded him as if they were familiar. Something about her had...compelled.

Ah! But he had not an essence to see into now. Least not inside of him.

He stroked a finger around his left eye, tracing the indented impressions of red, the mark of the banished. He could barely claim the name of his tormentor—Shinn—but for the pain he would never lose that memory, as he had lost so many other memories.

Shinn, a great lord of…somewhere…had banished him for…
something.

Faery, 'tis whence you hailed.

Yes, of course, Faery. An obvious deduction, for the wings that
endured the scratch of bone on his back. But difficult to recall the
reason why he'd been banished. He did rack his memory at times.
Just, *placed here,* was all he could summon. And he was changing.
Daily. Becoming something he knew. Comfort in his servitude. Red
capped his head and moved down past his shoulders now; but a
hand's-width of black hair remained.

He blinked a few times. A flicker of a different world—a different time—birthed in his vision. So beautiful, shimmering with
a fine mist of iridescence and coiled about by a massive and intricate system of…roots? Spectacular.

As she had been. *She?*

Banging his head against the marble wall, he fought to touch that
elusive sliver of memory. It lived there inside his brain, he knew,
but all thoughts were focused exclusively upon the task. And upon
his mistress.

Catching his palm against the cool white marble, he paused outside the door to the Collection. Flame held by Dionysius flickered
and seeped into his nostrils. The naked pin burned cold against his
cheek. No possible way around it; he was puppy toast.

The scent of his mistress's perfume, a heady mix of myrrh and
lemon, with a trace of dusty blood, swirled out from the crack between the door and the wall. She knew he had returned. No beckoning call for him. He had once already been led to the kiss.
Remarkable, she had commented that first time. They shared the
mark of the banished. However, she knew the reason for her banishment—had detailed the tragedy many times over.

Why could he not recall his?

Threading his fingers through the crack between the door and
frame, the pin man crept closer, easing the heavy door open with

his shoulder until the brightness of the room hurt his eyes. Never did she light candles. He could not explain the supernatural illumination that followed the Red Lady about, but she lighted every room she entered. Faery glamour, to be sure. A glamour only possible thanks to the many essences that kept his mistress alive— staving off the Disenchantment.

How he prayed for freedom. Perhaps a return of his memories?

As the pin man wandered out from the hall seven marble heads turned to follow. One stony watcher grimaced to reveal sharp teeth. A snort set the claw-held candle flame to a shiver.

"Come, Puppy."

The tone of her voice set his pulse racing and his mutinous desires to an expectant simmer. Excitement shivered through his being. She would expect him to stride in and prick the wall with a pin. Could he mime the motion? Mayhap she would not notice, for already there were so many pins.

"You've been a naughty puppy."

Clinging to the wall, his palms attached like barnacles, he slid inside the room.

Violet eyes surrounded by the snaking pattern of red dots locked to his. Not a smile on those cherry lips. Nor a frown. Oh, but he preferred some sign of emotion! Sprawled on all fours, creeping across the massive bed, her robe slid open to reveal the bone-white flesh and those delicious breasts he could suckle at for centuries. Too pretty to fear and too evil to love.

But oh, did he venerate her.

"Where is it?" She slid to the end of the bed, her legs flowing over the edge and her bare toes dangling. Twinkle twinkle, her toes tapped expectantly at the air. *Plunge forward, and suck them into your mouth. Love me, serve me.*

Resisting the urge to prostrate himself, the pin man remained at the wall, eyeing the glimmer of essences to his left. Wincing, he cringed, waiting the pain. Sure punishment.

"There were in-tru-truders," he muttered. Of a curious sort. *Did* he know that woman? Sweat purled down the side of his face. So intent she had been. Like she *needed* him to know her.

"What?"

"Intruders, my sweetness. Two mortals." 'Twas difficult to make himself any smaller. "They...kept me from the essence."

And then it struck. Flayed by invisible needles, the pin man screamed at the agony, feeling his flesh open and pour out his ichor. His muscles tightened then released. The floor caught his writhing limbs. Spasms bent and doubled, and then stretched him full-length. Palms slid through seeping—

Never any ichor.

Not even an open wound. He dripped out pain through his brain. It hurt there in his thoughts. She made him feel the torments without the physical wounds.

Bloody red bitch.

Strangled by the agony, the sudden creep of softness across his cheek stirred him to look up. She stared down at him, a sneer the closest thing to disapproval. He gripped her ankle, forcing his mouth to soften from the painful clench to kiss her foot.

All pain ceased. He collapsed at her feet, still clutching the cold white ankle. Whimpers, humiliating and unstoppable, leaked from his throat.

"What was it this time? An angry mob?" She tapped the foot he did not hold. "You disappoint me, pin man."

He cringed, hating it when she used that hideous moniker. Not an affectionate title.

Rolling to his back, he fixed his eyes to the one yellow light pinned higher than them all. *Mine.* Escape. A bittersweet end to the end he lived forevermore.

"'Twas a woman," he murmured, "and a man. She was strong, mistress. So strong!"

Where before had he seen that exotic brown stare?

"She kept me away while the Disenchanted one expired. I tried. I scrambled, I fought, I—I kicked!"

"But *she* defeated you?"

Keenly aware of his mistress's annoyance, he realized he had not come away without a prize. Scrambling to his knees, he shuffled in his pin sheath and produced the one tipped with glistening blood. Displaying it for his mistress to inspect, he smiled greedily. "Her blood."

The Red Lady strode closer, her alabaster skin supple and dancing with the colors of the undulating essences. Bending, she sniffed the pin, but made no expression of remark. And yet, she lingered over the point of silver, wondering perhaps?

"You can scent her?"

"Most definitely." He smiled up, waiting approval.

The Red Lady drew a finger along the length of the bloodstain, not touching, just discerning. "Good, Puppy."

Swinging around, she strode to the bed and stretched out across it. Patting the mattress beside her, she beckoned.

He needed no further encouragement. Scampering onto the bed, he tucked his head against her stomach and lifted his face to kiss the underside of her breast.

"A woman?" she said, threading her fingers through his hair. With a jerk, she directed his attention up to her eyes. "Mortal?"

"You would know if she were not."

"Indeed. Certainly it is a female's blood. You said there was a man?"

"Yes. He let the woman fight for him."

"Hmm… Handsome?"

Nettled at that question, he lapped at her nipple, producing a delightful shiver from her. "Not so very. He is ugly and pale."

As she pushed his head down to her loins, she cooed and stretched languorously across the satin bedding. "But…a man. Perhaps he will soon answer my call."

SIXTEEN

Gossamyr startled awake, to feel a tug at her jaw and a hand gently press her prone.

"Settle," Ulrich said. "Don't move your head. I wanted to put a few stitches to the cut on your jaw. You were out for some time."

Scanning overhead, she saw heavy oak beams, black with soot. Wide, rough ceiling boards seeped hardened plaster from above. Ulrich's face obstructed half her view. Inside, somewhere. Sliding her hands down the strange fabric—ah, the tight brown wool— her palms smoothed over the surface of the bench she lay upon. Sweet ash burned close by, fire crackles snapping.

"I don't need stitches."

"You do unless you want a scar." He smiled. "Such a warrior, my fine faery lady."

"I don't have time." She pushed up and straddled the bench. A glance to Ulrich's leg spied crusted blood below his knee. The hose were cut just above the knee to reveal a bare, hairy leg.

"I stitched myself," he reassured. "While you were out."

"Healer is another to your list of talents?"

He shrugged. "A man like myself can never be satisfied unless he is constantly learning." She shoved away his hand, needle and thread ready. He set the needle on the table beside a lit candle. "Very well, but you will need a poultice to that cut."

"If it is not too smelly." Testing the cut, Gossamyr touched it but felt no blood. It stretched from beneath her jaw to midcheek. "Healers are a rarity in Faery."

"A difficult profession?" He sorted through an array of brown glass bottles gathered at the edge of the trestle table, deciding on one with a smeared label and dark, clumpy contents.

"No. There are not many injuries, nor is there plague or common sickness."

"What of battle wounds?"

"The fée heal rapidly. Rarely are a poultice or surgical methods required."

Now she noticed the old man who sat across the well-swept room, his hands crossed in his lap and head bowed. Plain clothing, torn but neatly patched, and white hosen, with a hole in the largest toe. Thick white hair curled about his ears and brown spots littered his nose and cheeks. "Sleeping?"

"Indeed. My uncle Armand. Sleeping is a hobby of his—of course, it is late."

"What are those spots on his face?"

"Age, Faery Not. It is common for the elderly to display their trials and wisdoms upon their hands and face."

Tilting a curious eye upon the snoozing old man, Gossamyr wondered what the spots would feel like. That wisdom was revealed so clearly? Impressive.

"He gets around fairly well for his blindness," Ulrich said. "And he stews up a mean ale berry with sops."

"That is the smell? It is sweet like berries."

"Ale and spices and some such." Ulrich touched her jaw with a cool substance that smelled like mint. "I'll just smooth a thin layer on. There. It'll make the skin contract and knit together swiftly."

Did Shinn witness their companionship through the fetch? Her father would surely rage to see this mortal man touch her so often.

Let him watch, Gossamyr thought. If she were to serve Glamoursiège in any form, surely knowledge gained from this mission, and her introduction to mortal interactions, would prove a boon.

"Thank you, Ulrich."

"I did my best, but I still think it'll leave a mark."

"No worry." Her fée blood would not aid the healing. She bore a scar on her elbow to prove that. "Where are we?"

"At my uncle's."

"Yes, I've been introduced. But where?" Sight of the open saddlebag redirected her concern. Gossamyr shot across the table, slapping her palms to either side of the alicorn, which lay exposed across the black cloth. Bits of the horn lay in the folds of the cloth. "It is disintegrating?" She looked to Ulrich.

The man swiped a hand over his chin and winced. He looked off toward the fire. As if he had not heard her. There by the alicorn lay a knife.

"You cannot!"

"Just a few bits." Hurriedly, he rolled up the black cloth and clutched the alicorn to his chest. "It is required to help you locate the Red Lady."

"Required? You have damaged a sacred—"

"Gossamyr." He clamped a hand on her knee. So stern his face became, she ceased protest. "Do you wish to carry it?"

She shook her head.

"Then it is mine to own until I locate the unicorn. I shall do with it as I please."

"But—"

"Worry about your own troubles, woman." He shoved the alicorn into the saddlebag. "You could have been murdered had I not been there after you fainted."

"I did not faint. I've never fainted. I just…don't faint."

"Of course not. You are a warrior, a champion on a great and mighty quest—"

"Ulrich."

"Very well, but you were exhausted."

"No, I—" When last she remembered, she had to let the pin man go—without the essence.

Avenall? Her bruised heart had pulsed when she had looked into his eyes. Eyes that did not see the woman Avenall had once courted against Shinn's wishes.

Why did he not remember her? Did banishment erase a fée's memory?

The warmth of Ulrich's touch to her chin, to direct her gaze up to his, startled. "There is no harm in admitting you needed a bit of rest, Gossamyr. You've forged onward relentlessly since we met in that enchanted woods."

"But the pin man—" How strange to refer to one she had loved in such a manner!

"I searched after you fainted. There was no sign of him. You really think that strange being can lead you to the Red Lady?"

"I know he can. And he isn't strange!"

"He was there for the essence, wielding pins like a porcupine beast. His hair…it was unnatural red."

"That tells little of his alliance."

"Speaking of hair." Ulrich sat beside her on the bench and moved the tangled snarls of her hair back over her shoulder. "I've a comb. Mayhap I could plait your hair? I used to twine Rhiana's little braids. Even so young she had lots of hair."

His smile started in his eyes, attracting her to the pale blue iris like a flower to the sun. Impure, Ulrich would be termed by the fée. A mere mortal.

A mere mortal who had tended her and taken her to safety. And now he offered to tend her hair, as would a servant. It was odd to think it, but he reminded her of Shinn. A man who loved his daughter, though Ulrich's love manifested in tangible touches and emotion. Yet, they both regarded their daughters as the world. Did he offer that side of Shinn she would never have? The loving part?

"I think you will not find what you're looking for in my eyes."

Blue, so blue, and drowning in stark white.

Gossamyr startled, following with a chuff of mirth. "What makes you think I am looking for anything beyond the Red Lady?"

"How can you not be searching for something more? You've no home, no family, no place to call your own. And what of this wanderlust mother? Surely you must search for her?"

"There is no need to quest for a mother who did not love me."

"Mayhap she simply did not know how to love."

"Faeries are the ones who rarely love. Veridienne was mortal. She left Faery of her free will, leaving me behind."

"Yes, you mentioned something about a strange call?"

"The mortal passion. It is what called my mother away from me when I was yet so small."

"I am sorry you were not given the unconditional love you desired. Every little girl deserves love."

Gentled by his statement, Gossamyr nodded an agreement she wanted desperately. She had known love. From her father. Had she desired more than what she'd been given? Never. Until it had been taken from her arms. "Shinn loves me."

"Ah yes, so much he sent you off to your death."

"Death will not be mine." A grip of the air at her side did not place the staff to hand. It stood propped by the wall next to the door. "I will return home after the succubus is defeated."

And now there was Avenall to consider. Could she connect with him, make him see beyond the red gloss that filled his eyes? Would he remember her if she Named him? Of what use would the Naming serve if banishment would hold him for ever a prisoner of the Otherside? Unless the Red Lady had discovered a means to return. Why else would she collect the essences if not to gain enough glamour to serve her return to Faery?

A glance to the black cloth wrapped about the alicorn. So much the Red Lady could do with this powerful symbol of Enchantment. That Ulrich had damaged it...

Ulrich stood and went to a small carved box placed on the hearth. Drawing out a wooden comb he displayed it, his eye twinkling.

"Tip back a cup of aleberry wine, and let me work the tangles from your nest."

Before going at her hair he poured her a cup of wine from a dented pitcher. Inside sloshed a pale liquid that smelled of berries. It tasted weak but not awful.

Gossamyr closed her eyes. To the alicorn. To her immediate troubles.

The sensation of Ulrich's careful fingers touching upon her scalp, easing a comb through her hair, calmed. He started with the ends and combed so carefully she did not once wince from an aggressive tug. So many kindnesses he had offered to her.

He began to whistle a quiet tune, not waking the slumbering old man. Gossamyr could picture the soul shepherd sitting with a youngling on his knee, tending her curls. And the lightness returned.

She lifted one foot from the floor and pointed her toes, stretching out her muscles. Closing her eyes, she held out her right arm and tilted up her palm to wiggle her fingers.

"Feeling better?"

Stirred from her lull, Gossamyr reached for the aleberry wine. She swallowed back the wine and swiped her forearm across her lips. Lifting her right foot to fold across her left thigh, the brown wool rode up to her knees. She guessed her exposed legs were not seemly and stomped her foot back down.

Soft fingers strode along the surface of her scalp, following the wake of the comb. A prinkle fluttered along her neck. Ulrich weaved lovelocks into her hair. A mortal prince imprinting his favor with every twist of his fingers.

Would her future husband ever be so gentle? Could Desideriel open his heart to a wife that could never be what he wanted?

"So, Faery Not, tell me about your family. There is your father and mother. You left behind no…other? A…fée man you cared for?"

"Mayhap."

Gossamyr again closed her eyes…

Three suns and three consecutive moons witnessed her heartbreak. Tears flowed from her eyes, trailing warm streams down her cheeks and into her clothing. When her fine arachnagoss gown had saturated, the bed linens took on the sad liquid.

When on the third day Shinn finally entered his daughter's bedchamber, tears dripped from the bed frame and into a puddle upon the blue marble floor. No shimmer sparkled in the pool. When Shinn's toe brushed the edge of the liquid a mournful cry echoed up from the floor.

Her tears flowed without effort; mayhap she could no longer stop them. She did not know; she did not care.

"Please, child of mine, cease your mournful tears."

Gossamyr lowered her head and studied the pool that had begun to spill across the floor. So much then she had loved? Yes love, not the false love faeries know.

"I now know how you felt when Veridienne left," she said.

"Nay, you do not." Shinn's weight settled beside her and Gossamyr allowed him to lift her hand into his.

"I loved h-him." A choking sob pushed out a rapid purl of teardrops. "You will never understand."

"It is done. I…reacted," Shinn said. "I should have first listened to you."

"And then banish my lover?"

"Gossamyr." He pressed his forehead to the back of her hand.

Tentatively Gossamyr touched her father's head, trailing a finger over the short horn and around it as she had done so many times when she was younger, curious and fanciful.

Fancy had been murdered three days earlier by her father's ruthless lack of regard. The attribute that had made him a lauded warrior and commander of the now-defunct Glamoursiège troops also made him a devastating foe to his own daughter's heart.

"We are both alone now," *she said finally, resolute in her courage.*

Unwilling to forgive him, yet feeling in her heart the need to keep her family close, Gossamyr tilted Shinn's face up to look at him. "Perhaps love is not so favorable after all."

"Gossamyr? *Mon Dieu,* I wager Faery Not *did* leave behind a lover. Oh, Gossamyr?"

She blinked out of her state and homed in on the singsong tone of Ulrich's voice. He stood close. "Too close," she said and stood up and pressed her combed hair from her eyes.

"You left a lover?" He tipped the comb to his lips in thought. A nod confirmed some knowledge she could not know. "Mayhap that is what has hardened you so."

"What mean you?"

"Well, you are a warrior. Emotionless. Set on your course and ready for fight."

"One must dampen emotion to retain battle instincts."

"I see. Yet, so young and pretty to become a warrior. Pity." He patted the bench before him. "Sit and allow me to braid your hair. Just one braid down the back, yes?"

His hand, flat on the bench, asked so much of her. To sit. To place herself in his hands. To trust.

"So long as 'tis out of my face, it is bone." She did trust him, and so sat with her back to him, both legs to one side of the bench, as she deemed proper for a lady in a gown.

He started at the back of her head. "Tell me of this abandoned lover."

"He is—" swallowing at the sudden dryness at the back of her throat, Gossamyr pressed a palm along the cut on her jaw "—the pin man."

"What? You mean…"

"Yes, the man with the pins and the unnatural hair."

"But—truly? He is a faery?"

"Yes. Shinn found us together and banished him."

"For having relations with his daughter?"

There was a hint of tease in his voice. That he should ask such a bold question!

"We were not…having relations. But close. Shinn had refused Avenall's request to court me."

"Why?"

"Because he is a Rougethorn."

"Your father doesn't like Rougethorns?"

"It is like your Armagnacs and Burgundians. Of the same race but with differing beliefs. It is known they dabble in magic. After the Netherdreds, the Rougethorns are the most scorned tribe in Faery."

"I see. And yet, you continued to see Avenall?"

"Of course! He did not dabble. Avenall had come to Glamour-siège with his family when he was very young. 'Twas merely a fact of his birthplace that my father claimed him unfit to court me. Such ignorance!"

Ulrich tugged gently on her half braid, bringing her eyes back to stare up at him. "If you were my daughter I would have locked you up and tossed out the key."

"I would have screamed."

"Of course, Shinn could not deny you a thing, my spoiled faery princess—and I mean that in the kindest manner. So, to remove his one sore spot Shinn had no choice but to send away your lover."

"My father claims not to believe in romantic love. But I do."

"Is love such a unique concept to one from Faery? Do not the fée love? Or do they simply mate and exist?"

"I have told you they seek their life mate, and live together ever after. I feel sure love is mortal. How can it not be? But it is different for royalty and the upper caste—our mates are often chosen for us. And yet..." She thought of her father's choice. "Shinn chose Veridienne to wed."

"So he must know romantic love. To sacrifice for the love of a mortal? Was he not looked upon sorely for such a choice?"

"I had never noticed such when I was younger. It would not be wise to question the lord of Glamoursiège's actions."

Ulrich's fingers stopped, his palms resting upon her shoulder. "And yet your father is alone now?"

"Indeed."

"Perhaps a punishment for his loving a mortal woman?"

"I...had never thought of it that way." Had her father sacrificed for his love? He'd never implied that Veridienne's leave had been required, or forced. No more so than the resistance of the mortal passion made it a forced leave.

That this mortal man could conjure her to question her beliefs startled more than a little. So much he did claim to know of love. And to have it stolen from him.

Ulrich's touch called to her in a manner that did not trouble so much as intrigue. The light steps of his fingers working the braid down her back made her pause, counting each twist. Faster than her heartbeats; he had mastered the skill most impressively. Best not to pay attention to such a call.

"Think you there is a stable close by that will sell me a fine mount?"

"Just around the corner. Your faery coin still shiny?"

"It is."

"That's bone. And I am finished. Pluck that leather cord from the saddlebag and I'll secure it to keep you from spilling these luscious tresses."

Gossamyr smiled. The man should watch his words and the breathy tone with which he pronounced them. On the other hand, his comfort and lack of discretion around her made him real. No falseness to this man.

She twisted to draw out the leather cord, but Ulrich laid a hand over hers and settled onto the bench beside her. He still held her braid, and laid that hand upon her shoulder. "I don't know that this will matter at all to you." He clasped his fingers about hers and pressed it over his chest. Soft brows straightened and he bowed his head so close to hers, he might nudge her with his nose if he moved too quickly. "You have become the world to me, Gossamyr. You have been my companion for mere days, you have stood boldly and faced danger, and you seek a noble goal without veering from your path. For as confusing as you faeries make love to be, I love the woman that you are. It is a mortal love, mayhap more companion-like than romantic. As it should be."

"Ulrich."

"But…it could become romantic, should you allow." He kissed the back of her hand and with a sigh, stood and began to gather his things into the saddlebag. "Hungry?"

"Yes." Tracing a finger around the warm portion on the back of her hand where he had kissed her, she kept her silence. There was nothing to say. Her Faery heart protested his easy mortal confession.

But her mortal blood verily ached for the passion that had led her to journey to the Otherside.

After finishing a trencher of morning sops offered by the old man with wisdom spotting his face, Gossamyr pushed the empty wood bowl to the center of the table and, clasping her hands, bowed and rested her forehead there. She drew in a deep breath. Wine and burnt bread. Her mind aswim, she could not think to hold conversation with Monsieur Armand, for thoughts of her confession to Ulrich still haunted.

Never before had it occurred to her that Shinn might have sacrificed Veridienne for the crime of loving a mortal. Not a real crime, a punishable offense. But certainly those who did take a mortal mate were shunned. Unless, the fée was a great lord, wise and noble, who commanded respect no matter his liaisons. Shinn had loved. Deeply.

Of course the fée knew love! Gossamyr had loved. She had been loved. She was *still* loved.

It could become romantic, should you allow.

So the man did favor her? And why had she not immediately set him to right last night? Tell him there was not an inkling of interest in him on her part.

Could she Be here in the Otherside? If you Believe you will Belong. Surrounded by this air! Falling into the nuzzling warmth of the hearth fire. Holding hands with a mortal man…

No time! The Red Lady lurks and gains more power with each moment that she won from Time.

Peering at the top of her hand, Gossamyr traced the area where Ulrich had kissed her. Mortal touched. So fine. The voice that had initially bothered her now whispered inside her thoughts, deep and gentling—ever present. The weight of her braid, trailing down the center of her back, reminded of his careful attention. She would keep it so.

"You wish more, my lady?"

The old man held out a splayed hand. He sat at the end of the table. Ulrich was not to be seen yet this day. Bone. For she wasn't certain what reaction she would make to seeing his pale blue eyes, offering promises of romance.

"I've had enough, thank you, Monsieur Armand."

"Ulrich tells me you are in dire need of proper attire." He gestured to a chest near the hearth, where a soft yellow gown had been lain across the curved lid.

"Oh, but I couldn't," Gossamyr said, even as she stepped over for a look.

The fabric slid smoothly under her brushing fingers. Some sort of silk, though it did not possess the iridescence of arachnagoss. The neckline and bell sleeves were trimmed in a thin swath of brown fur. She could not guess at the animal, but sleek gold highlights glinted as she petted the softness.

"It is old," Armand offered. "My wife's. She passed decades ago."

"It is gorgeous. But——" Far from practical for the fight that yet waited her.

"Please, you must wear it for an old man's memory. I thought to sell it at the Monday market, but those greedy hawkers would never pay the coin it is worth. Ulrich tells me you would wear it well." He stroked the soft white hair of his beard. "I will take it as an affront if you do not accept."

Already holding the gown before her and checking its fit—the shoulders looked to span exactly to match hers—Gossamyr stepped over to Armand, gown held to her chest, and leaned in to kiss him on the forehead. "I accept. On one condition."

"Anything."

"I require braies, as well."

Armand chuckled. "Yes, Ulrich did mention your penchant to fight. He placed braies aside for you, but I'm afraid you'll still require the gown."

She thought of the saddlebag, where her purse yet rested. To give this man her mutable faery coin would be worse than his receiving an unfair price at market.

"Help him," Armand said.

"What?"

"My nephew. Help him to move on, is all I ask in repayment."

"To move on…where?"

"You know he has suffered. And now he seeks. You can help him find that solace."

I hope you discover the solace to the ache that has been your nemesis. It could become romantic, should you allow.

"I…will. Thank you, Monsieur Armand, I will dress right now." She stepped inside the cove of the doorway and within a leap of the man, tugged the brown wool from her body.

"My nephew tells me you quest?"

Dress spilling over her arms, Gossamyr nodded eagerly in response. "Yes. I seek…" Vengeance, valor, truth. "Truth?" The word had sprung from her mouth, unthought. Since when had she claimed truth over valor?

"Looks like it has already found you."

She returned to the table, preening over the soft fur at her wrists. "I don't understand."

"Sometimes the truth can be in your hands, yet you see only the dust from the road. Your past."

"You see nothing, old man." Then she blanched. Of course he could see nothing.

"I see Faery, splendid and bright."

"Truly?" Had Ulrich told him her origins?

Armand smiled. "I have been there. The last thing I looked upon before the Faery prince took away my sight was the emerald water flowing down a falls amidst a rocky outcrop glittering like diamonds."

The falls at midcenter of the Spiral forest. Many times she had swum in the waters, always fearful the rush of current would tug her under, but loving that fear for the adventure it proved. Of course, there were surely other falls throughout Faery.

"Why were you punished so? Did you enter Faery of your free will or fall into it?"

With a throaty chuckle, he explained, "I plotted and planned for decades, since I was a young boy. Finally I caught me a faery and bade him bring me to his home." He clasped his arms and brought them to embrace across his chest. Reverent in his memories. "He did. I lived there for what seemed like years. I would learn later, here in this mortal land but a day had passed. He indulged me in

sweets and kept me as his pet. Then as recompense for his show-
ing me the delights of Faery he took my sight and banished me."

That word—banished—how it etched at her heart. *Like red
pricks to flesh.*

"I remember his name...Shinn."

Clutching the gown between tight fingers, Gossamyr looked to
the floor.

"The Faery prince showed me the dark side of Faery. 'Tis a far
crueler place than Paris will ever be. I fear not the Armagnacs nor
the English." The old man laid a finger aside his nose, sniffing. "But
should I smell a faery I will turn and race far away, blindness be
damned."

If he could smell a fée... Had Disenchantment taken the scent
of Faery from her?

Troubled he was not struck by her presence, Gossamyr put it
off for a more immediate worry. She knew Shinn was generous
with his favors and ruthless in his repayments. That Armand had
tricked him required return punishment. And that Shinn had
granted Monsieur LaLoux the pleasures of Faery before stealing
his sight was his manner—his very right as a Faery lord.

"My nephew tells me you are the child of a mortal and a faery."

Gossamyr traced her neck; the blazon was no longer there, having been washed away in the stream by the windmill. So far from
home. Lost... "Yes."

"But you are more mortal than faery?"

"You...do not scent me?"

Armand tilted his head, appeared to be sniffing the air, then
shrugged. "It has been a time since I have been so close to one from
beyond. Wicked place, that."

"There is a balance between right and wrong. Good and Evil.
You cannot have one without the other, old man. Faery is no more
wicked than this mortal realm is pristine."

"Indeed."

She strode to the door, but clutched the frame, unwilling to dismiss him as would Shinn. "I am sorry for the loss of your sight. Where is Ulrich? We should be off."

"He is in a dark mood. He sits up the ladder dwelling on the past."

As she passed by, Armand grasped her wrist. His fingers were cool and veiny, loose with age. "Listen to Ulrich, and do not judge. Do not be blind to what he can offer you, child of the faeries."

SEVENTEEN

Skirts tugged to her knees, Gossamyr ascended the narrow ladder to the attic room mired with a dull light from the waxed window set into the gabled peak of the roof. She paused on the top rung and knelt on the floor, sure Ulrich remained unmindful of her presence. A fine sheen of dust coated the warped wood-slat flooring. It smelled like the musty underside of a toadstool. Simple this home, crafted of wood and bare of luxury, far from the cold elegance of marble. But she felt comfortable here.

Or was it the entire atmosphere that embraced with welcoming lightness?

Ulrich's footsteps made marks across the floor. Peeking around the corner, she spied him in shadow for the sunlight blurred dimension, but his hosen called out in bold defiance—yellow and black now; the left leg yellow, the other black—for he'd found replacements for the pair the werefrog had destroyed. He caught his forehead in his hands and let out a keening moan.

Gossamyr stiffened. Oh, these mortals and their delicate emotions!

"Gossamyr?" He snapped a yellow knee up to his chest. "I should have known. Only you could sneak up that creaky ladder without a sound. That gown!"

"Your uncle gave it to me. But see." He nodded as she revealed the braies—but she noted his lack of enthusiasm for her secret fortune. "Do you wish to be alone?"

His sigh settled heavily in her heart.

"I was thinking of her."

She tiptoed across the floor and crouched beside him.

Shrugging his fingers through his hair, a restless motion, Ulrich smirked. "I owe Rhiana twenty years."

"You missed those years, but yet…she did not."

"Logically, I should accept that truth. But logic has served me no boon of late. Hades, I should have remained in St. Rénan and…I don't know…slayed the bloody dragon! I might have saved her, Gossamyr! Don't you understand?"

"Dragon slaying be a miserable task." Rarely did the beasts come to Faery. And should they, they were revered and welcomed.

Ulrich gasped, clutching at nothing before him, but his shoulders sank as if a giant stood upon them. "Do you have no feelings? No emotions? Don't you know what it is like to feel guilt? Remorse?"

"Unnecessary feelings." Feelings she had known, surely, but would not succumb to their crippling force. She turned and tried to focus out the waxed window but it only allowed in the light, not a clear view.

Behind her, Ulrich rose and beat a fist into his opposite palm. Within a heartbeat he'd gone from agony to a strange anger.

"A man's greatest fear is loss of his family. For without people to love you, what can a man be?"

The time has come to release you from a father's protective obsession.

"To have family ripped from one's grasp, it is…devastating."

"Yet still you live." She spoke the statement, but thoughts of her father's devastation filled her vision. Still he lived…but for how long? Why did he rush her to marriage?

"What?"

"Your greatest fear has come to fruition, yet you remain standing. The fear did not defeat you, so it cannot be a true fear."

A frustrated clench of fingers shuddered near Ulrich's cheek. "How to make you understand? I have been changed, and I don't like the change, for it finds me standing alone, without hope."

"You've hopes of finding the unicorn. Your family may yet be returned to you."

"Never again the same, Faery Not. Never again."

Likely not, for a man's wish could not reverse time and place his wife at his side and his infant daughter in his arms. For would not the entire universe have to move widdershins, as well? A monumental event. Surely even a unicorn's Enchantment could not make it so.

Ulrich's only hope was to save his daughter from death. Twenty years must remain a sacrifice for what? A reunion with a child who might never recall her absent father's face?

"What do you fear, Gossamyr?"

"Hmm? Me, fear? Oh. Well…I… Nothing." Toying a fingertip in the soft fur circling her wrist, she attempted to dredge to light an answer. Despite his disbelief in her capacity to feel, Ulrich's fear was understandable. Loss of family? Not ever seeing her father again? Her heartbeats increased even to consider such. "Mayhap…losing a limb?"

"That is a ridiculous fear."

"Not so! A champion cannot—" That she claimed that title with such ease. Who be she but a lost bit of fée dust? Lost. *Without family*.

The prinkle returned to her spine. Ever there, that unease and uncertainty.

"You throw up physical walls of protection against your true emotions, Gossamyr."

He stepped beside her. Now she could verily feel the blood of him rushing through his veins, furious and bright. A match to her own inner turmoil. Fear?

"I think you fear feeling."

"Nonsense." How had he come to know her very depths in so little time? "I can feel."

"No."

"Yes!"

"She is dead, and I am not," Ulrich hissed. "And…it hurts. I made promises to Rhiana. That I would care for her, see to her education and upbringing. Now she is gone from me, I can never have her back. And I cannot imagine what it must have been like for her, to wake one morning to find the one man who should have been there for her gone. Do you know what it is like to love? To have loved and lost? Do you?"

"I have loved!"

"Oh? Ah, yes, your parents. The mortal mother who abandons her own for her pleasures, and a Faery lord who blinds an innocent man for his trickery!"

"How dare you!"

"Who would have thought I would meet up with the very child of the faery who destroyed my uncle's life."

"It was mischief that destroyed your uncle Armand's life!"

"That is his penance not mine. But do you see? Just as me, you fear loss of family. And look: Now they are lost to you."

He approached, stepping too close for her comfort. The angle of the roof prevented her from moving back. The length of her skirt was too long; her heel stepped onto the hem, jarring her to the side. "How does it feel, Gossamyr?"

She did not like his tone. She did not want this conversation. Not this thread of misery to be stretched out before her and plucked like a lute string. He thought to know her fears? *Yes, and what are they?*

Believe and you Belong.

Where *did* she belong now?

"Step back," she warned.

"No." He shoved her shoulder. "Does it hurt? Can you feel it? Right here." He laid a palm over her chest, between her breasts. "Here is where it all coils up and simmers, yes? Tell me you have emotions, Gossamyr. Tell me you are not some freak faery who masks her feelings and blinds men to satisfy their lust for mischief. Do you want to push me away?"

"Yes, blight you!"

"Bone! That is anger. What of pain? What will you do to show me your pain? Kick me? Knock me down with your mighty staff?"

"I—I will do you no harm."

"Nor will you step from your safe past to be. To feel! Gossamyr, feel! Be! Dare to be like me, a mere mortal who wants and needs and aches. What if I were to kiss you? Right now?"

"You speak nonsense." She stumbled but caught herself against the rough wood wall and slid to the right, closer to the ladder. The man followed, relentless in his futile mortal ramblings.

A kiss? That had naught to do with the angry emotions of which he spoke!

"I hunger, Gossamyr." He gripped her. His fingers splayed about her shoulders—revealed by the low-necked gown—claiming her in a way that added a shiver to her frightened heartbeats. "I hunger to take you right now. To pour my grief into you. Just…to share a part of me that aches. Can you understand?"

She shook her head. What had mortal lust to do with pain and grief? He was acting the devil he appeared.

"You hurt, Gossamyr. You ache. You weep. You can love. Show me! Show me your loss!"

"I have loved! And I have vowed never again to cry for such a loss!" She slipped from his touch and rushed to the ladder.

"All that pain," he called as she exited the room, "it gets caught up inside you, Gossamyr. It must come out sooner or later. It should have been sooner for me," he cried. "Mayhap Rhiana would still live."

Skirts lumped up about her waist, Gossamyr thundered down the ladder and outside. She did not break stride until her palm connected with the rough bark of a chestnut tree coved into the miniature courtyard out back of the house.

Huffing and blinking, she forgot to keep back the stream of tears relentlessly stinging. Salty liquid splat her nose and lips and seeped down her throat.

What had he done to her? She was not like Ulrich. He carried useless emotions for an event that could not be changed. The past would ever remain untouchable. He could never bring back his daughter. And yet he punished himself with hopeless desires. There was no sense to that!

Smearing the back of her palm over her cheek, she then stared at the wet on her flesh. Crying? No! She had expended that fruitless emotion long ago.

I know how to feel. I have loved!

And she had vowed to never again feel for someone so strongly…

From the corner of her eye she spied Avenall. Why did he not flee?

"Father, I—"

"Silence!" Shinn moved his gaze from Avenall to her, down her face and over her robe, which she clutched between her breasts. Could he know? But for the telling color of Avenall's wings he must know! "This man I have forbidden from seeing you stands in my home?"

"Forgive me, lord—"

"You have begged my forgiveness once, Avenall…of Rougethorn. I thought to respect your humility, but I see it was for naught. You lied to me when you promised you would not continue to court Gossamyr. You have debauched my daughter?"

"No, I merely—"

"*We were but kissing, Father,*"*Gossamyr offered hastily. "Nothing more.*"

Shinn tilted his head. Hard violet arrows shot through Gossamyr's heart. Betrayal, they spoke. You have betrayed me. His disappointment hung in the air like a choking cloud.

"*I...*"*Avenall managed. "I will leave.*"

"*You will,*"*Shinn spoke,*"*be punished for this betrayal. You swore you would not seek my daughter's favor.*"

Gossamyr cringed at the command. Rarely did Shinn raise his voice. Please, do not hurt him, she thought. Do not wound him.

"*For betraying my trust,*"*Shinn continued in the same abrasive command,* "*banishment!*"

"*No!*"

Gossamyr spun to Avenall. The Rougethorn fée stiffened, caught within Shinn's mighty glamour. He cried out as the red pinpricks of banishment bore through his flesh, circling his left eye and for ever marking him.

And with a sweep of Shinn's hand, Avenall was carried away, over the balustrade, up into the crystal sky, and finally he twinclianed in a minute shimmer.

Aghast and completely stunned at her father's quick and cruel punishment, Gossamyr stood there shaking, staring off into the sky. Her jaw hung open. She could not comprehend. Avenall had been here, in her arms, kissing her, loving her—now he was gone.

"*No,*"*she murmured, and swung to beat her fists against Shinn's chest. "Bring him back! You cannot send him off for loving me!*"

"*Love?*"*Shinn spat out a vicious snort of laughter. "Go to your room, daughter. Be gone from me now.*"

He actually shoved her from his body. And Gossamyr, lost in the devastating rush of the moment, fled from her mother's study.

But oh...it did ache there...right in the center of her chest where Ulrich had touched her bruised heart. Gossamyr clutched at the gown, her fingers filling with the soft brown fur. Seeing Avenall in the market square had shaken off the shroud of indifference she had built up. Emotions were mortal. Unnecessary.

Truly?

You fear loss of family.

She was all alone. So far from Shinn. To Be seemed the greatest challenge.

That Shinn had banished a Rougethorn… The only reason her father had the ability to banish one not of his tribe was because Avenall had lived in Glamoursiège since he was very young. He had lived in Glamoursiège longer—and so he was considered a citizen.

Avenall. The one man who had loved her had looked through her as if she did not exist. The Red clouded Avenall's vision.

Yet Ulrich saw her clearly.

He touches a part of you that does feel, the mortal part that knows emotion before your fée instincts ever could.

It would be simpler if she were completely fée.

You fit into the air here. No one looks upon you with a disdainful sneer.

Sliding down against the tree trunk, Gossamyr squatted and caught her forehead in her palms. Tears flowed through her fingers and dropped to the ground, wetting the soil.

Ulrich pushed away from the small triangle smoke hatch where he watched Gossamyr struggle with tears. He was halfway to the stairs, determined to rush outside and comfort her, when he stopped, and returned to the window.

"Let her cry," he whispered. "Let her feel the pain. It is good. You are learning, Gossamyr of Faery. Disenchanted? It is bone."

EIGHTEEN

As they gained the bell tower of St. Geneviève, Ulrich sprawled across the stone floor to rest. He had chosen the cathedral for, set upon a hill, it offered one of the highest lookouts in Paris. Excellent view of the entire city.

Having sprinted up the last dozen or so steps of the tower, Gossamyr closed her eyes and tilted back her head. The air up here was even lighter than on the ground. Sounds of humanity, the rush of horses and carts and carriages wobbling across cobbles, segued into but a hum. A nest of hawfinch chirped nearby, tucked away beneath the chin of a sooty gargoyle.

And there on the snout-nose of the gargoyle perched the fetch, its wings folded upward, obliquing in the midday sun. Always there, her father. *I have not lost family.*

She wondered now how Rhiana felt when she had thought of her missing father. To wake one morning and never again know the comfort of his presence? And, if she was ill thought by her mother, as Ulrich had explained, it must have been a lonely existence.

No, not gone, my family. Who then was she to claim such pain?

But it did pain. For she was alone, and the uncertainty of her return to Faery would not rest.

She must defeat the succubus and—then what? Would she Passage back to Faery? Where to find a Passage? Surely Shinn could merit a trip to Paris to retrieve her.

What if he were injured, or worse, the staunch Faery lord was killed battling the revenants? She would not know. Mince may not know where to find her. Had Shinn told Desideriel of her task? Certainly, the marshal at arms would never come for her.

Each day spent in this mortal realm challenged her beliefs. Where did she belong? And why had her conscious so suddenly altered?

"I hadn't realized there were so many steps," Ulrich huffed. He tipped over the saddlebag he'd carried up the spiraling stairs. "Must be hundreds."

"You are winded," Gossamyr said as she leaned over the stone balustrade and cast her eyes across the city.

"Not at all! Just—" *puff, puff* "—breathing in this fresh clear air. A man's got to do such, you know, for to tread the city, all close and dirty, tends to make one's humours sluggish."

Yet Gossamyr fancied she could leap from this tower and soar, so light and perfectly fit into this air stood she. Had she wings, flight would not require thought. One leap and she would soar over the kingdom, come hunting hawk or mighty dragon, naught would bring her down.

Dissected by the Seine, the city spread wide and vast. Narrow streets barely stitched demarcations between the dwellings. Stuffed tight within the bounds of the fortressed city walls thousands upon thousands of buildings fought story by story to reach into the sky for a breath of the light air. Great spires and towers and banners proclaiming royalty, religion and wares populated the sky. Sun glinted on red tile roofs and glittered upon the river. Great conglomerations of buildings hugged the cathedral, looking more to support than actually surround. Packed tighter than a honeycomb, the city, and as bustling and productive as a queen's hive. People were but gnats in colorful bits of fabric. Shopkeepers clopped about on red wood sabots. Archers bore a deer hung by its quarters from poles through the spiderweb of streets. Laundry flagged the stretches of cord from window to rooftop. And everywhere children scampered and dodged and shouted.

Surprising how a different perspective designed the city most beautifully. The intricacy of it all marveled. "Be that the royal palace there at the end of the island, where your king lives?"

Ulrich tilted his head, honing his directions. "I believe so. I don't much answer to King Henry myself. He is English."

"You mean the drunkards and——"

"And tails, my lady, indeed! One country isn't enough for him; he's got his grubby mitts on Paris, as well. Pray either the vulgar Burgundians or bloodthirsty Armagnacs take this city soon."

"You don't care which of the two?"

"So long as they are French, no. Though I do favor the Armagnacs, simply because our unseated French king sides with them. The village I am from is under his reign. He's a good king, so far as kings go."

Gossamyr propped her elbows on the balustrade behind her and eyed Ulrich's sorting about in the saddlebag. "Glamoursiège has been a place of peace since I can recall. Unlike the Netherdreds we value peace."

"Sounds like your Netherdreds would get along well with the Armagnacs. That is the tribe the Red Lady hails from?"

"So far as I know."

"What was the tribal name of your Avenall?"

"Rougethorn." She pronounced it as Avenall had. Rogue—Torn. A cad's dashing mannerism.

She looked down into Ulrich's expectant gaze. Stirring within the pale whites of his eyes swam a glitter not unlike mirth. It beguiled Gossamyr. Change had crept between them. In addition to being fascinated by her surroundings, Gossamyr found Ulrich held interest. A man alone and on a heartfelt quest. Of the tribe Mortal. An intriguing race.

"What the hell is that?"

She followed Ulrich's gaping stare to the gargoyle's chipped nose. "The fetch. You've seen it before. I've explained—"

"Yes, but you said it was a dragonfly." He stood. The sudden movement caused the fetch to flutter its wings, so Ulrich stilled. He embraced the air, pointing, but uncertain whether to let out a cry or swallow back a shout. "It be a dragon!"

"The size of a fly," Gossamyr said with a shrug. "What troubles you?"

"You! Faery! Tiny dragons and man-eating frogs?" He drilled his fingers into his hair and stretched out the curly strands. "What next? A hornless unicorn?"

"If you are vigilant."

A sigh preceded his accepting nod. "Indeed." He propped his elbows on the balustrade aside Gossamyr. A glance to the fetch— both summed up the other. "What wonders I have known and wish to ever erase from my eyes."

"The fetch is not so remarkable."

"So say you, lady from Faery."

She stretched her hand before her to encompass the city. "Here be true wonders. So many eating, sleeping, dancing, making love."

"Fighting, killing, maiming."

"Skipping, birthing and growing."

"Dying."

"Ulrich."

"I know. You see the wonders of a new world. I have closed mine eyes to all but strife."

"Anon," she offered. "Your heart will change if you see her again?"

He swung a bemused look at her. "Yes, anon."

Stretching out her arms, Gossamyr tilted her body forward. Standing on tiptoe, she moved with the sway of the air. Flight, she had never before known the sensation.

"Faery Not!"

Groping for the balustrade, Gossamyr teetered forward as Ulrich caught her ankle, catching her from a sure fall.

"What in all of Hades? Think you to fly?"

"Of course not." She smirked and made show of clutching the balustrade for support. No, and yes. Flight? What a dream.

Sighing, she knelt beside Ulrich to watch him sort through the various items within. The wrapped alicorn remained tucked inside the leather bag. After defeat of the Red Lady, there was the matter of returning the sacred object. Could she convince Ulrich to hand over the alicorn to her? Had she any right? It was his find. Only he held the power to claim his wish. And what a wish it was. Faery owed Ulrich for his stolen years. Haps 'twas intended the alicorn fell to Ulrich's hands as repayment for his suffering?

A mortar and pestle rolled to tilt against Gossamyr's toe. Tucking aside her skirt, she lifted the heavy polished bowl and smoothed her fingers inside the convex stone. "No wonder you're exhausted. This weighs half a stone!"

"Only now is the woman aware of the suffering I endure for her." He gestured she hand him the mortar.

"You suffer naught for me. It is for your distressed damsel whom you quest, and that is the proof of it."

"Indeed." He emptied a cloth bag of flaked herb into the bowl, but paused. "Do you think it wrong?"

"Most certainly. You cannot bring back the dead."

"And yet, you implied earlier it could be done."

"Be it possible to bring back the dead does not make it right."

Ulrich nodded. "And you can kill a soul sucker in the name of Faery, but that doesn't make it right, either."

"I will kill her. And it will be right. She threatens Faery, Ulrich!"

"And how do you plan to stop her murderous rampage? That stick of yours tends to only knock a man out for a time. She'll bounce right back up and suck out another soul from your Disenchanted brethren."

Leaning back on her palms, Gossamyr toed the base of the stone baluster. "I hadn't considered the method I would use to stop her."

"Truly, my lady, you continue to astound me. What was your father thinking to loose his spoil—"

"Don't say it. You do not know the truth of me."

"True, I do not. Yet, do you know the truth of yourself?"

"Of course I do. I am Gossamyr from Glamoursiège."

"Merely a title. You quest, fair lady. But not for blood. You seek. We all seek."

"There isn't a thing to be sought." And do not go on about my lack of emotion, she thought. She wasn't prepared to descend into strange territory this day; she must focus on finding the succubus.

From a tiny piece of twisted leather Ulrich dumped some fine shavings into the bowl of herbs. Had he intention to—

"You cannot!" Gossamyr slapped a hand over the bowl of glimmering shards. "It is sacrilege."

"Gossamyr, it is blasphemy merely to stand atop this cathedral and perform magic. On the other hand, magic and the church have a secret liaison far stronger than any Inquest will allow you to believe."

Cringing away from him, Gossamyr clung to the stone balustrade. Magic! A fée who participated in the deed participated in the destruction of the very Enchantment that was their life.

"You know magic harms Faery?" she whispered. The soul shepherd did not regard her as he continued to sort through the items. The black cloth was tilted over the mortar to sift the particles of alicorn into the mortar. "No!"

She leaped to slam her hands over the mortar.

Ulrich gripped the bowl and met her defiance with a leer of his own. "Now come, I cannot press it back onto the alicorn and hope it sticks."

"It is forbidden for a fée to dabble in magic."

"That is well and fine, for I am no faery. Let go! You needn't watch if that is what troubles you. Do you not want to find your Red Lady? Just a little magic to locate the succubus who threatens all of Faery?"

She relented and sat back on her haunches. Clamping her palms to each opposite elbow, she remained stiff. Surely it would be fine to tap a bit of Enchantment so the entire realm of Faery might be saved?

Would that she had stopped him before such destruction. He'd shaved the bits from the alicorn at his uncle's house; likely when she had been passed out—er, sleeping.

Always the Rougethorn tribe had been tolerated, but Shinn had never chosen to join troops for a tournament. Tainted, they were, for their dabbling. Yet, Avenall had been just like any other fée who had lived in Glamoursiège.

Ulrich ignored her, whistling quietly as he went about his magic. He was but one single man, and he had claimed to merely know a bit of magic. He be not a wizard or mage.

Gossamyr's curiosity got the better of her. She broke her stiff pose. "This spell will track the Red Lady directly to her lair?"

As he began to pulverize the mixture to a fine powder, Ulrich nodded. "I shall perform a discovery spell. It will track and mark any with Faery ichor in the city."

"What if there are more than the one?"

He shrugged. "Are not all Disenchanted?"

"Yes, but their ichor remains Faery."

"Your Red Lady is Enchanted bethanks to those stolen essences?"

"I believe so."

"Then she should shine brightest. Should at least give us clue where to begin the search. Darkness would have served far better to sight the charm, but clouds mar the sun this day. Trust me, Gossamyr." He touched the hem of her sleeve. In his eyes danced a trust that overruled the illicit touch. "I will help you locate this red lady."

She moved forward, bending, and brought her face directly before his—close enough for Faery. "And in return you expect me to lead you to the unicorn?"

"Sounds a fair trade."

"What if I refuse?"

Ulrich sighed and leaned back against the curved stone wall of the tower. "Then I wager I am on my own. But you may yet favor a guide."

"You are no more familiar with Paris than I, soul shepherd."

"Think you? You do not know the truth of me, faery princess."

With that curious comment, he unwrapped a length of dark twisted plant leaves. Cranesbill, Gossamyr guessed, for the pungent odor. A charm for the eye.

You commit a foul sin against your own!

But could it be so wrong if it ultimately served to save Faery from a dire fate?

"I do this for Faery, and Faery is my home," she whispered, "so I do this for myself. Selfish…"

"Yes, yes. But what makes Gossamyr of Glamoursiège happy? Do you even know?"

"A silent soul shepherd, 'tis what gives me happiness."

"Sorry, can't help you there."

"Can you be quick about it?" She scanned the sky, her sight fell on the fetch. "Shoo!" She flapped her hands, but the fetch remained.

"Your father watching?"

"He once banished a man from Faery simply because he was a Rougethorn. Rougethorns dabble in magic."

"I see. And so, your father will see you dabbling? Through the fetch?"

With one eye to the keenly perched fetch, Gossamyr vacillated for but a moment. "It is what must be done."

"I like you, Faery Not. Have I mentioned that? You're bold. And you sparkle. Now." Ulrich stood and handed Gossamyr the mortar. 'Twas heavy and cool in her palms like a river stone dredged up from the muddy depths. Inside, a fine dark powder glimmered much like the fée's natural blazon. "If you'll hold this while I summon the elements?"

"You can do this?"

"Have faith in me, fair lady." A glance to the fetch narrowed Ulrich's eyes. "Shinn, do not fault your daughter for this magic. It is a necessary device to locate your villainess." He tipped a wink to the fetch.

With a tilt of his head and a shrug of his shoulders, Ulrich began a strange ritual. 'Twas as if he were shaking and loosening every limb in his body.

Gossamyr watched with a mixture of doubt, mirth and interest as the soul shepherd went into a remarkable concoction of gyrations accompanied by strange humming. He spread his legs and shook out his arms and shoulders, the movement traveling to his head as he rotated and worked it upon his neck. Finally he snapped to a position and hummed. "Hmm… Hmm, hmm, hmmm."

Never had she witnessed such display. Once a wizard—a practitioner of magic—had infiltrated Faery and had been given the guest treatment by her father. She wondered if the old wizard still danced the endless dance. 'Twas very possible. The mortal had no right to enter Faery unannounced; that punishment had been fitting.

A funny noise brought Gossamyr's attention back to Ulrich. He blew air through his mouth, vibrating his lips. Just what were the requirements for magic?

Eyes closed, Ulrich then clapped together his palms. His arms splayed back behind him, he gave a jump and a spin to face her. Arching his back, he opened himself to the air. Spreading his arms wide out to his sides, he beckoned the elements and began the low hum in his throat.

"Spread far, dance wide, become my eyes." With a decisive nod, Ulrich silently took the mortar from Gossamyr and held it high above his head. "Track the faery souls—"

"Essences!" Gossamyr interrupted.

"Er... *essences* hidden in the shadows. Sift through the masks of the common and illuminate that we wish to see. So mote it be!"

The mixture inside the mortar fluttered upward, spiraling into a glittering swirl. Tiny stars fallen from the heavens, Gossamyr mused, seeking to claim their original position. A gust of warm summer air dispersed the spell. She dashed to the balustrade and stretched out her arms. The particles danced and swooped and began to descend over the city.

"It is working," Ulrich whispered.

"You are surprised?"

"Yes!"

Unaware of how close the man stood, Gossamyr jerked her attention from the bespelled particles and looked upon Ulrich's face. Awestruck, he watched his spell take shape. Slack, his open mouth revealed the gap in the upper row of brilliant white teeth. Not a single line of age traced his flesh. Very near to her age? Not with a daughter grown and gone. And yet, he had not lived those stolen years. Mayhap they two were peers?

She touched his chin, fine stubble wobbled under her finger pads. Startled, he turned to her, and Gossamyr repressed a sigh. There in the centers of his dark pupils glimmered a spotlight, the origin of the bespelled particles. *Exotic.* She tilted her head, meeting Ulrich's mouth with her lips.

Softly she accepted his kiss. Like fire sparkles to her being, the connection quickened through her. Prinkles of energy snapped all along her extremities. Buried desires emerged. She felt want, a pining, seductive want.

This mortal passion, it was sweet. So…natural. Easy to fall into.

Quickly, Gossamyr pulled back. The fetch was nowhere to be seen. Still lingering in the throes of passion, a smile could not be suppressed. A second brief but sweet kiss followed close behind.

"So mote it be?" Ulrich said with a charming grin twinkling in his eyes.

"I…" Startled at her brazenness, Gossamyr turned away, locking her arms over the balustrade. Still the smile would not leave her lips. In fact, a silly grin formed and she could but shake her head. "Forgive me, that was most uncalled for."

"Never."

"Ulrich! You are a married man."

"Whose wife has taken another man and chased me away with a huge, hurting stone."

Gossamyr reminded herself: The mortal was without ties. A giddiness filled her. Joy, such as discovering a secret hiding place. Yes, that be mine! I claim it.

He belongs to no one else.

She could secretly claim any man she wished. Yet she had been spoken for.

A kiss, one perfect kiss. 'Tis bone. Just…enjoy the feeling.

Indeed. Releasing a truly spontaneous smile upon Ulrich, Gossamyr said, "I liked that."

"Kissing has been known to bring great delight."

"But we must not do it again."

"Think you?" He leaned against the balustrade, casually crossing his ankles. "Saving yourself for a handsome faery man who will sweep you off your feet—literally?"

"No." Yes. The wedding had been arranged. Be the groom willing or otherwise. Face your truths! "Yes."

"What if you cannot return—" Ulrich tilted a look outward, scanning the cityscape. "Dragon piss!"

"What?" Gossamyr followed Ulrich's line of vision. Thin rays of sunlight bursting through the clouds painted the red-roof tiles a brilliant orange. Shadows stretched long behind jutting towers and chimneys. Everywhere sparkled the alicorn dust. Surely, hundreds of lights, like a midnight skyscape fallen to earth. "There are so many."

"The city is verily infested with those from Faery."

"We'll never find her now."

"Mayhap we can." Ulrich pointed toward the palace plopped at the end of the island. "Do you notice some lights are brighter than others? Only few really stand out."

"The weak ones must be the Disenchanted."

"I thought all fée in the city were Disenchanted?"

"Or very near. Perhaps the brighter are the strongest and newer fée. Disenchantment requires a few days. And if she is stealing the essence of the fée she must possess Enchantment untold. We must seek the brightest—"

"That one over there, near the Conciergerie."

"Where?" She knew not the city, nor the buildings, and followed Ulrich's directions as he pointed out next to the palace the Conciergerie—a jail, as he explained—then, across the bridge from another large cathedral, the wide-open square of the Place de Grève.

"Or there!" She pointed to a particular light twinkling brightly at the edge of the city.

"Doubtful." Ulrich sighed and settled his chin in palm. "'Tis the castle of St. Antoine—the Bastille. Another prison. I wager your bloody succubus has not hidden herself away there."

Gossamyr tried to determine where Ulrich looked now, but it seemed he stretched his gaze along *her* cap-à-pie. "What be to you?"

"Hmm? Oh. Er, *n'importe.*"

Avoiding the question. So unlike the man.

"Can you see my light?"

"Oh?"

Gossamyr looked over her body and all around and above her head. Stretching out an arm, she slid her palm over the soft yellow gown, hoping to see a glint from the spell. A frantic wave of her arm proved fruitless. The sudden disappearance of the sun behind a cloud shadowed her body. Not a glow, not a glimmer.

"I have not been marked, have I?"

"Well…"

"I am…unremarkable? Tell me true." She needed to know! This man was the only one she trusted.

"It is likely the Disenchantment. Mustn't worry, Faery N—er, my lady."

She nodded, and yet knew she had not been marked. That Ulrich would not tell her troubled. Why did he seek to protect her, and from what? The emotions he so relentlessly strove to dig up from her depths?

"I'm sorry, Gossamyr. I thought the spell would be successful."

"It has been." She squeezed his shoulder. "It worked too well. Let's begin with those sights close by."

He gathered his supplies into the saddlebag and they began to circle down the stairs. Disregarding the darkness and the cold stone, she traced her fingertips along the curving walls. The short steps and tight twists enclosed Gossamyr in her thoughts.

Do you know the truth of yourself?

Why had she not been marked? The Disenchanted had been. Was it her mortal blood? Did it alter the spell, blinding it to her fée half? Perhaps Ulrich had merely been too close? Close enough for Faery, not nearly close enough for her newly kissed desires.

"Likely we need to view my light from above," she called up to Ulrich.

"Certainly, that is the case."

As they gained the last dozen steps, Ulrich's voice was low but close to Gossamyr. "So, are we to pretend it never happened?"

Pressing to the wall and looking up to him, Gossamyr feigned ignorance. A teasing gesture. It took all her determination to keep the smile from her mouth. She picked at a tuft of fur at her shoulder. "What never happened?"

"That kiss. Two kisses, actually."

Ah. Touching her lips invited a silly grin to her face. "Of course it happened," she offered slowly. "I kissed you because I wanted to."

"Will you kiss me again?"

Blue eyes on a white sky. Exotic, he. "Mayhap. If you are worthy."

"Ah, I am always up for a challenge put forth by a beautiful lady. Were I a knight, I should wear your favor onto the tournament lists."

"Were you a knight, you should come to arms against me in the tournament lists."

Ulrich's chuckle echoed in the twisting stone stairway. His final step as he brushed past Gossamyr swept a shimmer of feeling through her. Touched. Connected. For a moment they two had spoken silently their needs. It was a moment she planned to hold for ever in her heart. A heart that would need sweet memories to endure a loveless marriage.

As he turned to bow to her, Ulrich misstepped and stumbled. The saddlebag spilled its contents.

Gossamyr lunged to catch up the mortar and pestle and the alicorn. The blade he'd been using to scrape at the base of the alicorn landed the ground at Ulrich's toe, but a hair from doing harm. Fine particles of the alicorn glittered upon the tiled stone floor of the cathedral. She scooped up everything.

The mortar tucked inside the bags, Gossamyr stood, ready to chuckle at the man's clumsiness and offer a chiding remark, when Ulrich's expression silenced her mirth.

"You cannot touch that thing without protec—" he started.
"You're holding it."

His sudden awe switched her attention to what she was doing.

"You are holding the alicorn," Ulrich gasped, "in your bare hand."

Indeed she did hold the unicorn's horn against her flesh. She'd picked it up without thought, hadn't been concerned the loose linen wrap had come off from the horn.

Not possible. She must not—

Suddenly a shock of power hit Gossamyr like a blow to the chest. Her arms stretched wide and her body tense, she stood within the vibrations, unable to move but feeling no pain. Something radiated through her being, seeping into her every pore and permeating her veins. 'Twas a remarkable sensation limned with a solemn fear.

She must drop the alicorn. This was a sacred horn. Only the pure could touch it.

"Gossamyr, are you...fine and well?"

Ulrich's voice barely edged the sensation surrounding her as if with a brilliant beam of cool light. She could not utter a reply. 'Twas as if all the magical lights Ulrich had cast across the city gathered in her breast, inflamed but not burning.

"You will lead the unicorn right to us!" he cried. "Keep hold of it, Gossamyr."

"No!" Voicing her fear released Gossamyr from the paralyzing stance. She was able to open her fingers. The alicorn landed the cloth Ulrich had kept it wrapped in.

"What be to you? Something great had begun. A signal or beacon was being sent. The unicorn cannot find us unless you keep hold of the alicorn."

Gasping in breaths, Gossamyr bent at the waist and caught her hands on her knees. "I will not be responsible for luring the unicorn to the Red Lady."

"But it is the only way the unicorn will ever have it back. Please, you must pick it up again."

"Ulrich." She straightened and, shaking off the lingering prin-kles, toed the cloth carefully over the alicorn. "I journey to the Red Lady. Any man or beast following me—particularly a hornless unicorn—will be endangered. I cannot risk it. In fact, we must hide the alicorn. Yes. Until we can return to it knowing the unicorn will be safe."

"Unthinkable." Ulrich wrapped up the alicorn and replaced it in the saddlebag. "I have taken a vow to protect this horn. It won't leave my sight."

"You *vowed* to protect it?"

"Yes."

"A few whispered words of prayer as you were being chased by the big bad evils?"

"About like that."

"Sacrilege!"

"To a faith that is not mine, faery! I will give up the search when the devil is blind. It has given me strength when I only wish to close my eyes and… Never mind." He stood and made to stalk off, but Gossamyr caught him by the arm. "It is human-emotion stuff," he spat. "Stuff you would never comprehend, so I will not bother to explain it to you." He tugged his arm from her grip and marched out from the cathedral.

Gossamyr sighed. She comprehended. And that knowing fright-ened her mightily.

After they had passed through the Porte St. Antoine, Dominique San Juste dismounted Tor and landed the cobbles. When he'd agreed to accompany Tor he'd thought the beast merely in need of a run. Not a trek to Paris. Relentlessly, the stallion had galloped straight on to the outskirts of the capital city. The beast had seemed to fly. Almost.

Now Tor stilled, pricking his tufted white ears. Clanging metal signaled slops being emptied out a window close by, and beyond that a baby wailed like the wind. With a glance to Dominique, the beast regarded the changeling with what Dominique had come to learn a very sad look.

"I know what you seek, fair friend." Dominique smoothed his palm across the base of Tor's neck. That one spot, there beneath the braided witch locks, pleased him so whenever it was itched. "I will accompany you evermore. Onward?"

The stallion snorted and pawed the ground, hooves scraping hard cobbles. Dominique remounted, and threading a hand through the witch locks—for he never reined the beast—he prepared for the ride. Tor stepped into a regal march. One step, pause to listen, and then another.

Sliding a hand up Tor's mane and leaning forward, Dominique wondered if the bare spot on the forehead of the beast wasn't shining more brilliantly than usual. Could it be Tor had finally located what he had been missing all these years?

NINETEEN

Ill-sprung, this carriage. His jaw clacked as each uneven cobble bit at the rotating wheels. The pin man drew a pin crusted with dried blood beneath his nose, remarking the scent as most curious. Female certainly, as his mistress had remarked. Though not the usual female scent. Strangely, it seemed familiar. Yet…exotic. How could that be?

And that the woman had spoken to him with some familiarity struck him harshly. She could not know him, for he did not recognize her. Much as he knew his memories of the past were blurry…

Pressing the heel of his hand to his brow, he winced as he tried to dredge up what he could not touch.

He knew he had been banished from Faery. The markings on his face were the same as the Red Lady's. But while she knew the reason behind her banishment, he couldn't conjure the memory— save for the name Shinn. And that name came to him only because his mistress used it so frequently.

Was the reason for his banishment so evil he'd blocked it from his mind? He did not *feel* evil. What be evil true? Blood and pain and wicked laughter? No. Something deeper, more visceral, like a slug that cleaves inside one's belly.

He did not subscribe to evil. Serving his mistress sickened him. The only reason he did so was because he craved freedom. And there remained the fact he had no choice. The red bitch held him in thrall, his very essence pinned to the marble wall like the others. But unlike the others she was able to keep him alive.

Still Enchanted.

The notion stabbed him like a spear piercing an iron-cold night. He had yet been Enchanted when the Red Lady had found him. She had been able to take his essence, but not his life, for the Enchantment kept him alive. A fée in a mortal man's world. Yet, he did no more feel out of place than he could fly.

So he must have fallen into the Red Lady's thrall immediately following his banishment. Not so long ago. He had only been assisting Her Divine Redness since the spring had pushed up vermilion poppies in the fields that bordered the embattled city. Intoxicating that flower's kiss, as was the succubus's kiss.

He traced a finger over the pocked marks curving about his left eye. Not deep, but permanent. Pores saturated with the Red. Not blood, but residue from Faery. *Painful. Do you remember?* He'd cried out in the moment of banishment. Small pokers searing a lasting punishment into his flesh. And then?

Do you not remember me?

He had *known* the woman who fought with the applewood staff? When? And where? In Faery? But she did not reek of Faery. It did not seem feasible…

"Need to remember," he muttered, pressing his fisted fingers to his temple.

"What did you say, Puppy?"

Myrrh tickled his nose. He sat alongside his tormentor and lover. "Oh, er, she is close, mistress. I can scent her."

"And with her the man always follows?"

"I wager so. You've only to wait, as is your exquisite role."

"Leave me then. You've the others to retrieve. Two of them for my collection. But remain within calling distance so you may track the mortal man when he leaves my arms."

"Ever your servant, most beauteous one." He kissed her lap, lush folds of scented velvet, and nuzzled his nose deep into her musky scent, then slipped backward from the carriage and silently closed the door.

"For now," he muttered.

Bells tolled in Notre Dame to announce nones. Jacqueline, Ulrich named the largest bell. Her voice carried across the city. They would first check the Place de Grève, an execution square, Ulrich had explained, just across the bridge from Notre Dame.

"An actual place for executions." A chill of morbidity choked in Gossamyr's throat. Such easy violence she had never known.

She looked over the cobbled square. Massive in size, it flanked what Ulrich had pointed out were the principal city buildings where the lawmakers and religious leaders and army generals knocked heads. A bustle of carriages and mounted riders wound through the square; unlit lanterns carried aloft on sticks dandled this way and that. A beruffled dog danced by on its hind legs, its master calling all to a comedy at the nearby theater. Here the air, soaked in stench of the Seine, felt heavier, sullen.

Leaving Fancy snuffling over a pile of rotten melons, Ulrich walked across the square, his head held high and his ears pricked.

Gossamyr slapped Fancy's flank. Road dust fumed from the dirty hide and made her sneeze. It was her first sneeze since arriving in Paris. Interesting. Mayhap she had adjusted to the Otherside?

Mayhap you belong.

She looked to the wandering soul shepherd. "Ulrich?"

Ignoring her completely, Ulrich tripped over a branch, but kept moving, as if compelled onward. He walked right before an equipage of six, barely avoiding the snap of an admonishing whip. A smithy cradling a horse's hoof in his black apron looked up at the sight, shook his head, then gave the hoof another pound. Scorched iron scented the air. Five long strides carried Ulrich into the shadows, where he disappeared into a narrow alley.

"What in all of the Spiral?" Tugging Fancy along, Gossamyr trotted across the square. Keeping her head down she dodged the crowd without rousing concern. She did not know to fear the English or the French more, and so obscurity was wisest for this lone woman.

The alley was narrowed by a row of parked carts, empty save for a few twigs of kindling. She followed him closely, down the aisle of buildings stacked three stories upon one another. Everything was so close, too close for a faery. "What is it, Ulrich?"

"It's so…beautiful."

At his slow recital Gossamyr dropped the mule's reins. The hairs at the back of her neck prinkled. The man was aware of nothing but that directly before him. Ahead, the alley curved. She couldn't see a thing that would attract—

"More lost souls?"

Ulrich shook his head. No.

He had so suddenly changed from alert to…led. To walk through the busy square as if he had been bespelled?

Tilting her head, Gossamyr turned her ear the direction Ulrich walked and moved in stealthy side steps. She heard nothing. Thick gray clouds twinkled with rays of escaped sunbeams. The soul shepherd stretched out a seeking hand and moved onward. It was very obvious he was being led somewhere. *Not* by a soul?

Gripping him by the elbow, she tugged him to a halt. "Be you pisky-led? Close your mind to whatever it is you are hearing."

"No piskies here. Far from Faery." He tugged from her grasp. Spreading his arms wide, he encompassed the unseen. "Can you not hear it, faery princess? It is like rain on a stream. Bells ring in my head."

"It is not the cathedral?"

"No. She sings to me."

"I don't hear— She?" Her heart thudding, Gossamyr twisted around and scanned high and low. Not a single face appeared behind the dirty windows. The fetch was absent. Quiet this street. "She? Here?"

The Red Lady plied her game of seduction, luring Ulrich into her deadly embrace. As she had lured him since he'd taken the alicorn into possession. Gossamyr should have persuaded Ulrich to hide it, to leave it at his uncle's home—no, the old man was far more susceptible to a Faery *erie*.

They rounded a turn in the street, Ulrich blindly pursuing the musical call Gossamyr could not hear no matter how she strained. Her feet tripped quietly over the cobbles. Stilling the clicking *arrets* at her waist—gown or not, she would not walk the city unarmed—she skipped onward, but maintained a distance. As well, her staff was always to hand.

While she must protect the alicorn from danger, it might serve to learn the direction of the Red Lady's lair. Could it be so simple as following Ulrich?

Two mounted riders clopped into view. Sensing danger, Gossamyr hiked up her skirt and tucked portions of the yellow silk into the waist of her braies. Freedom to dash or leap was imperative.

Staff at the ready, she focused.

Twin blood horses snorted and stomped the cobbles. No visible livery. Not the watch then. Fully armored, mail chinked with the horses' movements. The steel bourquinette helmets were open.

Ulrich walked right up to them, unmindful to their drawn swords. And their red eyes.

Was the man always so oblivious to danger?

More for you. Is danger not what you crave?

"Have at me."

Stabbing her staff into the ground, Gossamyr swung up her

body and caught one rider on the head with her heels. The bourquinette flew into the air. The force of connection toppled the rider to the ground.

The other dismounted with a fluid ease, and swinging his sword in challenge, let out a banshee yowl. No humanity in that voice. But a chilling reminder of Faery. Two of the succubus's victims, then.

Ulrich, his head erect and eyes forward, miraculously dodged a wild sword slash and kept walking.

Slapping her staff into both hands, Gossamyr barely avoided a slice to the head from a seeking blade. Thrusting high, the staff vibrated in her hands as steel cut into the hard wood—and broke the fire-forged applewood in two. The force of the blow unsettled Gossamyr from her stance. Her arms swung back, a serrated half of the staff swinging in each hand. She caught herself from falling by redirecting her balance.

So easily her best defense was destroyed? A simmer of fear surfaced. *What do you fear?* No! Danger, it was hers to embrace.

A step dislodged the skirt from her waist and it fell to her ankles. Ill outfitted for this challenge. From the corner of her eye Gossamyr saw the first rider remained on the ground, groaning and pulling at his eyes with cutting gauntlets. Already the red had begun to seep from his pores.

"Ulrich, no!" The soul shepherd listened only to the silent and beguiling song of the succubus. A song that planted itself in the skulls of Gossamyr's attackers and had fruited into a wild, evil thing.

Now there! The fetch swooped low to hover over the head of the other man. He swung his sword at the creature; the fetch dodged and flew off.

Gripping both halves of defense to her sides, Gossamyr announced to the standing attacker, "Deliver your best, blighted lackwit!"

Spinning one half of the staff in her right hand, she twisted at the waist and conked the armored beast upside the head with the other short staff. The bourquinette went flying. Another twist of her waist returned a blow to the crown of his exposed head. The hard wood connected with skull-cracking impact. Momentum pulled her around and she spun the short stick to a stop, stabbing the swordsman in the gut with the serrated end, just below the hard iron cuirass. With a jingle of circled metal, Gossamyr tugged the staff from the mail. A guttural squawk quaffed out from him. He landed the ground, gripping his stomach, but was far from defeated.

Using his momentary befuddlement, Gossamyr raced to the wall before Ulrich, blocking his path with her half staff. "Don't do it, Ulrich. She is calling to you. The Red Lady!"

"So pretty," he murmured. Tears streamed down his cheeks, drawing thick runnels through his dusty flesh. Bespelled then. How to break the succubus's *erie?*

"Jean César Ulrich…"

What was the remainder of the man's overlong name? The third…something. Blight!

Gossamyr used the only form of deterrent she knew would work. She blunted the staff into Ulrich's gut, folding him and bringing him down. His palms slapped the wall behind him for stability, yet found little as he slid to his haunches.

Now an attacker fixed to Gossamyr's back, the flat of his blade cleaving into her neck. She bent, heaving the man over her head and pushing away the deadly blade as he landed the ground. Raising the staff above her head, she prepared to bring it down onto his skull—but paused.

Red tears poured from the man's eyes. The neck muscles tightened to thick cords, then released, softening his flesh. His mouth gaped, releasing a torrent of ichor swirled through with vibrant crimson.

Remembering the last time she had witnessed such a death—Gossamyr scanned the periphery in search for the pin man. Did he lurk in the shadows?

She hissed an invitation to challenge. "You want their essences? You'll have to go through me!"

"Oh..." Ulrich stirred and, using the wall, managed to pull himself to his feet.

She dashed to him, lifted her skirts, and kneed him in the thigh to effectively pin him.

"What did you do that for? Ouch." He toppled into her arms and began to retch dry coughs over her shoulder. "That is the last time I kiss you!"

"You were under her spell." She embraced him around the shoulders and held him as he heaved. "I had to do something to keep you from the Red Lady. Steady, Ulrich. You are safe now—oh, my faery heart."

"What?"

"Look."

There, behind the mule snorting at a scatter of rotting hay, lay the first unfortunate fée she had laid out. And squatting over him, the pin man, a long steel pin held in wait. No hood concealed his hair this day. Capped in brilliant red, the long strands looked to be soaked by a bloody flood. Sunlight flickered across his face. The mark of the banished curled an arabesque about his eye.

"Avenall." The name fell, a stolen whisper, from Gossamyr's lips. The fear she'd previously pushed back clambered to the fore and set her to keen attention. *See me. Remember me?*

Still holding Ulrich, and feeling his body yet convulse in protest to the blow she'd delivered to his gut, Gossamyr remained at the wall. She did not want to frighten Avenall away.

Nor must she allow him to succeed in stealing yet another essence for his mistress.

As well, she wanted him to recognize her. Was he a slave to the Red Lady? His mind trapped in her wicked thrall? Could Gossamyr broach that invisible shield and draw Avenall out from the facade of the pin man? 'Twas sure a poke to his gut with her staff would do little but rile.

A small orange light emerged from the dead fée's skull, squeezing out in a globulus quiver and expanding.

"He's going to take the essence," Ulrich hissed. "Get him!"

"I…" Yet Gossamyr remained, strangely unable to move. For to do so would require force—against her lover.

At the exact moment the pin pierced the essence, the fée's armored body jerked. The shell of flesh and bone rose from the ground. Armor cracked and tore in a dull metallic rip. Out struggled a revenant from the rib cage. With a shrieking wail, the creature soared into the sky, away from Paris. Back to Faery to torment Shinn.

Her heart stalled, Gossamyr could but witness.

Releasing a squeal of glee, the pin man turned and scampered to the other body. The fée lay but a half-dozen strides from where Gossamyr and Ulrich observed. Intent on the task at hand, the pin man did not notice them. Or maybe he did see them, which is why he worked so quickly. This time a pale green essence seeped out from the body.

"Enough!" Gossamyr shoved aside Ulrich and pointed her staff at the pin man. "Move and I strike you dead. Look at me, Avenall!"

The pin man drew himself straight, taller than Gossamyr—as she remembered—and grinned so wickedly she thought any sane man's face should crack. Holding out his arms, he displayed a pin, decorated with an essence, in the left hand. Narrowing his eyes, he tilted his head and nodded. "I make no move, my lady."

Did he surrender so easily? What to do? To strike or speak?

Gossamyr maintained her pose, the staff—shorter, but no less effective to defense—ready for instruction. Her left hand strummed the chord of *arrets* at her hip. A step forward was halted by close-fitting fabric. Blight, this awkward gown!

"Tell me how you have my name?"

A conversation? Might be the thing to dissuade him from the burgeoning essence that sought a safe *twinclian*.

"I knew you when you lived in Faery, Avenall. I know the reason why you were banished."

He gaped. So he did not know the reason behind his banishment? Most certainly, for then he would know her.

She must tell him. Mayhap win him from the succubus's *erie*.

The green essence quivered, slowly rising between them. If he moved, Gossamyr would leap forward and crack open his skull.

Studying him, she saw he was dressed in the finery of Faery. Skeleton leaves frilled about his neck, and at his wrists, fée lace fashioned of delicate arachnagoss. Yellow rose petals had been sewn for a doublet, and amphi-leather hose drew her eye down impossibly long legs. If the Disenchantment had set in, surely the clothing would not hold—

Had Shinn the ability to send the banished straight to Paris, yet still retain their Enchantment? For so long? Even Shinn feared Disenchantment with an overlong stay.

"You…" he started, the pin held firmly in his left hand. A weapon, no doubt about it. "…know?"

"Do you not remember your life in Faery, Avenall?"

"Do not continue to speak that name!"

"It is your name."

"It means nothing to me."

Gossamyr blew out a breath. Indeed, she must Name him to break the glamour. "I name thee Avenall of…"

Of. Of what? Tightening her brows, Gossamyr searched her memory. Avenall… Why could she not place his name complete? She knew this man. She had once thought to give herself complete to him.

"I must go." Ulrich rose behind Gossamyr.

She reached back to grasp Ulrich's hand but touched only the flutter of his cape. "No! She calls to you!"

A squeal of triumph shot through Gossamyr's system. Not her own rejoiceful cry.

Avenall danced, his stolen prizes glowing, one speared on a pin in each hand. "She lies, the mortal warrior. She cannot name me."

In that instant the bell of the great cathedral on the island began to peal.

"Ah, Jacqueline!" Ulrich called, raising his hands to revere the distant bell. "So prettily you toll, but I've only ears for my lady's song. So sorry."

Gossamyr struggled to maintain hold on Ulrich and yet keep Avenall in sight. The man's name! She must conjure his name to restore his memory of their alliance.

A skin-prinkling howl burst up from the ground. The revenant clawed its way out from the husk of the Disenchanted. Flesh tore and clung to the bones, one last attempt to keep the evil at bay. Muscle stretched and snapped. Armor bent and ripped. Finally the revenant was free.

She must stop it from returning to Faery. She must stop Ulrich from going to the Red Lady. She must rescue Avenall from the wicked thrall. She must—

With no apparent intent to flee to Faery, this revenant turned and yowled at Gossamyr, revealing gnashing fangs and whipping wings. The creature was twice her size and loud enough to wake the dead.

"Ulrich!" Gossamyr yelled.

The man heard nothing but the Red Lady's call. He strode from the alley, oblivious to the danger that waited. What she would offer for a lost soul to wander across his path. "Right now," she muttered. "Can you hear me, lost souls?"

"Watch you don't get your head ripped from your shoulders!" Avenall called in a macabre song. Orange and green faery lights blurred across the stone building facades, a shadow of Enchantment stealing across their sealed windows.

Dodging the revenant's lunge, Gossamyr raced toward Ulrich, then realized her mistake as she arrived on Ulrich's heels.

The revenant screeched and followed.

"Get yourself gone!" She shoved Ulrich and he collided with the wall.

A swing of her staff connected with the revenant's fist. Bone-clean fingers clamped about the applewood and jerked, winning the prize.

"I am off," Ulrich muttered. "My mistress calls."

Gossamyr dodged the swing of her own staff, feeling the *whoosh* of air part the fur rimming her neck. Death missed. Had the weapon been full-length she might have received a blow directly to her skull. But it did hit another target.

Ulrich yelped as he received the blow intended for her against the side of his head. He went down like a felled tree.

The best thing she could do right now was to lead away the revenant. Bent at the waist, Gossamyr ran toward the square, luring the skeletal beast with her. *No, you'll lead it toward people.* Gossamyr stopped, jumping to turn and face the creature. Taking an *arret* in each hand she began to spin them.

The revenant hung before her in the sky, sunlight ripping through the slashed wings and glinting on the ichor-dripping muscle shreds clinging to the ribs. A shred of mail hung from one rib bone. It wielded her staff with such ease, transferring it from one hand to the other as if a mere toy. Not mindless then. It could remain if it so chose. And this creature sought some fight before returning to Faery.

Judging the best hit for her tiny obsidian blade would not be between a rib or on the tattered wing, Gossamyr thought to try the eyes. Nothing in the skull that she could determine, but it was worth a shot.

A death cry preceded the revenant's swinging attack. Gossamyr leaned back to avoid the hit. She swung, releasing the *arret*. It

soared through the open jaws of the revenant and out into the sky.
Blight!

If skulls could grin, the creature cracked a bitter smile at her.
Swiftly it returned the staff, bringing Gossamyr down. The *arret*
abandoned on the wet cobblestones, she rolled to her knees,
clutching her gut. The staff had connected directly. But she hadn't
time for pain, for the revenant attached to her back. Strength immeasurable pressed down on her spine. Bony fingers dug between
her ribs.

The thing thought to rip her apart!

And it would. Rolling to the side, the revenant clattered upon
the ground, bone against stone, but would not release Gossamyr.
She managed to slip a hand around and grip bone. Her finger slid
into—an eye socket. She felt the skin on her back tear. A cry of
pain escaped but was swallowed by the revenant's manic screeches.

Slamming hard, Gossamyr heard the skull crack. Working another finger into the other eye socket, she held fast. Repeatedly
she beat the skull against the cobbles. Each pound released the pres-
sure on her back until she was free. She flipped her legs out from
under the revenant. Using both hands, she made to pound the
skull one forceful time but instead pulled the head off complete.

Amidst the terror, Gossamyr found herself kneeling on the
ground, stunned to be holding the skull of a dead fée in her hand.
The jaw opened and let out a yowl.

Gossamyr whipped the skull across the square.

It landed a stone wall and shattered into a glimmer of dust.
Strange to think the sight pretty, but it was.

Now a skeletal hand groped her knee. Gossamyr stretched along
the cobblestones and grabbed her staff. The tip of a finger popped
through the silk skirt and opened her flesh. Smashing the staff in
a purely desperate move, she obliterated the offending arm and
hand. The hips and legs were put to end with a fervent pounding.
Faery dust rained upon her head and shoulders and legs.

Satisfied the beast was demolished, Gossamyr flung back her arms and lay upon the cobbles, heaving and panting. Dust coated her eyelids. Whimpers of pain punctuated her frantic breaths. Air wheezed from her lungs. Blood from her knee oozed down her leg and soaked her braies.

But successful, she thought. A smile was the only thing that did not hurt. One less revenant to torment Faery.

Avenall's face appeared above her. Insectile in his movements he looked over her. Streams of red-and-black hair tipped her aching muscles.

"Avenall," she gasped.

"Impressive, mortal wench."

"I am not…" Too exhausted to argue, she thought to expend her energy mentally. What be his name? He was of the tribe… Rogue. Torn. Not enough to invoke a reverse glamour, but certainly worth the effort. "Avenall of…Rougethorn."

But a single red eyebrow lifted. Considering? Remembering? Both brows narrowed to study. Gossamyr stared into the violet depths that, with a blink, were sluiced over by red.

"*Rougethorn,*" he said, trying the word, but not saying it as he'd once said. A thoughtful tilt of his head was followed by an adamant shake. "No. You shall not win the prize this night, pitiful one. Puppy must return to his mistress."

With that he dashed off, leaving Gossamyr sprawled in the center of the street, her arms spread wide and her body coated with the revenant dust.

Darting out her tongue, she tasted Faery. And for the moment she reveled in the shroud of glamour that revisited her home.

I am coming home. I will become the champion.

TWENTY

By the time Gossamyr reached his side, Ulrich was standing—wobbling and muttering a blue string of oaths about vicious faery women—and alive. Which, after that nasty club to the side of his head, is all Gossamyr worried about. Unthinking, she pressed both hands to the sides of his scalp—a Mince gesture.

"Ouch!" He wriggled from her touch and slid along the wall, his eyes manic on her. As if she had been the one to hurt him!

"I didn't—"

"It was *your* bloody staff!"

"Sorry." She twirled one half of her now-short staff and snapped it to hide behind her back. "'Tis gone, the revenant. Ulrich, I must go in search of Ave—the pin man. Can I leave you to find your way home to your uncle?"

"You *will* leave me, faery." He touched a stream of blood trickling from the depths of his tangled hair. "I've had enough of your danger. I'd rather defend the alicorn from a thousand wailing banshees than to stand again in the midst of one of your battles."

"Ulrich."

No time to argue. It mattered naught who was right or wrong, only that he was alive. And that she must move while she could. The revenant had pushed one of its fingers—bones—through the side of her knee. It hurt something fierce. If she did not walk the muscle, it would bind and ache all the more.

As well, the pin man would not get away this time.

"Sorry. I must be on to it." And with a long, fretful pause, looking over his skull—the blood no longer trickled, in fact it looked a scratch—Gossamyr scampered off.

"I would have preferred another Dance!" Ulrich shouted in her wake. "Damned bloody faeries!"

"Return to your uncle, Ulrich. Do not veer from your path!"

The pin man dropped from the painted rafters of a tanner's shed. The stench of urine did not bother, so honed his senses were to the task. Foolish woman. That he had slipped from her so easily with both prizes intact!

Clutched in his left hand he held two pins, each heavy with a fée essence. A smile curved beneath the scatter of crimson-and-black hair that spilled across his face. His mistress would be pleased this night. Good puppy.

In his right hand he drew out from his pin sheath the bloodied pin that reeked of the warrior woman's scent. He waved it beneath his nose, again trying to determine the curious origins of her essence. 'Twas not fée or troll or elf, but mysteriously, she did not seem all that mortal, either. Powerful, she. To have defeated that hideous skeletal monster?

I know why you were banished.

She lied. Even he could not summon the memory.

And she had Named him, or rather, called out a name. The name Avenall strummed within him, residing with little protest. Such ease it made itself home.

Rougethorn? It did not resonate as the other name did. Yet, he did remark the name; it was *her* tribal origin.

The warrior wench toyed with him. She sought to trick him, surely. Lower his defenses. A feeble mortal woman. She could not be anything but! Otherwise, the Red Lady would have scented her presence as soon as she landed Paris.

Could his mistress be slipping?

A delicious thrill shivered gleefully through him. Skipping merrily, he headed toward the succubus's lair, leaving all curiosities about his name to the stench of the tanner's shop.

Gossamyr followed the skipping man, keeping far enough back so he would not detect her. Ulrich had promised he would return to his uncle. She hadn't meant to hit him so hard, but when in the midst of battle, who was afforded the time to think? With rest the man would fare fine and well. There, he could keep the alicorn safe. There was no sense bringing it closer to the succubus who craved it.

As for herself, she gripped her pulsing knee. Every step shrieked with pain. Blood drooled down the back of her leg. Frustrated with the cumbersome skirts, she bent and gripped the tear through which the revenant's finger had poked. She managed to rend the entire hem away, as high as her knees. The braies beneath looked parti-colored, for blood stained the left leg.

Sniffling, she smeared a bloody fist across her nose.

Don't think about it. *Do not consider the pain pierces with each beat of your heart. You may hurt later.*

Avenall scampered, his posture bending and streamlining as he quickened his pace. She assumed being the Red Lady's minion required a subservience that would tax any man's posture. Held at each side, the glimmering essences called out his journey through the streets like a supernatural beacon clutched in the grip of a lantern man. The red flooding his hair shocked. A mark of the banished or the Red Lady's taint?

The pin man suddenly slipped inside a doorway and a crack of light closed behind him.

Gossamyr stepped up to an iron fence surrounding a stone and red-tiled manor. So this was the Red Lady's lair? Unremarkable. It was a small dwelling at the corner of three intersecting streets. A crossroads?

A shiver, in anticipation of unseen souls, prinkled across her chest, matching her lost blazon. The iron gate closed in a small garden rimmed with a pink shell path. Even the evil succubus would have use for a garden, for nature was a fée lifeline.

As well, stolen faery essences.

Carefully she picked across the shell path; her light footsteps made no sound. Gossamyr snuck into the shadows and limned her body to the limestone wall. The exterior verily hummed, she could feel Faery shimmy through her being. Enchantment within. Curious to find such a concentration in the depths of this mortal city.

Touching the crease between the door and the wall, Gossamyr contemplated what she must do.

The fetch landed Shinn's forehead, stretching its wings beyond his temples—scritch-scratch across the horns—and its elongated thorax down his nose. Closing his eyes, Shinn allowed the communion to begin. Images recorded from the Otherside flickered as brief and darting as a dragon's flight. A battle. Two Disenchanted, their shining armor decimated. Revenants taking to escape. Again, his daughter was the victor. But she suffered injury.

Another flicker focused a disturbing image in Shinn's thoughts. The soul shepherd kissed Gossamyr. A flurry of faery lights shimmering throughout the city ended the recorded communication.

Sending gratitude to the fetch, Shinn did not open his eyes until it had lifted from his forehead and *twinclianed*.

"She is in Paris," he murmured. "That kiss."

While he should be more troubled his daughter was forced to

face bogies and maniacal minions of the Red Lady, the image of that kiss disturbed him fiercely. Now was no time for Gossamyr to stumble. She risked much more than her life. All of Glamoursiège relied upon her success.

His deepest fear had come to fruition. The mortal passion had taken hold. She invited distraction when her goal must be focused.

"My lord." Desideriel Raine stood waiting in the great hall. The marshal at arms reported morning and evening now that the troops had been mustered.

"How many?" Shinn queried solemnly.

"Two, my lord. We've taken care of them. But their frequency increases. It is difficult to determine where in Glamoursiège the revenants will next arrive."

"How many casualties?"

"But two."

"Their essences?"

"Safe."

Shinn nodded and Desideriel bowed then left.

"You are so close," he said aloud.

Images of Gossamyr's determined grin fixed before him. How she loved adventure. But could she separate the adventure from true danger?

"Concentrate, child of mine."

The small outer manor deceived as Gossamyr tracked Avenall down a slanting, curved marble hallway until she estimated she marked out a path as vast as the market square where Ulrich had explained the Parisians hung their criminals. Damp and the scent of clay were eminent even for the marble that covered walls and floor and ceiling. Torches hissed on the walls and flickered as she brushed by them. Gargoyles, the torches; each of them holding an eerie glint in their hollowed stone eyes, for the flames flickered below their jaws.

The pin man danced joyously toward his destination, quite unaware Gossamyr had closed the distance between them. He had no sense of the man he had once been, a regal fée princeling. And despite his obvious change, Gossamyr still clung to that image of his former self.

Would he lead her to the Red Lady? Gossamyr's entry into the lair seemed entirely too easy. And she held but a short staff now for she'd left behind the other half. Where were the minions? Surely the succubus commanded an army of red-eyed sycophants. If there was Avenall, there must be others.

In the air hummed a strange susurration, like tiny whispers, secretive and stealthy. And beyond the murmurs the single tone of a harp string sung out from a dense and muting distance. Be this the sound that lured Ulrich? Wasn't nearly so sweet as a midsummer reel sung by a forest siren.

Avenall sang, tapping the heads of each gargoyle torch as he passed. "Seraphion, Martimanas, my sweets!"

Ahead, a flash of white light stretched down the pale marble floor. Gossamyr pressed herself to the wall behind a grotesque torch; the blaze of flame would hide her from discovery. Sweet the candle fire, flames melting honeycomb. A cool wind tickled the side of her neck. She slapped a palm over her throat and scanned the smirking gargoyle to her right. The tiny whispers had stopped.

Had the gargoyle——? No. Couldn't have.

Avenall entered a room and the door began to close. Quickly, she tiptoed to the door and pressed a palm to it. Though forged of marble and massive in size it moved on a whisper.

Tang of citrus and hush of myrrh drifted out from the room. Peering inside, Gossamyr spied a bed of tousled red linens. Elegant tapestry hangings, fringed in heavy gold tassels canopied the bed. No other furniture cluttered the vast marble floor. No succubus in sight.

On the wall opposite the bed there glowed such a marvel——Gossamyr gasped.

Hundreds of luminous masses glimmered on the wall. Here the song of Faery blossomed and cried out. Not fearful, but neither joyous. Tentative, the tones, so leery. This was the melody she had heard.

Avenall thrust one pin into the wall, securing the quivering orange essence with ease. Silver into stone? The second pin was secured with equal aplomb. Mesmerizing. In proof, Gossamyr watched as the pin man lifted his head and looked over the essences, his arms falling slack at his sides. Trapped in a pose of worship, his hair dusted the floor at his bare heels. It appeared the crimson had flowed even farther, leaving barely a hand's-breadth of black at the tips.

Did the Red Lady possess hair of such color? Shinn had not remarked such.

And there, from beneath the heavy fall of crimson-and-black hair, unfurled the gorgeous papilinod wings, spurred with wispy filaments. Not violet. Not iridescent, so drained of color they were—much like a revenant. Now she noticed his arms. The Rougethorn blazon girdled arms and hips. Banishment had not stolen Avenall's blazon, yet, it was pale, barely a shimmer of curling arcs and dashes upon his flesh.

Gossamyr drew herself into the room. Wincing at the sharp pain in her knee, her bare feet made not a sound on the cold marble as she crept around behind the succubus's minion. So entranced he was he did not notice her. The glowing, shifting orbs continued their weird humming. Was the sound a death cry, a captured fée essence, unable to journey to its final resting place? Did they suffer in oblivion? Would the revenant's death—somewhere in Faery—see an end to this captured essence?

No, for she had obliterated the one back in the square, and Avenall yet retained the speared essence.

The urge to leap forward and yank the pins from the marble flared in Gossamyr's gut. But she quelled the ache for justice. *Do not seek vengeance, hold fast to valor.* Be bold, be bold—until she knew where the mistress of this lair hid, she must be wary—be not too bold. *Seek the truth!*

Who was to know what their release would prove? Mayhap there was chance, with the revenant's death, the essence could then be granted the final *twinclian.*

For now, she was more concerned with Avenall's faculty.

Following the tilt of the pin man's head, she gathered he stared at the one essence pinned highest above all the others. A leap to touch the thick iron head of that pin. The essence there undulated lazily, fat and palest yellow, as the sun on a cold winter morn. It was different than the rest. Not as glimmery. More solid. As if…not filled with glamour.

For the Enchantment still reigned in Avenall? Of course, his blazon proved as much.

The softest of whispers gave away his fascination. "Mine."

"It is yours," Gossamyr blurted.

The fée startled, his wings twitching, but he did not turn from gazing upon the yellow essence.

"Be that how she keeps you?" Gossamyr approached the base of the curved marble stairs. Cool beneath her toes, the slick stone. "Is it your essence?"

"Oh, yes," he murmured in a reverent hush. Avenall stood tall and proud. The subtle sweep of his wings stirred heliotrope into the mixture of citrus and myrrh. Seductive. Can it be as it once was? Oh, but she ached for it to be so.

"Take it," Gossamyr said. "It is but a leap to your freedom."

A rabbity moan brewed in the man's throat. The filaments spurring his wing tips coiled tightly. He shook his head, dusting the cold air with his vibrant tresses. "It is too high."

Gossamyr strode up both steps to stand beside the man. It had been a time since she had stood alongside her lover. Anticipation thrummed her heartbeats. But here she felt his anxiety, a verita-

ble shiver emanated from his being. And there, the remnants of
desire yet cleaved to her bruised heart. Oh, but he must remember her!

The return of his essence—yes, surely that would make him
whole?

"It is but a leap. Shall I get it down for you?"

"No!" He clapped a hand over his scalp and winced, lunging forward in a moaning sway. "It is forbidden."

"I have not been told as much." Gossamyr stepped forward.

The pin man thrust out his foot, successfully tripping her.
She landed her palms and stared up at the humming, pulsating
wall. A reach away, one of the pins. The essence of her fellow
fée groaned and moaned before her. Life captured there. Stolen
life.

Gossamyr lifted a finger to touch. A strange reverence befell her.
How dare she touch another faery's essence?

"Sacred," she murmured at the same time Avenall skipped down
the stairs.

"Where is she? Your mistress?" Gossamyr spun up and stood.
"Quickly!"

"Away." The man clapped his hands over his head and did a spinning jig before the crimson bed. "Won't you stay?"

"I believe I shall." She released an *arret* but did not swing it to
full speed. Instead she spun it gently, winding it about her forefinger and then unwinding it.

Avenall's attention preened over her. Once compassion and a
fiery interest had glittered in his violet eyes, now a malicious spark
of red glinted at Gossamyr. He smelled of heliotrope and myrrh
and something so evil.

He asked, "What *are* you?"

"You don't know? Can you not sniff me out?" A lift of her chin
stretched the cut that slashed from cheek to jaw. She nodded toward the sheath of pins at his hip. "One of those is mine, is it not?"

"You reek of Faery," he said, pacing around her, cautious to keep his distance.

Gossamyr bent and sat on the lowest step, propping her wrists on her knees. She did not sense immediate danger from this man. Never had she felt fearful in his presence. But he had changed. She must caution herself to be wary.

"But Faery you are not. Nor are you an elf." He tapped his chin. "But mortal?"

She smirked at his confusion. "Your mistress would have me dead by now were I anything but mortal." How strange to feign mortality with the very man who had allowed her to accept her half blood as an exotic attribute.

"Mayhap she keeps you alive until she has pinned your man's soul to her collection?"

"She does not take mortal souls. Nor is he my man. Avenall! Look at me!"

The pin man merely glanced to the undulating yellow mass high above the others. "You are too familiar with my name, wench."

"As we have been familiar with one another?"

What power had the Red Lady over him that he did not recognize her? Or was it the mark of the banished, delivered by her father, that had erased his memory?

"The mortal is stalked by my mistress."

"Ulrich will not be fooled by your mistress's wicked cry." If Gossamyr could be there to keep watch over the man. Blight, she had so many to concern herself with.

"Oh, but it is a most delicious cry, fair lady. Irresistible and insatiable. The succubus can make any man want her, as well, hate her as he is kneeling before her pristine skirts."

A glint of malice iced the man's words. Gossamyr guessed at his hatred. So he was not entirely at the succubus's mercy? Bone.

"You despise her, don't you? You merely bide your time until you can retrieve your essence and escape."

"No."

"Oh, yes. Let me pull it down for you and send you on your way. Leave the Red Lady to me. She'll not pursue you for I'll remove her black essence and pin it to the wall before the day is through."

The pin man laughed and snorted and caught himself by clutching one of the wide marble bedposts. "Foolish wench, my mistress has no essence. Why do you think she has such a collection?"

"But she does nothing with them. What is the purpose of keeping them pinned to look upon?"

"She feeds off the Enchantment. Which in turn keeps the Disenchantment at bay. Do you see that one down there?"

Gossamyr looked to the green essence on the bottom, shriveled and flickering intermittently.

"Needs to be replaced anon," the pin man said. "As will they all."

"What of yours? How is it you survive without the essence?"

He lifted his chin defiantly. "My mistress…keeps me strong."

Gossamyr knew the answer. His time was limited. "Is it because you both bear the mark of the banished? Is that what binds you to her?"

Striding in a prancing arc before her, Avenall spun a pin in hand, the huge round head rotating in his palm. A twist of his head upon his neck aimed a hard glare on her.

"Why do you reek of Faery, strange woman? Yet I know you are not fée."

"Half—" Gossamyr started, but Avenall's wicked glee unsettled her. Could it be he did recall her, yet was unable to place that memory? It could merely be that the Disenchantment was so thorough. But no, he must be Enchanted for his wings. Did it matter? He had not recall of the two of them—she must help him to remember. With Avenall as her ally they could defeat the Red Lady and return to—

Gossamyr felt a twinge of regret at her lost ties to Faery. Is that how all fée felt the loss? But a mere twitch inside their gut? Surely it must be greater? Shinn should have prepared her...

"Shinn?"

"What?" Gossamyr squinted at the man. Where had he gotten the name— "Did you peer into my mind?"

"No need." He straightened his shoulders and clacked two pins together within his grip. "Your fear is tangible, daughter of Shinn."

"I do not fear— How do you know such?"

"So you are? Or rather—" he stretched his arms out and dashed a theatrical slide across the marble step "—claim to be when it is all a lie."

"Why speak you so, pin man? How can you guess such things? Do you lie about your memory of Faery?"

"Do you deny you are Shinn's daughter?"

"No."

She is queer-gotten—not of her parents' blood. Gossamyr shook her head, striking away Ulrich's tale of a daughter he claimed as his own though not a drop of his blood flowed through her veins. Strange to think it.

"But do you remember—"

"Shinn has made you believe you are truly of his blood? He has gulled you most effectively."

She stepped back, lowering her staff to her side. The *arrets* at her hip clicked. Essences danced on the wall. The melody of sadness wrapped about her shoulders. What lies did this leering thing speak to her? To trick her?

"They are not lies." The man stepped forward, a tilt to one of the pins glinting violet. Like a shard of Faery sight. "True blood wears the violet in their eyes," he said, a wicked curl crevassing the corner of his mouth. "Your eyes, warrior bitch, appear quite not violet to me. Brown, are they?"

Thud of heartbeats trammeled up her throat. Balance wavered.

"Stop." She would not listen to this foul attempt to weaken her.

To make her question. She swallowed back the rising panic. Of course they were brown; Veridienne's had been the same.

The need to help this pitiful excuse for a fée oozed from her intentions. The Red Lady was not here? She would go in quest of the succubus.

Spinning to leave, Gossamyr strode past the wall. Essences of the fée cried out in a purgatorial scream.

Brown, are they?

The pin man sang teasingly, "I know of you, mortal changeling."

TWENTY-ONE

Changeling?

Gossamyr pressed the heel of her hand to the cold marble wall. What play did the pin man attempt? Yes, pin man. Avenall was long gone. Not a lover. She wanted nothing to do with one who would tease her so cruelly.

Unable to take another step, she closed her eyes, wishing it were as easy to close her ears to the man's words. "How can you claim to know I am Shinn's daughter when you cannot recall our own connection?"

"We? Connected?" A flutter of his life-drained wings swept the foulness of bloodied heliotrope across their distance. "If there was such, memory was stolen from me upon banishment."

She let out a breath.

"I know only what I have been given." Drawing himself straight, his arms lax at his sides, the pins were forgotten for the moment. "After my arrival in Paris, my mistress told me much about Shinn of Glamoursiège. And his mortal daughter."

"Half-mortal."

"You are mortal complete," ground out in dripping tones.

Gossamyr made to brush off the impossible declaration with a brave thrust of her chin. "Lies spun by a banished succubus."

"Truth," the pin man hissed, "from a discarded lover." He twirled a pin between two fingers, a smaller version of her staff whisking the air to a violent and metallic hum.

"You honestly believe yourself a half blood?" He stepped right up to her. Not too close for Faery.

Gossamyr pressed her shoulder blades to the marble wall. Reaction fled. She could not scent him, save for the blood on the pins. She could but listen, stare into those violet eyes. Eyes that had once looked upon her with desire but were now clouded with a viscous red sheen.

A lover? Shinn and the Red Lady? He had not told her such!

Your truth will impede your safe return to Faery.

"It is most curious Shinn chose to keep the truth from you all this time. Quite the feat, I am sure. Though a mortal who lives very long in Faery does become Very Close."

"I am half-blooded," Gossamyr growled. Or she thought she spoke with a forceful snarl, but it seemed to come out as a whimper. "Fathered by Lord de Wintershinn and my mortal mother, Veridienne of…" Of where? Paris? Veridienne had never told her whence she'd come.

Steel pins clicked against one another as the pin man took one more step. Toe to toe they stood. He had gained presence in these few moments. A tilt of his head leveled his eyes with Gossamyr's. Menace glittered in the violet depths.

Kiss me.

Would a kiss bring memory flooding back?

Dare she?

Of a sudden the malice in Avenall's stare softened, and he smiled. "Shinn has not told you of your birth? Your…coming to Faery?"

"You cannot know things about me when you do not even remember we were once lovers!"

"Lovers? Indeed? Hmm." He strode a gaze over her body, his face almost touching her for their closeness. Sweet his breath, sweet with memory. But foul his hair, tainted with the Red that attacked the Disenchanted. "Mayhap. But you fight to change the sides of this exchange. Be you lover or warrior matters little to me of so pale memory. All I know is what she tells me. 'Tis only what concerns me."

"You should strive to remember."

"Have you not ever wondered why you are wingless?"

Heartbeats pounding in her breast, Gossamyr swallowed. Too close for her bruised heart. "M-many fée are wingless." Try as she might, she could not step away from Avenall. She wanted to stand close to him, in his scent. But this air—heavy, not right.

"Yes, there are wingless ones, but their eyes be not muddied by the Otherside."

"It is my mortal blood that makes them brown."

"Oh no, half bloods always wear the violet eyes of the fée."

"You spin tales for your mistress. Slave to a succubus! You will die pining for your essence, pin man."

"And you will die a mortal death, false daughter of Shinn." Now he pressed his palms to the wall above her shoulders. *Too close!* Hot breath hissed across her nose and lips as he spoke rapidly. "My mistress adored the pompous lord of Glamoursiège. They were to be wed—to unite Glamoursiège to Rougethorn. But when Shinn learned she dabbled in magic, he spurned her and took another. Yet the Red Lady remained his slave. He toyed with her affections, you see, trapping her heart for eternity, then discarding it as if a fall-sapped leaf. Shinn took Veridienne of the Otherside as his wife and she became full with child."

"Me—me," Gossamyr stammered.

"Oh, no, mortal fool." A silver pin tapped her chin. "The Red Lady pined for the love she once had. Shinn ignored her. So to avenge her broken heart she bespelled the child in Veridienne's belly. It was born a hideous changeling. Enraged, Shinn marked the Red Lady with banishment and cast her from Faery. The troop commander possesses a quick temper. He reacts without regard."

"No."

"Oh, yes! That much I do recall from my banishment. Swift and unforgiving."

Gossamyr gasped. Shinn had banished the Red Lady. But even more remarkable— They were to wed? To unite—

But—

Such knowledge pried into her courage with vicious precision. Why, to learn this from so horrible reminder of a bittersweet past?

...trapped her heart for an eternity...

Like Gossamyr's own trembling heart?

"You know it has been but a mortal year since the Red Lady was banished?"

Gossamyr lifted her chin, taking this announcement with a hard jaw. She had learned the measurement for *year*. It was not so long as to have occurred before she had been born. Yet, Ulrich's claim to have lost twenty years—it did not figure!

"Faery time is different from time here in the Otherside. So mutable, twisting this way and back, forward and then quickly past. Twenty years pass in Faery while one or two passes in the Otherside. Vice versa, widdershins and thus," he hissed into her face.

Time was indeed the enemy.

"H-how long have you been here?"

He shrugged. "That is not in my memory. A few mortal weeks? Less than a moon cycle."

Impossible! It had been so much longer... Gossamyr had aged many dozens of moons since Shinn had banished Avenall.

"My mistress strives to survive, but it is difficult. There are fewer and fewer Disenchanted who journey to this mortal city. What is it, changeling? Cat gnawing at your tongue?"

She wasn't hearing, for the title "changeling" stuck in her skull like the tip of an obsidian *arret*.

"Not a changeling." Gossamyr shook her head, unwilling to accept the man's lies. But knowing, for fact, Shinn had many secrets. "I cannot be…"

"No, you were not the changeling babe," the pin man spat, his breath covering her face with odorless heat. "You were the mortal exchange. You understand?"

She stared deep into his red-glossed eyes. A glint of humanity sparkled, drawing her into his truth, the will to believe, to trust and know. Could she make him believe his own truth?

Of what matter to her now? Be he enemy or lover, this knowledge threatened far worse than lost memories. Everything she had ever believed—had it all been a lie?

A wooziness shimmered inside her skull. Avenall's image blurred then sharpened.

"Shinn took his befouled babe to the Otherside and exchanged it for you, warrior bitch. Veridienne wanted a child—and if it be mortal, like herself, all the better. Shinn created a lie to keep you safe in Faery, claiming you were the child of Veridienne's belly, half-blooded, descendant blood to the Glamoursiège reign. Imagine that!"

Now Avenall pushed away from the wall and spun in a macabre dance step. Gossamyr could not focus for more than a moment. The weird blurring and sudden clearing of her sight made her nauseous.

The pin man stopped, crouched before her, wings flittering annoyingly, and then rose, a sinister grin curving his thin lips as he straightened. The Red Lady's influence grew into his dark hair, coating him with wicked red soot that befouled Gossamyr's memories of him. But the roots of the succubus's thrall dug far deeper, right to his being.

"You are mortal, false child of Shinn. Nothing but. Not a drop of Faery ichor runs through your veins. 'Twas the Red Lady who cursed Shinn, and you yielded from the exchange. Yes, you benefited! What a life to be raised in Faery! Oh, what I wouldn't wager to return."

"With your essence?" Gossamyr spoke, but the words weren't truly conscious. Benefited by the exchange?

Believe and you Belong. All this time she had believed—no!

"You spin lies! I—I will see you to the Infernal before I allow you to return to Faery. As well, your bloody mistress!"

"Ah? Cast your lover to the Infernal? Not very romantic of you."

"The succubus's *erie* has changed you. Blight, what is your name? Avenall of Rougethorn…"

"I see now why Shinn sent you," Avenall declared as he danced up and down the steps. The essences sung a frightened dirge. "A strong wench, be she!"

"I stand here on the Otherside of my free will. Shinn did not want me to leave…"

Had Shinn knowingly sent off his only daughter? A mortal, unable to return to Faery? A child born to mortals? …*to unite Glamoursiège to Rougethorn.*

Gossamyr felt her knees weaken. Icy, the pain streaking from her knee to her ankle. Bile curdled at the base of her throat.

"Indeed a wise choice," Avenall said. "The Red Lady would not recognize a mere mortal come sniffing about her lair. And what sweeter revenge than to send the mortal beast Shinn calls his own to avenge the Red Lady's curse!"

"No!" Peeling herself from the marble wall, Gossamyr swung her staff out before her, forgetting it was but half size. The serrated end swished the air. "It is all a lie!"

A changeling? She, a mortal exchange?

Rare, a changeling was born in Faery. Always they were swapped for a sickly mortal babe. It was the way of the fée. None of the mortal children ever survived longer than a day or mayhap a se'nnight...

It seemed an odd ritual now Gossamyr thought on it. Why a sick child? A healthy babe would survive— Had she been sick?

"No." Her voice gasping out in a dry breath, Gossamyr shouted, "It cannot be!"

"Embrace your truth," Avenall said and stepped to the bed, sliding his arm along the silk and stretching out on his back. Unfurled wings and red-and-black hair littered the counterpane. "And mayhap the Red Lady will prolong your life."

"By stealing my essence, like yours?"

"You've no essence to steal, mortal."

"Very well." Gripping the half staff in both hands, she worked at the wood until she felt sure the carvings would etch into her palms and out would pour blood. *Not ichor. You are mortal.* "I shall leave you with a bit of your own truth, Avenall of Rougethorn. It was my father, Shinn, who also banished you."

"This I know."

"And yet—do you know the reason you were sent from Faery without so much as a by-your-leave?"

Rolling to stretch on his side, he propped his chin in hand. "I guess you will tell me."

Gossamyr stepped up to the bed and gripped a thick spiral post fashioned of the same marble as the floor. She knew the Red Lady's heart was colder than the stone. If she possessed a heart. "I will, and then I will consign you to my past and think not another moment for your life."

Avenall sighed and spread out his arms in a waiting gesture.

"My father banished you from Faery because you chose to court his daughter after he had forbidden such a match. He would not have a Rougethorn marry his own. On the night we were to make love, Shinn sent you off. I loved you, Avenall."

Gossamyr turned and strode from the room. Her footsteps increased. Her arms pumped. And her heart pounded. She ran down the hallway. The gargoyles' flames flickered and brightened in her wake.

All this time—her father—

I will not have a Rougethorn in my family.

She entered the darkness of the Paris night with a cry that echoed out and spiraled into the heavens.

TWENTY-TWO

Dominique San Juste startled at the female cry drifting over all of Paris. He could not fix a location to the sound, instead it encompassed all, the air, the cobbles, the stone walls and creaking wooden signs, and finally, resonated in his bones. Mournful and vehement, the howl was tinged with a glimmer of which he had never known—but had always carried within him—Enchantment.

Unsettled, he stroked a palm across Tor's bone-white withers and searched the darkness.

"You feel it, too, my friend," he said to his equine companion. "What mischief have you led me to?"

The stallion bristled and reared upon its hind legs in brilliant display.

And Dominique sensed every moment that followed would place him closer to a most dangerous Enchantment.

"Where is he?" Gossamyr stumbled across the threshold into Armand LaLoux's home. The old man nodded toward the ladder.

Gossamyr scaled the rungs two at a time. Ulrich met her at the top. She plunged into his arms but took no time for courtesies. Pulling him across the floor toward the window, she stood for a moment, catching her breath. Not once had she broken her stride from the Red Lady's lair.

Manic visions twisted her thoughts here, there and widdershins. A changeling? Completely mortal? Believe and you Belong…

Where *did* she belong?

So much she had always accepted, thought to know as truth!

"What is it? Did you track the pin man? Sit on the floor, my lady, you're out of breath."

She followed his direction and sat, crossing her legs. When he remained standing, she clung to his wrist and pulled him down, leveling his face with hers. Gripping his head between her palms, she ignored his wince when she pressed upon the bruise staining his cheek. Heaving yet from her race, she was unable to get out the words.

Warm hands bracketed hers, pulling her shaking fingers from his face. "Gossamyr? If you do not speak I shall assume the worst. Have you been followed? Harmed?"

Harmed? Mayhap by the very man she had called father all these years.

"You are bleeding."

She shook her head that he should disregard that insignificant bother.

Oh, but an ache had begun to pulse in the depths of her being. The old wound had been scraped and now this new knowledge tore open her bleeding heart.

"Gossamyr?"

She shot a gaze into the man's eyes. "What did you call me?"

"It is your name."

Yes, her name. Was it? Gossamyr Verity de Wintershinn of Glamoursiège. Truly?

She had not been able to conjure Avenall's name complete. It was there, just at the edge of her mind. Ah! He had utterly changed. Physically and mentally. He knew nothing of himself. Puppy? Yet, he claimed to know much about her.

Could he speak the truth of her?

"Tell me you are not harmed elsewhere," Ulrich whispered. "You tremble so—"

"No!" That shout released her dry and twisted tongue, and Gossamyr began to cry long-buried tears. She could not keep them back. Be blighted, the champion, the wandering refugee from Faery simply needed to let out some pain.

"*Mon Dieu,* this is serious. Faery princesses are not supposed to cry."

Ulrich pulled her to him. His hair brushed her face and for a moment Gossamyr recalled that time long ago, when she had been but a child and had stood watching the dancer…

There in the center of the toadstool ring, his hands swaying in the air, a mortal danced. A male, for he was hearty and dressed in striped hosen and doublet. His head tilted back and mouth open, he laughed and giggled and shouted out in joy.

Gossamyr tilted her head, studying the mortal's movements. Almost as if commanded by the mistress of the Dance, a puppet dancing for the twisted pleasure of the masses. "Poor thing."

Gossamyr worked her way to the edge of the ring where the grass had been trampled to an emerald mat and stood, her bare foot propped on the head of a wide loamy toadstool. No one paid her mind. Even the piskies soared by without so much as a teasing thrust of their lavender tongues.

Splash of mead sprayed her cheek and she swept out her tongue to lick away the sweet liquor from the corner of her lips. Dozens of fée danced a tribal rhythm about the mortal, a circle of violet eyes. His own eyes were closed, oblivious to a danger Gossamyr could not know. But she sensed it.

Dancers spun past her in increasing speed, stomping and twirling and lifting skirts high to expose moonlight-pale thighs and bronze ankle chains. Fluttering wings swept the air in heady perfume of heliotrope, rosemary and rose.

She spied the mortal dance closer. For all matters he looked as all *fée* did, having two legs, two arms, a torso, head and hair—rusty hair. Wingless, as was she—not uncommon in Faery. But the eyes, when they flashed wide to take in the merriment, were not violet. A pale noncolor. From where she stood, Gossamyr could not determine what shade or tint

The wind of the Dancers' reel stirred Gossamyr's hair as the mortal passed her by, oblivious to all but the music. "An endless moment," she recalled Shinn once saying as he'd explained in few words her frequent questions.

Closing her eyes, Gossamyr drew in the heavy green scent of moist meadow grass. A musty aroma drifted up from the frilled underside of the toadstools. Blackberries crushed, spiced, and brewed to summer mead spilled down throats and from bronze goblets.

Drawing deeply, she sensed another aroma, a scent she had not before smelled. Earthy and tainted with the ripe lush dregs of crushed grapes. Mortal scent? She leaned forward. Delicious. Beguiling.

Stretching out a hand, she wished with all her might—and it happened.

The skim of hair across her fingers. Swift, but the moment slowed, so she could sense every individual strand and memorize the texture as if she had studied it for centuries.

Clasping her fingers to her chest, she closed her eyes and stood on tiptoe. The canorous swing of the revelers faded into the background as her wishes, her passion was born.

The Otherside. She would journey there someday, to explore and discover and learn all that she could of the beguiling creature called mortal, for she was part of the realm, as well—by half.

Staring at her fingers now, Gossamyr perused the lines of life. There, mayhap the trail of the Dancer's hair deepened that line. Reaching out, she touched Ulrich's hair. Overwhelming tears rushed to her eyes.

"Gossamyr?"

It was him. This mortal had Danced for her unknowing. Not so long ago, he would remark. Many dozens of moons, she knew. *An endless moment.* Tricksy, this time difference between Faery and the

Otherside, moving neither forward in synch, but twisting in and upon itself. Avenall had spoken the truth of Time.

Truly, this man was the mortal who had unearthed her passion for the Otherside.

And yet, be it only because she was mortal? Her passion for all things not Faery stirred up from the depths of her being? Had the mortal passion led her here after all? Why hadn't Veridienne told her?

Do you already subscribe to a truth you cannot trust?

Believe and you Belong.

Believe in what?

She did not want to belong—not here!

"Am I mortal, Ulrich?" She gripped his shirt, fingering the needlework dragonflies. "Do you think I am mortal? Not of Faery?"

"What are you babbling about?"

"Avenall—the pin man. He…he told me things."

"Bizarre things surely."

"You've said yourself, I am more mortal than fée."

"Yes, but you've told me you are half-blooded."

"You never believed me. And the spell in the cathedral tower, it did not locate me!"

"The spell—but I am not a mage, precious one. 'Twas merely a trick that may or may not have succeeded. Why are you so upset? You take the word of some minion who tries to make you believe such nonsense? Gossamyr, I saw you the moment you left Faery. I saw the blazon."

Conscious of her lost glamour, she smoothed a palm across the base of her throat and over her collarbones. "Any mortal who spends time in Faery develops a blazon. It is the glamour fixing to one's essence. Have I an essence? Or but a mortal soul? Oh, Ulrich, you must help me!"

"You need rest, Gossamyr. You have not rested properly since we have joined up. Your mind, it plays cruel tricks upon your brain."

"But the Red Lady told him about her banishment. Ulrich, the succubus was banished from Faery by Shinn. The very man who would call me daughter was betrothed to marry the Red Lady. Why would he not tell me? Why the lie?"

"You would believe a succubus's minion over your own flesh and blood?"

"I—I am not Shinn's blood," she whispered.

"What?"

"Avenall claims I am but a mortal exchange for Shinn's changeling child."

Ulrich sat back, his legs bent, forearms propped on his knees. The single candle's flame, set on the floor before the window, shadowed long lashes across his forehead.

"You have no answer for that."

"I don't know what to think. You have a relationship with this pin man that you call him by name? You know him well enough to trust his word?"

"I did once. We were…in love."

"Oh?"

"My father would not allow him to court me because he was not Glamoursiège but rather a Rougethorn, I told you that. The two tribes have warred against one another. And yet, they were to wed…" Impossible to imagine that Shinn might have once agreed to marry the Red Lady. And yet, she knew so little, mayhap it had been an easy agreement.

"But he did not marry her. Instead, he took a mortal wife. This mortal passion makes one do crazy things."

"Indeed. It will set a man on a deadly quest to find a hornless beast of myth."

Gossamyr sniffed and, only now realizing she cried, pressed the heels of her palms to her eyes. "You see I have emotion. Mortal emotions that run afoul with the merest of problems. Don't look at me."

"Be you mortal or be you fée you are still the same, Gossamyr. A beautiful warrior—"

"Sent by lies to exterminate my father's banished lover!"

Ulrich gave a low whistle.

"Bloody elves, does Shinn banish every fée who gets close to him and his own? Mayhap Veridienne was banished, too!"

"You don't believe that."

"I don't know what is truth anymore."

"You know your mother was mortal."

"Yes, but is Veridienne my birth mother or merely a foster mother?"

The clank of an iron pot below silenced them both. Armand must be to the evening meal. Counting her heartbeats, Gossamyr squeezed her eyes tightly shut to avoid the steady blue gaze bent before her.

"There is a way to know for sure," Ulrich said. She looked up at him. "Call out your father."

"To Paris? The Red Lady would scent him in a moment. Shinn would not be so foolhardy."

"Can you send the fetch to him?"

"I haven't seen Shinn's fetch for a time. But you!" She lunged and clamped her hands upon Ulrich's shoulders. "You can work a spell to see my truth? Yes?"

"I am but a mere shepherd of—"

"You can! You studied with a mage. Your spell in the cathedral was successful."

Vacillating with a noncommittal shrug and then a defeated sigh, Ulrich offered, "You are quick to use magic now."

"If I be mortal, it is my right."

"I would have to check my leech book."

"Then do it! Where is it? Here!" She dived for the saddlebag and upended its contents. The mortar and her sigil scattered. A small book of folded parchment slid out beside the candle and she paged through the stitched sheets. Black lines of flowing text darted from side to side of each page in a tilted manner that made it difficult to decipher the words. She knew the mortal script, yet this was erratic. Why did everything have to be so complicated?

From behind her, she felt Ulrich's arms embrace her and his hands move over hers, closing the book in her lap.

"Does it truly matter, faery princess?"

Do you know the truth of yourself?

"I am not fée. It was...*is,* and always has been, a mortal love."

"I understand now, the mortal passion you speak of."

"What of it?"

"It is love, Gossamyr. Love is the mortal passion!"

"I—" But it made sense, so much sense. Shinn's mortal passion for Veridienne. Her mother's love for her home. And she, she had always known that she could love, but had pressed it back as the mortal passion. "I think you are right, Ulrich."

Silence pounded in her ears. Her mortal soul beating within, seeking escape? *Your truth will be your end.* "But I must learn the truth. Help me, Ulrich."

"Very well." He drew her onto his lap and, looking over her shoulder, the two paged through the leech book. "There must be something in here."

"We must hurry. The pin man will tell his mistress who I am."

"Think you?"

"Yes. Though I did leave him with the truth of us, I wager he shall not remember. If only I could recall his name complete I might break the *erie.* Ulrich, as Faery slips from me, so too do my memories."

"You remember your father."

"How could I forget Shinn?"

"It is akin to asking how he could not love a child he has raised as his daughter."

Turning in Ulrich's lap, Gossamyr looked into his truth. Her

Dancer. His presence in Faery had forged her curiosity for the Otherside. Had he not danced, she might never have attempted to convince her father to allow her this mission. It could not be coincidence that had placed them together on this path to change their futures. Or be it the mortal passion that held her in its thrall?

She waited in the attic, twilight shimmering a thin silver line across the window. Cross-legged, she sat, and closed her eyes. Those three words from the dilapidated castle returned to her. *Vengeance, valor, truth.*

What word had vengeance replaced? Charity? No, there had been a single "r." Honor? And why had she claimed valor when all along the truth had dodged her like a fetch's flight?

She had not succumbed to the dreaded fée curse called the mortal passion. She was the antithesis of the malady. For in her heart, she already loved. A mortal who could love. So many unexplained things from her childhood could be answered with the simple statement: You are mortal.

She did never heal as did the fée; scars abounded on her legs and arms. Glamour had to be learned, 'twas not innate. No wings. Unable to *twinclian.* Not so tall as the lithe fée and not slender. Muscular and well formed, and as Avenall had remarked, breasts far too large to accomplish flight. Brown eyes. And how she had lumbered in the Faery air, not like here, where she positively fit.

Could Avenall's claim that her truth would be her end have some bearing on Shinn's silence? It made little sense a man who had claimed to love her for so long could so easily dispose of her. Was Shinn capable of wearing such a mask? Had he been plotting the Red Lady's demise, with Gossamyr as the weapon of destruction, since her birth? Why, if they had been affianced, had he not initially refused the betrothal? Rougethorns had always been known to dabble. Surely their union had taken that into account? Mayhap it had something to do with the rift? To combine magic with Enchantment to induce it to heal?

No, it did not seem like her father.

Every day she learned more of the lord of Glamoursiège's quick and bitter temper. What twisted reign did Shinn walk? He had no right to toy with love and desire. Had his own tragic love affair pushed him to be so protective of her? To jealously cast away her lover?

The soft footfalls of Ulrich's boots landed the attic floor. Gossamyr heard him shuffle a jumble of items in his hands as he laid them on the floor behind her. Pages flipped in his leech book. A heavy sigh weighed down his breath. He had gathered the required supplies to work the spell—one gray mouse tail, sleep dust (from Armand's eyes), fresh thyme and six strands of Gossamyr's hair.

"You can do this," she offered, turning to catch his reluctant, yet agreeing, nod. "What betroubles you, Ulrich?"

"Of course I can work the spell. Thing is, I don't know if I *want* to do this."

"You would refuse me help?"

"Never."

"Then what is the problem?"

Seriousness stilled his eyes. "There is a requirement to work the spell. You must present yourself to me bared of propriety and vestments."

"I come to you open and prepared for the truth."

"As well—" another sigh and a riffle of his fingers through his hair "—you must be naked."

TWENTY-THREE

Gossamyr slid down her borrowed braies. She hooked her fingers at the knife-ravaged hem of the silk gown and caught the stunned look on the man's face. "What?"

"I don't know if I can do this, Gossamyr. Don't. You… I can't—"

"You fear my naked flesh?"

"Fear it? Blessed Mary and all her veils, you really are an innocent, aren't you?"

"I understand much more than you comprehend. Are you so unpredictable you cannot look upon a naked woman without lust in your eyes?"

"That is about the mark of it."

"Bear up, Ulrich. Think of your wife."

"Do not bring Lydia into this, or you slay me with your unthinking cruelty."

Gossamyr tossed the gown and it landed Ulrich's head.

"Oh Hades."

"Hurry up, soul shepherd, 'tis drafty up here."

"You are naked?"

"Completely." She shrugged her hands over her arms, then down her thighs. Shiver bumps lifted in her wake. To stand naked so close to this man… "Start reciting."

"If I do not burn for my past transgressions, surely this one will cinch the deal for me. Very well! Pix, pax, abraxus!"

With the tip of the dagger Ulrich diagrammed a cross in the air above his head. Words—that sounded to Gossamyr like utter nonsense—were spoken with such command she trusted he did know the spell.

As he began to pulverize the items he'd gathered in the mortar, she stood and watched, her fate entirely in Ulrich's hands. She trusted him. They were inexplicably bonded in this quest for truth. Now, could he give her the answer she needed?

"I need your name."

"What?"

It took all his mortal strength and every moral muscle in his being to keep from turning to look at the naked woman who stood but a stride behind him. Ulrich could verily sense her nakedness. He could feel the swish of the single braid across her bare back and taste the gooseflesh coating her limbs.

"Your name complete," he forced through tight teeth. "I must speak it to make you my slave. If you are fée, the spell will work. If you are mortal, nothing I can command of you will make you act. You retain your free will."

"Yes, I…understand."

In the moment of her reluctance Ulrich felt his heart surrender. He had loved before and he had lost. Who would have thought love would once again be his to own?

Own? Be you very quick to replace your wife with any fine and pretty female who befriends you.

No, not my wife any longer. Yet how long must he honor her memory?

She is not dead, man!

"Ulrich? Yes, erm…Gossamyr Verity de Wintershinn of Glamoursiège."

He lifted a brow. Fine, pretty *and* a faery princess. "I command you, Gossamyr Verity de Wintershinn of Glamoursiège, to do my bidding. Be thee fée, you will grant me the truth. Be thee mortal, you will ignore my plea." He paused, and then entreated, "You ready for this?"

"Do your worst."

He had to smile at her gumption. Holding the mortar high above his head, he announced, "Kiss me, Gossamyr Verity de Wintershinn of Glamoursiège. Plant a fée morsel upon my mouth. I command thee, Gossamyr Verity de Wintershinn of Glamoursiège!"

Silence filled the room. Ulrich tilted his head, listening for the sound of bare feet upon the creaking boards. "Gossamyr?"

"I am not going to kiss you. Not like this."

"But you would if you were dressed?"

He turned, thrilled she hadn't completely refused his suggestion. And before him stood the most gorgeous being he had ever before placed eyes upon. The mortar settled onto his foot, but he did not comprehend pain. "Gossamyr." The name slipped from his throat and became a prayer in the air.

She lifted a defiant chin. But he had fallen into her spell, an enchantment of the soul that buried itself deep in Ulrich's being. He had no desire to step forth and touch her. To taste her mouth. To touch the full and perfect breasts. Nor to slide his hand down her flat stomach into the nether of her being. He wanted only to look upon her. Ever after.

"It must be so," she said on a wistful sigh. "I am mortal."

"A mortal with the power to enchant," he whispered, utterly beguiled.

But there, blood and dirt on her knee. The sudden jar of that foul evidence followed a rude tap from Gossamyr. Ulrich shook his head. "What was that for?"

"The spell worked." She bent to retrieve the gown. "And you were starting to drool."

"Was not." He dashed out his tongue across his lips. No drool. A man had to check. "Sorry. Gossamyr, you are wounded."

"It's from the revenant." The gown fell to her knees. A tug of the braies completed her renegade attire; the entire right leg was stained brown from dried blood.

"You must let me tend it. It looks bad."

"No worse than a bite from a werefrog. You did put a mustard plaster to your bite?"

"Anon."

She bent and ripped the front of the skirt all the way up to her thigh to allow her legs ease of movement, then grabbed the half staff leaning against the wall. A fistful of *arrets* was retrieved from the floor in a clatter of obsidian.

"Where be you off to?" He followed her down the ladder. "Shall I saddle up Fancy?"

"I go alone. Ulrich, you must tend that bite or it will fester."

"My uncle has prepared a plaster. Will you stop?" He sprinted to meet her at the front door. "There is danger. You need protection."

"From Shinn?"

"You go to call him out? But the city...the Red Lady... Will your father not be in danger?"

"I ride out from the gates of Paris. I must have answers, Ulrich." She smiled, a brief yet genuine smile. A touch to his hair, she drew in his scent. Ulrich closed his eyes and tried to scent her but smelled only the onions his uncle boiled over the hearth.

"You don't remember me," she said, "but I remember you."

He lifted a brow.

"When you danced. I stretched out my hand and touched your hair as you spun past me."

"You...saw me? Yet, I danced but a few days ago..."

"Faery time is confusing."

"Faery time is a bitch."

She nodded. "I truly hope you can get back that which was lost to you, Jean César Ulrich Villon III."

"Do you? I thought you against my quest to bring back the dead."

She shrugged. "I wish your twenty years returned to you. One way or another."

With that she leaned forward and kissed him aside his eye, right over the green bruise. Forgoing a farewell, she left without turning back.

"Would that you could help me, Gossamyr of Glamoursiège," Ulrich said as he watched her approach Fancy. "But I do not think a mere mortal will serve me now. If there is a unicorn to be found I shall just have to sniff it out myself."

The city gates were more willing to let one pass out of than into Paris. Reports that the Armagnacs were pillaging on the west side of the city provided little relief to the anticipation swirling in Gossamyr's gut. She traveled south but kept her eyes peeled and ears pricked for danger.

The evening beckoned with soft *schusses* of meadow grass and the brays of a flock of sheep waiting entry.

When Gossamyr reached the water mill where yesterday she and Ulrich had stopped, there was no need to summon Shinn. She dismounted, dropping Fancy's reins and leaving the mule to root at a patch of trampled grass. Striding toward the stream where she had bathed in the rain, Gossamyr fisted her fingers at her thighs and tightened her jaw.

Chiding words spoken by Mince visited her thoughts.

Do not react. Listen with an open heart. Your father acts only as his wisdom allows. He knows little of growing girls and their hearts.

And if their hearts be mortal?

The nemesis Shinn had bid her seek solace from had been placed there by Shinn himself.

Her strides were unhampered by the heavy gown, for the cut exposed her braies to the thighs. *Arrets* clicking at her hip, there was no need to call out to announce her presence.

Shinn did not turn around. Cloaked by the feathered cape, his broad shoulders squared him, increasing his presence. Hyacinth perfumed the air. So very light, the paleness of sky that surrounded the formidable Glamoursiège lord. Truly, a man who could command troops with but a word.

Gossamyr faltered as she gained him. Was that it? Shinn was a leader, not a compassionate father. He had lied to her only because that is all he could muster.

Not an excuse.

Fisting her fingers at her sides, she opened them, then closed them tight. If he did love her, then he owed her an explanation.

"I would beg your forgiveness," he said as Gossamyr stopped behind him. He swept out an arm and lifted an entreating palm upward. His blazon, which ended in his palms, sparkled with the rays of the setting sun. Still he did not turn to face her. "But I have never been one to beg. And I fear your anger is too strong to allow such mortal emotional fumbling."

The fetch had clued him to all.

"Why did you not tell me? Ever? When I was younger?" So wanting to beat upon his shoulders, to empty out her anger, Gossamyr suppressed her rage—for the truth. But not all of it.

She gripped him by the shoulder and shoved. He turned to her. Fine lines creased from the edges of his eyes and mouth. And his hair! She had not remarked it, but—it was silver. Now the small horns had darkened and tightened in, standing out against the long strands of faded hair. Bronze glinted in twists about his crown. "Wh-what happened to you?"

"I have been battling the revenants."

"I have been gone but a few sunsets!"

"Many more moons than you can imagine have risen in Faery."

"Be time so mutable as to steal many moons from me? To do this to you?"

She thought of Ulrich's horrid dance and all the time he had lost here in the mortal realm. And Avenall; he had stated but a mortal year had passed since his mistress had been banished; less than a moon since his banishment. How to comprehend?

Had she lost Time since Passaging to the Otherside?

"My trips to the Otherside are risky in that the passage of Time takes from me that which Faery holds off—mortality. You will not understand, but I have mourned your absence far too long."

"An absence you could have prevented!" Clutching her chest, she gasped at the weight of her heartbeats. Such pain did pierce her there in her heart! So much she needed to learn, and yet she should have known all along.

Shinn turned a stern eye on her. "I did not want you to leave."

True. But he hadn't been overly aggressive at making her stay. Mayhap that is how he erased his mistakes, by sending them to the Otherside? To think of herself as such, a mistake? No, if she truly was a changeling, that would mean she had been chosen. Yet, would not Shinn have expected her to perish? *They take sick mortals.*

"You knew the Disenchantment would be permanent. That, as a mortal, my return to Faery could prove devastating."

"I took a vow never to reveal your truth."

"But why?"

"To keep Time from you!"

"Time? I—I don't understand. Shinn, you sent me off for ever!"

"The rift will allow your return—though it may yet prove dangerous."

"Then why did not Veridienne return?"

"She is dead."

"So you say." Did he keep that truth, as well? This man she had trusted!

"I made a vow to Veridienne, Gossamyr." He closed his eyes. The muscles on his face tightened, the vein in his temple pulsed. "Veridienne so wished to break our marriage vows that she would sacrifice for her return to the Otherside."

"Sacrifice?"

"The mortal passion was strong, so strong." A falter in his voice.

Gossamyr stepped closer. "The mortal passion...it is love, yes?"

A smile, so small, but tremendous in meaning, curved Shinn's mouth. "You are right about that. Veridienne loved the Otherside. I...loved her. I did not want her to leave me. But even more, my mortal passion for you was great. I could not bear to see her take you away from me."

"My mother—Veridienne, she wanted to bring me to the Otherside with her?"

Shinn nodded. "Of course."

Such discovery made Gossamyr wobble. The air, once so light, settled heavily in her lungs. She had always thought Veridienne had not cared. Yet she had loved her so much as to— "Why did she not?"

"It was her sacrifice. You for her freedom. She sacrificed one love for an even greater love."

And the stunning realization of her father's cruel dichotomy cleaved a sharp blade into her heart. *The Faery prince took my sight for the wonders I had seen.* Twenty years stolen for a few moments of revelry. A child sacrificed for the freedom of one's homeland.

"You forced her to leave her child behind? How dare you!"

"You are my child, too!"

Shaking her head vigorously, not wanting to allow the truth to settle in, for then it would be so, Gossamyr stomped against the pain. "I am not your child! I am not Veridienne's child! Why keep this cruel secret for so long?"

Still so utterly emotionless, Shinn answered, "Before she left, Veridienne begged me to keep you safe. To not reveal the truth, for she feared such knowledge would hurt you more than help. She feared knowing your mortal heritage would increase your risk of succumbing to the mortal passion."

"And so you allow me to believe I am something I am not? You have known of my mortal passion with the Otherside. It is as if my very being were trying to make me understand. I am what the fée so fear!"

"I could not have prevented you from leaving. I thought to keep the truth from you would keep you safe. So long as you never left Faery your Enchantment would remain." He sighed. "You would have never stayed in Faery. Admit it."

"I did desire adventure." Drawing a staunch face, Gossamyr wrestled with the inner struggle of emotions. Yes, emotions.

Fear was key. So little she knew, and yet, had thought to know! What now would become of her? She could never regain her Enchantment when returning to Faery.

Anger swirled around the fear. If she had known before leaving that she was mortal, would she still have left Faery? To fight for a land that was not even her own? So many lies told, all to keep her from knowing love. The mortal passion. A crime to the fée, but to a mortal? Was it not a birthright?

As well, pity and a very slippery bit of hope fought with Gossamyr's darker emotions. Self-pity was not a familiar mien; yet it stabbed at her gut, weakening her stance. Why her? Why had the Faery lord chosen to toy with her life?

"I should not have left."

"You wanted to prove yourself," he quickly answered.

"Could you not have sent me to a dangerous task in Faery? A quest to defeat a root lamia?"

"Gossamyr, you pleaded for this chance. You were the only choice to send after the Red Lady."

"You mean, your disgruntled lover."

He lifted a gray brow. "You have spoken to her?"

"Spoken? You say it as if I would converse with the bitch before I destroy her. Curse you, Shinn! I have not. But I know all. That you two were to be wed. That she was the reason for my being brought to Faery. That you banished her. It is all because of a lovers' spat that I now find myself neither here nor there. She— she is a Rougethorn!"

"Yes."

"I thought her a Netherdred."

"Why?"

"I don't know, I assumed. Where else could something so evil reside?" In a fée lord's heart? The flickering thought gave cause to wonder. "I thought it because the Rougethorns practiced magic— but the only reason you hated Avenall was because he was from the same tribe as your lover?"

"That is not fair."

"But it is true!"

He splayed his hands between them. Blue-black raven feathers listed in the breeze. So close she stood, and yet, not too close for Faery. It was hard for her to step into Shinn's air. "Why did you two not marry?"

"She dabbled."

"An excuse! You had to have known such before the two tribes were even brought together with the banns!"

He nodded and sighed, unwilling to speak. Difficult for him? She would not relent until the truth was hers. It was owed to her. This may yet be her greatest challenge.

"You must have once loved the Red Lady, to have agreed to wed."

"Lust, Gossamyr, no more than that. The Red Lady...I was drawn to her. Compelled by the succubus's song. She is a dangerous lure to any fée male. But I will not claim lack of defense; I wanted her. It was a time when the Rougethorns had only begun to dabble. Discussion to unite the tribes was so new. The Faery elders believed uniting the tribes would bring the Glamoursiège morals to Rougethorn, prevent them from following the darker arts of dabbling. They are no lesser than we…only very few have established alliances with mortal wizards and witches.

"My sudden distaste for my betrothed had nothing to do with her dabbling—she did not participate in magic at the time. It was, as you have learned, the sudden onset of my mortal passion that turned my lust from her. I had visited the Otherside and fell in love with Veridienne. 'Twas the first time I knew my feelings for a woman were true—in the deepest way, the way mortals love—so unlike the lust I had felt for Circélie."

"Circélie?"

"The Red Lady."

Gossamyr swallowed to hear her father name—so personally— the enemy she had stalked. An enemy, she realized, who had dabbled in Gossamyr's very fate.

"Circélie was persistent," Shinn explained, "and sought my continued affections. And so, when Veridienne was with child Circélie kissed her; a cursing kiss, you understand. When our child was born 'twas a changeling."

"That was the child—"

"That I placed in your mortal mother's cradle," Shinn said.

That he had not named her as the child broke the truth wide open. Gossamyr began to sink below the surface, groping blindly for hold, but sensing no matter how hard she struggled, or how long, she would never simply float. Never again would the mortal air feel light.

"In exchange, we took the female babe lying in the cradle back to Faery. You, Gossamyr."

She could not conjure the scene. A mortal babe lying alone in a cradle. Was there not family about? Not a mother's watchful eyes to protect her babe from mischievous faeries? How had Shinn decided Gossamyr would be the one?

"You…knew I was healthy?"

"No, we expected you would live but a few days, so sickly you were at the time. You surprised us both. Never doubt my love for you."

Turning away from Shinn she looked up to seek the sun, but as it set so its color was muted and pink. Not bright enough to bring tears to her eyes. The tears were there, but she sought camouflage. Faery love was false, a device modeled after the real thing, but never equal. *Not the same.*

"You know it is not the fée nature to love as the mortals do." Shinn's voice trickled over her scalp. So strange the fée lilt sounded to her now, and here on the Otherside. Alien. Not right. She craved the rumbling tones of Jean César Ulrich Villon III. "We are…fickle."

"Oh, I know that now."

"But you…you knew love, Gossamyr. You have always had the capacity for it. I saw it in your eyes when you spoke of him. He—Avenall—woke the love buried in your mortal heart. Which is why I discouraged your courtship. To love as a mortal, and have your heart broken, would have proved painful."

She spun on his erratic explanation. "Should that not have been my decision?"

"I only wanted to protect you. Desideriel Raine is a good man."

"I know that!" She turned and lowered her head. Picking at the fur flowing over her left wrist, she could but summon anger. A bold and furious rush that made her jitter and fist the air. He had thought it all through so carefully. Thinking to protect her from a broken heart? Shinn thought only of the political alliance her marriage would promise Glamoursiège. Desideriel was Wisogoth; the ancient faery tribe aligned to Glamoursiège only promised a brilliant future.

To ever keep the Rougethorn taint from Shinn's life had meant keeping it from hers.

"He excels in battle," Shinn continued. "Desideriel takes command—has even bested me more than once—and shows no hesitation to do so. He is the only choice to lord over Glamoursiège when I am gone. We have discussed this."

"I do not doubt Desideriel's qualifications—" *...to lord over Glamoursiège...* "You just placed Desideriel to the throne instead of me? I understand now." She approached him, anger keeping her stiff, sharpening her words. "You cannot have a mortal sit the throne and so you must marry her to a full-blood fée. Have you planned this since the day you brought me to Faery, Shinn?"

"Not so long as that. Gossamyr—"

She put up a hand, hoping to silence his insincerity in her booming heart. But those violet eyes gazing upon her with such sadness, and that sweet hyacinth aura, betroubled her and challenged her need to remain angry with him.

"I begin to understand the strange workings of your twisted faery love," she said. "That is why you wish me to marry a man who can never love me—because I shall never love him. Hence, the mortal passion would remain buried."

Shinn nodded. "It is for Glamoursiège."

"Indeed. Isn't it always for Glamoursiège? Unless Lord de Wintershinn finds a mortal woman he can love over the chance to unite two tribes."

"That is…"

"Not fair? Oh, yes, the fée always require balance. For every good there requires ill. For every trick a trade. For every broken heart…what? It is too late. I know love, Shinn. The deep, gorgeous, and yes, even painful love that faeries fear. You could never stifle my truth, yet in attempting to do so, you caused the very tragedy you sought to prevent."

"It was done to protect you, Gossamyr. Should you learn the truth Time will catch up and… The glamour—"

"You worked a glamour on me? Is that why I wore a blazon, because of faery glamour? Why? Why not simply return me to my mortal parents after you saw I was not to die? Should they not have had the right to raise their own child?"

"The d'Ange family was carefully chosen. They were not to survive long after your birth."

"Carefully— They did not— D'Ange?" Unsettled, Gossamyr groped for purchase on nothing more than the air, but stood without falter. Ulrich, where be he to? She needed him to stand by her, to support. *It could become romantic, should you allow it.* "That is the name of the family you stole me from?"

"Not so much stole, as—"

"Be honest! It is a Faery rite to steal mortal infants to replace sick changelings. Give and take! Good and ill!"

The feathered cloak fluttered out; beneath, Shinn's wings coiled open and beat the air once. Trying to maintain calm. Gossamyr knew that telling sign. *Please, Father, just open up and give to me my truth!*

He gripped the air before him, clenching—keeping back his truths—but spoke yet with calm. "If Circélie did not tell you, how then came this knowledge to you? Who revealed your truth?"

"Avenall."

The Faery lord gaped. Not an expression Gossamyr had ever before seen.

"Yes, my banished lover-to-be has joined forces with your banished lover. Marvelous, eh? But he does not remember me. Yet you left your lover with her memory intact, for that is the reason you now battle the revenants. To think you could have prevented this war with but your own discretion!"

Yes, wince, she thought. Show me emotion. Confess to your indiscretions! To your lies!

"Avenall Éloi Papilion," Shinn muttered, marking each name slowly. "I made it so."

"Of course..." Gossamyr whispered. "Papilion. That is his name complete. I had...forgotten. The succubus has him in her *erie*. Circélie?" She must remember. And: Avenall Éloi Papilion. "Avenall does not remember me. And he's changed so much. And how…how were you able to banish him from Glamoursiège when he was a Rougethorn?"

"I have command over all who have settled in Glamoursiège. Avenall has been there since he was very small."

As she had suspected. "Yet, you deemed him unfit for me with so little time as a Rougethorn?"

"Forgive me, child of mine."

"How can you name me that after all has been revealed?"

"I love you."

"Oh?" His admission meant so little right now. It felt little more than a tap from a damselfly's wings to her nose. Irritating, if truth be confessed. "Well, I hate you, Shinn. I hate you for your lies. I hate you for sending me away. I hate you for your smugness and your supremacy. And I hate you for the truth!"

The commander lifted his chin, catching the setting sun in a glitter across his throat. "Your hate, it is just."

Gossamyr stepped around to catch his straying gaze. "So I will wither and die as a mortal? Is that not the way of all mortals? Such a truth is not so fearsome."

"Remember, I have always told you to believe."

"Yes, yes."

"You believed you belonged in Faery and that is all required. The blazon of glamour was yours with Belief. But now…to know the truth…"

"I have not aged since arriving in the Otherside. Time has not touched me."

Gossamyr turned away and twisted her head down against her chest. Tears flowed freely. Shinn would be horrified. Ulrich would dance a merry jig at her plunge into emotion. But it felt right to cry. Because she hurt. Deeply. So deep it seeped from her chest and swelled into her heart and gut. Oh, but the ache had been put there by the only person she had ever trusted! How many more times would he wound her with his mistruths and abrupt reactions?

"I should leave," Shinn said softly.

Gossamyr stretched out her arms. "No! We are not finished. There is much to be said. Twice now you have hurt me with your indifference. Look at me! You witness my pain. A pain you put here." She pounded her chest with a fist. The inability to squelch emotion made her lips shiver as she spoke. "It seeps from my heart, Shinn."

He tilted his head inquiringly. So dispassionate. "Does not your hate for me close the wound?"

Cruel, emotionless fée.

Then he did something remarkable. Shinn reached out and touched her face. He traced the curve of her eye, wetting his fingertip with her salty pain. Drawing it before him, the sun caught in the glint of her teardrops.

"Worth so much," she said, challenge sharpening her tone. "Mortal tears."

"Worth nothing when I am the cause." He swiped his finger down his cheek, wiping off her tears on his flesh. Briefly, the salted trail sparkled like his blazon before fading and twinkling away.

Shaking her head, Gossamyr wept. "I hate you. And…" She fell to her knees and clutched Shinn's legs. All that she had known was her father's heart. And for every ill there had been a right so perfect she had never once doubted his love. "I love you."

Love and hate. Impossible to separate the two emotions, for they were alike in intensity. Both birthed from her heart. Both gushed tears down her cheeks. Both were…so mortal.

Fingers touched her scalp, gently easing into the motion of comfort. Gossamyr continued to sob, pouring out her loss, her reality, into her false father's arms.

Shinn knelt and tucked her head against his shoulder. And for a long time the two embraced, Gossamyr's sobbing filled the air, salting it and painting it heavily upon her heart. The rose-colored sky darkened and crickets began to chirp. And with that plunge into evening, and the release of her pain, Gossamyr settled to a sniffling acceptance.

"It was not indifference that hurt you, child of mine, but fear. I feared losing you so much—"

"So you kept a lie in hopes I would return to live ever after in Faery by your side."

"Selfish of me."

Only when Gossamyr heard Shinn's sniff did she look up into his watery violet eyes. "You do love? But...I am not your own."

"You are as my own flesh, Gossamyr. The day I sent you to the Otherside I wept. For the first time in my life. It is most...uncomfortable." He touched the corner of his eye and studied a teardrop, jiggling on his fingertip as if an alien thing. "I deserve your hate, but never your love."

And he would have her hate. But she would temper it with the inexplicable compulsion to cling to the only constancy she had ever known—her father.

"What of my mortal parents?"

"They were murdered a few years back."

Gossamyr's jaw fell open.

"I am sorry. The d'Anges. The—that is the castle where you stopped. I saw it through the fetch."

"I was drawn to my place of birth?"

"It is not a wonder."

"But what I found there. It was destitute. The destruction. Do you know how they died? Have you watched them? Are they all lost to me? Please tell me, Shinn, I must know."

"Very well. The d'Anges were murdered by a dark lord, who later fell at the hands of your mortal sister. She yet lives under the watch of an Enchanted, though I know not where."

"I have a sister?" She splayed a hand across the membrane of

Shinn's wing, which curled around her back. Warm and soft, like an arm hugging her close.

Completely mortal. And a family? A sister? How had her real parents died? Had they suffered? Had they mourned her absence? What had her mortal mother's hands felt like? Had she loved her more than Veridienne ever could?

"I always felt you had a better life in Faery. It pained me, your fascination with the Otherside. But I knew that the mortal passion had been yours to own since birth. In a manner, this mission was my gift to you."

The gift of freedom. The price? Truth.

To age and die? "Can I return to Faery? Will Time age me so quickly as it has aged you?"

"I have lived this aging, child of mine. I cannot guess what Time will serve you now that the truth is yours. It is legend a mortal who knows he does not belong will perish once returned to Faery, for the aging takes with great lust."

"That is why you kept the truth. To return to Faery now, I would…"

"I guess you would age as you should have here in the Otherside."

"But it has not been so long. Avenall, he claims he has been here less than a mortal moon cycle."

"Time twists widdershins and thus, Gossamyr. No man, beast or fée can stop or control it. While you have lived in Faery, many mortal years have passed, and yet, so few."

Gossamyr heaved in a shivering sigh. Her tears depleted, she could feel but an emptiness. But yet, 'twas as if that hole had begun to fill by that bit of wonder that had ever traced her heart. *What is the mortal passion?* Love.

How she fit into the air here in the Otherside.

"You placed me in the Otherside for a purpose. I have not given up the fight."

"And the man…"

"Ulrich?" She chuckled, mayhap because that was the only emotion she had yet to loose. "But of course. I suspected as much when in the forest. You enchanted him into my life. Did you think I needed protection?"

"Compassion. He has not proven me wrong."

"Do you know he is a Dancer?"

"Yes, and he possesses the sight because of it. I know you witnessed the Dance, Gossamyr. I saw your foray into the mortal passion."

So she had guessed correctly. "He is a good man. Though I dare not leave him alone too long. I fear he will succumb to the Red Lady's seduction."

"He is more susceptible with the sight."

And determined to follow the lure—

"Shinn! He carries an alicorn."

The aging fée warrior drew in a hissing breath. "This I have not seen through the fetch."

"It is what will heal the rift, I know it! Ulrich wants to return it to the unicorn in exchange for a wish granted. His daughter, she was sacrificed to a dragon, and he wants her back."

"He asks far too much with its return. One must not raise the dead."

She had believed much the same, until she had learned to know Ulrich. *You think a man cannot love a child not of his blood?*

Ulrich and Shinn, they two were alike.

"It gives him hope. A purpose."

"Mortals have always aspired to purpose. As have you, Gossamyr. I had only thought to give you that purpose. But this alicorn…you must not return it."

"What?"

Wind sifted Shinn's gray hair across his staunch jaw. *Not the same.* How many of her father's moons had been stolen from her with his Passage to the Otherside?

"Gossamyr, as it stands now, I can bring you back to Faery. As my daughter, whether blooded or not, you belong in Faery."

"But I will age?"

"I can return your glamour, though it will not be fixed by Enchantment. There…is the marriage to consider."

"Of course." The two tribes must unite. As well, Glamoursiège must eventually receive an heir to the throne. "How selfish of me—"

"Gossamyr."

She pushed out from Shinn's wing embrace and strode toward the stream. Another reason her father did not want her to leave his side—the business of securing the Glamoursiège reign—yet he would never put that into the air.

"Why should I return to marry and to rule a land not my own?"

"Because Glamoursiège is your home!"

"Oh?"

"It is the only home you have ever known."

"But you schemed to place Desideriel at my side. It is imperative I marry a full-blood fée. Does Desideriel know? That I am but a mortal changeling?"

"Gossamyr—"

"Tell me!"

"He does not. He believes you half-blooded. And should evermore."

"More lies! When will the truth ever be safe? Yet my return will see my swift decline. How soon before the aging reduces me to but bone? You ask me to sacrifice for the good of Faery."

"I should not ask so much of one I love."

"Faeries know not how to love," Gossamyr spat.

"Why can you not believe a man is capable of loving someone, of caring for and raising a child not of his flesh?"

"Because…"

Ulrich's situation flashed before her. The man quested to bring his daughter back to him. A child whom he did not know to be his or another man's.

Never had she felt Shinn was being false with her. His cruelties never weakened his kindnesses. He could speak the truth. She wanted him to speak the truth. Why now should he lie?

"Very well. I…accept that you love me. And that Veridienne loved me. But what has my return to do with the alicorn?"

"If you heal the rift, you close the means for your return. I will be forever sealed off from you."

And the marriage would not take place.

"But the fée can always Passage to the Otherside. You could…visit me, as you do now, without risking Disenchantment."

"My next visit may be my last." He stroked away a strand of hair from his face. Had the wrinkles deepened? He was aging before her eyes.

"You ask me to keep the rift open, to allow the revenants continued return?"

"Your defeat of the Red Lady will stop them." He bowed his head, clenching his fists near his face. "I don't want to lose you, Gossamyr."

"But Faery—it will suffer for—"

"For my selfish desires."

For a father's love. For a marriage that would crown Shinn's successor. Both noble desires. And since when did she ever believe that she could choose a life of her own making? The truth should not change any of that.

"Shinn, I don't know what to do."

"You know my wishes. You know the fate of Glamoursiège lies in your hands. But I will not keep you from doing what you feel is right. You are truly a champion. Valor has always been yours."

"Valor," she muttered, remembering the words painted on the dented shield. "And vengeance." *Your mortal sister killed him.* "And the truth. Have I the truth?"

"Truth is your name, Verity d'Ange."

"Verity? That is a part of my—"

"Gossamyr Verity de Wintershinn. Veridienne and I felt you should retain that part of your heritage."

"My, my mortal name." The knowledge landed her, light as a feather, to her shoulder. So precious, and she had held such all this time.

He lifted her hand and pressed it to his cheek, which momentarily brightened the tear trail. Not warm, Shinn's flesh, but neither cold. Drawing her hand away, he clasped it between both of his. "Now you have the truth. All of it. You must not worry for the world, Gossamyr. Think of yourself."

"Myself?" Verity d'Ange. Mortal. "Yes, so much I have wanted. So much I have received."

But there were others. "Can Avenall ever remember?"

Shinn shrugged. "I could make it so. Do you wish it?"

"I'm not sure." *Not the same.* "What if I Named him complete?"

"You might try. The Red Lady's power over him is great with the essences that feed her."

"What is her complete name, Shinn? You must know."

"I do, but the Naming will not command her. Circélie made a pact with a witch for her Naming. A foul mix of glamour and magic shield her from any Enchantment I might wield against her." Now he touched her forehead, connecting. Lowering his head, he kissed her in the wake of his thumbprint. "If I could have used the truth, I would have. Never forget I love you. I do not know how to hate you."

"I cannot forget something that lives in my heart. Thank you and…curse you."

With that, Shinn shimmered through the curtain that separated the Otherside from Faery. And Gossamyr fell to her knees and caught her hands at the edge of the stream.

A wavery reflection of a woman stared up at her. Silver light glinted in the purling waters sparkling like a crown about her blowsy tresses. Perhaps a remnant of her bath to wash away the glamour. If only she had known then she might have clung to the Enchantment a bit longer.

"No," she whispered to the woman in the stream. "This be who I am. Mayhap I have always known. Only now can I accept the truth." She speared a finger into her reflection, dispersing the regretful moue on the woman's lips.

There were things to do. Action to be taken.

But.

"Is my path now the same?" she wondered as she rose and scanned the wall of the city that had kept attacking enemies at bay for countless mortal moons.

The enemy was already inside the gates, safely shrouded within walls of marble. Walls undulating with the stolen lives of the Disenchanted. Shinn's lover. A vindictive succubus who would make her Faery father suffer for deeds he could not undo. How he must have felt to look upon his newly born child, a changeling cursed by the Red Lady. Then was when Shinn's heart must have broken.

Had it ever healed? Or had Gossamyr's difficulties in adjusting to Faery, and her ultimate mutiny, ripped Shinn's heart to irreparable shreds?

Had the man the capacity to love as only Gossamyr knew she could love? *I kept the truth to keep you in my heart. You are my mortal passion.*

Yes.

Gossamyr smiled at the voice inside her head. Shinn's voice. He was with her. And that knowledge comforted.

"Faery might not be my home, but it is in my heart. I will not step away from my quest."

TWENTY-FOUR

The shimmer was as a fallen star, or a portion of moonlight hovering in the mute shadows between two buildings. Ulrich, clutching the saddlebag covetously, stepped forward, his mouth agape. The brightness softened and he was able to look directly at the image for more than a few blinks.

Slowly the brilliance shimmied and moved and began to form. A man?

But of course. He doubted no strange creature. Had he not seen, in the past se'nnight, more than any sane mortal should see for a lifetime?

Thinking to turn away from witnessing, from pressing further into his memory visions of Faery, Ulrich splayed his hand before his face.

Yet a male voice, calm and rimmed with the remarkable jingle of Faery, stirred him to look fully into the face of a most marvelous being. A head taller than he, the creature. Glints of bronze and crystal gleamed with the illumination of Faery there at his brow and on his shoulder and lower, rimming his cloak. Streams of silver hair listed in the breeze. Small horns sprouted at his temples, glittering with so much Faery glamour. Regal, spoke his carriage; melancholy spoke his face.

Ulrich knew without thinking who stood before him. Impulsively he clutched the saddlebag tighter until he could feel the hard form of the alicorn cleave into his ribs.

The lord of Glamoursiège extended his hand. Ulrich flinched and stepped back.

"Jean César Ulrich Villon III."

"You—you know my name?"

"You see me?"

Ulrich nodded effusively. If he ran, would the Faery lord give chase? What was he doing here in Paris when Gossamyr had been emphatic regarding her father's aversion to the city, his risk to Disenchantment? And hadn't she just gone to seek him?

Remain, Jean César Ulrich Villon III.

The Faery lord had named him complete. Ulrich could but stand. And admire.

Do not move.

The urge to run slipped away like rain purling over a blanched skull.

Moving more upon a glimmer than actually stepping, Shinn swayed closer.

His fingernails digging into the leather bag, Ulrich felt the inexplicable urge to bow, to coil into his torso and prostrate himself. But as his knees wobbled and his stomach roiled, he found the fortitude to remain standing.

"A strong mortal. You are not afraid?"

"You are...Gossamyr's father."

The Faery lord tilted his head. Violet eyes touched Ulrich there— his heart pulsed madly—just on the chest, before moving up and meeting him eye-to-eye. A vision of the Dance flashed in Ulrich's forethoughts and he spat out, "They made me dance! For so long."

Shinn nodded, an understanding parent. "You are the soul shepherd who accompanies my daughter."

Huffing out a breath of the ages Ulrich felt, for the first time in over a week, a strange calm. "I am. I didn't mean to step into Faery. It was merely an accident. I was not looking where I wandered. I meant thee no harm!"

"The Dance is long past."

"Long past? It has been but a se'nnight! You stole so much from me!"

Shinn inclined his head. The slight movement straightened Ulrich and he sucked in a breath. *Settle. It is the past.* Mustn't anger a being whom he had learned was quick to temper and even more vile when doling punishment.

"You carry the alicorn?"

Ulrich looked aside to the ground.

"I will not take it from you, mortal. It is yours to command. You must study your heart and decide whether or not your original intentions will bring certain improvement or sure failure."

"I— Just want to see my daughter. One last time. And…I want Faery from my eyes." He clutched the shape of the alicorn in the saddlebag. Did he smell flowers? The scent seemed to drift from the Faery lord himself. "Gossamyr tells me to return the alicorn would seal the rift. If such an event occurs, she will not then be able to return to Faery—"

"You know far too much, mortal."

"—to you!"

The Faery lord bowed his head and the gleam of the bronze band about his forehead momentarily blinded Ulrich.

Ulrich touched his right eye, smoothed a finger over the ache, but with a blink he focused on the faery. "I want my daughter back."

"As do I," Shinn said loudly and abruptly.

"We both love a child not our own."

"Do not presume to compare two opposite beings."

"Mayhap in flesh and the internal soul we are opposite—" Ulrich pressed fingers to his chest. They shared much! "—but not in heart. I know you love Gossamyr. This alicorn, it is the key to my love."

With a disdainful sniff the Faery lord resumed composure and nodded. "It is not for me to command you, Jean César Ulrich Villon III."

Quiet acceptance swept over Ulrich. Glamour seeped into his pores. "Know only I love my daughter as you love your daughter."

The gleam surrounding the faery brightened. When Ulrich thought Shinn would flitter away, his light softened and he stood immediately before him. He hadn't seen him move. So close, these faeries, so close.

"Tell me, Jean César Ulrich Villon III…" Shinn's voice oozed through Ulrich's conscious, touching the resistance and softening with a sigh. "With which eye do you see me?"

"What? I see you plain as any man, standing far too close for my comfort."

"You but see me with one eye, mortal. Which one?"

Shaking his head, for he did not understand, Ulrich shrugged, but then thought to test the faery's suggestion. He closed his left eye. Shinn's calm countenance remained before him. So close he could feel the man's breath, warm as a summer breeze and tinged with—the scent of a flowered meadow? *Not too close for Faery.* So Ulrich opened his left eye and closed his right. He turned his head. Where had the man—opening both eyes, he saw Shinn had not moved.

"My…right," he offered. "I but see you with my right eye—"

Before he could finish, Shinn's fingers moved over Ulrich's face. Gripped in the faery's hold, he felt a cool touch of breath as Shinn blew into his right eye.

A blue ache crackled across his eye and moved around and behind into his skull. Cold, so cold. A momentary wave of pain, and then it dissipated with a jingle of the Dance, a remnant of all that had irrevocably altered Ulrich's life. *Never again the same.*

But do you desire sameness?

Shinn released him. Ulrich wavered then righted himself. Still there, the saddlebag. He could not see the Faery lord standing before him. Had he glimmered off so quickly?

"Shinn?"

"Never call me by name," the faery's voice answered from what seemed to be right before Ulrich.

Cupping a palm over his right eye, he searched the dimming light with his left. Shinn was not to be sighted. But his presence; he could verily feel the faery's presence in his blood.

"I cannot see you. My eye...what...I cannot see with my right eye!"

"Fair fall you, Shepherd to Lost Souls."

"No." Ulrich lashed out with a clawing hand and touched nothing but air before him. At the periphery of his vision he saw the flash. "You bastard! You have taken half my sight but you'll not take my determination. I will have my daughter back!"

Basking in the illumination of the multicolored essences, she stretched languorously along the silk linens soaked in myrrh. Puppy tended her desires. Perched at the end of the bed, he lapped at her bare toes, sucking each one inside his warm bud of a mouth. She neared the edge; release shimmied in her groin. Oh, but the lash of his tongue tip along the high arch of her foot!

"Oh, Pup-eeeeeeee..."

He knew not to speak, but to tend her unceasingly until the climax overwhelmed. Clenching thick wodges of silken sheet and pillow in her fists, she began to surrender. The moans of the pinned essences chanted an eerie background. Ah, there. A high, shimmering note vibrated from afar...

"What?" Snapping upright on the bed, she pricked her ears for the neuma of tone that clutched her passion and thrust it to the side. "Cease!" She kicked at Puppy, drawing out her largest toe from his mouth in a tooth-scraping tug. "Listen."

Her lover cowered at the bed's edge, his fingers clawing into the scarlet sheets, his eyes underlined by the rumpled linens.

Drawn from the manic magic that should have enthralled her, she slid off the bed, her parted robe scouring over Puppy's stream of hair. But the tips were black; soon he would be red complete. Red. Then gone. She disliked them after the transformation for they were so obsequious.

Stopping before the marble wall, she splayed out her hands, as if to command the essences to silence. They continued their dirge, unmindful of her efforts.

Tilting her head, she managed to fix upon that unique but so familiar vibration.

"Shinn?" she gasped, unbelieving if it were true. "In the Otherside?"

Sprinting out the door and down the marble hallway, she was aware the pin man followed like the puppy dog she'd named him. He remained silent. Good puppy. Passing by the seven sleepers, their murmurs halted and the candle flames heightened. Attention drew to her, as it should.

Had the Faery lord come to Paris? To become Disenchanted? No. He would not risk such a fall.

Mayhap he sought her? Could it possibly be after all this time her lover wanted her back?

Flinging wide the doors to the outer streets, she stepped onto the cobbles. The night air gloved her bare flesh, raising prickles upon her belly and arms and neck.

"Mistress, come back inside!"

Ignoring his pleas, the Red Lady sent out a call. An answer. *Come take me, I am here. I have never stopped loving you…*

"I will retrieve a dress and call for the carriage," Puppy muttered.

* * *

Ulrich paused just off the courtyard that preceded the Petit Pont. A torn banner whipped in the breeze, belatedly marking the Monday market. It was difficult to navigate with but one eye, but he was determined. Avoiding a fast carriage, he skipped backward and barely managed an inelegant jump over the center gutter. Thrusting an angry fist in the carriage's wake, he suddenly paused. He tilted his head to focus on a sound that did not fit amidst the shouts and brays and clanks of metal.

Insinuating himself between two close buildings, he shuffled the length of them to the opposite end where he stood alone upon the twilight-shining cobbles. There echoed the most elegant note, wavering and rising and finally settling into his chest.

So lovely the sound. It seemed to say, "I am…here…loving you."

Ulrich searched the sky, one-eyed as he could, unable to determine the direction of the call.

You are being pisky-led!

Pixies—or piskies, whatever the Hades they were—did not possess such beautiful song.

It is the Red Lady.

Well, she must be very beautiful, for her voice rivaled an angel's song. Or so Ulrich wagered. And she sang to him of love. Loving *him?* How he desired a kind, loving touch, a kiss to erase the bruise that yet colored his face with the sting of an accidental betrayal. This faery song was not the same and never to be the same.

Do not listen! She is evil.

Ulrich ignored his conscience, which sounded much like Gossamyr of Glamoursiège—daughter of his cruel tormentor—and sought out the origin of the compelling song.

He was not blinded fully and kept a wall on his right side, gliding his palm across the plastered limestone to support, for his lack of vision caused him to waver and stumble. Cold, the area surrounding his eyeball. Blinking at the brimming moisture that pooled in his blinded eye, he shook his head to fling away the wet, then proceeded onward.

The sonorous song filling his ears led him down a narrow passage darkened by buildings, four levels stacked one upon the other. Ulrich homed in on the music, succumbing to the heady surrender to ecstasy. She awaited him. A lover. Her kisses promised passion. It had been so long since he had known such. Twenty years. Or merely a week. He did not know anymore.

Sliding a finger under his right eye, he wiped away the stinging moisture.

The hunger for love grew. Already he could verily taste her, slipping across his tongue, gliding like fine wine down his throat and easing the ache in his belly.

Around the corner he spied a black lacquered carriage parked outside a manor stable. Not yet set out on journey, he suspected, for a coachman did not sit upon the driver's high perch.

Ulrich pushed aside the iron gate and walked up the crushed-shell path to the stable. His leather soles crunched the pearlescent shards in squeaking outbursts. If he kept his arms splayed and hands flattened, such did not tax his balance.

Drops of the stinging liquid running from his eye slipped into his mouth. Tasteless, unlike tears. Would he cry a saltless river from this day forth? Damn the Faery lord, Jean César Ulrich Villon III would not for one moment longer aid his daughter's quest. A mere mortal woman who could no more attract a unicorn than she could fly?

All for Ulrich now. He must focus on his wants.

A lava of pale velvet skirts spilled out of the dark-bodied carriage. The elegant twist of a feminine hand, gloved in softest gray kid, beckoned him forward. Alabaster and clouds and fresh clean eggshell, those were the colors of her gown. Yet— he could not see flesh. Or even a face. 'Twas the costume but no body!

The glove reached for his face. The touch of her, so delicate, shimmered through Ulrich's being, startling him madly. Like a bang to an elbow that vibrates shock waves, but this touch pleasured with its lightning path of pain. Pulling away, she held her finger between them, coated with the saltless tears that glimmered with the sheen of Faery. Shinn's trail? The finger moved in a fanning motion before what should have been her face—mon Dieu, but the wake of her movement showed red eyes and nose and smirking red lips! Wherever his tears touched revealed that part of the faery he could not see. She pushed the finger into her mouth and closed her eyes. Jubilation.

Strange as the vision was, to stand before him, partly seen, her costume draped in places where he should see flesh, Ulrich could not deny her beauty.

Banished for loving the cruel Faery lord? He reached to touch the blossom of vibrant red mouth that curled into a smile. His movement dislodged the leather saddlebag from his shoulder. Oblivious to the contents that spilled at his feet, Ulrich held out his hand, pleading for one touch of the delicious skin—so exquisitely pale—and to trace the dotted marking. *To recompense for love lost.*

Suddenly her crimson eyes widened and she drew in a hissing breath.

Ulrich looked down the shell path to where his seducer's eyes focused. Tilting his head, he spied what held her fascination. The alicorn lay unbound from its wrapping.

TWENTY-FIVE

Gossamyr strode toward the city walls where she knew Ulrich's uncle lived, her heels barely touching the cobbles. The wound on her knee stung. It was a struggle not to limp, but yet the air lightened her steps.

An ever-flowing stream of her mortal tears for a bit of glamour right now—though the tears be valuable only to the fée. Anything to make her less vulnerable. She should have remained in the Red Lady's lair, waiting to end it, to take her out.

Had it been fear for Ulrich that had hastened her away from the marble-lined walls? Nay, fear for herself.

Blight, that was it. She was afraid.

The realization stalled Gossamyr in her tracks. Fear? Ulrich would be most pleased. She pressed her knuckles, half staff in hand, to the stone wall at her right. Heavy breaths huffed from her lungs.

You are not fée. Not even half-blooded!

Believe and you Belong.

Shaking her head, Gossamyr struggled with voices crying out from her past and the future that beckoned with a strange crook of its bony finger.

Believe? In what? And where to belong?

This mortal world—no, she was not fascinated by it—horrified her. It offered nothing but filth and depravity and war. The people were not friendly; they did not look at her with smiles but downturned faces. They did not care about Gossamyr, daughter of Shinn. They struggled to survive.

As would she. She could not believe in this mortal realm. But no longer could she believe in Faery. Or the idea that Faery was her home.

When you stop believing you cease to belong.

"I want to return," she whispered. "I do believe. I will always believe."

But she could not return should the alicorn be restored to the unicorn. Could she stop Ulrich from seeking his wish? Had she any right to keep him from summoning his daughter from death?

So important, family. Hers had suddenly been yanked away. *Not even a real family.* Yet, according to Shinn, Gossamyr had family she had not even known.

The d'Anges were murdered.

Verity d'Ange. Such a peculiar name. But it intrigued in that it *belonged* to Gossamyr. Her birth name. Verity—a secret name that had always been hers.

No!

She could not belong to a family that no longer existed. But there remained a sister—this unknown sister might be all Gossamyr had now. Might she ever hope to find her? For Shinn's betrayal had cleaved Gossamyr from Faery.

You love him despite his cruelties. He is all you have ever known.

They did love one another, had grown closer following the departure of Veridienne. Gossamyr had learned to love—the faery way. A surface emotion that never truly rooted. Or had it? She was not capable of hating Shinn. Love, the mortal passion. "It has always been mine."

She thought now of the decimated castle she had explored. How might her life have been had she grown up on the d'Ange demesne? Would she have romped through the meadows with a sister? Were there other siblings? So much to wonder about.

"I want to know them." The words slipped from Gossamyr's mouth without volition. She wandered forward, not really seeing, her mind stuffed with noise from the past.

"Always mortal?" She tripped, but braced herself, both hands to each end of her staff against a pole fleched with torn public announcements.

To her left the careful clops of horse hooves neared. Measured, almost as if the beast was…looking. Timing its steps. A massive animal, for the echoes filled the air with a march worthy of a gallant parade.

Gossamyr straightened, listening. The back of her neck prinkled, akin to fear, but more so, anticipation.

A force approached. Be it good or evil? Armagnac, Burgundian, or English? Either would taste her skill with an *arret* to the skull.

Abandoning foolish wonders about her stolen past, Gossamyr slid her hand down the silk bodice of her gown and unhooked an *arret*. She began to spin it for release—but immediately relinquished her defensive stance at sight of the brilliant white horse that advanced. No, not a horse. The beast verily gleamed in the clouded twilight, its snow-white hide casting about it an aura of illumination.

A rider sat upon its back but Gossamyr could not drag her attention from the beast. She held out a hand, thinking to touch its pale pink nose. Long witch locks, elegantly braided with fine strands of silver threading, hung between the animal's violet eyes.

And there, between the plaits of mane and above the eyes shimmered an ovular spot, the hide bare of hair and looking pink and open. Like a wound, but not seeping.

Sucking in a gasp, Gossamyr recoiled. Realization felled her to her knees before the magnificent beast. Bowing, she pressed her forehead to the cold dirty cobbles.

The rider's dismount clacked boot and spur against cobblestone. "My lady?" a deep male voice inquired.

Rising, but slinking backward, Gossamyr hissed at the insolent, "How dare you?"

The rider, cloaked in black and hooded, tilted his head wonderingly. Dark stones set about the perimeter of the hood clacked, glinting in metallic rays with a strange beauty of their own.

"You ride the unicorn!"

A smile eased onto the rider's face and he stroked a gloved hand across the unicorn's braided mane. "You are most perceptive, fair lady." He eyed her staff and looked over her motley clothing, assessing but not judging. "I ride Tor because he allows it."

"T-Tor?" came out in but a squeak smaller than a mouse's sigh.

The gall of this man to be so casual about the sacred beast. Lacking an alicorn. This be the one Ulrich sought!

Or had the unicorn come to her? She had held the alicorn, had felt the power. Had that moment drawn the creature to her? But she had not thought a unicorn would ever allow a man to ride—

Stepping closer, Gossamyr examined the man's face, finding his movement tilted his eyes out of the shadows and into the pale light of evening. They were deeply colored a darkest violet.

"You cannot be here," she gasped as another awareness struck. "You dare to approach the Red Lady's lair?"

"I know naught of a red lady, *demoiselle*. I go where I will. Rather, this journey finds me following Tor's path."

"But you…you are fée?"

Another bemused smile curled his lips. A handsome man— fée—Gossamyr corrected her silent summation. *Or is it Verity?*

"It surprises me you know so much. You have sighted a unicorn and a faery in less than a breath. I have always thought the common man blind to our true identities."

Gossamyr straightened, one hand fisted about each end of her staff and leveled at her hips. "I am not common."

"Indeed not." The man bowed and offered, "I am chevalier Dominique San Juste. You have already met Tor. We've been on a journey—or rather Tor has. I suspect he seeks the missing alicorn."

"I know he does." Gossamyr made to pet Tor, but recoiled once again. She could not touch the unicorn. 'Twould be sacrilege. But oh, did her fingers itch for one stroke of the silken moon-bright hide. "I know where it is."

The faery lifted a brow. Tor whinnied and stomped the ground with a fine hoof.

Gossamyr nodded in answer to both.

And so fate had been decided for her. 'Twas destiny had brought the unicorn to her.

Goodbye, Shinn, she thought wistfully. *I do love you. But I choose to do what is right.*

Gossamyr beckoned as she started down the street. "Come. I will take you to what you seek."

Hands clutching the air before him, his neck stiff from the tilt of his head, tears spilled down his cheeks and sweet liquid seeped into his mouth. The false child of Shinn had thought to touch it! His!

"Mine," he hissed.

It glowed seductively. Palest of yellow. Thick and full. Unlike the others. His mistress had not drained it. She wickedly teased him by keeping it whole and out of reach. Dare he take it back? Could he? He lingered in a purgatory of not-dead and not-life. Yet he did not dissipate or rot as he suspected he should. Nor did one of those skeletal creatures lurk within him. Mayhap.

Alive? No. But neither dead.

So long as it glowed and no one pulled it from the wall, he remained.

"Mine," he whispered again, savoring the sound of the word, floating on the resonance of that claim. *His.* 'Twas all he owned. Yet even that he could not touch.

Ah, but he had gained a new possession, yes? Information. How his mind bounded with such!

The Red Lady would be pleased to hear Shinn's false child had been here. But sporting such revelations?

I know you, Avenall. Do you not remember me?

Yes.

No?

Pretty Faery lord's daughter, pristine in her blue marble castle. Don't touch. Exotic...

No, not a faery! She is mortal. A changeling!

Exotic? Why did he want to remember those muddy brown eyes?

You are Avenall of Rougethorn...

Rougethorn? It was familiar because his mistress so often mentioned it. He muttered it slowly, over and over. Rougethorn. Rouge. Thorn. Rouge... Rogue. Torn?

Avenall shook his head, rocking the provoking memories about in his brain. Rogue? Rogue. Torn.

Avenall?

He wondered.

Hmm. Yes. Avenall.

"My name."

A smile curved his mouth. The realization put him straighter, sucked in a breath and filled his chest with air. Yes. "Avenall...of Rogue—Torn."

Indeed, he had come from the place named thus. Rougethorn. The tribe whence his mistress had hailed. Yet, there remained a missing piece of his name....

He had courted—

The clatter at the door bent him into a crouch. All productive thought dissipated. The Red clamped hold of his volition and he hobbled over to greet his mistress. Regal and lovely, she stood in the doorway, alabaster shoulders erect and one long leg bared to reveal a slender ankle ringed in silver chains of mail. Something dangled from the fingers of her right hand. A…head. Attached to a body.

She deposited the limp body of a man near her feet. He rolled down the step, arms slapping the marble and skull thudding, and landed the main floor on his back. Parti-colored black and yellow hosen wrapped his legs. One arm splayed above his head. Blood purled from his lips. And there, drawing a slug trail across his cheek, glittered a hint of Faery. It was the man who had earlier kept Avenall—yes, Avenall!—from pinning the essences. The man who accompanied the female—Shinn's daughter.

Do you not remember me, Avenall?

Yes…I…I courted you.

"Puppy?"

What distraction was this? Had not the Red Lady gone in search of Shinn? He looked up into her red eyes.

"My new pet," his mistress announced with a flirting air.

The satisfied curl on her lips dug into the thrill Avenall had felt at gaining his name, mayhap even more— *New* pet?

"No. My lovely pretty. I—I am your puppy."

Striding past him, her plush skirts sweeping his face in a brushing slap, she paced before the wall of essences. "Worry not. You will always be my puppy. I will make this new one my…kitten."

"No!"

She waved a naughty finger at him. "Ah, ah, ah. Mustn't be jealous."

"Do you not know who he is? He be that woman's man!" Yes, Gossamyr!

No. Avenall coiled into himself. *Only for Puppy's ears.* He would not give her a name. She did not deserve it now. Oh, cruel mistress!

"Yes." Pausing, she considered with a sad moue. "Her man... So little you know, Puppy."

"I know you were led from your goal by this insignificant mortal!"

"I had thought to draw Shinn into my arms, but instead this bit of skin and bone wandered up. Useless, I had initially thought, until——" Avenall's mistress drew an object out from her sleeve; a bit of black cloth wrapped about something narrow and long. She tapped it against her chin. Menace glittered in her eyes. "I must keep him alive for the moment, for that will bring her to me. Or, if Fortune answers my beckon, it will bring Shinn to me."

He shrugged. There was that.

He'd be damned if he'd tell her the wench had been here not an hour earlier. Nor would he mention her strange tale of them having been lovers. If they had been lovers—— *I think we were. I don't know...*

Kitten? "You—you have kissed him?"

"Not...completely."

She teased the tip of the wrapped thing near one of the undulating essences. The viscous blue essence actually cringed, then it brightened to a marvelous indigo, expanded, and suddenly, it burst, showering the Red Lady's face and shoulders with a mist of glimmer. The essence pure. She licked at the splatter, sighing and giggling at the wonder.

Stretching the cloth-wrapped item high in triumph, she announced, "Lovely thing, this!"

"But." Avenall sank to the bottom step and tucked his arms

about his bent knees. A forceful breath blew a hideous strand of red hair from his face. He glanced to the sprawled mortal. "You...*plan* to kiss him?"

"Did you not listen, pin man?"

He cringed deeper into this new misery.

"I must keep him alive until we've lured the female here. I know not what her intentions, but I suspect it has something to do with this."

"She—" Avenall bit his tongue. No. His mistress was undeserving of his confidence. So much she knew about Shinn. Could she confirm his connection to the warrior bitch?

Now she beckoned him closer with a crook of her finger. Balking—she had brought a new pet into her lair!—Avenall finally scrambled up and knelt before her, the wall of essences but a reach to his side. Sniffing, he detected no discernible odor from the cloth bound about her new toy, save the remnant of mortal aroma. The man's scent.

Avenall sneered and crossed his arms over his chest. "What is it?"

"You must guess."

"I don't want to. It reeks of that man. You are most cruel to your puppy."

"You wear jealousy like a silken robe, sweet one. I want to devour the fire I see in your eyes."

She bent to tap his forehead then teased her fingernail down the center of his nose. A lunge and she lapped up the slide of his nose with her pink tongue. He snuggled his face into her palm, seeking assurance of her love.

The inadvertent touch of the wrapped thing to his chest ignited a violent spark. Avenall was flung backward, landing against the wall, the cold caress of a violet essence hugging his cheek. Scrambling away from the slimy coldness, he pointed to what his mistress held. "It is powerful!"

"Very much so." She teased it beneath the tumescent curve of a pink essence until it looked ready to burst, then withdrew. "With this, I can draw all the Disenchanted I need to my lair. And I won't have to leave my bed. They will line up at my door. You, my puppy, have but to sit by and watch them wither at your feet. They will journey from far lands to taste my kiss."

Avenall whirled to face away from his mistress. A shiver of blue ice traced his scalp. He shook his head. Flash of an embrace—

—*my father is away, he will not discover us.*

—*I love you, Gossamyr.*

What is this? Avenall clawed at the wall. Struggling to grasp hold of the flickers of what could only be memory, they danced just beyond his reach. And then a face appeared in his mind's eye. The warrior bitch. Smiling at him.

Loving him?

How to take in this information? Had the touch of that strange object released a picture of his past? Or had he merely been tainted by the warrior's suggestion?

The man on the floor moaned and shrugged a hand over his face.

"This," the Red Lady declared, the horn held high and her strides moving her before the wall of essences, "is my triumph over Turiau de Wintershinn of Glamoursiège."

Glamoursiège? Another strange but compelling word.

Beside his face, Avenall felt the hissing burn of the object. The thing was unwrapped, but held by the cloth to protect his mistress's hand. It hummed. Its voice filled the room, overwhelming the death sobs of the essences. More seductive even than his mistress's call. He jerked his head to the right.

"No!" cried the man from the floor.

"Oh, yes," whispered the Red Lady into Avenall's ear. "Time to play."

The welcome shimmer of Faery caressed him from head to toe, moving across his face and around his shoulders—then the reemergence stopped.

Shinn, restrained between Faery and the Otherside, compre-

hended the inexplicable barrier that would not allow him to complete his *twinclian* to Glamoursiège.

Something had named him. A most powerful force.

TWENTY-SIX

Tor led the way to Armand LaLoux's home. Gossamyr had once seen a unicorn—she must have yet been a youngling to tether. Her father had spoken in a silent conversation with it while Mince had held her back from a gurgling toddle to embrace the beast.

That Dominique was fée explained why the unicorn tolerated him riding it. Almost. Unicorns were not beasts of burden. Mayhap the missing alicorn gentled the unicorn's nature? Sir San Juste seemed so mortal. His eyes—normally fée possessed brilliant violet eyes—were violet yet dark. Not true blood?

"Ask me," Dominique said as they neared the door to Armand's home. "I feel your curiosity. I am ashamed."

"I mean you no disrespect." But curiosity stirred. "Very well. You are true fée?"

"Yes. But."

She quirked a brow.

"I am a changeling. I was laid in a mortal infant's crib after I was newly born. I know," he said. "I should have perished. Or so say the tales I hear."

Gossamyr had always thought Faery changelings died. On the other hand, mortal exchanges were supposed to die, as well. Yet here she stood very much alive and well.

"But my fée mother had darker reasons for hiding me away. I have never been to Faery. Though I can feel it all around." He scanned the alley, reaching to touch the cool stone wall of Armand's home. "Not in Paris though."

"Never," Gossamyr agreed. "So you were…raised by mortals?"

"A fine set of parents. They raised me as their own. De- spite—" he shrugged, easing his shoulders up as if to work out an itch on his back "—my differences."

"You are winged?"

He nodded. "You must know how difficult it is for a faery to walk unnoticed in Paris."

"But they do."

"They are able to work a glamour for so long?"

Gossamyr nodded. "Most mortals cannot See a faery should they spread their wings before them. And when the Disenchant- ment sets in, well…their wings, they dissipate. Why is it you still have yours?"

"I cannot say. They've never disappeared, much as I wished for such when I was a child. I only wanted to run and play with the others," he said. He drew the cloak out along one arm. "This is my disguise."

"It serves to hide your nature well. But with the Red Lady hold- ing court, do you know the danger you are in?"

"I know nothing of this red lady. I am not of Faery, *demoiselle*. I am fée, but…an outcast. I can never have Faery. I function as a mor- tal with some of the powers of glamour. I suspect this red lady, if it is fée she seeks—"

"The Disenchanted."

"Disenchanted? The woman will not recognize me as one?"

"Perhaps not, for you were never Enchanted in the first place,"

Gossamyr said, understanding growing. One must live in Faery to be Enchanted. Yes?

"It pains me to hear you put it in such a manner."

"Forgive me." She felt the wall of a house behind her and pressed her hand to it. She was so stunned to hear this man's confession, and yet, curious. He was she in every opposition.

"What troubles you? My lady?" He searched her face. A look that gentled even with its curiosity.

...a fine handsome faery man to sweep you from your feet—literally?

She stretched a look to the unicorn, which stood outside the door to Armand's home. Peaceful acceptance glittered in the beast's pale violet eyes. Perfection destroyed by the mortal who would take its horn for devastating magic. She must return the alicorn immediately.

But you vowed to help Ulrich. Gossamyr stilled. Indeed, she had made a vow.

Close, the presence of this stranger. He reminded her of Faery—at least the semblance of her former home. *Your truth keeps you from returning.* She wanted to be there. To touch it. To feel the comfort of her home. A home she might never again visit.

It is not your home! It was never yours!

"How long before you learned the truth?" An abrupt question, but she hadn't time for dally.

"I have always known I am a fée in the mortal world. My mortal mother made sure I knew whence I came. Though she knew nothing of the faery ways and could not teach me."

"You were fortunate to have the truth."

Do you know the truth of yourself?

Verity d'Ange. Always she had carried that bit of her truth, unknowing.

You have the truth complete now. You are the truth.

"Remove your cloak. Please," she pleaded.

He balked, placing a hand to the hilt of his sword. Not a menacing move, merely, unsure.

"I—I just need to see. To…to remember. Please?"

"To remember?"

"Since I have been in Paris, the Disenchantment…I think it draws away memories. I simply want to believe."

"Ah." He unclasped the silver agraffe at his neck and swung the cloak from his shoulders. Behind him unfurled shimmering violet wings, quarter-sectioned like the fetch, and her own tribe—but the upper wing was larger than the lower, unlike the symmetrical wings of tribe Glamoursiège. Such wing structure identified him as from an old and revered family.

"Wisogoth." Not troopers but ancient earth dwellers who lived in great underground caverns lit by crystals and iridescent rivers. Desideriel's tribe.

The span of Dominique's wings fluttered in the still air, gushing a sweet breeze across Gossamyr's face, a summer meadow rich with clover. She closed her eyes and drew in the aroma of all she had once had.

To seal the rift would for ever close your access to Faery.

"What is Wisogoth?" he asked.

"It is a Faery tribe. The oldest in Faery. Your tribe, I would judge from the form of your wings. Have you a blazon?"

"I know naught."

"It is…the Wisogoth blazon covers the back. It shimmers with glamour. A permanent marking."

"I have nothing like that."

"Perhaps you are not Enchanted?"

"Yet, I've glamour. That damned dust constantly spumes from me at the most inopportune moments."

"Interesting. I cannot figure this." How to possess glamour without Enchantment?

"You know Faery?" he inquired softly. "Tell me who you are, *demoiselle*. You are on a quest?"

"I am come from Faery," she confessed. "Glamoursiège, a tribe that borders the Netherdred. But I am mortal. Like you, I...am a changeling."

He tilted his head wonderingly.

That she had spoken the word secured it into her soul. A completely mortal soul. No essence of Faery within.

In a rocking sway of unstoppable comprehension Belief altered.

Lost to you now...Faery.

I bid you farewell....

Gossamyr stroked a finger under her eye. No tears. Just the memory of pain. "I am mortal, stolen from my cradle as a child and taken to Faery. I have lived there all my life because I...believed."

"Wondrous."

"And now I do not belong."

"Why not?"

"Because a mortal must Believe to Belong." Gossamyr twined her fingers together before her and pounded her balled hands to her forehead. "I have always believed myself to be born of a mortal woman and a Faery lord; only recently have I learned I am true mortal—that my birth parents are no longer."

"I am sorry."

Bouncing on anticipatory footsteps, she shook out her fingers and entreated, "Did you ever meet your faery parents?"

"Yes. My mother lives close to me now. My father...is dead. For the best; he was not fée."

"I see."

"That may be the reason I have glamour while you deem me without Enchantment. My father, he was...cruel. Of the angelic ranks. I am..."

"Quite astounding," Gossamyr offered.

Charmed by his smile, an easy charm and not gratuitous, Gossamyr knew she had found a friend.

"Why have you come to Paris, my lady?"

"I have left Faery to seek the Red Lady and destroy her. My father sent me, knowing no fée could approach the villainess without her seducing and killing them."

"You possess the powers of the fée?"

"No. I am Disenchanted, stripped of the little glamour I once held."

"Ah." He curved his hand before her, looking to caress her cheek, but he did not touch her. Only he smiled upon her with a calm look of peace that reassured he was friend not enemy. "What is your name?"

"Gossamyr," she said, and then looked to the ground. Overwhelmed, that is all she could feel here in the presence of such a regal man and the unicorn. Gossamyr Verity de Wintershinn of Glamoursiège, false child of Shinn. Avenall's words cut to her tender heart. Who was this Verity d'Ange?

The unicorn snorted at the sudden appearance of a man in the doorway. A froth of white beard tufted the door frame. Ulrich's uncle tilted his head, sensing those around him. "Who is about?"

"Monsieur LaLoux." Gossamyr approached the old man. "It is Gossamyr. I've come for Ulrich. Is he inside?"

"Ulrich? I've not spoken to him since last he was here with you, my lady."

"I told him to return anon. Where could he possibly—" Spinning her half staff, Gossamyr looked both ways down the dark street. "Oh, no."

"What is it?" Dominique calmed Tor with a palm to the beast's muzzle.

"She was calling to him earlier," Gossamyr said. "I should have never left her lair. The Red Lady has likely lured Ulrich and the alicorn to her."

"The alicorn?"

"Yes." She started walking the cobbles. "My friend was on a quest to return the alicorn to its rightful owner. I must hurry."

"I shall accompany you!"

"You cannot," she called to the changeling. "You would put your-self in harm's way should the Red Lady recognize you are fée. Stay with the unicorn; protect it."

"Very well," the changeling called. "But Tor does not take or-ders. He will go where he pleases, there is nothing I can do to stop him."

Gossamyr winced. A unicorn anywhere near the Red Lady was surely a dead unicorn. "If the beast knows what is good for it, it will stay far from the Red Lady's lair."

A protesting whinny and clomp of hooves preceded the charge of the unicorn. He cantered past Gossamyr. Close behind ran the changeling.

"Very well," Gossamyr said, picking up her pace to match the others. The smile of adventure emerged. "To charging head on into danger!"

The world undulated away from him. Or rather, he was being dragged, arms wrenched overhead and wrists clasped by pinching fingers. His muscles, stretching from pit to torso, screamed. Too dazed to struggle, Ulrich remarked the thick white candles flash-ing fire sparkles across the walls. Stars stolen from the sky. The flickers of light moved away from him, appearing from wherever it was he was being dragged.

At his feet trailed a disturbing vision, the succubus who had kissed him—briefly. Not really a kiss though, more like she had moved close enough to kiss and had...inhaled his essence. *Your soul, lackwit! She draws out your soul!* Even so, that blithe moment had lit-erally left him drained.

Lifting a knee, Ulrich thought to kick out, to put a stop to this.

"Ah, ah," the lady with the red marking on her face cooed—still he could but see a swath of her face where she had wiped his tears; it floated mysteriously above the white dress. She poked Ulrich with the tip of the alicorn.

Such fire! 'Twas as though he'd been pierced with a flame-red poker, when all she had done was touch it to his knee.

Drowsy with pain, Ulrich muttered, "Gossamyr?"

"Be that her name, then?" The Red Lady danced the alicorn in the air gaily, drawing a circle of iridescent glamour in its wake. "Gossamyr, Shinn's false daughter?"

"The man knows not what he mumbles," the unseen voice from above Ulrich's head snapped. "Gossamyr is a common name."

Something gave a tug to one of Ulrich's wrists, making him cry out. He could not see who or what held him. A faery thing, curse them all!

"Why do you hide things from me, Puppy? There, in the torture chamber."

Torture? Where was the danger-loving Faery Not when he needed her?

An icy blackness ignited to a dull glow as the alicorn was touched to an iron torch on the marble wall.

"Shall I chain him to the wall?"

"I don't think it necessary." Two glossy red eyes peered at Ulrich, the alicorn drawing a line below her pouting lips. To but see a part of her face, from cheek to cheek and eyebrow to lower lip, distressed him. "He's weak. Nor will he run without trying to retrieve his prize, yes?"

Yes, he'd run without the prize. The loss of his wish seemed ultimately more tolerable when compared to the evils this nasty half-faced bitch could work upon him. Ulrich had seen the wall of pinned essences. Souls of faeries the succubus had sucked to a slow and painful death. Could she do the same to him? Steal his soul and pin it to the wall? And then, would one of those skeleton creatures emerge to battle Gossamyr?

A dead soul shepherd would not then be able to retrieve his lost daughter.

"My kitten will be a good little boy."

The woman's touch felt like ice. No longer did the soft, susurrating tingle of the divine attract him. Nor could he smell the myrrh that had filled the halls of this lair; naught but terror filled his nostrils with a sharp cloying odor.

He saw the tip of fingers coated with the glimmer from his eye swipe across the air to reveal her neck and the serrated curves of her bosom.

"Methinks you should not play with kittens," the man he could not see said as he dropped Ulrich's feet and legs. "They have nasty claws that will tear my mistress's dress and make her bleed."

"Oh, Puppy. Come to me."

"Not when you've that horn in hand. It hurts."

"I'll not let this prize from my sight, so you'll have to learn to live without my touch. Leave him. Shinn's daughter will seek him, I am sure of that."

"I mean nothing to Gossamyr," Ulrich managed.

"So she *is* Shinn's daughter?"

Hades, he shouldn't have said anything. Ulrich choked back risk of exposing further knowledge.

"Your silence speaks volumes."

For once he prayed for a rogue spirit seeking direction to float on by. Could he use it as a weapon and send it through the succubus's being?

The fire burn of the alicorn tingled along Ulrich's brow as the Red Lady drew it slowly over his face. "To what purpose do you serve Shinn's false daughter, hmm? You are completely mortal, this I know from your plain scent and unremarkable appearance."

Summoning the few remaining threads of courage, Ulrich worked up his saliva and spat. Direct hit above and between the Red Lady's breasts. The globule landed a part of her flesh he could not see, so it appeared to float.

"Wrong answer." She summoned the minion who lurked in the shadows with but a flick of her fingers. Footsteps shuffled over. Ulrich saw the tips of black hair revealed as they wiped her breasts clean of spittle. "I see we shall have to restrain the miserable mortal. But I don't want to take away his soul, not yet. So…just a little kiss."

Ulrich struggled as she leaned over him, but the melody whispering from her mouth captured his mind in a vise hold and quickly becalmed him to a ragged mass of muscle and bone. Unable to move, he moaned as cold lips pressed upon his and summoned the passion in his groin.

Oh, but it was so sweet, her kiss. *Take me, drink me, suck out my soul…*

TWENTY-SEVEN

"I know it is this way." Gossamyr strode ahead of Dominique and Tor. "East from the edge of the city. I remember the spire of that great cathedral was in view."

"This man who has been accompanying you," Dominique called from behind. "What were the reasons the two of you joined forces?"

Inexplicably compelled, she looked at her palm, the lines deepened with memory. He'd danced the mortal passion into her soul. Love? "We were destined to come together. Though I cannot be sure my father did not place him in my path. Ulrich is a good man."

"As a mortal he will be safe from the succubus's evil?"

"Not sure. The man who serves at her right hand is fée—and she holds him in an *erie*. His essence is pinned to her wall."

"And that is a faery soul, as you have explained. Incredible. You teach me much in so little time."

Time. The unrelenting enemy.

Gossamyr stopped, stretching out a hand to give the others silent orders. Tor's hooves clopped to a halt behind her and the hematite stones on Dominique's cape ceased clacking. The caw of a crow, unseen, but close, made her tilt her head to the side. The air smelled clean, strangely so. They were far from the market-place, but close, the calls of rivermen, as their skiffs sluiced silently through the dreadsome dark waters.

The warm huff of air at the back of Gossamyr's neck danced through her system, invigorating and smelling of summer mead buzzing with honey-dripping humble bees. She reached back. Tor pressed his nose into her palm. Hot suede. Huff of misty breath.

She and Dominique exchanged glances.

"He trusts you," the changeling offered.

"If that be so then I beg the unicorn remain far from the Red Lady's lair. If she has Ulrich, no doubt she holds the alicorn."

Dominique shrugged and smoothed a hand over Tor's braided mane. In response, the unicorn stomped the ground twice with its foreleg and dropped into a regal bow, nose to the cobbles and fettered forelegs bent.

Fearful of such deference from the sacred beast, Gossamyr managed a bow and gestured the beast rise. But Tor did not. "What is he doing?"

"He will yield to your request. Many years Tor has searched for the alicorn."

"Time be tricksy."

"He knows it is close, but is aware of the risk. Evil cannot be calmed when such power lies at hand. Do not lead us astray."

"I will not. I have seen and touched it. I will bring it back to you...er, Tor. I pledge my honor to you."

The beast rose and reared up grandly upon its hind legs, stretching twice the height of Gossamyr. It then turned and cantered off down the street.

"He will remain close but unseen," Dominique said as he gestured they continue. "Are we near to her lair?"

"Too close." Gossamyr walked up to the iron gate surrounding the humble manor. Four guttered candles lit the shell path to the stables. And there, at the edge of the stable lay a puddle of darkness. Gossamyr rushed across the path, her bare feet making little noise, and plunged to the fabric that resembled a slick of mud. It smelled earthy. "Ulrich's cloak. She has him."

"I...can feel her."

Gossamyr spun around to spy the changeling standing in the center of the shell path. The dark cloak listed on the wind, skillfully disguising wings. His eyes closed, he pressed forth a palm to caress the air before him, feeling, scenting—

"No!" Gossamyr shoved Dominique out from the succubus's *erie*. "She is calling to you. Do not listen. Don't—blight, perhaps you should remain out here."

"I will not abandon you now."

"But you hear it?"

"A call? Yes. Gorgeous and seductive."

"I can do this on my own."

"Oh? You remind me of my wife. Headstrong and stubborn, she is always getting herself into a fix." He cocked his head, closing his eyes. "So...gorgeous."

Swinging her staff to gently land Dominique's chest, Gossamyr said, "Please, you need to understand the power of her call. It can devastate."

Dominique blinked from the reverie he'd slipped into. "But you said I am in no danger. If I have never been Enchanted...?"

"A faery essence lives inside you. A sweet waiting to be plucked by the Red Lady."

Dominique nodded, agreeing. "Very well, Tor and I shall stand guard outside."

Pausing before the door to the lair, her hand pressed to the base of a stone gargoyle with horns curled about its ears, Gossamyr surveyed the darkening perimeter. Thick vines grew over the garden and sweatered the side of the mansion. Their leaves were sharp and smelled foul. She had not before noticed them. The stable door hung open, revealing the carriage but no equipage. Dominique strolled outside the gate, arms akimbo, his head twisting. Dark hair listed across his cape. Had the changeling resistance to the Red Lady's allure, he might have proven a boon to her. But knowing little of the glamour he held——Enchanted, Disenchanted, or mayhap Celestial?——she could not trust he would be resilient.

Facing the door, she summoned courage. It no longer mattered that she defeated some evil force and made Faery safe. Nor did it matter that she returned to her father's side, valorous and proven. *A champion.* Her own desires mattered little.

Ulrich, the truest friend she had ever known, needed her. And mayhap there was yet hope for Avenall. Avenall Éloi Papilion of Rougethorn.

"Be strong," she muttered. "Be bold, be bold…" She would not speak the final "be not too bold."

Gripping an *arret* to the ready and tucking her half staff under her arm, she kicked the door open and marched over the threshold.

Gossamyr strode forward, passing the leering marble gargoyles that clung to the walls as if captured midscamper. Constant whispers tickled her ears. Did the stone creatures speak? The chill of such a notion shivered through her limbs.

She pressed onward but indecision slowed her pace. Would she find Ulrich there in the room filled with moaning essences? Would the Red Lady leave such a well-marked path to her destruction? If only she could *twinclian* into the room, remain small and scope it out.

Touching her neck where the distinctive blazon had once shone, she felt nothing. Mortal now. *Always had been, and always will be.* So powerless without the blazon of Faery.

And yet…still a force.

Shinn had trained her to jump out in the face of danger and offer it up a challenge. And that was what Gossamyr intended to do.

The whispering had stopped. A movement at the corner of her eye snapped her gaze to the left. Just in time to see one of the gargoyle torches move its horned head. Watching?

Testing, she tapped the head of a stone beast with her staff. No movement.

"Methinks I am being tapped by souls unseen," she murmured. "Blight! Be to it!

"Where are you!" she called out, announcing her arrival. "Show yourself, banished one."

A shove of the staff tip against a door to her right opened into darkness. Cool air crept out, fluttering the candle held by her stone watcher. The stone claw faltered, dribbling candle wax onto the floor.

Gossamyr strode onward, her wake whipping the remaining torch flames in a mad dance. Stabbing open the door on her left revealed a thin stream of light cutting across the marble floor. Peering through the crack, Gossamyr spied a single form suspended in the center of the empty stone-walled room.

"Ulrich!"

Rushing inside, she skidded to a halt before the soul shepherd. His body, stripped to but his parti-colored hose, hung suspended by nothing more than the succubus's *erie*. The weight of his torso stretched his arms; they had turned unnaturally inward at the shoulder. His head hung upon his chest but his eyes were wide. Fingers twitching, he moved slowly in a circle. "I will get you down from there."

"No." Weak and barely there, his voice. His thumb twitched. A miserable moan preceded his whispered, "Let me...die."

"And have you forfeit your chance at a reunion with your daughter?"

"I will see her...anon. If Heaven will admit a miserable soul such as mine."

Gossamyr stepped beneath Ulrich. He was very high.

"Gossamyr, save the alicorn. I am not worthy… I just want to die. Rhiana waits for me…"

He wanted to be with his daughter. His *dead* daughter. "Has she taken away your soul?"

"Not…yet… She comes!"

Leaping high, Gossamyr managed to brush the toe of Ulrich's pointed leather shoe. She landed in a crouch.

A wide sweep of white light flooded in through the doorway.

Gossamyr looked up from her crouch, into the blood-red eyes of her father's disgruntled lover. Pinpricks of red circled her left eye and arabesqued onto her cheek, a match to Avenall's mark. Hair the color of scarlet anemones poured over her shoulders. The simple white plush gown caressed her body and was cut high to expose her legs to the thighs. She drew a silver pin beneath her nose, tipped with brown. Dried blood, most likely. Gossamyr's?

"Delighted you could join the fête," the woman purred in a sensual stir of tones reeking of Faery. "I have looked forward to meeting Shinn's false daughter for quite a time. Pity we cannot speak as allies."

Gossamyr stood upright. A glance to the ground spied her staff, too far to grasp.

"You have an interest in my pretty, mortal kitten?" The Red Lady gestured to the suspended soul shepherd.

"He has done nothing to you; release him and you shall have the alliance you have waited for."

"Mmm, no." The woman drew out an object from her wide-cuffed sleeve and pointed it at Ulrich's form. "I am not finished playing with him."

A fine stream of glimmer shot from the alicorn's tip and zapped Ulrich into a spastic disarray of jerks and twitches. "Nor you." She turned the alicorn toward Gossamyr and winked. "Gossamyr de Wintershinn of Glamoursiège, you will do my bidding!"

TWENTY-EIGHT

For a moment the entire room stilled. Gossamyr gripped her chest, anticipating the inexplicable pull, the *erie* to melt over her with the recital of her name. The vile red creature had Named her.

Gossamyr de Wintershinn of—

Wait.

No urge to prostrate herself before the woman befell. Not a single muscle flinched. Breath held, Gossamyr sucked in deeper. Was that a prinkle racing up her spine? No.

Named, yet— *Her Faery name.*

You are mortal complete!

Not her true *mortal* birth name.

The smile of adventure, of dangers yet mastered, crooked Gossamyr's mouth. "Think you?"

The Red Lady's jaw dropped. Clearly she had expected Gossamyr's submission. "Gossamyr de Wintershinn," she repeated thrice quickly.

"Not the right name, bitch!"

Fire blazed in the red pupils fixed in the Red Lady's alabaster mask. Lifting the alicorn high, she incited its power with a few words. "Faery forged with glamour bright and magic bold. Tell me your mortal name!"

Gossamyr dodged the stream of power that shot from the alicorn's tip and rolled beneath Ulrich's dangling figure to the far wall. There, she gripped her staff and jumped to defense just as another wicked bolt of forbidden magic crossed the room.

She spun the half staff up to protect her face and caught the mixture of glamour and magic within the ribbons of carved applewood. Gossamyr could feel the wood bend and change, briefly, and then the strange mix shot out from the carved ribbons at each end. To master the alicorn—so much power the succubus drained from the essences!

"You do not want me dead," Gossamyr called. Moving deftly, she sidestepped another blast. "I am your only connection to Shinn!"

The room silenced. Gossamyr had played the one weapon she could guess would harm the woman. Love.

Drawing back her stolen weapon, the Red Lady gained in height and volume almost as if puffing herself up with air. An illusion, Gossamyr knew, but still impressive. Her pale flesh shone. And now, peeking through the decorative cuts of white fabric, the blazon that girdled her waist glittered brightly. The air tickled with sharp bites—Enchantment bound by a darker force. What wicked magic comes this day?

"Shinn is in Paris," the succubus announced. "I don't need you, silly mortal."

Could he yet linger in Paris? Gossamyr prayed not, for her father risked far too much. He had aged; a stay in the Otherside would weaken and further age him.

"I know as much because I control him at this moment," the Red Lady announced. "Turiau de Wintershinn of Glamoursiège—"

"No!"

Too late, her father's name had been invoked, mayhap many a time previous to this moment.

Please stay away, Shinn. Fight the allure.

Easing to the left, Gossamyr worked slowly toward Ulrich. A keen eye to the alicorn ensured it hung at her enemy's side, for the moment forgotten. She could feel the subtle wind of Ulrich's feet swaying overhead.

The urge to strike stirred in Gossamyr's breast. If she rushed forth right now, she could pin the woman to the floor and be done with her. But the unknown held her at bay.

If the Red Lady died would her glamour then die? All those pinned essences…would they be obliterated? And Ulrich, he may perish, as well. What of Shinn? He would be released from the suc-cubus's *erie*. But—possibly Disenchanted—could he then return to Faery?

And where was Avenall? The pin man must lurk close by. Had her confession to their past stirred his memory?

"Call Shinn to you," the Red Lady commanded in her cool growl, "and I will release the mortal man."

"Promise?" Gossamyr knew it would not be so easy. Nor would—or could—she summon Shinn into this dangerous nest of tainted Enchantment.

"You have my word." The succubus bowed her head and looked up through dark-shadowed eyes. "The Faery lord for your mortal lover."

"Your word?" Gossamyr laughed. "Nay, that I should trust thee! You be the one who doomed me to Faery through your spurned heart."

"Doomed? You did not favor your home?"

"Well…"

"Should not I bear the right to exact punishment against *my* heart? Come, child—" the succubus tilted her head, eyeing her with curious malevolence "—you know the sharp pulse of a wounded heart." She drew a blood-red nail along the curve of her pale breast.

Speared expertly through her bruised heart, Gossamyr flinched. The succubus knew of her and Avenall's relationship. She knew of her birth and origin. The enemy grew more powerful with every bit of history she claimed from Gossamyr's soul. Yet, she did not wield her mortal name, and that promised hope.

"Are you not willing to do *anything* to make your mortal heart whole?"

"It is…" Gossamyr shivered at the quake moving through her body. It is whole!

Have you no feelings? Your truth…you are lost to Faery.

"My heart…" She stepped twice to the side, swayed, but righted herself. "No," she gasped to herself.

A beautiful song, rich in volume and melody, filled the room. *Come to me,* it uttered in lyrical tones.

Gossamyr blinked and yawned. Falling, she. So pretty, the surrender.

Her muscles stretched and loosened. The staff stabbed her foot.

The blurry figure of another, a man, bounced in behind the Red Lady. Wings spreading, he fluttered them, his position gifting the succubus with false wings. Flash of silver glinted in Gossamyr's peripheral vision.

"Surrender your heart, pitiful one," the pin man hissed in glee. Tapping a pin aside his jaw, his wings, lucid and tattered, flapped once. "She wants you."

Pulled into the song, Gossamyr again swayed. "No, Avenall…" she managed to say. "Av…enall…"

"Surrender," danced the delicious tones tickling into her ear.

Yes, to the Dance. Merry be and merry will, dance away your life you shall!

No! Gossamyr gathered a breath and shouted, "Avenall Éloi Papilion of Rougethorn!" She fell to her knees as the whinny of a horse startled her.

Awaken.

Gossamyr shook her head. It felt as though she were shaking away a hard shell of opaque glass, seeing again, coming back into her soul. *Your mortal soul.*

In the doorway appeared Dominique, and behind him Tor raced past, his glossy white hooves clacking against the marble. Had the—yes—the unicorn had spoken beyond the *erie* and wakened her from it.

The Red Lady spun and pointed her Enchanted scepter. "The unicorn!" she announced, and then scurried from the room in a flight of flowing white skirts.

At the touch of the alicorn, Dominique flew into the air. Connecting to the wall with a sickening crunch, he slid down to land in a tangle of legs and wings.

Gossamyr ran to the doorway. The duo—pin man and Red Lady—were on to the room filled with essences.

Scampering back to the center of the room, she retrieved her staff and glanced to Ulrich.

"Leave me," he whispered.

"And when did you become such a pitiful excuse?" Planting the staff before her, she leaped, using the short bit of applewood to lengthen her distance. Arms stretched, she straightened her legs upward and kicked Ulrich in the gut. The blow released him from the *erie*. He landed the floor less gracefully than Gossamyr's crouch.

A yelp and a moan clued her the man would survive. She had been rather rough with him of late, poor thing. He deserved only kindness.

"Dragon piss!" Ulrich whined. "When will you see to leaving this poor old man in peace?"

"When you are poor and old and worthy of ignorance. Are you all there?" She pressed a hand to his bare chest. "Soul…intact?"

"I think so."

"Did she kiss you?"

"A bit."

"A bit?"

"Once or twice."

"Hmm." She touched his cheek, tilting it to a side. His eyes fluttered, but beneath the nervous lids vivid blue flashed. "Yet you are still whole."

"Yet." Probing over his body with his fingers, Ulrich finally nodded and let out a sigh. "I may be beaten, Faery Not, but I am far from broken."

"That is the Ulrich I like to hear."

Flinging her arms about him, Gossamyr hugged him, drawing him upright to clasp to her chest.

"Faery Not?"

"Yes?"

"You are...hugging me."

"I know." And she gasped out a happy sound. "I would kiss you, as well, but we've more urgent needs."

"Must we? I could manage a kiss."

Gossamyr forced their separation, but Ulrich touched her face.

"What of you? I thought you were off to find your father." His head lolled, but he snapped it level. Remnants of the *erie*. "Did you speak to Shinn?"

"I did." Softly, she touched the green bruise on his cheek. That a woman could hurt this man! A charming smile managed to stir up a smile on her face. "You have taught me much, Ulrich. I do believe that a man can love a child, even if she is not of his blood. Shinn thinks love is elusive, but it was love that kept him silent about my mortality. He has always had the mortal passion, as have I."

Two blinks offered a silent agreement. Still woozy from the Red Lady's *erie,* surely. A film of glimmer purled a trail from the corner of his right eye.

"What be wrong with your eye?"

"Nothing that hurts overmuch. Don't touch it! It seeps...glamour, I think."

"Glamour?"

"I spoke to Shinn, too."

"My father— When?"

"Mayhap right after you did."

So Shinn had sought Ulrich. There was no reason—

"He took your sight?"

"Just the one eye. Blessings, but I cannot see faeries now. Though, I did see the red bitch, or at least, part of her. There is another whom I cannot see."

"Avenall."

"Ah." He held up a swaying finger. "Your forgetful lover. Do you count him as your enemy?"

"No." At the moment she needed any would ally themselves to her. Sure, he stood at the Red Lady's side; but for now— "Ready for some danger?"

"Does that bitch yet hold the alicorn?"

"She does."

"Then I'm right behind you."

"Let's be to it!" Gossamyr dashed out into the hallway and slid to a stop. She glanced back; the soul shepherd rolled to his knees.

"Right behind you!" he called.

The white marble halls twisted into dark curves and long stretches of cold blackness. When Gossamyr felt sure they had passed the same horned gargoyle torch, candle held in claw, she turned to find the scent of myrrh drew her forward down the hallway, dark on the end she and Ulrich stood, and bright a short dash onward.

The clomp of hooves alerted them both. Sliding to a halt, Gossamyr pressed back a hand to still Ulrich at her side.

"The unicorn. Slowly, Ulrich. We don't want to frighten it."

The beast paused at the T at the end of the hall, shook its head and stamped the floor. Tor's brilliant luster illuminated all.

"That be a unicorn?"

"Shh."

"It's…why, it is but a white horse!"

"Sacrilege! Oh!"

And the beast was off, snorting its displeasure.

"You've chased it off with your unthinking words."

"But it looks like any other—sorry." Ulrich pushed the staff from his bare chest. Offering compliance with splayed hands near his shoulders, he said, "Whatever you bid, I shall do. Lead on, champion."

Tempted so suddenly, Gossamyr kissed him. Quick. A reaction to her heart. A mortal passion she had no desire to avoid.

"Remember your eye, Ulrich. You can no longer see the Enchanted. Mayhap that is why you see but a horse."

"You've got a point— Gossamyr?"

She turned another corner and strode ahead, her focus, finding the Red Lady.

Left standing beside the hot flicker of gargoyle flame, the fleeting warmth of a woman's kiss quickly receding, Ulrich surveyed his surroundings.

Empty hall…that led to another empty hall.

To the right, one Faery Not—not skipping down that way. (She needn't his interference.)

To the left—one white horse?

"Here, pretty, pretty…"

Gossamyr ran into the pin man outside the door protected by the seven gargoyles. She remembered this place. The room filled with essences was just through the huge marble door. "Avenall?"

A beastly yowl startled her thoroughly. One of the gargoyles tossed its candle at her. Flame burned her elbow. Sulfurous sparkles tainted the air. Spatters of fire licked up her back, tracing the length of her braid.

A force hit Gossamyr's chest. Avenall flung her to the ground. Their bodies crushed together, Gossamyr yelped as the hard surface battered her bones. The roll snuffed out the flame. Tickles of red hair swept her face.

"Avenall!"

He stood and, fisting his fingers in the air, roared and kicked the stone beast.

The gargoyle opened its stone jaw and silently yowled back.

With another warning hiss to the stoic torch, the fée minion knelt at Gossamyr's side. One of his wings bent and brushed her cheek. So dry, the once supple wing. Violet eyes, more red now, blinked as he surveyed her body. "You are fine and well?"

"As best possible." Snapping her right shoulder forward tugged what felt like a dislocated bone back into place. Sitting up, Gossamyr touched the lifeless wing skimming her side; it was cold, not at all warm or iridescent. "You...remember me?"

"I did not remember for so long. Now I do." A quick smile was destroyed by a confused wrinkle of brow. "She took it all from me. Gossamyr?" Red tears streamed across his pale cheeks.

"You remember."

"Yes, Gossamyr Verity de Wintershinn of Glamoursiège. I know your name. I remember. I remember you. We...loved."

"Yes!" She reached to embrace, but he jerked into a defensive crouch.

The shivering minion shook his head and his wings coiled tightly. "But a fée heart knows not love."

"If you believe, Avenall, you can, you can know love. It is..." So he had the mortal passion, as well. He'd suffered it unknowing.

"I..." A tilt of his head swept thick red hair tipped with black across Gossamyr's thighs. "I...saw you as no other. It mattered little that you were not full-blood fée. Why did your father despise me so? I only wanted to court you."

"My father...had his reasons."

"I did not dabble!"

"Shinn knew that. He—"

"Shinn." He nodded, knowing. "A mighty fée lord. Together we betrayed his trust. Oh." His wings curled about his shoulders as he inclined forward into a rocking bow. "My mistress," he hissed in a reverent sigh. "She has taken so much from me, much more than my essence. Memories of you. Our kisses."

Gossamyr clasped her fingers up through his hair and drew his forehead to her cheek. Heliotrope, his aura, deliciously reminiscent. "Yes, many kisses. Your touch made me light, as if I had wings."

"Exotic."

She nodded. A burst of nervous laughter calmed her fears.

Manic and red, his eyes, he shuffled back and pressed himself to the wall. Wings made a papery crunch.

"We must get the alicorn from her. Is there a way? A weakness?"

A male cry echoed down the hall. Not Ulrich, but the changeling.

The collection room undulated with humming essences. The unicorn was nowhere to be seen. Dominique, his cape abandoned at the doorway, slowly approached the Red Lady. She lured him with her call. Volition abandoned, he strode with head up and arms stretched to caress. Vibrant violet wings curled forward to receive her strokes.

Wielding a spinning *arret* Gossamyr dashed forward. She did not aim for the Red Lady; it would serve little against her powerful mix of magic and glamour.

The obsidian arrow released, it connected with the back of Dominique's left thigh. He cried out and gripped the injury—direct hit, for he was pulled from the succubus's lure.

The woman hissed at Gossamyr and twisted the alicorn in her fingers like a marshal's baton readying the musters for the call to attack.

Another *arret* hit its intended mark—the Red Lady's wrist—sending the alicorn flying against the wall of essences. It landed point first next to the yellow essence that had been pinned highest of all. Knocked loose, the essence began to fall, ever so slowly.

"Oh, Hades." Ulrich stumbled into the room and sucked in a gasp. "So many of them!"

Keeping an eye on the Red Lady, Gossamyr called to the soul shepherd. "Do you feel them? Can you command them?"

"I can feel them...all." He plunged to his knees. "There is one..."

The yellow essence floated past the Red Lady's grasp. Shimmering, floating on wings unseen, it bounded above Dominique's head. The pinned entity soared toward Gossamyr, a strange weapon aimed for her heart.

"What is it?" Dominique called.

Dodging, Gossamyr avoided getting hit, and at the opportune moment managed to reach out and catch the yellow essence. It shushed between her fingers, but the pin did not wound nor tear the essence asunder. Heavy, its weight, and scented with life—heliotrope. Humming loudly, the essence did not make to leave her carefully netted fingers.

"Mine!"

From behind the curtained bed Avenall rushed toward Gossamyr. Eyes red with rage, he dodged Dominique's attempt to deter him, only flinching as the soul shepherd's fingers skimmed his wing.

Gossamyr could not stop her lover as he plunged into her. She felt resistance, and heard a strange mellow sigh—a return.

The point of the silver pin exited Avenall's back and he collapsed into her arms.

TWENTY-NINE

"Avenall!"

Gossamyr juggled the oozing yellow essence and the wobbly limbs of the pin man. Avenall had speared himself upon the pin in a manic sacrifice.

Now the pale-winged fée, quivering and slipping his fingers into the viscous essence, looked up to Gossamyr. A smile, so bright, filled his violet eyes. Red spilled down his cheeks. "Thank… you…"

"No!"

"My…Gossamyr," he said on a gurgling gasp. Red splattered her breast as he spat out the words. "I have loved…you. So. Exotic."

A death sigh escaped. With that breath the yellow essence seeped into the fée's body through his pores. Gossamyr watched the mark of banishment gleam and lessen and vanish.

"Puppy!"

"What is it?" Ulrich asked. Of course he could but see the essence she held in her arms, not the faery.

"Avenall," she whispered. "He is speared upon the pin."

The Red Lady stretched out a hand, butchering a flock of essences as she slapped the marble wall.

"Please, Ulrich, come to me." Dead in her arms, Avenall was released into Ulrich's hold. "Can you feel him?"

Ulrich wrestled with holding the fée, but Avenall's shoulders slipped against his chest and he nodded. "Got him."

"Gently, please." Drawing in a choking breath, Gossamyr raised her sight to the succubus.

He held a being. He could not see it, but he knew whoever it was had meant much to Gossamyr. The pin—suspended in nothing, it appeared—wobbled between his curled arms. Ichor oozed from the pin, spilling over a shape of a body, yet unseen. Pierced through the heart, Ulrich guessed. Final remnants of the essence dissipated, mayhap seeping into the dead fée's body.

Now he felt the fée's very being tap him and seek guidance. A familiar call. He would not refuse. Drawn into the Send, he directed the essence onward. Heaven or Hell? No such choices.

"Go in peace," he whispered. "Ever after in his grace."

The body fell limp and began to slip from Ulrich's arms. Hooking under the invisible arms, Ulrich held strong. Together, the two men slid to the floor.

Arret spinning, Gossamyr spared a moment to turn and look to Ulrich. Avenall lay limp in the soul shepherd's arms. But peaceful, yes? A horrid loosening of tears pushed from her eyes. It was not fair that he had suffered for loving her! Be this his punishment for the mortal passion, a cruel sacrifice always demanded of the fée.

But there, the glimmer of Faery burst out from Avenall's chest. It stretched the height of the room, and then with a blink, spanned horizontal, running the length and out the door into the hallway. Bathed in the golden glow of his essence, Gossamyr closed her eyes and smiled. With another blink, the glimmer dissipated.

"The final *twinclian*," she said. *I love you, Avenall.*

"Not my puppy!" the Red Lady spat at Gossamyr. "You have taken much from me, warrior bitch."

Wiping spittle from her arm, Gossamyr approached the succubus. "No more than you have taken from my father."

"Shinn's cruelties touch all. Why is he not here to answer to his crimes? Does he hide behind a helpless mortal?"

"Helpless? You must have lost half your sight too, red woman." She spun the *arret* into a frenzy. "I've yet to fall babbling from your pitiful song."

"My puppy is gone!"

"You killed Avenall."

"You were the one who wielded the pin!"

"You took his essence and taunted him. He was dead long ago."

Avoiding contact with the wall of essences, Gossamyr stalked the succubus widdershins toward the edge of the marble steps. If she could throw her off balance she gained opportunity to strike. But how, exactly, to take her out without a sword or weapon larger than an *arret*? She seemed impervious to the staff and its stealthy blows. Must she kill the woman?

Either that or be killed, Shinn's words revisited Gossamyr's thoughts. Or had she heard them, plain as ever?

Her aggressor stood stunned, yet a malicious grin stretched her lips to an open smile. It was then Gossamyr felt the new presence.

Shinn stood in the doorway.

THIRTY

His presence filled her heart, pounding, expanding, urging… All she had ever known—a father's love—overwhelmed. Gossamyr wanted to rush to Shinn and embrace him. To plead, "Take me home; I believe."

She believed in love and that it knew no bounds.

She glanced to Ulrich. He gathered Avenall into his arms as gently as a father would a child. He had fathered a child not of his blood and had loved her.

Yes, she felt loved. And why not? She was Verity d'Ange: mortal.

Vengeance, valor—and now, the truth.

But in her heart she could not abandon her mission to such foolish emotions.

Keeping the *arret* spinning and ready for release, rage over Avenall's senseless death worked tears at the corners of her eyes. Courage shimmied through her being, far more powerful than any glamour. And fear loomed close. Not fear of the enemy, but fear for the well-being of Ulrich, and now Shinn. Why had he come here? He risked Disenchantment, or worse, the Red Lady's bane.

"Father?"

Shinn lifted a hand. "Gossamyr, stay back. Would I had done this before, I would have never had to send you off on such a mission."

"But—"

"You've come for me, Turiau de Wintershinn of Glamoursiège?"

At the succubus's announcement, Gossamyr saw Shinn stiffen, fighting the *erie* of his Naming.

The Red Lady glided across the marble base, the essences quivering with her pass, right up to the staunch Faery lord. "So little time has passed, and yet—" she sneered, displeased with what she looked upon "—you have aged centuries."

"I have not come to welcome you back to my bed, Circélie Sangreul of Rougethorn. I banished you with good reason, and the banishment holds."

She pouted out a thick red lip. "Your recital of my name wields no power against my magic. What do you desire, Turiau? Do not tell me you've come to rescue your false mortal child."

"Never false in my heart."

"Ah. So honorable, to the bitter end. Such a horrible confession to love a mortal makes me quiver, Turiau. Twice now. But you are too late. She knows her truth; Faery will now only eat her away."

"Enough!" Shinn nodded toward the wall, high above. "The alicorn's power is not for you to possess."

"Who sayeth?"

Gossamyr eyed the pinioned alicorn. Using her staff—even half-size—for a levered jump, she might make the leap.

Shinn's voice boomed throughout the room. "Me for the alicorn."

"No," Gossamyr gasped. 'Twas as if the gargoyles' flames sizzled in her throat that she could not speak another word.

"Oh?" The Red Lady spun around. Malice twinkled in the look

she speared at Gossamyr. A twist at the waist turned her back to Shinn. "You offer your…essence?"

"The Disenchantment has yet to touch me; I offer you an essence strong and capable—"

"—of seeing my return to Faery?"

"If that be your desire."

"But you are not so strong, I see you age before my eyes."

The Faery lord spread his iridescent emerald wings wide. Hyacinth perfumed the room. A swoosh of his wings breathed a strong wind, stretching out the Red Lady's hair and skirts from her body. He spoke forcefully, "Yet strong."

The Red Lady clapped her hands overhead and spun. "Yes! I will agree to the exchange."

"Gossamyr! Retrieve the alicorn," Shinn demanded.

While her body moved toward the wall, Gossamyr felt heavy tears streak her cheeks. The burning in her throat, acid and hot, choked her from crying in protest. Shinn must not sacrifice his essence to this wicked succubus! Nor could he allow her return to Faery!

She stopped beneath the alicorn and looked to Shinn. In her father's eyes she saw the mirror of her tears. With her truth, he had sacrificed something greater—his own truth. For he had fallen to the mortal passion by loving her.

The Red Lady whisked between the two of them. "Take it then, false child of Shinn. Be quick with it."

"Turiau de Wintershinn," sang the succubus, "bold lord of Glamoursiège."

Shinn stiffened, his jaw hard. He could not move, Gossamyr knew, so great was the Red Lady's hold.

You can overpower her.

"Don't," Shinn croaked as Gossamyr lifted her staff behind the Red Lady's head.

I love you, she mouthed to the Faery lord as the Red Lady approached him, her palms rising to bracket his face. She would kiss him, suck out his essence. Gossamyr knew not how the foul extraction manifested, nor did she wish to witness.

She jumped and missed the alicorn.

Landing the floor in a graceless sprawl, she spied as Ulrich carefully arranged Avenall upon the crimson bed. A man blind to the figure in his arms, yet he managed to remove the leather hip sheath of pins.

She jumped again and her fingers skimmed the alicorn. A vibrant burst of Enchantment drifted from the horn. "Achoo!"

"Take this!" Ulrich called. He pulled out the clacking pins and tossed the leather bag to her.

As Gossamyr turned to catch the bag, she saw the Red Lady press her lips to her father's mouth. And she froze in that moment, a reluctant witness to her father's sacrifice.

The mighty Faery lord, arms spread wide in resistance—you shall have me, but you shall not have my fealty—took the kiss without moving. Clinging to her former lover, the Red Lady kissed him for what seemed to Gossamyr, evermore. *Too long.* A heart pulse caught up in a net.

In that instant the fetch buzzed into the room and swept over Shinn and the Red Lady's embrace. The dragon fly fluttered before Gossamyr. *Look away.*

And so she did.

She turned and leaped again, this time snagging the alicorn with the bag. In that moment she felt the vibrations of Enchantment. She did not want to hold this object. It was not hers to own. Where had gone the unicorn and the changeling?

With a deft balance to keep the alicorn teetering—without touching it—she slipped it into the leather pouch and ran down the steps to Ulrich. "Take it."

He shoved the pins into her hand, exchanging them for the leather bag. Gossamyr was pulled about by a mourning cry from her father. His body plummeted, falling straight backward, arms still out at his sides. Wings drained of life were useless against the fall.

The Red Lady, unloosed from her deadly kiss, staggered and coiled into a fix of squirming limbs. She moaned with such pleasure Gossamyr felt she witnessed a private act.

"Shinn!"

"No."

She wrestled against Ulrich's attempts to hold her back.

"This is your chance," the soul shepherd pleaded. "She is in a wicked sort of sexual thrall. Take her out!"

A glance to Shinn. He lay perfectly still. Wings flattened upon the cold marble. The fetch landed his forehead. Dead?

"No," Gossamyr moaned in a rabbity cry.

And in the next instant her fingers clenched about the silver pins. Gathering the dozen long needles with both hands, she pointed them outward and rushed the writhing succubus. Racked with a pleasure most wicked, the Red Lady danced and sighed along the wall, clinging and undulating against the essences. Viscous fluids splattered her arms and neck and face as her movements burst the struggling essences.

Gossamyr wielded the pins overhead and, just as the Red Lady's arm whipped backward, twisting her chest up and high in a spasm of pleasure, Gossamyr drove the weapons into her chest. Silver pin to faery flesh. Pins slid freely through ribs, others, Gossamyr had to shove hard to pierce the resistant bone cage.

The force of the act blasted Gossamyr backward. Flung unfettered and uncontrollably, she landed Ulrich's body. The two slumped to the floor in a tangle of limbs.

Maniacal wails filled the room. The succubus's body shivered upon the wall as if an essence for ever pinned between the Celestial and the Infernal.

"Will she die?" Ulrich whispered over Gossamyr's shoulder.

"I—"

The succubus spat out oaths tinged with the Red and then ceased movement. Ichor poured from her chest, glistening ooze dripping from the heavy iron balls that tipped the pins. Her head slumped, folding onto her bosom.

And the wall of essences stopped. All became quiet.

Save the glimmer parting Shinn's chest. A brilliant essence of violet and emerald emerged and severed from the Faery lord's body.

"No, go back!" Gossamyr lunged to her father's side. She reached for the escaping essence, then paused to consider. Should she touch it? She did not want to risk a revenant. Carefully, she placed her palms above the essence to shield it from rising any higher. The cloying aroma of hyacinth set loose tears. "What should I do, Ulrich? I cannot put it back in the body."

"Let it go!"

"No!" Gossamyr clasped the essence to her body and felt it seep into her clothing, through her flesh and into her body. "Oh!"

"Hades," Ulrich moaned.

In the next instant the revenant's bony fingers reached out from Shinn's chest and sprang, fully formed into the room. Heart beating heavily, Gossamyr knew then she should have allowed the essence to leave of its own. She had prevented the final *twinclian*.

Now she held her father's essence within her. She could feel it pressing inside, filling and glowing. It sought freedom. From a species so foreign?

The revenant spread out its wings. A shriek rattled Gossamyr's concentration. It slapped one wing back against the wall, crushing several stilled essences in a spray that showered distorted rainbows upon the Red Lady's bowed head. Shinn's revenant—it sought an essence to achieve the final *twinclian*. It would be off to Faery!

Gossamyr reminded herself it was not Shinn, but a creature. Only when united with the essence would it become Turiau de Wintershinn, lord of Glamoursiège. Her father.

The revenant's skull bobbed, searching the room. Hollow red

eyes focused first on Ulrich, then Gossamyr. Clutching her chest, Gossamyr's terror mixed with the strange filling sensation that glimmered throughout her being. A fée essence cleaved to her insides. Her *mortal* insides. She could gauge the strength growing in her muscles. Her thoughts wavered, parting to let in another. Shinn inhabited her. Though her mind remained her own she experienced an overwhelming calm. Of being touched by a being that could only communicate love. Faery, so rich and luscious. Shinn's final gift to her—light.

She began to rise, floating up from the floor.

The revenant slashed out with a long, clawed hand, missing Gossamyr's face by a breath. But she did not dodge. Still rising, shoulders straight, she hung before the creature, ready. Dropping the two remaining pins, they landed in a clatter.

"Gossamyr, no!" Ulrich cried. "You are...do not sacrifice!"

Delicious warmth seeped throughout her. Shinn would protect her. She believed.

Yes, Father, I do belong—in your heart.

"Take the essence if you can!" she defied the shrieking revenant. "No!"

She ignored Ulrich's protest. If she did not do this all of Faery would suffer.

"I love you, Shinn," she murmured. The vibrations of her voice echoed in her bones and the glowing, shimmering essence inside her twitched in response. "This is for you!"

Stretching out her arms wide, Gossamyr lifted her chest, opening herself completely to the oncoming attack. A macabre grin cracked the jaw of the skull that flew toward her. Fingers of sharp bone moved through her ribs. The pain was real, tearing her open and parting her chest. All she could do was gasp as the revenant, its hand embedded deep within her, held her suspended before the wall of stilled essences.

To her right the Red Lady still shivered and fought against death.

Ichor glimmered in a stream from her mouth. And peaceful upon the bed lay one she'd loved, gone to the Celestial.

The hand inside her twisted and began to probe, to summon and gather.

Gossamyr let out a yowl that birthed from a mortal midnight that saw her stolen from her cradle and secreted away to Faery.

Verity d'Ange...

...this day we baptize you in the name of our Lord.

She is so precious. Do you like your little sister, Seraphim?

She's stinky.

Verity is ours to love...bless us all.

The shimmering feeling began to subside, to give way from her extremities, pulling, balling and forming into a central mass. Gossamyr felt the revenant's bony fingers curl and scrape against her spine to clasp. In that moment she looked up into the fathomless red eyes of the skull and saw the circumference of the pupils begin to fill with violet. Faery seeped back into the revenant. Shinn returned.

And in his wake, Verity d'Ange rose up from the remnants of Enchantment.

Lifted high, her feet dangling above marble, Gossamyr thought the beast to fling her across the room—but instead it lunged toward the bed. Gently—the hand still within her chest—it laid her upon the red sheets beside Avenall.

As the revenant hand withdrew, Gossamyr groped at the opening in her chest. Everything moved slowly, lengthening the pain. Bones moved out from her body, the creature, not Shinn. And grasped in the skeletal hand the violet and emerald essence.

When the essence pulled free from her body, it brightened and expanded and began to overtake the revenant. Enthralled in a tornado of the brilliant violet and emerald essence, the revenant spun, moving across the room like a windstorm. Past Ulrich, who clung to the bedpost, and above Shinn's empty body.

Gossamyr, eyes fixed to the vision, clutched her chest. The

gown had been rendered wide, but beneath, her flesh bore not a mark. A deep inhale renewed her vigor.

She pushed up to the edge of the bed just as the essence devoured the revenant and twirled into a long thin beam. Ulrich's touch stopped her from rushing forward.

The essence poured into Shinn's prone body, covering the Faery lord over with its glimmer. The fetch, fixed to his forehead, fluttered its wings and took to flight. And then, the glimmer dissipated, leaving the dead fée in its wake.

Tears coating her cheek, Gossamyr stepped over to her father's body. "You sacrificed for me." And she pressed her head against his gut and began to cry. She had witnessed his final *twinclian*.

"Gossamyr!"

At Ulrich's cry, she looked up from Shinn's body. There, pinned to the wall of exhausted essences, the Red Lady's essence began to emerge from the pinnacle of her skull. A dark crimson thing oozed slowly into the atmosphere to hover above its mistress's head. Taunting, as only the succubus could.

"Shall I get it?" Ulrich wondered from over her shoulder. "I'll take your staff and smash——"

"No." She reached for Ulrich's hand and turned to sit at the edge of the marble steps. "Just…witness."

The blood-red essence remained above her head for so long Gossamyr thought the revenant might climb out and smash the thing itself. But suddenly the red globule popped.

"Dragon piss," Gossamyr muttered. Feeling every muscle in her body tense she prepared.

"The revenant?" Ulrich said.

"Soon," she called. "Stand back!"

Approaching the Red Lady's body, Gossamyr stood over the limp heap of white velvet speckled with gobs of the shattered red essence. "Have at me," she whispered. "This is what I've come for."

It did not claw its way out from the body. No, this revenant shrieked and flew from the cage of bones as if shot out from a cannon. It touched the ceiling of the collection room, floated momentarily, its red eyes surveying the floor, and then dived.

This one was not a skeletal clatter of bones. This revenant was fleshed with red muscle and long glinting claws. A result of a succubus, or that of a succubus's dabbling with magic?

It mattered not.

Gossamyr swung her body in a circle, drawing the staff straight out. Connection thrust her against the wall of essences. Cold goo oozed over her shoulder. A shriek to raise the dead pierced her ear. The revenant slashed the wall. Its claws cried to the Infernal as they destroyed essences and neared Gossamyr's face.

Leaping forward, Gossamyr gripped the waist of the creature. It flew high with her clinging and kicking at the muscular legs. A shake released her hold.

Falling, she let out a cry. "For Glamoursiège!"

Her body hit marble. Briefly her sight blackened. She lifted her hand, still clutching the half staff. It connected with something solid.

The revenant cried out and the staff jiggled in her hand. Gripping it with both hands, Gossamyr wrestled with the speared revenant. Claws hissed through the air and the foul stench of decay spewed over all.

"The alicorn, Ulrich!"

Releasing the staff, Gossamyr rolled on her side. She slid ungracefully down the two marble stairs. Behind her the revenant banged its shoulder against the wall as it struggled with the staff fixed in its chest.

Sliding to a stop at Ulrich's foot, Gossamyr felt the alicorn slap into her palm. "Get back!" She rolled to her back and aimed the alicorn toward the revenant.

Not a glimmer of Enchantment beamed from the horn.

The revenant, aware now, tilted its head curiously.

"Ulrich, I think I need some magic to destroy this beast!"

"I'm not sure—"

"Grab my hand!" She scrambled backward and when she hit Ul-rich's leg, she leaped to her feet. It was wrong to include Ulrich when the most possible outcome could be his death. But there was little choice—this revenant had been forged of both Enchantment and magic.

The revenant lunged for her.

Ulrich slapped his palm to hers.

Believe, Gossamyr thought to herself. And then she shouted to Ulrich, "You must believe!"

The wind of the revenant's savage growl bruised her face. Star-ing at slimy maws, Gossamyr lifted the alicorn and drove it up through the revenant's throat. The tip emerged at the top of its skull. She felt little resistance. But a spark of dust sifted from the alicorn's tip and floated over the revenant.

Keeping hold of the alicorn, Gossamyr shoved Ulrich behind her but kept his hand in hers. She could feel it. His truth. His be-lief flowing through her arms and out her other arm to focus in the alicorn.

A brilliant crackle of bone and muscle exploded before her. No glimmer. Not a single glint. Particles of bone clattered to the mar-ble floor.

And it was done.

"That," Ulrich gasped over her shoulder, "left a mark."

"We're safe. Circélie Sangreul of Rougethorn has had the final *twinclian*."

With a shimmering flight over their heads, the fetch landed Gossamyr's forehead. So brief the touch, and yet, in that moment she saw a flash of the time she had cried three days. And follow-ing, Mince storing her tears away in a crystal vase, where they hard-ened and sparkled like quartz. That was all she saw before the fetch alighted and *twinclianed*.

Dominique entered, the unicorn in tow. The changeling took

in the destruction, glancing to the body of Avenall, and sneering at sight of the Red Lady, yet pinned to the wall. Red had begun to trickle from the pinprick marks around her left eye. Finally Dominique's eyes fell upon Shinn.

"Your father?" he said as he knelt beside the Faery lord. "I am sorry."

Involuntary shivers rode Gossamyr's spine. She could not force herself to speak, to offer an "I know, he sacrificed for me." Instead, she fell into Ulrich's embrace, tucking her face against his shoulder. The soul shepherd stroked her arm and kissed the crown of her head. Bare of shirt, his flesh felt ridiculously warm and so very…like home.

"He must be returned to Faery," Dominique said softly. "I will prepare him for the journey, if you will allow."

Gossamyr simply nodded. She knew that without Shinn's assistance there was no Passage back to Faery for her. Though the rift yet remained open.

When you return to Faery you shall age and wither. Belief had been altered. No return, ever. And yet, someone must now sit the Glamoursiège throne.

From the corner of her eye she observed Dominique as he stood over Shinn, finger to chin in thought. Devising a plan? Tor walked up to the changeling and nudged a suede nose into his palm.

"It *is* a unicorn," Ulrich's hot breath whispered reverently.

Dominique looked over his shoulder at her. Then he turned back to Tor, pressed his forehead to the beast's nose, right between its eyes, and held there. Communicating? Mayhap, and similar to Shinn's communication with the fetch.

Why had the fetch shone her a picture of all her tears?

A twist of her waist focused her gaze on Avenall, laid carefully upon the bed. Glimmer of faery dust sparkled there on his chest where the pin had pierced through flesh and heart and married his stolen essence with the body.

"You remembered," she whispered, "just before you died. I hope it was a good memory."

"He loved you, Gossamyr," Ulrich reassured. "As did you him."

"Call me...Verity."

"Why?"

"It is who I am, who I have always been."

A sigh sloughed out final tears. She pulled from Ulrich and touched the leather saddlebag.

"I know," Ulrich said. "We should return it now the unicorn is here."

"Not we. You, Ulrich. You have journeyed far for your wish."

"Tor is aware the alicorn is within reach," Dominique announced. "But not here in this lair of evil. We must to a place of calm, far from Paris and closer to Faery. He will bear Shinn and the other on his back. We should be off."

And so the threesome carefully secured Shinn and Avenall upon Tor's back and left the Red Lady's lair as it was. The essences that had not burst were rapidly dissipating. One after another gave a bright twinkle before finally dissolving to but a whisper of dust. Gossamyr could not guess if it be the final *twinclian* or merely a sigh of final release.

She strode from the room without looking back.

As they emerged from the depths of strange darkness and despair, the chill of the morning reawakened their senses. Tiny chirps from a hidden nest brightened the sweetness of the dawn. Clasping a hand to her breast, she only now realized the gown had been rent wide, revealing the curves of her breasts.

Dominique stood waiting with his cloak, which Gossamyr gratefully accepted.

Ulrich embraced her. "Your father truly did love you."

"I wish he had not sacrificed himself before I could tell him I understood. He kept his secrets thinking to protect me. I could have lived forever in Faery without knowing."

"We must all bear the cross of our lacking wisdom, Faery Not."

"Do not call me that."

"Very well, champion."

"I am not a champion."

"Oh ho?" A dramatic gesture of arms to the air revisited the good-natured Ulrich she had first met. "You defeated a vicious succubus and rescued all of Faery from those manic revenants. You were prepared to give your life so others may live. I'd call that a champion."

"The man speaks the truth," Dominique echoed from the other side of Tor.

She tugged the soft wool cloak high, pressing one of the cool hematite stones against her chin. "It is not important anymore."

"So what is?"

She glanced to Tor, who ambled ahead by a few paces toward the gates of Paris. "Seeing my father returned to Faery. And..."

"Yes?"

She must wed Desideriel to place a successor to the throne. But how to return yet alluded her scatter of thoughts. And there were other desires—new to her—but strongest of all— "Finding my sister. I have one, you know?"

"I did not."

"You will come to my home in the Valois woods," Dominique stated as he strolled off. "I want you to meet my wife. She will be pleased to know you."

"Sure," Verity answered. "But I shall seek my sister first."

"I can help you," Dominique stated.

But it was Ulrich's eyes that held her transfixed. She wondered, "You up for a holiday in the woods?"

"Are there any wicked red faeries lurking within, waiting to kiss me to death?"

"I don't expect so."

"Then I am willing. You would have me accompany you?"

"I couldn't imagine leaving you behind, Ulrich. I...I favor your company. That is, if you favor mine."

"I think what you are trying to say is you like me?"

"Er, I do."

"I like you as well, Gossa——Verity. I may even love you."

"You——you do?" She grinned and felt her smile grow loose and wild. The heat of her blush startled her. She pressed her fingers to her mouth and glanced down.

"You are sweetest when you are out of your element, Verity. I love you for that."

"I shall always and ever be out of my element."

"I will help you to adjust. If you will allow it."

"I wouldn't have it any other way. Shall we to the unicorn?"

"Indeed," Dominique called as he began to follow Tor's gait. He turned a curious gaze upon Gossamyr. "Did he name you Verity?"

"It is my mortal name," she offered.

"Ah. Well then, my wife will certainly be pleased to meet you."

Tor led them out from the gates of Paris and to the edge of a forest bisected by a stream. Far from the dangers of marauders, here in the peaceful meadow the sun danced upon the leaves and grass, and butterflies flittered deliriously, unmindful of those congregated around the white beast.

Shinn was laid upon the ground and Gossamyr crossed his hands upon his chest. She touched his face; it was still soft and a little warm. His hair, so white now, flowed across a crush of fragrant heather. Touching the short horn at his right temple, she smiled to remember the many times as a youngling, when she had grabbed hold of both and rode upon his back as if he were a beast. They had laughed until Shinn would fall to his knees and gently roll over her and tickle her to oblivion.

To Shinn's side had been laid Avenall. Gossamyr felt sure now Shinn would not mind the Rougethorn being placed aside him in death. They two had loved her; Shinn knew that.

"This Rougethorn was fine and kind," she said to them both.

"It will be well," Dominique said as his shadow drew over Shinn's legs. "Trust that it will."

"I know." Gossamyr stood, and stepped back from the two men she loved. Of a sudden the fetch *twinclianed* before her. The creature lumbered in the air. She noticed a small stack of crystals in the harness strapped to its back. "What is this?"

She did not touch the fetch or the crystals, but further observance deduced something most remarkable. "My tears?"

And the knowledge became hers as if granted by the fetch. Her tears would provide her means to return to Faery.

"I can use my tears to *twinclian* back to Faery."

Ulrich strode up beside her. "You said there was a danger in your return."

"Yes, but mayhap if my visit is brief. I am willing to risk the danger. There are things to be tended. Desideriel, my betrothed, must take command."

"Your betrothed?" She turned and found herself in Ulrich's arms. Pale blue eyes rushed across her face. How many times had she looked upon that animated mouth and only now did she see it frown. "My lady, did you not reveal all your truths?"

Stroking her fingers through Ulrich's tangled hair she noted a new bruise at his left temple. An excellent companion he had proven for this journey. Not afraid to stand at her side, nor had he feared to step back and allow her the fight. A good man, he. A fine mortal.

"Yes, my betrothed."

Ulrich but held her gaze, no admonishment, yet little compassion in his look.

"Shinn had arranged our vows. It has been so for many Faery moons. We will wed..."

"I see."

She could not prevent a sigh. He could never understand, though it was his right to know all. "Desideriel...does not favor me."

"As I do," he answered in the smallest voice.

"Yes, as you...do." She smiled, but mirth slipped from her mouth so quickly, she felt the pain of its departure. Mortal touched meant that she was loved by this man, and she in turn loved him. "But he is a good man. An excellent leader. Shinn would want Desideriel to replace him as lord of Glamoursiège. It is necessary."

"Yes."

"Ulrich, I love you."

"Ah?" A touch to her lip. Difficult to put off the exquisite feeling of being loved. "So much that you would marry another?"

"I love Faery even more. It is the only home I have ever known. So much that I would offer my hand to a loveless marriage."

"But if you return—did you not say you would age?"

"It is a chance I must risk."

Cleaving together, the twosome kissed, and falling they went, falling, deep into oblivion. No need for words. This contact bonded them, soul to mortal soul, mortal heart to beating mortal heart. Light in Ulrich's arms. Light in this world.

Here is home.

To be kissed ever and anon by this kind, gentle man returned the smile to her lips. This feeling of safety and acceptance she could believe in ever after.

"Thought I'd try to convince you to remain," he said, pulling back from their embrace. He sought her eyes. "How did I do?"

"Very persuasive." She touched his mouth. "But—"

"Say not another word. I understand. Verity, is it? I am a better man for knowing you."

And he stepped away, turning to acknowledge the changeling who waited beside Tor.

So simple as turning away one's head, their departure?

Yes, and keep it so.

Gossamyr clutched her chest. There is where it pained. Many men that she had loved, and all of them, taken from her. Was it fair that she must sacrifice so much to save a realm not her own? No.

Champions are made.

Indeed. And champions be as lonely as an innocent mortal woman coming into her own.

She gestured to Ulrich to bring the saddlebag to her. The two knelt in the meadow before Tor. Ulrich carefully extracted the wrapped alicorn from the leather bag and laid it upon the blades of boot-crunched grass.

"You do it," he said to her. "Unwrap it. It is not my place." He looked to Dominique. "Unless you wish to?"

Dominique nodded his head. "Neither is it my place. Only the pure of heart may touch the alicorn without risking grave harm to the Enchantment pure. Lady d'Ange?"

How perfect that name felt. Not new, but always hers. Here did she belong, in the Otherside. Yet now she must sacrifice to make things right in Faery.

"I'm not so sure how pure I am." She had kissed a man—two men. Did that not lessen her purity? Only a maiden could enthrall the unicorn. "I am," she murmured, ruefully, "I am afraid. Besides, Ulrich, you must have your wish."

A thick rusted brow arched aside the new bruise. "You must do it. And you have overlooked the fact that I be no virgin, Faery Not. Would that I had realized such before I began this quest, eh?"

"But you have traveled far."

"Truly, it is not right to bring back the dead. I must be satisfied with my memories and know that Rhiana did live for twenty-two years. Pray it was a good life." Ulrich's hand on her shoulder anchored a rich warmth in her chest. "You are the champion, Gossamyr of Glamoursiège. I bid you, Verity d'Ange, return Enchantment to this beast."

She nodded, and as Ulrich stepped back to stand beside Dominique, she knelt before the alicorn and touched the wrapping. Beside her, Tor snorted softly; not impatient, but calming. Ready.

She held the ability to grant this beast a return to Faery. With him, Tor would bring Shinn to rest in his rightful place. As well, Avenall would be returned to Rougethorn.

Pulling back the cloth, she revealed the glittering alicorn. Dominique's gasp placed a smile to her face. Time to give back the gift of Faery and to seal the rift. And she? She would marry Desideriel and place a new lord upon the Glamoursiège throne.

All would be right, save, her heart.

Standing, she bent and gripped the alicorn. The power of the object—Enchantment pure—susurrated through her arms and down her sides, stiffening her carriage and flexing her limbs straight out in surrender. Verity rode the wondrous wave of power for but a moment.

Not yours to possess. Return it!

Finding she could move, she placed the alicorn to the raw oval on the beast's forehead. It sealed. And the unicorn reared onto its hind legs, whinnying triumphantly. The witch locks that had once protected it from harm unwound and the lush long mane splayed out at neck and tail. Awareness tapped all creatures. Insects buzzed up from the green-ribbon grasses, clouding in a whoosh of wing and clacking shell. Squirrels chattered in the trees, and in the distance a lone fox howled.

And for a moment Verity saw the world in all the vibrant colors of Faery. The sky intensified and became like indigo glass, liquid and smooth. Clouds dissipated. The grasses swayed and sang a canorous song.

The unicorn's forelegs stomped the ground. The bass pulse of the earth echoed with each stomp. Verity, frozen in place, smiled as a soft wet nose nudged her face and a rough tongue lapped her chin. Kissed by Enchantment.

The last taste she might ever know.

To her side, Ulrich threaded his fingers into hers and Tor moved to stand before the soul shepherd. The unicorn bowed its head and pressed the length of its nose to Ulrich's face, a strange communion that held the man in a shuddering reverie. Shaking minutely, Ulrich stretched out both arms, releasing—and gaining. With a snap of its head Tor pulled back.

Ulrich collapsed forward onto the ground, palms catching in the grasses. In the next moment he exclaimed in effusive gasps, "She is alive! My Rhiana! The unicorn bid me see her. She is—not safe—but yet lives! Oh, my, such dragon fire."

The unicorn turned and, going down on one leg, bowed before Dominique. A dust of white-plumed mouse flies sifted skyward. The beast bristled and shook its head. Dominique bowed.

In a storm of lofting butterflies and bees and scuttling field mice the unicorn took off at a gallop. It charged the meadow then turned and cantered toward Shinn and Avenall. Powerful forelegs beating the earth, the sound of its pace drummed the air. A leap passed the white stallion over the Faery lord's body. But it did not land the ground. One moment the unicorn beat down the grasses with powerful legs and dancing head—

—the next moment it was gone.

Returned to Faery. Re-Enchanted.

Shinn had gone to rest in the place of his origin. Avenall would be returned to Rougethorn.

Iridescent wings fluttered over Gossamyr's head. She tilted back her head, catching the sharp tinks of her crystallized tears upon her eyelids and cheeks. Contact softened them and salty liquid slid over her flesh. The sound of love lost cried out across the meadow.

Verity turned to find she stood before the blue marble castle. "Oh."

Flutter of the fetch's wings glittered in her peripheral view— but began to fade. All began to blur and soften at the edges like ripples on a pond distorting a reflection. Time here would be limited. Soon she would lose all sight of Faery, and in turn Faery would rob her of life.

Now, to find Desideriel.

"I have worried a pacing trail across the room!" Mince scampered out from the castle entry. "You are home."

Home, yes, in Mince's arms. And in her father's closed eyes.

The same, this castle. The same, her maid.

Mince fussed and tugged at her motley clothing and commented when she saw her burnt hair. But Gossamyr could only wrap her arms about her and hug. Close, here in Faery, and better for it. Ever the same.

"Lord de Wintershinn?"

Gossamyr gulped at the heavy air. "He has had the final *twinclian,* Mince."

"Oh, blight!" The maid faltered, but Gossamyr caught her by the elbow and walked her toward the castle.

Never had she truly belonged. She believed in the Otherside now. Her side. "The wedding must go on. Shinn would have wanted that. Though I doubt I shall live long after. Time will make that decision for me."

"Nonsense!"

"I am mortal…you know. The rift has been sealed. My time is limited."

"Oh? Oh, yes, yes." Mince clasped her arm tight to Gossamyr's and leaned upon her as they walked. "Oh, Gossamyr?"

"Verity."

"Oh?"

"My mortal name—"

"Nay, you must not speak a Name from the Otherside or you will—"

Perish. The unspoken word.

"You may be safe—hold back Time—if you do not utter your mortal name complete." The maid nodded effusively, and then…

"Mince? I cannot see you."

"I'm right here, precious one. Oh, we must hurry you to Desideriel!"

* * *

Desideriel Raine stood in the cloistered tower, looking out over the rose garden. He wore battle gear, armored gauntlets, a leather cuirass strapped across his broad chest, and greaves on his shins. Brilliant periwinkle wings folded down his back and thighs.

Gossamyr, quite in a hurry, but slowing her approach, paused some good distance from him and bowed. Still garbed in the tattered fur-trimmed gown and Dominique's hematite-rimmed cape, she had allowed Mince to untwist her plait to survey the damage from the flame. A perfect mess, she appeared.

If Desideriel took notice of her he did not show it.

She hadn't time for his refusal to recognize her as a viable mate. Her staff, it was not to hand, and she felt not whole without it. With immense regret for what she planned, Gossamyr stepped right up to Desideriel—close enough for Faery.

"Lady de Wintershinn," he offered, looking down upon her. He did not move, but neither could he summon a bow. But his eyes did widen and his nostrils flared. Disgust. "It has been many moons."

"But a few mortal days," she said. There was no time to wonder about the erratic effects of Time.

"Shinn left a full moon cycle previous," Desideriel said. "The revenants, they have ceased. I have waited for Lord de Wintershinn's return."

"He is dead."

Desideriel stepped back, obviously taken with her abrupt announcement.

"Forgive my rude manner," she spoke quickly, but with the authority her position afforded. "I am not long for Faery. Before my father died he explained much about…my origins."

"He is dead?"

"Sacrificed himself for me."

"I see." Was that genuine concern in the violet depths of Desideriel's gaze? "Then you have returned to take the throne?"

"Listen to me, Desideriel." She approached the crenellated marble and swung to face him as bravely as she could muster. No, bravery was not required, she had that. It was fortitude. "I cannot rule Glamoursiège, nor do I wish to. Shinn chose you."

"To stand at your side as your adviser."

"No, to rule Glamoursiège."

"I don't understand."

"Despite your lack of regard for my half blood—" Drawing up straight, she settled into her mortality with ease. This is who she was. Mortal, and not about to regret that fact. For so many she had loved because of it. "—you were the only choice to take control of the Glamoursiège reign. Will you do as the former Lord de Wintershinn desired?"

"I...yes. I will. And I do not hate—"

She put up her hand again. "I see your truth in your eyes. Do not make it peccable with falseness."

He nodded. Not about to admit what she claimed to know. It only made what she must do all the more trying.

"We should marry quickly. As I've said, I've not time. The rift has been sealed. I should not have returned, but to see Glamoursiège crown a new lord I have risked it. You will gain a wife who puts the disgust to your eyes, but worry not, I shall perish soon enough, leaving you to reign."

"We shall wed this evening."

"Splendid." So cold, his quick plans. But not unexpected. An excellent commander Lord Desideriel shall make. "I'll have Mince gather fitting vestments for we two, and you shall see the proper authorities are summoned.... Desideriel."

"Yes?"

"We must both enter the agreement knowing the other's truths. I know you do not favor me. I find you a fine and powerful warrior, well qualified to stand in my father's wake—but, my heart belongs to another."

He lifted a brow.

"As well, I have learned I am mortal complete. An exchange

taken to appease a changeling birth. I cannot stand upon the throne of Glamoursiège. It would be sacrilege. But my marriage to you will grant you that reign."

"I begin to understand—"

"Far more quickly than I could, I guess. As well I have learned my real name." She touched the hard leather curve of Desideriel's armor chest plate, carved on the dextral side with the Glamoursiège crest, and on the sinistral, a smaller version of his homeland crest, the Wisogoth. "I will tell it to you as a trust to honor our vows."

Both knew to Name her complete—a mortal in Faery—should condemn her to the Otherside evermore.

"I will never utter it, my lady, as my trust to our vows."

"Thank you." And she went on tiptoe and whispered her mortal name to him, then begged he begin to arrange for the evening's ceremony.

Gossamyr looked over the blue marble balustrade to the Passage below. Bright crimson toadstools formed a perfect circle within the vibrant emerald grass. A passage to a land she would recall with pride and such wonder. Her home. Ever a part of her heart.

An evening breeze perfumed with scythed grass and primrose hushed over her face and lifted the long trailing sleeves of violet arachnagoss as she spread her arms out to her sides. Faery, filled with memory, times she would not trade for even a glimpse at the mortal life she might have lived.

Vows had been spoken beneath the splendid light of a thousand beeswax candles carried aloft by a muster of violet-tongued piskies. A bronze circlet grasping rose crystals had been placed to Desideriel's head where the smooth tips of horns were just beginning to sprout. He had kissed Gossamyr beneath a swag of fragrant laburnum, merely display to those who witnessed, she knew. For she had not felt a thing during that kiss.

No, that wasn't right. In that moment she had felt much. Loss.

So many she had truly loved—Shinn, Avenall, and yes, Ulrich— all to remain only in her heart, never again in her arms.

A great feast had been brought in upon crystal platters. Minstrels had fluttered over the keep, dancing and singing praises of the new lord. Those fée who had ever looked upon Gossamyr with disdain had not changed their looks now she was the new lord's wife. It mattered little; Gossamyr knew who loved her, 'twas enough.

They were delivered to a flower-bedecked bedchamber and toasted with mead. And now the revelry was but a minute pulse to the beating of Gossamyr's heart.

"I will never lose you, Ulrich. For you live here." She pressed a hand over her heart. "Next to my father and Avenall."

Behind her, Desideriel approached, the ceremonial evening garb of crystal-trimmed arachnagoss revealed his bare chest and wide sweeping wings. He carried an applewood staff—one Gossamyr had not before seen—and displayed it across his palms for her.

"It is very fine." Tracing the carved design with a finger, she noted the inlaid crystal. "This pattern looks familiar."

"It is your father's blazon."

"Oh." Bewildered by Desideriel's kindness, she, with a look for permission, accepted the staff and turned from him to spin it thrice. The applewood sang brilliantly in her hand. It was who she was, this warrior wielding a staff. And it felt right. "A very fine piece."

"It is yours," he offered as she leaned against the balustrade and he joined her side. "You will need it."

"Certainly, I shall cherish it. As for *needing* it, the revenants have been defeated. With the rift sealed, Faery is no longer threatened. I have but to serve as your wife now, no matter how far in the background. You won't even notice me, I promise."

He tilted up her chin with a finger. In Desideriel's violet eyes she saw her own reflection. The proud warrior remained defeated even after triumph. But this is how it must be.

"The vows have been said. The Glamoursiège throne has been seated," he said. "You, my lady, are quite unnecessary."

She tried to look away, to hide her bruised integrity, but he held her firm.

"Would that I could keep you here," he said. "But I know your heart belongs elsewhere."

"My heart desires to do Shinn's bidding."

"And you have. You must return, Gossamyr."

Verity, she thought. "But—"

"You deserve a long, rich life. Already I have noticed…" He traced the corner of her eye where even Gossamyr had noticed a crinkle in the flesh. Age, racing quickly against her mortal heart. "Though I would offer you my attention, my care, my trust and my admiration, I could never give you my heart. I will never succumb to the mortal passion."

"I know that. I should never ask so much. I have explained I will turn my cheek when you seek another."

"Gossamyr, you are a princess. You should not have to turn your cheek. You deserve love and respect. I think you might find it in the Otherside."

He would allow her to return? Never to find her way back to Faery. "Mayhap."

"There is a man, yes? A mortal man who interests you?"

She shrugged.

"I am jealous."

"You are not."

"Oh, but I am. That a mere mortal can attract my lady wife?"

Did he work to make his voice sound so teasing? Almost flirtatious. Impossible.

"Who is but a mortal herself and who only draws pity from her husband's gaze. But my leaving will change nothing—we will be married still."

"As it must remain. It is not a requirement that the lord of

Glamoursiège has a wife to stand at his side. I vow to you I shall not interfere in your mortal affairs."

"You do?" That this man would sacrifice for her? How he had changed! "It is too much to give, I do not deserve—"

He pressed his forefinger to her mouth, silencing her protest. "Return you, to find love and a long life."

Gossamyr clutched the staff, wanting to hug him, to let out a cry for joy. To simply thank him for understanding. For no longer did she belong. Yet she knew his truth in her heart; to release her was not a sacrifice—he put her from his sight as would please him.

He gripped the staff and stepped up to kiss her. A kiss good-bye, an acceptance of sorts. A seal to their agreement to join hands across the distance.

"I should ask to visit you from time to time?"

"Whatever for?"

Desideriel laid both palms to her shoulders. Not a single tingle in that touch, Gossamyr noted. "You are everything your father is. I looked up to Shinn, almost as my own sire. He lives within you and in your strength and fire."

She nodded. "Suits me fine and well. Send me off. I don't want to lose another mortal moment!"

Staff clutched in one hand, she stretched her arms out and tilted back her head. Gossamyr felt her body lift into the air. Propelled by Desideriel's glamour, she soared over the balustrade and ascended slowly to stand in the center of the Passage. Looking up, she waved to the new lord of Glamoursiège.

"Verity d'Ange!" he announced. "Verity d'Ange! Verity d'Ange, claim your birthright now!"

And stabbing her staff into the ground, she suddenly wobbled but caught herself with a balance of her hand.

"Achoo!" Faery dust misted about her head.

Verity smiled and leaped from the toadstool circle. Her bare toes touched the familiar red dirt path and instantly she sensed the pounding approach of a horse and rider—a lick-for-leather approach.

Danger?

A smile curled onto Verity's lips.

But barely able to stumble backward, she caught herself from falling with a stab of her staff into the ground. A black palfrey, rider crouched and focused, galloped past.

"Kind sir—" she tried, but the rider did not slow.

He hadn't noticed he had almost galloped right over her!

"Mortals," she said, then laughed at herself. "They be a strange bunch, eh? Achoo!"

It felt grand to be back on the Other— "Home!" she shouted and spun a merry whirl until one foot stepped upon a toadstool. Veering from the spongy mushroom, she bowed to the Passage, acknowledging the gift Desideriel had granted her, then skipped across the path to the knee-high grasses.

So light! This was home!

The snorting, pounding approach of yet another rider alerted her. Spinning to witness the unwavering strides of a mighty stallion and his—

As the rider passed, Gossamyr scratched her head. Twice now. The horse had been black both times. The rider, merely a black blur for a cloak billowing about his shoulders, had looked…familiar?

It could not be possible.

On the other hand, this wood was rife with Enchantment.

Planting her feet and staff, Gossamyr waited. She didn't have to wait long. Again the horse and rider sped past her. So determined he was to get where he traveled! And if it truly be Ulrich he had found himself a fine destrier. Had so little time passed? Could it have been but one sunset since she had been to Faery?

Too much to hope for.

When the rider approached for the fourth time, Gossamyr decided to intervene. "Lest I be here all the day watching the dizzy circles of this rider unawares."

Springing to the edge of the path, she thrust out her staff. The beast stopped abruptly, its sweat-glossed breast heaving but an armshot from the staff. The rider sailed over the horse's head and landed a thicket of grass. But a single cry echoed up from the ground, in that deep, familiar tone Gossamyr knew.

Gripping her long wedding skirts in one hand, she scampered over to Ulrich. Leaning over his head, she stared down the length of his body. The same. Blessings, but he was the same!

"Who be—" Blinking and patting his chest, Ulrich finally looked up and above him to her face. He closed his right eye and cocked his mouth open. "Faery princess?"

"Yes, 'tis me, Ulrich. Be you fine and well?"

"Fine, yes. As for well, I've just flown like a faery through the sky and landed on my bottom." He eased a hand over the mentioned bottom. "It aches, but I don't think it'll leave a mark."

She offered both hands and he stood and flipped his cloak back over his shoulder. "You're...here?" He looked her up and down, touched her sheer sleeve and stepped back a stride to take it all in. "Looking the faery princess that you are. But still the same! The same, my precious one."

"Be you the same, as well. Save your blinking eye."

"Can't see a damned thing through it. Blind as the devil to fire."

Gossamyr's feet were lifted from the ground as Ulrich spun her and sang of her sameness and how gorgeous a dress made her look.

"Not that you were not gorgeous before," he added as they spun to a stop and he finally set her down.

"You've found yourself a fine mount."

"Fancy did not want to leave Paris. Uncle Armand kept her."

"You were in a hurry. Did you not notice me thrice over standing here?"

"Nay, I— You mean it happened again?" Swaggering a few steps, he held a hand over his brow to shield the sun as he looked over the forest wall. "I might have traveled all the day around and about? Ah! I am in a rush, so I thank you for stopping me."

"Why the hurry?"

"Rhiana, she is yet alive."

"Yes, I remember the unicorn told you. So, no time has passed since my departure?"

"A few days, but…" He touched her cheek, trailed a soft finger up under her eye. Noticing the fine lines of age. "Not the same. Is that why you came back?"

"Do I look so old to you?"

"Mayhap the same age as me now. But yet young! You are back for ever?"

She nodded.

"Well then, you must come with me. There is room on my mount, as you can see."

"And your family?"

"I want to see Rhiana safe—be it from a distance—and my heart will be whole. But what of you? Did you not marry the faery man?"

"I did. Desideriel Raine is now lord of Glamoursiège."

"You have a husband."

"And you have a wife."

"Yes, but— Ah! We two are in such a fix! This husband of yours, he approves your coming to the Otherside?"

"He was the one who sent me here."

"I see. So…is it the same?"

Ah, that sound of desire. Of mortal passion all coiled within, waiting for release! "Is what the same?"

"Us?"

Pressing up on her tiptoes, Gossamyr leaned in to kiss Ulrich. He embraced her, shaking her from balance and toppling the two of them into the grasses. With laughter and kisses, they two rolled upon the ground.

"Is it Gossamyr or Verity?" Ulrich asked, one arm propped on an elbow as he lay over her.

"Verity. I like the name. Verity d'Ange."

"I will take you to meet your sister."

"You found her?"

"Dominique introduced me after you left. He is married to her!"

"You speak the truth? Why did he not tell me before?"

"He wanted to honor your quest. And then you left before he had opportunity to say anything. He suspected you would return."

"So you have met my sister. Is she lovely?"

"Very. But not so lovely as you. Her hair is dark and short and she is tall and strong like you. A warrior, the changeling affectionately called her. But I must to St. Rénan first."

"Then will you take me to my sister?"

"I vow it, faery princess."

"Then let's be to it!"

Lifting her in his arms, Ulrich spun once and handed her up to sit the waiting destrier.

"My staff!"

"Ah!" He retrieved the abandoned staff. "A new one, methinks." He handed it to her and she tucked it under her arm.

"Can't go anywhere without my big stick."

"As well—" he tipped the *arrets* at her waist "—will you teach me to use these?"

"Of course."

He mounted before her and took up the reins. "Such times we will have together."

"I look forward to them. Oh!"

"What troubles thee, faery princess?"

Verity gripped the sleeve that had come away from the seam at her shoulder. "I think I shall need your cloak."

"Again?" He twisted to look at her dismay. Shrugging off his cloak, she wrapped it about her shoulders and moved close to slide a hand around his waist as the destrier took to the path.

"Indeed, the same," Ulrich sang. "And we are off to adventure! The soul shepherd and his naked faery princess."

* * * * *

What has happened to Rhiana? Find out in spring 2006!

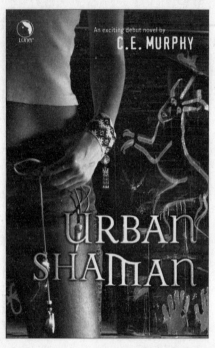

614-771-
9900

Ohio
  Fabric Farm Interiors,

item #
WR 80
grommet Tape.

Winter, 1433—and Jeanne d'Arc's ashes still glow with unsettled embers...

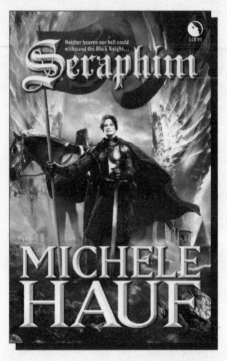

In a land where the battle between good and evil is always near, the Black Knight's sword fells enemies with silent grace. The Black Knight, Seraphim D'Ange, has sworn vengeance on Lucifer de Morte, the fallen angel, and she is determined to end his reign of terror.

Neither heaven nor hell can withstand the Black Knight....

On sale now.
Visit your local bookseller.

LUNA™